pulped

a simeon grist novel

Books by Timothy Hallinan

The Simeon Grist Mysteries

The Four Last Things
Everything But the Squeal
Skin Deep
The Man With No Time
Incinerator
The Bone Polisher

The Poke Rafferty Bangkok Thrillers

A Nail Through the Heart
The Fourth Watcher
Breathing Water
The Queen of Patpong
The Fear Artist
For the Dead
The Hot Countries
Fools' River

The Junior Bender Mysteries

Crashed
Little Elvises
The Fame Thief
Herbie's Game
King Maybe
Fields Where They Lay

pulped

a simeon grist novel

Timothy Hallinan

Print: ISBN: 978-0-9828302-7-7
MOBI: ISBN-10: 0-9828302-6-2

Cover design by James T. Egan of Bookfly Design

Print layout by booknook.biz

For Munyin Choy
for everything.

prologue

Before the Beginning

WITH HIS EYE PRESSED AGAINST the small hole he'd torn in the newspaper that covered the window, he watched her pick her way across the sand, head down as she scanned the area ahead for snakes, rocks, and the occasional cholla cactus, knee-high and lethal. Slender, lithe, long-waisted, with hair chopped shorter on one side than the other, a crude way to blunt her beauty. Why was she so uncomfortable about being beautiful?

It took nothing to make her blush.

He inhaled the scent of the newspaper, perfume to him although the newsprint was yellowish and brittle from its decade of keeping out the desert sun. The headline read, as always, LOST CHILD FOUND. He'd asked himself for more than a year now, every time he watched her leave, whether a lost child who had been found could properly be called a *lost child*. He leaned toward the window again and filled his lungs with the fragrance. If he never saw her again, he thought, this smell would always bring her to mind.

But of course, he'd see her again. So *Au revoir*, he thought a bit self-consciously, watching her follow her short shadow—the sun was high—toward the scratch in the sand that marked the road where she'd parked her car.

It was *crazy* to think he'd never see her again. He'd seen her four days a week, every single week of the fourteen months and nine days since she'd been hired—the four days each week when their shifts overlapped. Sometimes he'd make an excuse to put in an unpaid hour or two on his days off.

Crazy.

3

He thought he heard a noise from one of the other rooms in the shop. He stood there a moment, checking his memory to confirm that he'd locked the front door, and then he shrugged and went to take a look.

part one

the imagisphere

1

When It Turned, But

THE HAWK WAS WHERE IT always was.

Day in, day out.

The same hawk. Motionless. In the same sky.

In the same center of the same window.

Seven days a week, if we even *have* weeks wherever this is.

It was exactly as exciting as it sounds.

Yeah, yeah, I know. This is no way to start a book. A book is supposed to start with conflict, with a *hook*, with some dazzling string of words and images that grabs the reader and drags him or her across the exposition and the weather and the half-assed writing and the failures of imagination and all the carpentry and infrastructure that get slapped into place while the writer tries to think of something interesting.

And if the writer isn't capable of that, he or she tacks on some half-assed prologue about a character we won't meet again for a hundred pages to get the reader's attention. So see? Maybe I didn't really *write* the six books that were told in "my" first person, but I was *there* as Hallinan unspooled me and all those other folks onto the page. I *learned* things. Not that I actually knew I was being written back then—we don't have any idea of that, none of us. The biggest, cruelest joke is that we think we're *real*. But I sensed it even then when things were going flat, when I wanted a sharper scene, an unexpected twist, a snappy comeback, a dame in a raincoat.

I never did get a dame in a raincoat.

So anyway, without even knowing it, I picked up some point-ers about what makes a story happen. Okay, maybe my writer wasn't very good, but I like to think his shortcomings actually made *me* better, more aware of what works and what doesn't, more likely to jump in and try to tidy things up. If he'd been a better writer, I might not have figured all that stuff out.

Of course, if he'd been a better writer, I wouldn't *need* to fig-ure it out because I'd still be in print. But instead, I'm up here, rudely interrupted in mid-sentence. (The sentence, which Hallin-an was writing at the moment everything ended and the pulping machine closed its steel jaws, was for a book that he never sold. The sentence read: *I lifted the door handle a tiny bit to keep it from squeaking when it turned, but*). At that instant, instead of experi-encing whatever was going to happen on the other side of the door—as soon as Hallinan figured it out—I was snatched upward by the nape of my neck, ending a career he had thought would eventually fill entire shelves.

Instead, it lasted exactly six books, and then the contracts weren't renewed. But he persisted, bringing a whole new dimen-sion to the phrase *futile gesture*, downing gallons of cheap red wine and smoking his lungs into beef jerky as he took three whole years to write the Great Lost Simeon Grist Novel, *The Wrong End of the Rainbow,* hammering away at a mystery he never quite solved while the six books that had been published went through their backward metamorphoses, turning from hardbacks with ugly covers into paperbacks with uglier covers, like butterflies that created cocoons to be transformed into caterpillars, and then, one by one, like little stars blinking out, went out of print. Even the cheapest of the paperbacks.

And finally, as he put my hand on that damn doorknob, the last unsold copy of the final book in the series—*The Bone Polish-er*, a pretty good one, I thought—was pulped.

Pulped. Even now, even here, the word gives me the jukes. All those books, those gratifyingly thick copies of me doing the same things over and over again with minor variations and iffy dialogue, were ripped apart, shredded, and mixed up any old way with the absolute dregs of literacy: men's adventure magazines, coupons from Bed Bath & Beyond, instructions for assembling barbecues, faux-Regency romances, and (for a specific kind of fiber) used facial-quality tissue. Then the whole glop was bleached repeatedly to rid it of any traces of my friends and me, and fed into the maws of an infernal machine that *pulped* it, chewed it into molecules, mixed it with liquids of questionable origin, and pressed it flat to become huge rolls of newsprint. Fish wrapper, the cheapest and least durable of all the noble varieties of the world's most time-honored non-digital writing surface.

Me; my girlfriend Eleanor Chan; the irrepressible Dexter Smif; my indispensable cop friend Hammond; plus all the bad guys and girls, momentary love interests, thugs and angels, suppliers of drugs, exposition, and local color; and the whole environment we inhabited, the streets of Los Angeles, the chaparral-furred folds of Topanga—all of it, our lives and our world—reduced to *newsprint* to carry classified ads for failing businesses, misrepresented used cars, ads for payday loan companies, life-insurance scams. All the trivial ephemera of dodgy basement-level capitalism.

Once in a very great while, when fragments of our bleached-out pages have somehow clumped together and come through the pulping process without getting separated before they're pressed into a page of newsprint, we—we characters, I mean—get a watery glimpse, like a vision, of someone who's opened to that page. In my case, I got a heartbreak glance at the one and only "erotic masseuse" in a small town in upstate New York, a sad, lonely, tired-looking Korean woman who'd married the wrong American soldier and gotten stranded in the Land of the Free, now with a little too much beef on her and strands of gray in her hair, checking *The Syosset Shopper* to make sure her ad was in the right place. The sigh of resignation she heaved when she saw it was almost enough to startle me out of my self-absorption. That's one of the two ways we can be linked with the so-called "real world." The other one is much more vivid. More about that in a bit.

The long-distance encounter with the sad masseuse startled me because I wasn't expecting it; just one *more* thing I wasn't expecting. It happened soon after I found myself here—just *pop*, one moment standing there in Hallinan's imagination with my hand on that doorknob, and the next moment *up here*. It was more than a little unnerving. It was, in fact, terrifying. The big machine took its bite, and I was instantly back in the Topanga Canyon shack Hallinan wrote for me, bewildered and disoriented. Nothing to do. No case to go on. Not quite clear on where all those cases had come from in the first place. Not, in fact, clear on much of anything, except that everything I'd thought was my life was actually imaginary.

And it wasn't even *my* imagination.

But I'm getting way ahead of myself. Let's retreat to the most relaxing kind of narrative, chronological order.

Those first days—however many of them there were—were deeply rattling. For lack of anything familiar, I grabbed onto what I had and tried to take comfort from it. This house, which appeared to be real and pretty much as it had always been, except for rather conspicuous differences I'll probably tell you about later. That damn hawk in the window. No one I knew anywhere. My books, my bed, my gun. I maybe spent a little too much time with my gun, although I have no idea whether I even *can* commit suicide. Doesn't that require a life?

I was well into a really solid and possibly permanent panic attack when a complete stranger, a fourteen-year-old kid, dropped by, Welcome Wagon-style, to usher me into my new world.

2

Welcome to *Here*

NO ONE HAD EVER KNOCKED on the door before.

I wasn't in the best shape. I was, in fact, half-drunk. One of the things I'd discovered was that the rickety little refrigerator in my kitchen *up here* would always hold the three bottles of Singha beer that had been in it when I left the house that final time, when I still thought I was real. Three bottles, no matter how many I drank. Along with whatever else had been in it, which made for really, really boring meals. But the beer made them a little better, and I'm afraid I had drunk maybe six or seven since getting out of bed that morning. What the hell *else* did I have to do?

So when the rap at the door came, I literally fell over.

I was going to grab *another* beer and was in the process of getting up from the old couch, just as uncomfortable here as it had been there, and I was in one of those in-between poses that you live through mainly because you keep moving before gravity can take charge. But I froze at the sheer unexpectedness of the knock, my body weight badly distributed and my balance impaired by beer, and I was deposited back on the couch. By the time I could summon the equilibrium to get up again, I heard footsteps going away from the door.

Here's as good a place as any to describe the house or, as some have called it, the shack. It's a wooden structure shaped like a U. The upright left arm of the U contains the bedroom and bath-

11

room. In the right upright are the kitchen and dining nook, which is kind of a grand way to say a piece of plywood nailed to a frame to create a table. The bottom of the U represents the living room. In the living room's right wall was the window where that fucking hawk was always motionless in the sky. In the middle of the room's bottom-most wall was a doorway that opened out to the roof of a little room built just down the slope, a roof that gave you the best view in all of Topanga Canyon, which was saying something.

Running up the empty space between the arms of the U was a narrow, rickety, badly roofed passageway with firewood stored behind uprights along the left side, a virtual theme park for black widows. At the end of the passageway, on the right as *you're* facing the U but on the left of anyone who came in via it, it, was the door, which opened into the kitchen.

The door, obviously, was where the knock had come from. And now I could hear someone creaking away down the wooden walkway.

I attempted to shout, "Wait," but I hadn't used my voice since I got here, if you don't count the occasional scream of despair, and all I produced was phlegm and air. I tried again, choked out an actual word, creaky as an old gate, and listened to the footsteps pick up their pace. A despair-fueled lunge brought me to my feet and propelled me across the room in the direction of the hawk's window, windmilling my arms and trying to stop until I collided with the massive fake-Victorian sideboard that lives against that wall. I held on for a moment, panting, then ran to the door, yanked it open, and shouted, "*Hey!*"

"On the doorknob," a girl called, but the person hot-footing it away seemed to be a smallish male, about five feet tall, wearing a khaki outfit made up of a long-sleeve shirt, a pair of creased shorts that ended above the knee, and a flat-brimmed stetson. A kid, in uniform. A kid whose voice hadn't changed.

"Please," I said, and then, acting on a subconscious memory, I said the magic word. "I need some *help* here."

The kid stopped as though he'd run into an invisible wall, one foot literally frozen in mid-air. He turned to face me, a plump, ordinary-looking, freckle-spattered boy who had tugged the flat brim of his hat down to conceal his eyes, and whose mouth was pulled sharply over to the left, an expression I remembered occupying my own face when my mother was about to ask me to do something I didn't want to do.

"It's on the knob," he said.

"What is?"

"Welcome flyer." He turned away again and raised an arm in parting. "Okay?"

"Hang on a minute. You want—" I broke it off. You didn't offer a Boy Scout a beer. Especially not *this* Boy Scout: hanging beneath a little swarm of sewn-on badges that celebrated various kinds of probity was a red, white, and blue ribbon with a gunmetal grey, vaguely Nazi eagle hanging from it. I said, "You're an *Eagle Scout?*"

"Eagle Scout Bradley Zipper," he said in a weary tone. "I don't have to salute, right?"

"No," I said. "Nice of you to ask, though."

He blew out a bunch of weary-sounding air. "I'm going to make a suggestion," he said. "If the Pope or anyone ever offers to make you a saint? Throw him or her out of the highest window you can get to."

"Because."

He tilted the hat back just enough to give a me look at his eyes, which were green and furious. "Because if you *let* them, from that moment on, any time some idiot makes an outrageous request—'My son is going to be shot at daybreak. Will you please take his place?'—and you decline, they'll immediately say, 'You know, *you're* no saint.'"

"Got it."

"Why don't you just read the orientation sheet?"

"I will. But I might have questions."

"No kidding," he said.

"So *can* you help me?"

"You keep using that word."

"It's not a complete accident. I still remember the Boy Scout Oath." In my backstory, Hallinan had given me a short, unhappy interlude in the Scouts.

"Well," he said. He put both hands in the pockets of his khaki shorts and rocked back and forth, heel to toe, for a moment. Then he met my eyes and said, "Got any beer?"

* * *

Dear **Simon Grist**, it said, proudly putting the first mistake right up on the very first blank on the sheet. *Welcome to* **here**. I said, "Here?"

"They haven't named the place yet." I was on the couch. Eagle Scout Bradley Zipper was sitting cross-legged on the really filthy carpet. It was saturated with Topanga dust, but when it (and I) had been *down there*, every vacuum cleaner I'd ever plugged in had blown out the ancient fuses, so there hadn't been one in the house when I got pulped. But there was *dust* up here. Lots of it. If there'd been a body of water nearby, I probably could have shaken enough sand and dirt out of the rug to create a beach.

I said, "And it's been here how long?"

"Since about 1922." He tilted the bottle back, swallowed, and burped. "There's a couple of girls here who were the first people to arrive. Sisters. Twin sisters. Really *snotty* twin sisters. Like having been someplace awful for a long time somehow makes you better than people who have been there a shorter time."

"Who's the *they* who haven't named the place?"

"Who knows? Keep reading."

You may have questions, but be patient. They will all be answered in time. In the meantime, the resident who handed you this brochure will be your first new friend.

I said, "You're my first new—"

"Yeah, yeah," he said. "Don't take it literally. I delivered that thing, I didn't write it."

"You're hurting my feelings," I said.

"Then you're in for a tough forever. Keep reading."

You'll have lots in common with the people you meet. We are all detectives—

I said, "Shit."

"Got to the 'all detectives' part, huh?"

"That's what made me *interesting*. That I was the only detective in my books."

"Well, *yeah*," Bradley Zipper said. "Interesting compared to everyone else our writers could squeeze out. In my series, some of the secondary characters, to pay them a compliment, managed to be thinner than the page, like the page was *dimpled* every time they showed up. It wasn't like we were in lit-fic, where the characters are multi-layered and, uhh, leap off the page. I haven't read any lit-fic, but that's what I hear: the characters are multi-layered and leap off the page."

"Sounds like it'd get crowded." I looked at Bradley Zipper as he upended the bottle and drained it. I was half a bottle behind him. He looked every day of his fourteen years, but no older. "So that means, this sentence, here in this brochure, means that *you're* a detective?"

"Was," Bradley Zipper said. "Same as you."

* * *

"*The Troop 24 Mysteries*," he said. He was lying on his back with the empty beer bottle balanced upright on his forehead. "By

Edwin G. Werfel. There were eight of them and a few stories in Scout magazines. How many of yours?"

"Uh," I said. "Six."

"Any stories?"

"Not exactly."

Bradley Zipper's unblemished brow furrowed. The beer bottle wobbled. "What does that mean?"

"It means 'no.'"

"Oh, well. We had less competition. There's 100 books written now for every one that was written in the thirties. Some of the new people up here tell me that." He took the bottle off his forehead and looked longingly toward the kitchen. "I really like your fridge. Wish I'd been old enough to have beer around when I— well, *whoosh*."

"Yeah. Whoosh. You got up here *when?*"

"Nineteen thirty-four. Listen, you don't want to read that whole thing and I don't want this to be the last beer of my day, so why don't we make a deal? I'll go get another one and tell you what all this is about, and then you can ask me three questions—"

"Why three?"

"It's *always* three. And then I'll take another beer for the road and get on my bike."

"To go where?"

"Home. I'll tell you about it, how you get from place to place, I mean. You just hold on." He got up and headed for the kitchen. It took me a moment to recognize the sound he was making. He was clinking the neck of the bottle against his front teeth.

"I'd love another one," I called after him.

* * *

"So here's the deal," Bradley Zipper said. He was back on the carpet, reclining on his side and up on one elbow, another half-beer down. "If this sounds kind of lawyerly, it's because I've said it about a thousand times and I've accidentally memorized it. Some of it's really obvious, but just let me keep going so we can both get to the next part of our story, boring as it's likely to be. Any questions will count against your three, and don't think you can ask me to help you again because it doesn't say anywhere that we have to be *infinitely* helpful, you got that?"

I said I had it.

"Okay. You see, we exist at our fullest level, thinking everything is real, only in *four places*: in between the covers of our books, in our writers' imaginations, in the imaginations of the people who publish and sell our books, and in the imaginations of our readers. That's when we're at full strength, and it lasts right up to the moment that final unsold copy of the last title in the series is pulped, at which point one whole energy source—the work of the people who published and proofread and sold our books—disappears in a snap. And then we're instantly in the aptly-named *here*, and we're here forever, as far as we know, since the budget for this place doesn't seem to include fortune-tellers. We're just stuck up here, writerless and sharing a sort of genre slum with hundreds of other heroes and heroines from series that stiffed. I don't know how good a writer your guy was, but some of the ones I've met, well, I wouldn't have read their books if they'd been the only ones on the shelves of a desert island. And suddenly, we're all neighbors up here, yanked out of our stories like flowers that got pulled up by the roots, looking at each other and trying to think of something to say."

"What happens if we're republished?"

"Is that your first question?"

"Sure. What the hell."

"Did you just ask *What the hell*?"

I raised both hands in self-defense. "It had a period after it."

He shrugged. "So you mean, what happens if you go back into print? Well, there are the *franchises*," he said, his tone acidic enough to be mistaken for envy. "The Hardy boys have been back and forth so often this is like a vacation home. Other than that, it's only happened to a couple, three people, that I know of in the 80 years or so I've been here. They get snatched from here just as rudely as they were snatched from there in the first place. One of them, Elegant Eddie Lathrop—you know about him?"

"Not unless Hallinan wrote about him."

"Right, right. When you've been here a while you'll get some content of your own. I mean, Hallinan didn't write me, right? But here we are, talking to each other. Only thing I knew when I got here was that damn Scout pledge, how to build a fire with two sticks, and to stay the hell out of caves. Well, Elegant Eddie was kind of a rip on Fred Astaire in a series written back in the forties. He was a movie-star tap dancer who solved mysteries in Hollywood. All the books had some kind of dance in the title, *Fox Trot to Fear, The Jittery Jitterbug, Tapping Toward Terror, Hokey Pokey Dead*—"

"Why do writers do these things to themselves?"

"Masochism. And publishers like predictability. Anyway, in the 1990s, an African-American dancer, a Broadway star, bought the books and sold it as a TV series, you know, crime, dancing, old-time glamor, and racial prejudice, set in a time nobody knew much about, when theaters in the South were all segregated and the studios used to bring in black actors after a movie set closed down at night and shoot a quick, cheap version of the same story for the black audiences in the South. The producers hired someone to revive the books too, like a spin-off."

"But in the first books, he was white, right?"

"Yeah. But they kept the name Elegant Eddie. And now that the *second* series is out of print and pulped too, we have two Elegant Eddies up here, one white and one—"

"Do they get along?"

"That's your fifth question. The answer is, they avoid each

other, and it's awkward because they live in the same house." He rolled over and got to his knees, sitting back on his heels. "So, summing up. You're here, and you're stuck here unless you come back into print. Cheap as this house is, it'll stay up until, I guess, the Great Fictional Detectives' Plague strikes and this whole place vanishes. You'll meet other people because they're as bored as you are, and they're sick of everyone who's already up here. Wait, you can ask me one more question if you'll answer one of mine. What's with the stuffed hawk?"

"He's not stuffed," I said, "although I suppose he might as well be. Hallinan was always short on visual detail. Whenever his editor wrote, 'What the hell are we *looking* at?' which was pretty often, he stuck the hawk up there, usually held aloft by some poetic active verb. So there it is."

"I'll bet it gets old fast."

"I've tried to shoot it," I confessed.

He shook his head. "You got your gun up here? Lotta the others don't. But anyways, even if you blew the bird's head off, it would still be there. You can't change anything. It's here the way it was written, and that's how it'll stay. Do you think I'd still be wearing this fricking uniform after all these years if I could put on something with a little flair?"

"Fricking?"

"I have my gol-dang vocabulary limitations."

"Okay, other than being published again, is there any way to get back down?"

He crossed his legs. "I'm not allowed to talk about that."

"So there *is*."

"Look," he said. "You've never been down there when your story wasn't being written by someone whose job was to keep you alive and who could *rewrite* in case things didn't work out. You'd be hopeless on your own. And some of the ones I know of who tried—two, anyway—well, they disappeared."

"What does that mean?"

"Okay, okay. I'm not actually supposed to tell you this yet, but it feels good every now and then to do something I'm not supposed to do. I said we were alive in four places, right? In the books, in the—"

"It wasn't that long ago."

"Well, if you lose *more* of those places after you're pulped, your signal sort of dims. If your writer dies, you get a little, I don't know, transparent. Light sort of comes through you. If people stop reading you, you don't have the energy to move very much. We got people up here just hanging around like faded gauze curtains. If all your books somehow disappear forever, you're still transparent and motionless, but you also get really little. Like postage-stamp little. People will step on you."

"Not something to look forward to."

"But if you go back down there—and I'm not telling you how—and something—something *goes wrong* down there, then poof."

"Poof?"

"Nothing. You don't exist. You never existed. Your books were never written. Your writer has no memory of you. There isn't even a smear to show where you were erased."

I said, "Yikes." I reviewed it for a second. "Then how do *you* remember them?"

"They were up here. I don't know, it's like a glitch in the software. I know of four who went down, and only two who came back. So—" He got up easily, elastically young forever. "You don't want to try to go down there. Seriously. You don't." From the kitchen, he said, "Wish I had this refrigerator."

3

A Lot of Time Passed

A LOT OF TIME PASSED, and it passed slowly. I got almost used to things.

I figured some stuff out. Despite his promise, Bradley had escaped without telling me how to get around. My second visitor, a Brooklyn vampire detective named Tony Romero who'd had a brief nonlife during a momentary publishing enthusiasm for mixing genres, had told me all I had to do was think of the person I wanted to visit—"C'mon, I mean, you know," he had said, ramping up a little velocity before tackling the steep uphill climb of an actual thought, "we're all, like, *imaginary*, right? I mean, *duh*. Once you got the person in mind, all you gotta do is walk."

It was a little disconcerting the first time I did it, because there were these cheap D-movie special effects, a sort of scramble of words and word fragments in front of me, accompanied by a kind of card-shuffling sound and, at the far edges of my vision, a flicker of movement that proved to be the fanning of semi-transparent pages.

An amateur detective who had been a film critic in his day job said he'd seen better effects in Ed Wood movies. But I was learning, gradually, that cheapness was one of the really pervasive characteristics of this—this limbo.

If I didn't want to walk the eight to ten steps it took me to get anywhere, I could also drive my car, which was parked at the top of my nearly vertical driveway, where Hallinan always put it, but the experience was just too depressing. I turned the key and there was a scratchy recording of a car starting, and then I wiggled the steering wheel back and forth like a kid's bumper car, and the pages started flickering at the edges of my et cetera et cetera until I got there. There was no actual sensation of movement; the rear-view mirror seemed to be aimed at the inkiest, farthest stretches of intergalactic space; and the scenery through my windshield was as generic as the backgrounds in a low-rez Super Mario Brothers game. In the books, I'd always loved driving Topanga's suicide blind curves. By comparison, this was like that little wobble-car you feed quarters into outside the supermarket to divert your two-year-old.

In short, things were *boring*. Time, as physicists like to say, is elastic, and boring time is the most elastic of all. When I learned that it took *months* to deliver the amount of action I was used to in, say, two or three pages, I despaired. I felt as though it would have been more merciful to preserve me in amber; at least then I wouldn't have gone on hoping that something, especially something *interesting*, would finally happen.

And then something did. And to prevent you from having to endure any more of my boredom, I'll get right to it.

* * *

To set the stage, by the time it happened, I'd been in a state comparable to being on hold with your cable TV provider ever since—well, since *The Bone Polisher* was pulped in 1998. Same house, same rooms, same books on the shelves, same food in the refrigerator. Same Los Angeles out there, although the only parts of it that I can visit are the ones I already visited in the books.

Same me.

And I know you get bored too, but oh, poor you. I sneeze wetly in the direction of your boredom. I was trapped in a fic-tion-thin shack in a fictional Topanga Canyon with one window that you can always see a hawk through and a refrigerator full of leftovers that will never spoil. It you want a tiny sample of what it's like, *you* eat rewarmed lasagna for dinner several hundred nights in a row.

Raymond Chandler, a writer to whom Hallinan was occasionally (and not usually favorably) compared, once wrote, "When in doubt, have a man come through the door with a gun in his hand."

And that day, right on cue, someone rattled the handle of the door.

4

A Bunch of Traits
Everyone Else Had Rejected

I COULD HAVE DARTED INTO the bedroom and grabbed the Glock. I could have quietly positioned myself behind the door with a cast-iron frying pan or a carving knife in my hand. I could have given the fire extinguisher a shake and pointed it at the doorway. But by then, my expectations for visitors were somewhat lower. What I did was remain sprawled on the couch and say, "Yeah, yeah, yeah."

I heard the door open, out of sight around the corner that leads to the kitchen, and a Basset Hound trotted in, gave me an unaffectionate once-over, and looked back toward the door. A woman whose voice sounded something like a flute being played underwater said, "Everything all right, Billy?" and Billy, the Basset, glanced back at me with a *look-what-I-have-to-go-through* expression, flopped onto the carpet, and began to lick himself someplace I can't lick myself.

"Thank you, Billy," said Lobelia Twombly, still hidden from view. "One can't be too careful."

"Of what?" I said. "Bumping your head on a dangling participle?"

"Oh, *someone's* in a bad mood today," Lobelia said. She trundled into the room, a little gingerbread cookie of a woman with flyaway reddish hair floating above a figure like two sets of parentheses stacked one above the other, with the lower quite a bit wider. Lobelia had legs, of course, but for all I knew there were four of them because they'd never been described; she was invariably written swathed in floor-length skirts in mottled earth tones. She also wore a great many scarves which fluttered around her even when the air was still. Her author had been quite insistent about the fluttering, and it was irritating as hell. In her hand was a wicker basket with a red-and-white checkered cloth napkin covering it.

"I felt like baking," Lobelia said. "Like I always do. I hope you like butter cookies."

"I have no idea," I said. "Hallinan never wrote a scene in which I ate one."

"Well, you can try them now. Tony Romero—do you know Tony?"

"Sure. Mr. Cool Black Leather. Fangs. I don't hang with him, but—"

"Tony had never eaten one, either—"

"I didn't know Tony was allowed to eat anything that doesn't bleed." Tony's author had begun what was supposed to be a long-lasting series about a vampire detective with the snappy title *Once Dead*. He'd called the second *Twice Dead*, and then struck out on three. *Thrice* and *Triply* didn't seem so punchy, and he couldn't come up with an alternative his publisher would accept. As a result, Tony had lasted only two books, so I could look down my nose at him. Behind his back, I mean.

"Well, he didn't actually *eat* any, silly," Lobelia said. "That's why I brought them to you. But he said they smelled good." Lobelia put the basket on the warped sideboard in front of the window with the hawk in it, and pulled the cloth off. "This is one of the recipes from my first book, *Bassets and Liabilities*. The secret is half a ton of butter." She batted down a corner of one of her scarves, which was floating around the tip of her nose. "Dora wrote a *lot* of butter."

Lobelia and Billy, her mind-reading Basset Hound, had been featured in four cooking cozies written by Dora Wainwright: *Bassets and Liabilities, Frozen Bassets, Basset Management,* and *Tangible Bassets.* They'd done all right saleswise, the audience for cooking cozies featuring a clairvoyant Basset Hound being larger than I would have imagined, but then Dora Wainwright had died of a heart attack. According to Lobelia, she'd had an actual stick of butter in one of her arteries.

"Don't indulge in unkind thoughts about Dora," Lobelia said, lifting the cloth. "Even if I *did* say it first."

"How did you know what I was think—Oh, right. *Thanks,* Billy." The dog averted its eyes and put its head on the carpet. It sighed.

"I *know* it isn't fair," Lobelia said, taking the words right out of my mind, via Billy. "But I can't help it."

"You could keep quiet about it. I'm already having a crisis about being boring, without having to make conversation with someone who already knows everything I'm going to say. I feel like I've got a stutter and you're rude enough to finish my sentences. Thank God I don't tell jokes. I can't imagine anything—"

"—worse, no, probably not," Lobelia said. "Whoops. Force of habit."

"Can you tell Billy to turn it off?"

"I could, but you wouldn't know whether he actually did, would you? Just forget he's here."

Billy growled.

"There, there, Billy," Lobelia said. "Simeon's just *thinking* about doing that, he's not going to do it. Here, Simeon, have a cookie."

She trotted across the room, scarves wisping around her face, and held out the plate. I sat up and took one, and—not sure what would happen, because things up here, while boring, are occasionally unpredictable—put it in my mouth. It went in, and when I chewed it, it did all the things it was supposed to. It got wetter, it got smaller, it went down. "Tastes like butter," I said.

Lobelia sighed and sat next to me. It was a good-size couch, and Lobelia took up a lot of it. She looked idly out the window in the opposite wall, where the hawk hung in the watery, half-bright sunlight, like light on an undistinguished early winter morning before the low clouds burn off. The light I looked at all day long, every day.

"Really crappy light," I said.

"You should see it over in Literary Fiction," Lobelia said. "They've got a sun so bright and yellow it looks like a first-grader drew it. And the light *changes* as the day draws on."

"We've always been a low-rent sub-genre," I said. Then I said, "How do you know what the sky looks like in Lit-Fic? And, by the way, *draws on?*"

"Ah, well," Lobelia said. "One doesn't always associate with the low-lifes of crime fiction. Sometimes one needs richer conversation."

"Something good and bleak, I'll bet. Something that sounds like it was translated from a Swedish movie in black and white, a low-key chat between a sensitive hunchback and the Spirit of a Stone. Something rich in Larger Meaning. And then the child's bright shoe floats in on the tide."

"I have to tell you that hawk is enough to put me off my appetite." She took another cookie and offered me one.

Around the cookie, I said, "Even the field mice are used to it. They stand around in plain sight as the day draws on, and make raspberries in its direction."

"Really. Dora gave *me* an absolutely adorable little mouse named Mrs. Danvers. Lives in the cutest little hole in the baseboard, all lined in gingham. Wears a weensy little apron, nibbles cheese in its tee-tiny paws, walks around on its hind legs, offers occasional cooking advice. If I could get my car into the living room, I'd run it over."

"Wouldn't work," I said.

"I know. We're stuck with them." She took another cookie, and when it was halfway to her mouth, she said, "*What*, Billy?"

The dog had gotten up and was facing the window, its pendulous ears raised half an inch or so, making worry lines in its forehead that probably would have made it look intelligent if I hadn't known better. It was staring at the hawk, or at *something* out there, and from its chest came a low, almost subsonic growl. Its earlier growl had been a grumble of irritation, but this was the real thing, a warning to whatever was coming toward us that it should change course *right now*.

"Oh, my," Lobelia said, the cookie forgotten in her hand. "Look at that."

The sky was brightening, going from a sort of tarnished pewter to the gleam of silver under water. The light had a *direction* to it, for a change: it shimmered along the tops of the hawk's wings and glinted off the cruel hook at the end of its beak. The hawk turned an ice-cold eye on me.

"Oh, I'm so glad I'm here to see this," Lobelia said. "I was afraid no one was reading you anymore."

"Hey," I said. "I'm the one who got reviewed in *The Wall Street Journal* and *The Chicago Trib*. As I recall, you got your starred reviews from *Quazy Quilting* and Betty Crocker."

The sky was quite bright now but starting to flicker like a loose bulb. Looking at it, Lobelia said, "Don't forget all those recipes in *The Huffington Post*."

Dark holes began to appear in the sky. They blossomed and spread like burning film, black at the edges and gray inside.

"I don't know how to break this to you," I said, "but Betty Crocker is a fictional character."

Lobelia said, "Look who's talking. Anyway, I still get read quite a lot. Sometimes. Once in a while."

Then the sky vanished entirely, taking the hawk with it, and the window had become a flat black rectangle of nothing, no reflections on the glass. Swimming up through the darkness came an oval something, emitting an orange-red glow like the bars in an electric heater. It was as soft and diffuse at the edges as a swarm of bees, but as it grew larger, its outline hardened, and then the space around the glow brightened to fill the window, and I saw bookshelves, lots of them, crammed with books jammed in any old way. I could almost smell the dust. Although the room we were seeing was dim, it looked passably bright by contrast with the black it had replaced, and the reddish oval had resolved itself into the back of a man's head. He had a monk's little bare circle of scalp at his crown, which I was pretty sure he thought was a lot smaller.

"It's Ferdy," I said.

"Ferdy?"

"Ferdinand Carvalho. Got a name like an opera cape." Our perspective changed as Ferdy opened a book, and we were looking straight up at him as he lifted the open book toward his nearsighted eyes until he came into focus, squinting down at it, as unimpressive as ever. Ferdy looked like he'd been put together from a bunch of traits everyone else had rejected: he had chipmunk cheeks, bad skin, protruding front teeth, and hair that was already receding both front and back although he was still in his early thirties. I couldn't see his body because the book was so close to his face, but I knew from times when he'd put the open book down and walked away from it that he also had narrow shoulders, wide hips, and soft, damp hands that, I was sure, creeped out the female characters in the romances he sometimes read. I'd found myself wishing on several occasions that he wasn't

drawn to romances. We all like to think that our fans have superi-
or taste.

"A loyal reader?" Lobelia said. "He's sort of, umm, moist,
isn't he?"

"Oh, eat a cookie. He works in a used bookstore in Joshua
Tree. That's the high desert, in California. He's in the back
room, on a break, probably." I closed my eyes for a moment and
"heard" what he was reading—the quotation marks are there because it was actually soundless, and, no, I can't explain it any better than that except to say it was a little like eavesdropping on his
mind. "He's reading *Everything But the Squeal*."

"Was that a good one?"

"I don't know. What I remember was almost getting killed.
But some critic, Dick Adler maybe, called it *compelling*."

Lobelia jostled me for a better view, leaned forward, and said,
"It seems to be compelling Ferdy."

And indeed it did. His tongue was protruding and his eyes
were bulging.

"Sex scene?" Lobelia asked.

"For Christ's sake. I pretend to be familiar with your books.
You could do the same with mine."

"Ummmm," Lobelia said. "No one ever looks like that when
they read me. Unless they're on a strict diet."

I was up, although I didn't remember standing, drawn toward
the window even though I knew I wouldn't be able to see anything more, no matter where I stood. The rectangle of sky wasn't
something that was actually on the other side of the window; it
was sort of a rear projection, and so were my readers and the
rooms they were in, when they showed up. I could make it a little
bigger by getting right up against the glass, but it wasn't much of
an improvement.

But then the picture shivered and tilted dizzyingly down, and
as the book slipped from Ferdy's fingers, I saw the hands around

his neck. Big hands. The book plummeted toward the floor, bumped against Ferdy's copious stomach, and landed face up and wide open, so we were looking up, as though the page was a window in the floor, up at the Leaning Tower of Ferdy as he swayed, prying limply at the fingers digging into his throat, and then as he collapsed, not toppling over but rather folding up like a marionette until his face slammed into the page, eyes wide open and rolled back. Ferdy in profile. Forever.

Behind him, someone lifted a foot and kicked him in the back. Ferdy shuddered with the impact but it was physics, not life. The legs behind him turned and left, giving me a quick glimpse of cowboy boots. Big cowboy boots.

"Jeez," I said. "I think I just lost a reader."

5

They Have Sound in Lit-Fic

FOR QUITE A WHILE, NOTHING happened. I stood at the window, looking through it and the book that was open in Joshua Tree, watching Ferdy not breathe, while Lobelia stood beside me, metronomically eating butter cookies and exhaling on my shoulder.

Time passed, and I have no idea how much of it there was, unless you measured it in butter cookies. It was quite a lot of butter cookies, but then, I was eating them, too. Then, 30 or 40 butter cookies later, a pair of small running shoes tied in decidedly girly bows appeared at the right edge of the frame, behind Ferdy, and froze. They shifted anxiously from side to side for a couple of seconds and then turned and vanished.

"No sound?" Lobelia asked.

"Does yours have sound?"

"No. But I hear they have sound in Lit-Fic. With a music track, even."

"Probably played by a live orchestra," I said.

Lobelia gestured at the window with a cookie. "*What* was his name?" And then she nodded at the dog and said, "Right, Billy, thanks. *Ferdy*. How long had he been reading you?"

"This was his third book. He read *The Man With No Time* first, and then *The Four Last Things*."

"Terrific books," Lobelia said dutifully.

"Oh, give it a rest. You've never read a word of me."

"I spent a lot of time cooking. And there *was* the occasional murder."

"Had to play with your mouse, too."

"Stop that. I've heard quite enough condescension from you hard-boiled knuckle-busters. You think cozies are *easy*? You think just anyone can make a perfect Bundt cake and solve a locked-door mystery at the same time? Without swearing?"

"I know I couldn't."

"Look, since we're a persecuted minority, I mean *all* of us in crime fiction, wouldn't it make sense to stop all the quibbling and sort of hang together? You don't pick at us about recipes and quilting and talking cats and Colonel Mustard in the conservatory with an exotic Amazonian blowgun, and we'll leave you alone about your cop friend and the empty bottles and the ongoing Bleak Night of the Soul and all the recycled wisecracks."

"Fine," I said. The woman in the running shoes, which I was thinking of as pink, hadn't come back.

"Boy," Lobelia said. "He really *is* dead, isn't he?"

"And the laws of nature mandate that he will remain so."

"I suppose the girl with the frou-frou shoelaces has gone to call the cops."

"Seems like."

"Got coffee?"

"Sure, I've got coffee. Who doesn't have coffee?"

After a pause two cookies long, Lobelia said, "May I have some?"

"Of course, you may. Beans are in the freezer. Grinder's next to the stove. And no, I'm not going to go fix it for you. What do you think, we're coming up on a commercial?"

"It's not very interesting. In a movie, we would have cut away a long time ago."

"I want to see how they handle it. This is one of my readers we're talking about."

"An endangered species," Lobelia muttered peevishly as she went into the kitchen to make her own coffee. "Rarer than the Tennessee Speckled Cave-Darter."

I aimed a thought at Billy.

"Really?" Lobelia said, turning around. She spread her skirt with both hands. "It makes me look fat?"

I said, "Play nicely."

"Oh," Lobelia said. She shook her head in what might have been admiration. "How clever of you. Do you know that Dora never had a character do that? Lie to me via Billy? Not even once, in any of the books."

"She was probably thinking about dinner." The room on the other side of the window brightened suddenly.

"Somebody's turned on the lights," I said. "My guess is, the cops have arrived."

"Do a play-by-play for me. I need coffee."

"Okay. Big hand on Ferdy's shoulder. Guy's got a lot of hair between his knuckles."

"Yet another attractive masculine trait." Lobelia was unfolding the top of the bag of coffee beans.

"You want details or not?"

"Of course, I want details," she said. "I'm a detective, too."

Billy whimpered.

"I didn't think that," I said immediately. "Okay, he's rolling Ferdy over. Now we see Ferdy's dramatically thinning hair and his left ear. Oh, no. The cop's a uniform. They didn't even send a detective. Cop looks about thirteen."

"George Bernard Shaw said that's a sign you're getting old. When the police look young, I mean. Mmmm. Brazilian dark roast. Expensive."

"It's fiction, remember? Costs the same as Dunkin' Donuts. Boy, is he mucking up the crime scene. He's moved Ferdy, he's getting his big cop shoes everywhere. Man, Hammond would have his ass."

"Hammond?" The electric grinder whirred into life.

"Al Hammond." I raised my voice over the sound of the beans being pulverized. "My cop friend."

"Ah, yes, the invariable cop friend."

"If you're going to solve crimes," I said, "a cop friend seems like a more useful accessory than a copy of *Cuisine Française* and a bottle of dog shampoo."

"Where's the French press?"

"In France. Just boil some water, put the coffee into the filter cone and pour the—oh, Lord, he's picking up the book." The cop's face filled the window as he brought the page up to read it. A lot of the room came into view behind him.

"He's kind of cute," Lobelia said from the kitchen. "In a worn, bleary way."

"So is she." I pointed at the young woman watching the cop from the doorway. Mid-to-late twenties, a ragged, asymmetrical chop of brown hair above bright, intelligent eyes and sharply angled cheekbones.

She said something that I couldn't hear, since there was no sound, and the cop turned and closed the book.

The hawk was back, in exactly the same place.

"Well," Lobelia said. "*That* was interesting. Sort of like old times, a murder and all."

"It's getting foggy outside," I said.

Lobelia put the pot on the stove and I heard the *poof* as the gas caught. "It doesn't do that here."

"No," I said. "It doesn't. But it's getting foggy anyway."

"Hmmm. What an unusual day." She stood there, plastic filter in one hand, looking at the counter as though cockroaches were square-dancing on it. "Just put the filter cone on top of this awful-looking carafe?"

"I thought you were in cooking mysteries."

"I'm surprised you don't just boil the grounds with some eggshell. That's what they do over in the cowboy ghetto."

"What's the eggshell for?" I was watching the fog gradually obscure the hawk. For a moment, it seemed to me that the hawk's eye swiveled and found me again, a sharp dart across the distance, and then the bird disappeared into the milky air.

"How would I know?" she said. "A bunch of old cowboys aren't going to tell a little woman their coffee secrets."

"Probably not." I felt sour and grimy. I'd just seen someone killed, someone who liked me, who gave me the hours of his life it took to read the books I appeared in, and I'd had to watch his death helplessly, through a dirty window. I hadn't even been able to tell him to look behind him.

Lobelia came back to the window. "It'll boil eventually if I don't look at it. Really *is* foggy, isn't it? I haven't seen this before. And I've been here a while."

"Maybe it's a metaphor," I said. "For my state of mind."

* * *

The fog was ropy and drifting, although I couldn't feel a breeze. Lobelia had toddled down the unpaved driveway, her silhouette swallowed up by the mist beneath the dark masses of the pepper trees, and I'd grabbed a second cup of coffee and hiked the driveway as it continued uphill past my shack, to the vacant housing pad that someone had bulldozed into the top of the hill, back when it seemed like all you had to do was plant a house somewhere, like a lima bean, and watch the money pour in.

Those times had returned but the thwarted builder hadn't. As a neighborhood, Topanga is rich in people who begin things and then walk away, diverted by something else.

It had gotten chilly, which was also unusual. This was the first time I'd been cold since I got here. I pulled the cuff of my sweat-shirt down over my empty hand and wrapped the other around the hot cup.

Lobelia's coffee was a *lot* better than mine was.

Seeing the cop screw up the crime scene was almost enough to make me miss Al Hammond. He was up here but not handling it well, drinking way too much at a cop bar from a book written by a Joseph Wambaugh wanna-be who hadn't made it. Every fictional cop up here hung at that bar, so it did a booming business. I'd seen Hammond a few times in the last however-long-it-was, but it had been depressing. He looked worn and frayed and unfocused, and although he'd been on the dour side in the novels, this was different, more depressive. I could sympathize. I hadn't actually realized how much fun I was having in the books until I wasn't in them anymore. Of course, that was in retrospect. During the books I was mainly trying to stay alive, or what I *thought* was alive.

Something scraped something in the fog.

The sound came from my right, where a big fragrant sage grew, a bush much beloved of rattlesnakes. I'd seen a couple of big ones there and, once, a baby no more than ten inches long and sort of cute, if you didn't know that the little ones are more venomous than the big ones. But whatever made the noise was bigger than a rattler.

Coyotes are bigger than rattlers, but coyotes don't scrape against things. The average coyote could sprint through a forest of wind chimes without a single ting-a-ling.

I smelled something musty, like a pile of old paperbacks that's been stored someplace damp for a long time, the kind of damp that would be swarming with silverfish. The smell came from the same direction as the scraping sound.

This did not feel good.

I backed away from the smell until the heel of my boot hit the old tire that's been up there since before I moved into the house.

There's a steering wheel and part of a front seat on the dirt next to it, which has made me wonder hundreds of times what happened to the rest of the car.

Whatever was out there, it moved. This time it crunched. The sole of a shoe on rocky soil.

And then something thickened and materialized in front of me, advancing through the fog and homing in on me as though the mist didn't exist for it, as though I was standing in clear morning light. I was squinting, although it didn't help, and what I saw was a man, wearing a heavy corduroy jacket and corduroy pants, the pants making that *whisk-whisk* sound cords make when you walk. A man taller than I was, slender and slope-shouldered, with a narrow face and a sharp needle of a nose.

A man who had once—with every indication of enjoying it— pushed the tine of a fork under several of my fingernails.

6

Sometimes It's Nice
Not to Have to Fight Fair

"OH, GO AWAY, FOR CHRIST'S sake," I said. "Haven't you learned *anything?*"

Villains and secondary characters were up here, too, but just. There was barely enough solid stuff, atoms or whatever else it might have been, in the crime-fiction ghetto to give solidity to the protagonists and their environments. The secondary continuing characters, like Al, were kind of shadowy, but generally speaking, the villains—who'd usually appeared in only one book and only for a few scenes—were as thin as a frame of film, so insubstantial they didn't even really have adjectives. Old Needle-nose —his real name was Barry—bore a grudge against me, with good reason. He'd materialized a couple of times already, but he didn't have enough substance to do much of anything except glare at me. When he'd tried to hit me, I'd felt something like a soft breeze.

I was thinking, perhaps a bit late, that I'd never heard one of the villains make a *noise* before, when he raised the branch he was carrying, rifle-style, over his shoulder and clobbered me with it.

It hit me hard, the blow cushioned only slightly by the leaves and twigs. I spun away from him. It wasn't a skilled, strategic evasive move, it was just the direction he'd batted me in. He'd caught me high on the left arm, and some of the hot coffee slopped unpleasantly on my shirt, which reminded me I had the cup in my hand. I completed the turn and threw it at his head.

I half-expected it to go right on through him, as though he were made of the surrounding fog, but instead it made a nice, solid sound like someone dropping a frozen steak on the floor, and his head snapped back and he got a faceful of coffee. He bellowed something, but whatever he said, I was distracted by the sound: it was *wrong*, it seemed to come from farther away than Barry was, and that encouraged me; maybe he wasn't as present as he seemed. I bent down, picked up the tire, and heaved it at his chest.

It hit him low, in the gut, and bounced back toward me as he said, *Huhhhh* and folded his arms over his midsection, fighting for breath. He still had the branch in his hand, and from the look on his face, he had plans for it, so I grabbed the tire again, lifted it high above my head, leaped across the distance between us, and brought it down over him like a big doughnut, pinning his arms at his sides.

Since he couldn't hit me back and nobody was looking—after all, I wasn't the hero of a book anymore—I punched him a couple of times in the face. Sometimes it's nice not to have to fight fair.

His head rocked back in a really gratifying fashion. My knuckles hurt but I hit him again, still angry about what he'd done to my fingernail with that fork in *The Four Last Things*, a score I didn't really get to even in the book. He opened his mouth to shout. I could see his throat constrict, but it was a second before I heard him. He was turning a little shimmery at the edges, as though he were dissolving into the fog, so I just kept hitting him until my hand went through him and the tire dropped to the ground and I was alone on top of the hill.

The shout faded until it sounded like it was coming from the next mountain and then it disappeared.

I thought, *What the hell?*

The fog began to lift. A snake rattled a warning beneath the sage. A warning seemed appropriate.

One of my readers, killed before my eyes in the real world. An old villain from *The Four Last Things*, the first of my books, materializing out of the kind of fog I'd never seen up here, trying to do me harm. And almost solid enough to succeed.

As the fog dissipated, the farther hills, maybe a quarter of a mile away, came into view, pretty much where they always were, but—how can I convey this?—in high-def. When I'd lived among them in Hallinan's books, they'd been pretty fully imagined—for him, I mean, and remember, I had nothing to compare them with then. It was the only world I knew. But he'd written lots of detail: individual plants and flowers, the occasional dog or coyote scampering or slinking, respectively, between them. Since I got here, those hills had looked more like a printed backdrop, like scenery in a 19th-century melodrama.

And suddenly here they were, in detailed, three-dimensional glory, and there was even a breeze stirring some of those distant plants.

Faced with this substantial boost in production values—not to mention solid, moderately dangerous villains—the only thing that came to mind was that there'd been some sort of *imagination boost*. I still wasn't clear on how most of this worked, but it seemed likely to me that I was being *concentrated* on. Eagle Scout Bradley Zipper had said that people up here dwindled away as various streams of imagination were withdrawn: our publishers', our writers', our readers', and so forth. Maybe it worked in reverse, too; we and our worlds got more solid as imagination flowed in, so to speak. Hell, maybe Hallinan was writing me again. Maybe, if I went inside and checked the window, I'd see half a dozen people reading me simultaneously.

I thought, why not go down and look? And at the instant I

began to head down, something *else* moved on the hilltop, way back in the brush. The idea of going back to the house suddenly seemed doubly appealing. So I scuffed back down the hill to the shack, and once I was inside I tilted a chair against the doorknob.

In all the time I'd been here, the place had been as unchanging as a flower inside a ball of solid glass. I'd chafed at it, the sheer, static, unchanging *boredom* of it all. No excitement, no threats, no challenge to rise to. Suddenly, I thought, that might actually have been a selling point.

7

Imagisphere

I REALIZE THAT I KEEP saying "up here," but that's just a verbal tic, probably the vestige of some childhood image of heaven. But I have to say that if this is what's meant by "heaven," some of the world's religions are a very elaborate setup for a limp punch line. As for "up," I have no reason to believe that this world is literally higher, in terms of elevation, than the one occupied by readers and their mouth-breathing brothers, sisters, and cousins who are indifferent to books.

In other words, I'm probably not really "up here" and you're probably not really "down there." It's more likely, I think, that we co-exist in different *atmospheres*. I've come to believe that the earth has at least two atmospheres. There's the one that stars on The Weather Channel, the atmosphere that totes clouds around, that occasionally whips itself into a frenzy and flattens trailer parks, and then turns around and caresses your cheek with the perfect breeze when it's April and you're in love. The atmosphere in which actual events (whatever "actual" means) take place. History, the rise and fall of empires, and all that.

Then there's what I think of as the *imagisphere*, the dreamy, transparent envelope of imagination that surrounds the planet as surely as air does. It's a rich mix of hopes and wishes and fears and ideas, inspiration, desperation, dreams, nightmares, the occasional mistake and the infrequent gleam of solid gold: Beethoven's Violin Concerto in D, the concept of the expanding universe (as opposed to the expanding universe itself), formulas for baby powder and the hydrogen bomb, Philip and Christopher Marlowe, the secret of the cathedral arch and the blunt ambition of Albert Speer's Nazi monstrosities, dance notation and romance languages, Botticelli's Venus, the magic of harmony on stringed instruments, *The Odyssey*, all the books ever written.

This place is *in there* somewhere, I think. And it's like people used to say, or maybe still say, about cosmic string theory: up here, all these dimensions are curled up inside each other, like that ripple-curl giftwrap ribbon, so we've got *our* place and Lit-Fic has *its* (apparently considerably nicer) one, and way over there, rolled as tightly as an umbrella in yet another dimension, Shakespeare and Sophocles are discussing act structure with Neil Simon, and somewhere else Pythagoras is arguing with Richard Feynman over the time signature of the Music of the Spheres. There's apparently a way to get from one of these ribbons to the others, at least if Lobelia meant it when she said she occasionally palled around with the folks from Lit-Fic.

Oh, and since you still may be asking what it's like up here, it's—*partial.* Obviously our lives are somewhat limited, since we can't go anyplace our writers didn't put us unless we're with a character from another series, when (most of the time, anyway) you can explore each other's neighborhoods as long as you're together. Makes you feel a little like a realtor: "And down this lovely shaded street, someone came after me with a straight razor. Great neighborhood for straight razors." Sometimes, it doesn't work—sometimes you can't actually experience the other character's neighborhood. I don't know exactly how to explain *how* it doesn't work. Here's as close as I can get: When you push your way in there, it's like you're wearing special lenses that block out everything but shadows.

But most of the time when you get that resistance, you don't even try. This might be the place for a homely metaphor. I once had a dog who knew he wasn't allowed to go any farther from the house than the bottom of the driveway. He'd sit down there, his front paws *exactly* on the line between yes and no. When I came home, that's where he'd be waiting for me. Obviously, when I wasn't home, no one was going to yell at him if he crossed the line. He just didn't. And sometimes, when you're exploring another character's world, you suddenly realize that you, too, are at the line between yes and no, and in danger of crossing it.

And you just… don't.

Let's see. You know about the hawk, and whatever else I've told you about. You know about the boredom. Here's something. Everything here is *rougher* than in the real world. Even surfaces that would normally be smooth—glass, for example—are a little rough to the touch. Wood feels like sandpaper, bedsheets might as well be burlap, although one female detective up here, who was a personal shopper who doubled as a private eye (each of the books' titles contained the name of a department store, *The Macy's Murders*, *The Skull In Saks*, and so forth), has Egyptian Cotton Sateen sheets from Sferra Milos, and she says they're smooth. Despite the tone of voice in which she shared that information with me, I'll take her word. I have no idea what would happen if I were to get entangled with someone up here.

It's a *sparser* world than yours. My guess is that we're missing about half, or even two-thirds, of the atoms that make up your world. Everything probably weighs less, too, although we don't sense that since we're just as diminished as everything else is. And as I said earlier, the minor characters and villains—well, they might be missing five out of six atoms. Most of them, as I said, can't even make noise.

But as of that encounter on top of the hill, my corner of this world was feeling more solid, more detailed, more finished, almost threateningly so. It felt less like a quick first draft.

Back in the days before he wrote me, Hallinan worked as a

consultant for a theme park company. They'd show him these amazing plans—say, a hotel with a nine-story internal atrium, complete with a waterfall pouring all nine stories down to a "Little Mermaid" rock pool. Then, a couple of years later, he'd go to the completed hotel and it would, sure enough, be nine stories high, but there'd be no waterfall, no rock pool, no Little Mermaid. When he asked about them, he'd be told they'd been "value-engineered." In English, they'd been abandoned because they cost too much. The whole time he was writing me, he tried to work *value-engineered* into a book but he never found a way to do it.

So what I think: I think this world has been value-engineered. More severely, apparently, than the limbo, or whatever it is, for literary fiction. And now, for some reason, my little corner of it was feeling better built. Maybe we'd had some kind of imagination transfusion.

But that's just my guess. And judging from everything that had just happened, my guess was probably worse than yours. Also, if my specific corner was suddenly drawing attention, whose attention was it?

8

The Precise Slope of a Sagging Roof

TWO HOURS LATER, MY LIVING room was full.

That's not saying much. Remember, the living room was just the bottom of the U that the house formed. A big party in that room was eight people. A door three steps up in the center of the living room wall led to the roof of the leaky, sagging room added decades later, a little lower down the slope. The room was a dead loss but the roof served as an uneven deck that offered the spectacular views I mentioned earlier. Hallinan didn't actually make the place up. He lived in the real-world version of it back when he was writing the books.

On this extremely unusual day, the place was jammed. Lobelia had pulled together quite a crew on such short notice. I still hadn't met a lot of people, but Lobelia was gregarious, as are most heroines in cozies, which take place in a relatively friendly world if you don't count the murders. When she and I decided that our own *personal* murder, the one we'd seen through the window, was in fact the beginning of a mystery, she remembered that the one thing we had a surplus of was detectives.

So, the living room: Lobelia had claimed half of the couch she and I had sat on earlier; there was also an old wooden carriage seat from a movie buckboard that offered an uncomfortable perch for two; then there were the coffee table, a couple of folding canvas director's chairs, and two tarnished chromium bar stools that were usually parked at the kitchen counter. Bradley Zipper had

47

declined to attend; Lobelia hadn't known to use the word *help*. Looking around the room, I missed him.

"Here's what I don't get," Tony Romero was saying in his best Brooklynese. He was all alone, and for good reason, on one of the director's chairs. "What I don't get is how you know what book he was reading." He shrugged his black leather shoulders and crossed his black leather legs. Tony had been a vampire all the way through those two paperback originals, and he seemed to take it to heart. In a corner, being studiously ignored by everyone in the room, was a heavy paper bag, stapled shut, that rustled every now and then. It contained Tony's lunch. He had promised to eat it outside.

There was an awkward silence while people tried to figure out how to deal with Tony tactfully. I came out of the kitchen and handed a cup of amaranth tea, whatever that was, to Genevieve Winterspoon, shimmering away in the other director's chair. I got an angelic smile in return, which made sense since she was an angel, one editor's idea of what might be a good answer to all the vampires before it became apparent that the answer to the vampires was more vampires and, later, zombies. She'd folded her wings modestly behind her. She and Tony were as far apart as possible, and she'd moved her chair all the way across the room when his lunch bag rustled the first time.

After a long and awkward pause, Jack Money, who'd been written before political correctness and didn't worry about embarrassing anybody, pushed back his snap-brim hat, circa 1939, sat back on the buckboard seat, and said, "Ya poor mug. Don't get read much, do ya?"

Tony gave Jack a hiss and a glimpse of the fangs. "What'sssss that sssssssupposssssed to mean?" He went a little snaky when he got upset.

"Aaahh," Jack Money said. He shifted his weight on the wooden seat, which was dramatically uncomfortable. "Sittin' up here on your black leather *tuchis* and never getting a look at the real world. That's 'cause nobody's openin' your poor little books."

"Oh, listen to Mr. Great Depression," Tony sneered. "You haven't seen anything *down there* since they were lining up for apples."

"I still got readers," Jack said. "Unlike some I could name."

"When somebody's reading you," I said to Tony, nudging Lobelia aside to make room for me on the couch, "you look up at them through the page, and you can hear the words in your inner ear. There's no actual sound when I see my readers, but I can follow along as they read."

Tony did a quick look around and said, "I knew that."

"*I* hear them in my own voice," Jack Money said. His suit was shiny with wear, his chin had its perpetual crop of stubble, and he exuded an almost visible aura of bourbon. Jack was *noir* to his toenails.

"Are you first-person?" Lobelia asked with professional interest.

"All *real* PI characters are first-person," Jack said. He looked around the room, daring anyone to contradict him.

"I was in omniscient third," Genevieve said, making it sound like a beatific state available only to ancient Hindus, and probably only on Wednesdays.

I was interested in spite of myself. "What do you hear when they read you?" I asked Genevieve.

"Allura's voice." Allura Brightleaf, nee Sophie Mertz, had written Genevieve's four books, the most famous of which, *Murder in Eden*, had taken place not (as you might assume) on Adam and Eve's back forty, but in a Topanga nudist colony. Not having read it, I wasn't entirely clear on what an angel had been doing at a nudist colony or how much she'd shown everyone if she'd played by the rules. "She speaks the Words," Genevieve continued, somehow capping the W in a voice that might have come out of a carnation, "as though she's telling a story to an innocent child."

Lobelia made a discreet hairball sound, and Jack pulled out a hip flask and unscrewed the cap with a certain grim purpose. In the interest of amity, I said, "Anybody need anything?"

Nobody did so I volunteered, "I've got three beers."

"Socko," said Jack Money. "One over here."

"Fine. Anything else? Anyone? As long I'm getting Jack and me a beer?"

No takers. I went into the kitchen and opened the refrigerator while Lobelia took charge in the living room. "So here's what we've got. The crime scene is a bookstore in some desert town in California. The victim was a fan of Simeon's named Ferdy Carvalho. Portuguese or something. He was alone in what looks like a back room—"

"Was the store open?" Jack Money asked.

"We don't know," Lobelia said. "There were no windows that we could see, and the only light seemed to come from overhead fluorescents. We couldn't tell what time it was down there."

"Was he an employee or a customer?" That was Genevieve.

"Employee," I said, carrying the beers in. "My guess is that he thought he was alone in the store and he was taking a break. I've seen him do it a bunch of times. Maybe he locks, sorry, *locked* the front door when he did it."

"Why do you think that?" Lobelia asked.

"Just a guess. It's a shop with more than one room, since the one he read in didn't have any windows, and it seems to me the front room of a bookstore would have windows. Store might be an old house. So if he was going to leave the main room with the cash register and everything, he'd probably lock the front door. Twice before today, he looked over his shoulder while he was reading and then closed the book. One time he came right back and once he was gone an hour or more. I always figured someone had knocked on the door, rung the bell."

"How many employees?" Jack asked.

"Two, I think. Ferdy and a young woman."

"Cute little number?" I wasn't sure whether Jack clung to language like that because it was the way he was written or because he knew it irritated women from a later period.

"She's an attractive young woman," I said carefully. "Late twenties, interesting face."

"Interesting in what way?" Lobelia said.

"Looks intelligent," I said. "She's the reason I think the front door might have been locked. Before, when he seemed to hear something, he stopped reading. This time, he didn't, and it must have made noise, his getting killed, so she wasn't there when it happened. She showed up a while later and found him. So I think the door was probably locked and she had a key."

"So," Genevieve said, stirring her tea, which emitted a golden light. It illuminated her face from below, which seemed to piss Tony off. "You're suggesting that the killer was already in the shop when... what was it? *Ferdy*, when Ferdy locked the door."

"Killer could have had a key," Tony said.

"Surely," Genevieve said without looking at him, "if Ferdy were an employee and he'd closed up the shop for a reading break, when he heard the door unlock he would have closed the book and tried to look busy. It might have been his superior."

"The boss," Jack Money clarified.

Genevieve said, "*Thank* you," in a tone with a little un-angelic rasp to it.

"You think the babe is the boss?" Jack asked.

Genevieve closed her eyes and exhaled for a surprising length of time. Tony's lunch scuttled in its bag. From the size of it, it might have been a pigeon.

"She was the one who found him," I said, as the door into the kitchen opened and Al Hammond came through. "As I said, my guess is that she had a key."

"So was the killer still in there?" Lobelia asked.

"You know," I said, "to give you anything more than a guess I'd have to see the layout of the store."

Hammond was wearing his raincoat, and it was wet. It wasn't raining outside—it never did—but he'd been written with a wet raincoat so often it had stuck. Also, his general mood up here probably overcame the sunshine in his vicinity. He glared into the room, said, "Beer," and went into the kitchen. Even the set of his shoulders, the precise slope of a sagging roof, telegraphed despair.

"Well, you can't do that," Jack Money said to me. "See the layout."

"I'm keenly aware of that."

Coming back in with a beer in hand, Hammond said, "So?" He sat on one of the bar stools.

Lobelia recapped where we were, what we'd seen and guessed.

To me, Hammond said, "How do you know the female employee is the one who found the body?"

"Let me restate it. She was the first person to come near enough to the body for her shoes to be seen on this end."

"So you *don't* know," Hammond said in a tone I'd gotten a lot of in my books. "Somebody else coulda seen him on the floor, from the door, maybe, and not got close enough to get into the picture. Just went and made the call to the cops. Then your girl comes in, and she has to go take a look at the stiff."

I said, "Right."

"In fact," Hammond said with some satisfaction, "you don't know shit."

"No," I said, biting it off a bit. "We're making *hypoth*—"

Tony sat up straight and said, "Hey. Lookit that."

I followed everyone's eyes to the window, where the sky was once again warping and blistering, and the hawk was on the fade. I was looking at two fuzzy bars of light that quickly congealed into fluorescents, chalky and depressing. A man leaned into the picture, staring down at the page. He was about fifty, with a long mournful nose and an upper lip with that pronounced center "V" you sometimes see in trumpet players, He had a great many folds of skin, like someone who'd dropped a third of his body weight, and the pained eyes of someone who had dropped it on his toe.

"He looks like Billy," Lobelia said, and in fact there was a certain Basset Hound cast to the man's face.

"He's a cop," Hammond said with great authority, "and he's—"

He went silent. The upper left corner of the window had gone misty, like someone had breathed on the glass, and then the misted area spread until only about half of the man's face was visible. He leaned in, studying the page so mournfully it might have predicted the date of his death, and then part of his hand came into sight with a spray bottle in it, and the whole window suddenly seemed to be made of frosted glass.

"Ninhydrin," Hammond said. "He's trying to lift some prints."

"From paper?" Jack Money asked. "They can do that now?"

"Hey, Jack," Tony said. "They got all sorts of stuff now, radio and everything."

"At least he's a detective, not a uniform," I said. "I think the murder of one of my readers deserves a detective."

The window got a little mistier, and that was it for a few minutes. Nothing happened. Then, through the mist, the room kind of dipped and swam, and everything went black.

"He put it in a humidity chamber, set to about 185 degrees," Hammond said. "It'll stay black until he opens the door to see whether any prints have come up." Nobody sat up straight or did anything else to betray interest in what he was saying. "In the old days," Hammond added into the silence, "they used a steam iron."

The window remained black. The energy level in my living room dropped. Billy snored.

"Just a regular old steam..." Hammond said, trailing off. He drank again.

People looked at each other without much interest; they seemed to have reached an unspoken consensus that things had indeed gotten boring.

Right on cue, a man came through the door with a gun in his hand.

9

The All-Seeing

AND NOT JUST ANY MAN, either. A pale greenish giant, at least seven feet tall, his bare chest as heavily oiled as a Formula One car, wearing knee-length pants made from a single piece of silvery cloth that had been wrapped somehow around and between his legs. It looked like it would chafe. There didn't seem to be any pockets, so there were at least two reasons the style hadn't lasted. Hanging from his neck on a heavy gold chain was something that appeared to be a human eyeball, but about five times bigger, somewhere in size between a golf ball and a tangerine. It swiveled back and forth in front of his gleaming pectorals with some rapidity, apparently surveying the group. The giant's slippers curled up at the ends, a scimitar hung low on his hip in a bejeweled scabbard, and the gun in his right hand was a World War I German Mauser.

He stood absolutely still, his face inclined downward as though he were studying the floor, keeping the Mauser trained on everyone as the Eye probed the corners of the room. The spaces where his eyes should have been were empty, just featureless skin, sunk in deep green shadow. The rest of him was the green of that unwholesome sheen you sometimes see reflected on the surface of bad meat.

The silvery pants had bits of bark clinging to them and he had a long, fresh scratch on his arm. After a moment, he said to someone who was still outside, "No one. You may come." It was kind of a Schwarzenegger accent, if Schwarzenegger had been an Arab and a tenor.

Lobelia sighed. "Ahmed the All-Seeing," she said *sotto voce*, but not very *sotto*. "Talk about overkill. But if you want *them*, you have to take *him*."

"Nice pants," I said to her. "Too bad they didn't have the shirt in his size." The Eye whipped around to me and hung there, vibrating slightly.

"I asked them, but I didn't think they'd come," Lobelia told the room. She sounded pleased with herself. "And I certainly didn't expect all this whoop-de-do for a simple drop-in."

"Fly into a goddamn woodpile," complained a childish voice outside. "Thtoopid, thtoopid."

"They?" Genevieve said, her eyes absolutely circular. "*Really?*"

Tony said, "Them? You're shitting me." He had the dazed look of someone just beginning to realize that the wrong party might be the right party, after all.

Even Jack Money seemed impressed. He said, "Aces."

"The whole goddamn mountain," the child continued outside, "and he had to hit the woodpile."

The giant quivered slightly. The Eye on the chain suddenly found something interesting on the floor.

"Three years here," Genevieve said, her face translucent, "and I've never seen them." She hugged her shimmering teacup to her heart with elegant, tapering fingers, and I heard Lobelia hack up another discreet hairball. On the floor, Billy got up with a sigh, turned his back to Genevieve, and lay down again.

"You go firtht," lisped the very young voice from outside. "I'll be picking thplinters out of my ath for an *hour*. And I don't even know why we're *here*." The voice seemed to have been canned improperly, shelved in the dark, and left to marinate in resentment for, oh, maybe a century, the italicized words like pedal notes on a pipe organ of grievance.

"We're here, as always, dear sister," said a voice that was identical but for the properly pronounced "s" and the tone. *This* tone was a sort of amplified butterscotch, in contrast with the lemon drop who had spoken first. "To offer help and succor to those in need."

"Thucker ith right," said Lemon Drop. "You thtay and offer whatever, and I'll ride Ahmed home. If he can take off without hitting the goddamn houthe."

"Now, now," soothed Miss Buttercup. She cleared her throat. "*Ahmed?*" A little bit of steel under the sugar.

The Eye on the chain rotated to the door. It looked anxious.

"What are we *missing?*"

The Eye glanced quickly at us, hoping no one was watching.

"Ahmed," said the Buttercup, sounding weary. "The spindrift, please?"

I said, "Spindrift?" and Ahmed raised the hand with the Mauser in it, looked up, switched the Mauser to his left hand, and used the now-Mauserless right to make a sweeping overhand gesture, an elliptical arc that scraped his knuckles on the ceiling. Zillions of tiny particles sprang into being above and behind the moving hand and dropped in a curtain, a shower of diamond splinters, to create a storm of falling sparkle between him and the door.

"*Hey,*" I said. "I'm the one who has to clean that up. And I don't have a vacuum."

I was cut off as Genevieve, who had the clearest view of the door, said meltingly, "So *sweet.*"

And so she was as she shimmered into the room: Louis Carroll's Ideal Edwardian Child, maybe eleven years old, golden curls to mid-back, wearing a flowing gardening outfit of cream-colored linen—a loose, big-buttoned blouse over wide, perfectly draped pants. Topping off the outfit was a broad-brimmed picture hat swathed in shell-colored chiffon, knotted beneath a pale chin. She was the whitest child I'd ever seen in my life, the product of an entire planet with only about nine genes, all Scandinavian.

"Oh," she said in a reasonable semblance of sheer amazement, "what a *ripping* gathering."

Genevieve put her teacup on the battered sideboard and curled her fingers to touch her knuckles together over her chest, a praying stance for some off-brand religion. The Edwardian child gave her a very quick glance, seemed to decide *no, thanks,* and smiled at Jack Money. The smile got a little strained, and just before it would have started to look silly, she said over her shoulder, "*Now* would be nice, dear sister."

I smelled tobacco smoke. Nobody up here smoked.

Chains jingled.

And through the door, looking neither right nor left, came an exact duplicate of Louis Carroll's Dream Number One—eleven years old, golden hair, skin like milk with a high cream content, and so forth. But this one was wearing ripped black jeans with chains dangling from the belt loops, a black leather jacket with about a hundred safety pins piercing it, and an additional safety pin through her perfect little nose. Her hair had been gelled and pulled away into sharp-tipped spikes, and an unfiltered cigarette sent up smudge from the corner of her mouth, hanging at the perfect Jean-Paul Belmondo angle.

"How *very* 1970s," Lobelia said, taking in the safety pins, and this time the *voce* really was *sotto*.

"I'm Patsy," the proper Edwardian girl said, tilting her head to one side and winsomely pointing at herself to enlighten the slower among us. She extended a hand, palm up, like someone indicating a refrigerator in a giveaway show. "And that's Pansy." Her sister shouldered her slightly, pushing her a half-step to her left, and cut through the room, heading straight for the door to the roof. "We're the Parker Twins," Patsy finished, and made a curtsy.

"Loother," her sister said, stepping up onto the roof. "Bunch of lootherth." A cloud of tobacco smoke drifted back into the room. "I'll be out here until it'th time to get on the *Titanic* again."

"We had a *weensy* accident," Patsy said, with a quick little glance at Ahmed that missed being mean, but not by much. "But we laugh at adversity, don't we, Pansy?" She released a lilting triplet of a laugh, three descending notes. Pansy, on the roof, said something unprintable.

"One *hundred years*," Genevieve said, shaking her head in amazement.

"Hundred and ten," Pansy called from the roof. "Get it right, Galadriel."

"Genevieve," Genevieve said.

"Whatever," Pansy said. More smoke.

"My sister keeps track," Patsy said fondly, as though to say *what an endearing trait.* "It was 1902 when Mr. Stratemeyer wrote *The Parker Twins at the Seaside*—"

"Thee-thide," Pansy snapped from the roof. "You alwayth forget the goddamn hyphen."

"At the Sea-side," Patsy said, not rolling her eyes.

"*Edward* Stratemeyer?" I asked. "*The* Edward—"

"Yes, Mr. Stratemeyer. In the full vigor of his—"

"Vigor," Pansy sniped, following it with a raspberry.

"*All right*," Patsy said, containing the snap nicely. "He was young, okay? He was strong. In the flower of his—"

"Probably a bachelor'th button, the old queen," Pansy said.

"Pansy bears a *weensie* grudge about how we were shunted aside," Patsy said. She patted the center of her chest to calm herself, although her pulse didn't seem to be racing. "Actually, as far as we know, Mr. Stratemeyer never displayed any inappropriate interest *whatosever*—" she shouted the last word in the direction of the cigarette smoke—"in members of his own—"

"The *Hardy* Boyth?" Pansy spat the words into the room with such force they could have bounced on the floor. "I mean, ith that Freudian, or what? *Hardy?*"

"It's just a name," Patsy said, blinking quickly.

"Tom *Thwift?* Don *Thturdy?* Do we thee a pattern here? Bomba the *Jungle Boy?* In a *leopard bikini?* Written under the name Roy *Rockwood?* Give me a fucking *break.*"

A whole cigarette's worth of smoke billowed in, followed by the rasp of a match.

"It was a boy, you see—" Patsy said.

"—That little creep, Bert Bobbthey—" Pansy interrupted.

"—who replaced us in Mr. Stratemeyer's affections—"

"—*affections?*—"

"—after our somewhat limp third outing, *The Parker Twins and the Hollow Tree—*"

"—he took a perfectly good book with a really crappy title, *The Parker Twinth: Merry Dayth Indoorth and Out*, and—"

"—and he gave it to—to the Bobbseys," Patsy said, pressing an open hand to her chest and lifting her chin bravely in a gesture that owed a great deal to silent movies. "And that came out in 1904. Mr. Stratemeyer decided he liked the dynamic of boy and girl twins better than two girls—"

"—*big* thurprithe," Pansy said.

"And we were never written again," Patsy finished. She looked winded. "The last new book was pulped in 1916, and we were up here."

"All alone, you poor things," Genevieve said.

"It wath heaven," Pansy said from the roof. "*Real* heaven, no *angelth*, no *vampireth*, no *catth*—"

"Cats," Patsy translated.

"We *owned* the plathe."

"Of course, we were bitterly lonely," Patsy said. "Many was the pillow I soaked with tears. We had always been surrounded by love and laughter…"

She raised her eyes toward the ceiling. A gentle light settled like a shawl over her head and shoulders. From a great distance, as though heard through a heating vent from thirty stories below, an organ softly played.

"Cut that out, Ahmed," Lobelia said. The Eye hanging around Ahmed's chest jerked around at her. The light faded. Lobelia said to Patsy, "Many *was* the *pillow?*"

"Oh, thank you," Patsy said crisply. "One does so *wish* for one's grammar to be corrected."

"Excuse me," I said. "*The Hollow Tree? Merry Days Indoors and Out? At the Sea-side?*"

"*He* got it," Pansy said from the roof. "There'th a *hyphen.*" Then, from the sound of it, she hocked a loogie.

"Was that a display of memory?" Patsy asked me unaffection-ately. "If so, it was ripping."

"Those don't sound much like mysteries." Patsy was looking squarely at me, in a way that made me wish she was a little farther away. "Just, you know, judging from the titles."

Patsy looked out through the door, presumably at Pansy. Pansy, still offscreen, so to speak, said, "We were mithfiled."

I said, "Mis*filed?*"

"The Library of Congress," Patsy said. "They hadn't gotten around to cataloging us—we were, as Pansy is so fond of pointing out, *girls*, and we hadn't sold very well. But the libraries kept buy-ing us, and by the time we were cataloged, Mr. Stratemeyer was identified with mysteries, action series: the Rover Boys, Tom Swift, The Hardy Boys—"

"*Hitth*, in other words," Pansy said.

"Well," Patsy said, and for the first time she looked downcast. "Yes. Hits. And when they got around to us, they looked at all his other books and classified us as mysteries."

"The *irony*," Pansy said from outside.

I said, "That's terrible." Neither twin acknowledged my attempt at sympathy so I said, "What about him?" I raised my eyebrows at Ahmed.

"He arrived in 1939," Patsy said. She held up the usual number of fingers and began to tick them off.

"Three books: *Enter Ahmed the All-Seeing, Ahmed the All-Seeing and the Whispering Sands,* and *Ahmed the All-Seeing and the Secret of the Vanished City Beneath the Pyramid.*"

"Titles are getting kind of long," I said.

"Well, *yeah*," said Pansy from the roof.

"And then, *pulped*," Patsy said, brushing her hands together as though to get dust off them. "Poor Ahmed."

Ahmed's head was still down but the dangling Eye was following the conversation.

"And how'd he wind up with you?"

"Ahmed is—put your fingers in your ears, Ahmed."

Ahmed put his fingers in his ears but the Eye was practically straining on the end of its chain to follow Patsy's lips.

"*Conspicuous*," Patsy said. "He didn't fit in."

From the roof, Pansy said, "Duh."

"And despite his awe-inspiring size, he's as sensitive as a child. And alone in the world, we took pity on him—"

"A giant can be really *utheful*," Pansy said. "Or would be, if he had a dethent navigation thythtem."

"And now," Patsy said, as though no one else had spoken, "he's like family." She tilted her head winsomely and gave him a fond smile.

"Well," I said, "does he ever get to sit down?"

A tiny wrinkle appeared on Patsy's flawless brow. "Sit down?"

"You know, like in a chair?"

"He can thit on the woodpile, if it'th thtill high enough," Pansy said from the roof.

"Of course, he can sit down," Patsy said sweetly. "Ahmed,

take your fingers out of your ears." Ahmed took his fingers out of his ears, and she said, "Sit."

Ahmed sat on one of the bar stools. Jack Money, who was on the short side, sighed in relief.

"Hey. Look," Al Hammond said. Everyone looked except Ahmed, whose back was to the window, but the Eye floated up above his shoulder and turned to check the action.

Light flooded the window and a hand in a latex glove reached in and picked up the book. The ceiling of—I supposed—the police lab floated by as we looked up as the detective carried the open book to a table where he swiveled a lamp and directed it down at the page. The lamp somehow made things darker.

"If we could see it in color, it would be green," Hammond said wistfully. He sounded envious. "The print, if there is one, will show up under green light."

And suddenly, there it was. I was looking up at the cop through a fingerprint on the surface of the page. Others saw it at the same time I did, and there was a general murmur of interest.

The mournful detective leaned in, studying the print, and then disappeared. A moment later, he was back with a little digital camera. The lens, which had to be a macro, came down within an inch or two of the surface of the page.

Jack Money said, "Jivin'."

The book was closed and the sky flickered back into place, with the hawk in front of it. It was getting dark out.

"He got a print," Hammond said, shaking his head admiringly. "At least a good partial, or he wouldn't have shot it. How about that? He got a print." He almost sounded like the Al I'd once known.

There was a jingle of chains from the door that led to the roof, and Pansy Parker stood there, framed against the dimming evening sky, looking directly at me through a curl of cigarette smoke.

"Tho," she said. "Want to thit around with thith bunch of

lunkheadth and hope they give you an idea, or do you want to get down there and find out whothe fingerprint it ith?"

10

Wolves and Crickets,
Sid and Nancy

AHMED THE ALL-SEEING WAS snoring as gently as a young girl. The curled tips of his silvery slippers gleamed in the light of a fat half-moon, and the Mauser glinted coldly in his hand. Billy was curled up beside him, black nose shining in the moonglow. Through the center of the sky, like a vein of shotgun silver, staggered the Milky Way.

"I don't usually get this kind of night sky," I said.

"We brought it with us," said Patsy Parker. She was sitting beside her twin at the edge of the roof, her legs hanging over, her broad-brimmed hat in her lap and her hair a pale cascade over her shoulders. Now that the others had left, more or less shooed out by Lobelia and a barking Billy, Patsy was working on an un-filtered cigarette, borrowed from Pansy. Occasionally she flicked ash into the brim of her hat. Glowing against her Edwardian garden linens, the cigarette looked like bad Photoshop. "We've had a lot of time to figure out how to improve things. If I'd wanted to make all of you jealous, I could have turned the Seeing into color."

"The Seeing?"

"You know, that thing through the window. That wrinkly, doglike detective with his green light and his purple fingerprint. I get those in color."

"We," Pansy said. She took a drag off her own cigarette and streamed smoke at the stars.

Patsy closed her eyes tightly for a moment and released an irritable little series of *p's*, as though she hoped her sister would be gone when she looked again. "Sorry, sister. We, of course."

Pansy said, "I am tho thick of *we*."

"I get a little red at the beginning," I said. No one cheered. "So you understand how that works? The Seeing?"

"More than you do, anyway," Patsy said.

"You went out of print so long ago," I said, yielding to a twinge of malice. "Not to be tactless, but I'm surprised you still *have* Seeings. There can't be many copies lying around."

"Not many," Patsy said.

"Well, then. No copies means no readers, so no Seeings. How do you have Seeings?"

"It'th been a while," Pansy said, staring at the coal on her cigarette. For the first time she sounded more sad than bitter.

"How long?" I asked.

"Nineteen-seventy-four," Patsy said. "Should I tell him?"

"Why not?" Pansy said. "Who careth?"

Patsy settled in and took a professional-looking hit off her cigarette. "There was an English punk band, all girls."

Pansy said, "The Penith Pumpth."

"And they got invited, the Penis Pumps did, to some twit's country house to do a show for the silk shirt and tennis-racket set. There was a copy of one of our books in the library. *The Parker Twins and the Hollow Tree*. A first edition, actually."

"The only edition," Pansy said, "and one of the band memberth thtole it. They uthed it in their act. The lead thinger would read it out loud, thcreaming into the mic and cutting her arm with a razor blade while the guitaritht and the drummer played thrash."

"Not exactly what Mr. Stratemeyer had in mind," Patsy said.

Pansy said, "Fuck him. It wath the only interethting thing to happen in a thentury."

"So," Lobelia said as she climbed up onto the roof, "that's where your, um, fashion sense comes from."

"You can only walk around for tho long looking like an immature pre-Raphaelite."

"I'm sure that's so, dear," Lobelia said, doing motherly. She turned around and bent down to get something, and when she was facing us again, she was holding a platter, one of my mother's old pieces of blue-and-white willow ware. I smelled ginger and nutmeg. "*He's* resting comfortably," she said with a glance at Ahmed.

"He hathn't got much to think about," Pansy said. "He'th like a thwitch. He'th homithidal or he'th athleep."

"Poor thing," Lobelia said. "We're so much at the mercy of our writers. That old hack Westmore didn't even think to write a holster for that stupid gun. The poor dear has it in his hand all the time."

Pansy toyed with the safety pin in her nose. My own nose let out a sympathetic twinge. "He'th better off now than when he arrived. Nobody would even talk to him."

"Just because he was a giant?" I said. "I mean, this isn't exactly Mount Normal. We just kicked out a vampire."

"You don't know, Simeon?" Lobelia extended the platter, which was piled with rectangles of gingerbread. Patsy took two, and Pansy gave out a solid, derisive snort that had serious rejection energy behind it.

"Generally," I said, taking a piece, "you don't ask a question to which you already know the answer. It's a shortcut to a dud scene."

"The problem was only *partly* that he was huge and green and didn't own a shirt," Lobelia said. "The real problem was that he was the first spin-off *ever*. In 1930-something."

"Nine," Patsy said, getting her teeth somehow into a word that's hard to bite. "I already said that."

"Thirty-nine, thank you, darling." Lobelia extended another piece of gingerbread, a peace offering. "Ahmed was created for a movie serial. *Rip Baxter and the Mountain of Doom.* He was supposed to be the sidekick, but Rip was such a stick that Ahmed stole the show. Rip barely had a walk-on in the second one, which was called *Ahmed the All-Seeing and the Silken—the Silken…*"

"*And the Thilken Claw,*" Pansy said. "And we were going to be in *Merry Dayth Indoorth and Out.*" She mimed blowing her nose. "Doethn't it make you want to heave? *The Thilken Claw,* that'th a *title.*"

"And it was a hit, too," Lobelia said. "So the studio decided to make some extra bucks out of Ahmed via the pulps, where they didn't have to make a movie or even pay an actor, and that idea resulted in three wretched novels by that idiot Alan Westmore. A duffer who'd already ridden two franchises into the ground, *Doctor Terminus* and *The Jasmine Peril.* And he wrote Ahmed into remainders around 1936, and three years later, old Ahmed was up here—"

"And everybody's nose was in the air," Patsy said. "'You're not a *real* character, you're from the *movies.*' So we made friends with him."

"Actually," Pansy said, smashing her cigarette flat, "we enthlaved him. But he wantth tho little—to be taken out and ridden onthe in a while, to flash the gun around, do a little cheap magic, get hith chetht oiled. It maketh him happy. And big ath he ith, he doethn't eat much of anything."

"The occasional steer," Patsy said. She was studying the moon as though she thought she recognized it from somewhere and wished she could go wherever it was they'd met. "And the magic can be helpful."

"How do you know all this stuff?" I asked Lobelia. "About Ahmed and everybody."

Lobelia wiggled a finger at me. "No more pretending you've read me. My backstory was that I became an amateur sleuth in the first place because I had read everything—and I mean *everything*, all the way back to Poe and that stultifying Auguste Dupin. I was a librarian who cooked and read mysteries. In every book, I adapted the methods of one of the classical detectives to solve the crime—Holmes in one volume, Nero Wolfe in another. And the recipes were appropriate to the detective to whom we were paying homage. For Mickey Spillane I created a meat dessert."

The premise seemed so awful that it required some sort of response; silence would have been insulting. "But Nero had Archie. Holmes had Watson."

"And?"

"Well, you don't have—I mean you don't seem to—"

"I have *Billy*," Lobelia said, glancing at the dog, who hoisted his pendulous ears slightly as he sensed our attention. "Billy was Archie, Billy was Watson. With the added plus of being a telepath."

I said, "Mmmmm." It was the most tactful thing I could think of, but Billy growled anyway. "So," I said to Patsy and Pansy. "You brought this sky along?"

"I said so," Patsy said.

"Very cool," I said.

Pansy said, "Want to thee more?"

I shrugged. "Why not?"

"Did your writer ever give you cricketth?"

"Yeah. Once. In a scene where I was going to kill someone, I told him he might want to keep track of his remaining moments, and since he couldn't use his heartbeat because it was about to accelerate, I suggested he should use the crickets, because they didn't give a shit."

"Okay," Pansy said, and before she'd finished the second syllable, we were awash in crickets, a whole orchestra of them fiddling away by the thousands all around us.

"Very nice," Lobelia said, conducting with a hand that had a baked good in it.

"It has to be something that was written for me?" I asked, slightly disappointed. "You can't whip up something I never experienced in a book?"

Pansy said, "How about a wolf?" A wolf immediately howled on the hill above us. The moon went from half to full and a ragged Lon Chaney cloud menaced it. The wolf howled more loudly and several others joined in, creating a full, shivery wolf chord. She turned up a palm. "*Voilà.*"

"Very impressive. So you weren't just blowing smoke when you said that thing about me being able to find out whose fingerprint that is."

Pansy turned to Patsy. "I'm helping him *why?*"

"Because, under that smelly leather and those stupid safety pins, you're written that way."

"Okay." Pansy turned to me and gave me a once-over that made me feel like sale merchandise. "How much do you know about thith plathe?"

"Well," I said. I suddenly realized how stupid my insights would sound out loud.

"Oh, come on. Jutht take a crack at it. No matter how thilly it ith, the truth is thillier."

"I doubt it, but here goes." And I told her what I've already told you. When I'd finished, she and Patsy shared a long glance.

"The Imagithphere," Pansy said. "Not bad. And you're right, there are a bunch of platheth like thith, for different kindth of imaginationth. Okay, here'th the part you may not have figured out. Imagination ith a *conductor*. Like copper—"

"Or water, for electricity," Patsy horned in. "Everything that

happens in the brain is electricity, right? It's little electrical im-
pulses that take different paths through the brain."

"Excuse me," I said. "Not to interrupt, but how does an elev-
en-year-old Edwardian girl know about this?"

Patsy and Pansy sighed in unison, and I had an inkling of
why Mr. Stratemeyer might have grown weary of them.

When she'd used up her sigh, Patsy said, "We've been to other areas of the—what did you call it?"

I said, "The Imagisphere."

"Isn't that interesting," Patsy said. "As long as we've been up
here, we've never named it. So, to keep it short, we've learned to
venture among the various areas up here. I've had fascinating
chats with people over in science, for example."

"And they talked to you?"

"I can't say I'm fond of your tone. It's *amazing* what people
will say to one when one is polite and interested and arrives on a
green genie who's seven feet tall. Yes, thought processes are all
electricity, and imagination is a conductor. That's why creative
people make *connections* other people don't. For most people, the
electricity flows through cords, to stretch the metaphor, that connect various parts of the brain to each other. Might connect seven
or eight places—or more, if it's something the person has thought
a lot about. But for a *creative* person, the electricity flows in the
brain the same way it flows through water, or through a cloud. It
can touch on thousands of connections."

I said, "Okay."

Pansy said, "And it conducth *between* people, too."

"Between good collaborators," Patsy said. "Mr. Gilbert and
Mr. Sullivan, for example. Two minds behave like a single mind.
Together, they generate a sort of shared field of imagination, and
ideas flow back and forth between them."

"That'th kind of what happenth in a theeing," Pansy said.

I said, "It is?"

"Plus," Patsy said, "you're already down there."

I said, "I am?"

"Of course. You're on the *page*."

I said, "Oh, yeah." I needed better dialog.

"And where *else* are you?"

Patsy's tone was one I had learned to hate by third grade, the tone of someone who's asking a perfectly simple question and is dead certain you're going to flub the answer.

"Ummmm," I said. "Up here?"

"Exactly. Here's what a Seeing really is. It's you, on the page talking to yourself up here, through the medium of a reader, conducted by the imagination, first, that the reader uses when she reads the words and, second, the imagination that forms this place. So there you are: you, up here, seeing the reader through the eyes of you, down there on the page."

"And that's why I know what book it is and which passages they're reading."

"They?" Patsy said wistfully.

"I've got a couple of dozen."

The twins let a mournful moment pass. Billy used it to fart.

"I've been trying to figure that out since I got here," Lobelia said, fanning her hand beneath her nostrils. "He didn't do it in the books."

"Yes, well—" Patsy began, and Pansy hauled off and kicked one of her sister's dangling legs, a *shut up* if ever I saw one, and Patsy said immediately, "... well, that's what's so *perpetually* interesting about this place. One surprise after another."

I said, "That hasn't been my experience."

"You probably had a more vivid life before you got here than we did," Patsy said, in a tone so acidic that she might have borrowed it from Pansy. "We went to the sea-shore, and he got ninety pages out of it."

"We didn't even get in the *water*," Pansy said.

"People had more time then," I said. "They read until they died. But listen, one of my readers has been killed, and I want to do something about it if that's possible. So if we could, like, hopscotch a little through the Edwardian pacing, how the hell does my being able to watch someone *read* me help me get, uhh, down there?"

"We all say that," Patsy said. "*Down there.*"

I said, "Glad to hear it. You want me to take a note?"

Patsy looked at me for a long moment and then nodded slowly, as though she'd come to a decision. It was a little stagy. "It's not just seeing," she said. "There are people down there who are like... like *sensitives*. They give out and pick up *signals*. A little bit the way psychics were supposed to, but real."

"What kind of people?"

"*Think* about it," Patsy said. "People who *read* all the time and recommend books to their friends. Really good librarians. People who own independent bookstores, just because they like to be around books. Some bookstore employees, the ones who can actually recommend something to you based on what you like to read. Even a few publishers. *Book people.*"

Pansy horned in. "They're, like, *open* to uth."

I said, "*Like?*"

Pansy blinked. "I picked it up from the Penith Pumpth."

"And you're lucky that's all you picked up," Patsy said.

"Oh, yeah," Pansy said. "It's *much* better to thpend eternity looking like thomeone who'th thearching for a thilver unicorn."

"And?" Patsy said, in a tone like someone gargling barbed wire. "I suppose British punk is *au courant*? Sid and Nancy are still alive? You look like something that died on the sidewalk on Melrose Avenue in 1979." She'd raised her voice, and Ahmed shifted slightly, the Eye on his chest rolling around as it checked us out.

"My, my," Lobelia said admiringly to Patsy. "You're *not* just the insipid twin."

"This is all very nice, very enlightening," I said. "Good to know about conductivity and everything, but what do you mean they're open to us? And how do you get involved in what's happening down there? Because that's what it sounds like—what you said, I mean. It sounds like there's some way for me to find out who killed Ferdy."

"You know," Patsy said, still riled up, "this took us years and years to work out. We don't actually *have* to share it at all, even if Mr. Stratemeyer would want us to. And even if we do want to—"

"You brought it up, dear," Lobelia said sweetly.

The twins looked at each other. Patsy smoothed the wrinkles in her linen, just displacing a little frustration. "This could have been a great scene," she said, still looking at Pansy. "I had a smashing twist in mind."

I just let the moment stretch out. Something was clearly happening between them.

The wolves howled again, and the twins broke their eyelock. Pansy's gaze drifted to Ahmed. She lifted her chin in a silent question. The Eye on Ahmed's chest flicked back and forth between her and Patsy. It seemed nervous.

Patsy sighed again, this time a sigh of acceptance, and nodded. She put out an immaculate, perfectly ironed linen-clad sleeve, an open hand at the end of it. "Ahmed," she said. "The Eye, please."

11

Sensitives

AHMED HAD GROWN BLUE EYES.

Within about 30 seconds of Patsy's removing the chain from around his neck, the blank spaces beneath his eyebrows turned an energetic pink, the healthy pink you see when a cut is healing, and then the area went kind of translucent, and I could see sky-blue eyes, wide open beneath the skin. I must have blinked in self-defense because the next time I looked, he was staring back at me out of a perfectly ordinary, if exotically shaped and colored, pair of eyes.

"This is what you need to do," Patsy Parker said. She handed the chain with the Eye on it to her sister. The Eye hung as inert as a fishing weight, devoid of its former animation. "Think about the place where your reader met his tragic fate. Do you know where it was?"

"Sure. The Pack Rat used bookstore in Joshua Tree. In California. I've probably driven past it."

"Close your eyes. Can you visualize it?"

I closed my eyes. It was dark. "Only the room I saw, the back room, I think, where Ferdy always read me. And even that, only a little." I tried to summon up the room I'd seen, beginning with the bookshelf that had usually been behind Ferdy, and suddenly I caught a very clear and very short glimpse of it. I said, "Whoa."

"What we need is an entry point. Like the first tile in a mosaic. We'll fill in the ones around that one and then work our way out. Try to bring back everything you saw. Any views you might have got when he tilted the book or when a cop picked it up. You want to be able to sort of turn your head and look around a part of the room. But *don't open your eyes.* Can you see it?"

And suddenly I could. "I can sort of imagine the, uhh, the corner where he usually read. Pretty sketchy, though. So now what do I do?"

"You can't hurry this," Patsy said. "Just hold the image and *keep your eyes closed.* Get what you're seeing as clear in your mind as you can, and then try to expand your sense of it. Not seeing it, just *sensing* it. The way you can hear and sense what's going on in a house even when you can only see the room you're in. Or when you think you hear something in the dark."

"Got it." I felt like the pores of the skin on my arms and the sides of my neck had opened wide.

"What you're looking for is *a point of warmth.* A fuzzy kind of radiance, something you might be able to warm your hands at if you could get close enough. You might see it as a faint blob of colored light somewhere in your field of vision."

"I don't know—oh, wait. Maybe I've got one."

"Well, don't try to focus on it. You know how you look at something in the dark by looking to one side of it because you can actually see it more clearly that way?"

"Yes."

"Like that. Remember, eyes closed. How bright is the spot?"

"Compared to what?"

"Right," Patsy said. "You don't have anything to compare it to. Well, when you find a sensitive who's read you, he or she will seem brighter, and more orange than red."

"This one's kind of orange." A few moments passed. I tried to hold the image of the bookstore in my mind's eye while remaining aware of the fuzzy spot, which sort of shimmered. It began to seem a little silly.

Billy whimpered.

"Take this seriously, Simeon," Lobelia said. "He was *your* reader."

"I'm trying. But I feel like I'm at a séance."

"The *warm spot*," Patsy interrupted sharply. "Is there *one*, or are there more?"

"One. Wait. Oh, my God, it's moving. Toward the left. That would be, ummm, the door, maybe? It's—it's leaving."

"That warm spot is, or was, the nearest Sensitive, and if it was orange, it's probably read you. It doesn't matter if it's on the move. Just stay exactly as you are. Take a deep breath and hold it, and don't lose the image of that back room. Pansy is going to touch you now, but try not to move or get distracted. Pansy?"

I smelled the tobacco on Pansy's breath, and her fingers brushed my skin, and then there was something cold and heavy on the back of my neck and the whole world began to spin, as though the house were rolling onto its side and we were all in danger of sliding off the edge and plummeting through the hundred and fifty feet of vertical canyon off to the right.

I said, "Uhhhh."

Patsy said, "This is normal. Maintain your concentration. *Don't open your eyes.*"

I did what I could to stay in the bookstore, but there was an immediate distraction.

"What do you see?" Patsy asked.

I said, "My knees."

"*Men*," Patsy said. "You lost your focus."

I said, "I've never seen my knees from this angle before."

"That's because the Eye is in the middle of your chest."

"You can open your eyeth now," Pansy said.

I tried, but no go. My eyelids wouldn't respond and my vision remained locked on the fold in my right knee. I reached up, to where my eyes normally were, and it was all smooth skin beneath my brows. I emitted what I suppose a minor writer would describe as a strangled sound.

Pansy laughed, an unpleasant little nutmeg-grater of a laugh.

"This is not even remotely funny," I said. "Give me my goddamn eyes back."

"Shhhhh. What I'm about to tell you is an anachronism for 1916," Patsy said, "but we're all going to have to live with it. The Eye becomes your default vision system the moment it's hung around your neck. It shuts down all the other optical circuits. You know how the speakers on your computer shut off when you put earphones into the jack?"

My computer had been a creaky old two-drive that fell behind me when I typed, but I remembered the headphone jack. "Sure."

"Like that."

I picked up the Eye and aimed it at her. She looked as innocent as unsalted butter. "That's all? I mean, losing my eyes is *normal?*"

She shrugged. "Normal? It's the way that idiot wrote it."

"And when I take the thing off?"

"Your eyes will come back. Just like Ahmed's did."

I reached back to lift the chain off my neck. "Good deal."

"*You don't want to do that,*" Patsy said as a scratching sound indicated that Pansy was lighting up another one. I swiveled the Eye to verify it and she gave me hard Barbara Stanwyck eyes over the match. "What you *do* want to do," Patsy said, "is go back in your mind to that bookstore and look at what you were imagining before. Just concentrate, exactly like you were doing a minute ago, and see what happens. And you don't need to move the Eye with your hand. Just let it hang, and think in the direction you want to look."

I wasn't quite sure how to begin. I couldn't close my eyes because I didn't have any, and the Eye didn't have lids. At first, nothing happened except that I became aware of how badly my trousers bagged at the knees. Then my legs got a little wavy and kind of insubstantial, like a theatrical scrim that appears solid until the lights come up behind it and turn it transparent I said, "Hmmm," and then my leg disappeared completely and so did the roof and the hills and all of Topanga Canyon, and I was looking up at the ceiling of the bookshop, just as I'd seen it through the book when Ferdy was reading it, but in glorious color, or as glorious as a back room in a used bookstore can be. "I see it," I said. "Just like I'm really there. Hot damn, I see it."

"Now look around the way you did before. Remember, you don't have to turn your head. You just think a direction and it'll look there."

I thought *left*, and my perspective shifted left. More bookshelves came into sight.

"I can do this." I looked more closely at the shelves. "Wow. I can even read titles."

"Good," Patsy said, "Now what you need—"

"They've only got three of me," I said. "Three titles, I mean. They've got two copies of *The Man With No Time.*"

"Are mine there?" That was Lobelia.

"Skip the titles," Patsy said. "You've got work to do."

"Well," I said. "They did have one more of mine, the copy the cop took. So that's four—"

"Are you listening to me?" Patsy's voice had been heavily starched.

"I'm there," I said. "I am *so* there. Titles, schmitles. Ready to go."

"First trick," Patsy said. "Change rooms."

"Change... okay, got the door now. Just wobble on over to the—"

"Not the door," Patsy said. "Forget the door. You're not a

pedestrian. What would you call the room on the other side of the door?"

"I'd call it the front of the store," I said, feeling like the teacher had, for some reason, slipped me an especially easy quiz.

"Then just think *front of the store*," Patsy said.

"Zounds," I said. "Here I am."

And I was. And not alone, either. The detective with the doleful Basset-Hound face was there, talking to a nervous-looking guy, balding and with an Adam's apple like a little tent, who was on a stool behind the counter. The place was a dump, old books stacked everywhere. "Two people," I said. "The cop and another guy."

"Look at their headth," Pansy said, sounding interested. "Look clothely."

"I am looking at their heads."

"Are you getting anything? Thoughts, words, feelings?"

This was new territory. It seemed to call for additional stillness. I almost stopped breathing. "I get some nervousness, some irritation, from the one who might own the place. Little zitzes of nervous energy, kind of reddish. From the cop, nothing."

"The cop's not a Sensitive," Patsy said. "And the store owner has what the Penis Pumps called a contact high. He's around books so much, even just as merchandise, that he can't help being a little bit open. But he's not the orange spot you found before. He hasn't read you, and he's not the one who can help you."

"The orange spot left," I said.

"That's right," Patsy said. "You said that. Okay, sit up straight. Make sure the Eye is hanging free. Breathe slowly two or three times. Get ready to go."

"Go where?"

"Wherever the Sensitive went."

"And we know where that is?"

"Sure, thilly." Pansy said. "It'th *down there*."

part two

joshua tree

12

Too Much Time Alone

THE SCREEN DOOR, SWINGING BACK at the command of its hyperactive spring, bumped Madison on her butt as she turned the knob of the heavy wooden door behind it. This happened every day, and every day Madison kicked backward to knock the door away, leaving her leg extended behind her to keep the door from bumping her butt again. And, as also happened every day, the bottom edge of the door bit into the tender skin covering her Achilles tendon in revenge.

Madison said a word of which her mother heartily disapproved. Then she shouldered the front door open and scooted through it before the screen door could attack again.

She stood there, centered in the rectangle of yellow desert sunlight that fell through the door, feeling the weight and heat of it on her shoulders, and surveyed her once-tidy living room. But what she was thinking (to her surprise) was *Poor Ferdy*.

A quick internal hypocrisy check rated the thought, which had come out of nowhere, as 40% hypocritical and 60% sincere. But, she figured, since she hadn't said it out loud (and there wasn't anyone around to hear it even if she had) that 40% wasn't *real* hypocrisy. It was *faux*-hypocrisy, not meant to fool anyone. *Except myself,* she thought, observing herself thinking *Except myself.*

"I am spending *way* too much time alone," Madison said out loud.

The living room echoed the sentiment from all directions. It echoed it in the slop of junk covering the coffee table, in the clutter crowding the couch, in the spilled-juice stain on the once-immaculate rug, in the crooked pictures, in the film of dust on the windowsills. When Madison was a little girl, she had thought dust fell from fairies' wings as feathers did from birds'. She tried to rekindle the belief now in self-defense, but the needle on the hyp-meter zoomed into the red and banged against the screw that marked the top limit. She should probably dust.

Ferdy, she thought again. The thought, which had popped into her mind unbidden, was shouldered aside by the realization that she'd forgotten something, and she turned around and went back out into the heat so she could get the mail out of the clay pot she used as a mailbox. The fern that had thrived in the pot back in the cool moisture of San Francisco had shriveled into a brittle brown skeleton by the end of the first week she'd lived here, its thin green vegetable screams almost audible at night, the tight, defensive curls of its fronds reminding her of the clenched fists of burn victims. The mailbox screwed into the wall beside the front door had been locked when she moved in and she hadn't been given a key, so she'd yanked the dead fern from the pot, its sad, dried dirt-plug coming up as intact as a cork, and told the postperson to drop the mail into it. The mail got dirty but it stayed down there, even when the wind was blowing. As it did approximately 92% of the time.

She fanned the day's mail, reading fast. It was all from corporate entities with their dry little corporate hands out, groping blindly toward her pockets. As she went back in, turning over the stuff that was upside down, she slowed at the sight of a plausible envelope, and the screen door caught her on the elbow. She dropped not only the mail but the book she'd been carrying sandwiched between her arm and her body. She said, "I *hate* you" to the screen door, kicked it once, stepped safely out of range, and bent to pick up the stuff she'd dropped. The promising envelope was a pitch for a magazine subscription. She closed the front door, tossed the mail into the wastebasket that she'd put against the wall for just that reason, and went to the window to turn on the air conditioner.

She got a grunt, a thump, a groan of operatic protest, and then a stream of hot, dry air with a staggeringly high dust content that slowly cooled and eventually stopped smelling like lizards. Madison stood in the air stream, the book in her hands, letting the moving air flutter her damp blouse and rill the skin on her arms into delicious goosebumps. God, it was wonderful to be cold.

Ferdy's cold, she thought, with a sensation that the words had been shoved into her mind like someone pushing a piece of furniture from room to room. This time, though, she stayed with it. The thought of Ferdy led her to the book, and she glanced down at it: *Skin Deep, A Simeon Grist Mystery* by someone named Timothy Hallinan. A ratty-looking hardcover copy with a creased, faded dust jacket that showed a nineties guy with dark shades and a lot of pathetic faux-Bee Gees flair, with a *hot chick*—no other term would do—hanging adoringly on his arm as though she had no idea that she'd be better off with almost anyone else in the world. The two of them were reflected in what appeared to be a glass of bourbon, and there were shadows of palm fronds all over the place, which meant that the book was set in Los Angeles. Palm fronds were the first thing a book designer thought of when he or she was given a book set in Los Angeles and had been told that the publisher's budget didn't include the licensing fee for the use of the Hollywood sign. Cheap genre fiction was what the book looked like to Madison, although Ferdy had been trying for weeks to get her to read one of the titles in the series.

"He's better than you'd think," Ferdy kept saying, meaning the writer. He'd seemed sincere, but she'd thought at the time it was just a conversational ransack, the result of a frantic search for something, anything, to say to her. He was continually searching for something to say to her.

The furniture mover was back, shoving words in. *Poor Ferdy.*

She opened the book and looked at the left-facing page where the publishing info was always printed. It said FIRST EDITION at the bottom, a sad little flourish of bravado that implied the thin possibility of a second edition, the publishing version of an act of sympathetic magic, a sorcerer's gesture toward the God of Luck, the maker of bestsellers. A genuine first edition, in its original dust jacket, worth every penny of—she flipped back to the first page, where she saw in pencil, *$4.95.* An earlier price, $5.95, had been crossed out. Where was the God of Luck when you needed him?

Where was *everyone* when you needed them?

The temperature in the room had dropped into double digits, and she went to the cluttered couch, cleared a Madison-size space, and sat, the book on her lap. It definitely did not exert the solid, reassuring pressure of the Balzac she was reading in the bedroom. The evening yawned in front of her, as empty and featureless as the desert on the other side of her windows. *Dinner* presented itself as one possible way of consuming some of that inexhaustible time, except that she'd overeaten at lunch. She felt like her entire lunch, plus the lunchbox she'd carried it in when she was a child, was lodged sideways just below her breastbone. She'd turned the shop over to Ferdy—*Poor Ferdy*—and gone to the Merry Go Round, as usual, for the usual lunch, hoping, as usual, that she wouldn't run into Jake there, and she hadn't, and that had upset her so much that she'd had a piece of peach pie.

That's right, she thought, watching herself think it. *I didn't want to see Jake and I didn't, and the disappointment at not seeing the person I didn't want to see made me overeat. There must be a medical name for this condition. Maybe it's something new. Maybe it'll be called Madison's Fattening Dementia. Maybe I'll be famous. I'll have a reality show with other people who have a disease named after them. We could call it "Sick and Famous."*

Other people, she thought, *real* people, didn't worry about how to fill their evenings. Other people didn't have any time to fill after the fascinating, all-engaging, world-changing things they did. They leaped up at the last moment and ate standing at the stove, their minds still engaged in something bigger and more interesting than they were. Or than *she* was, at any rate.

She gazed ahead into time, thinking it was probably a straight line but hoping it was actually curved so she could believe that the thing that was coming toward her, the thing that would change everything, that would broaden and enrich her life, was just around the bend, just *barely* out of sight. Coming into view any old minute now.

Without even looking down, she opened the book.

13

This Wretched Salt Lick

"WHOOO," I SAID. "SHE'S KIND of a ditz."

"She'th *your* reader," Pansy Parkinson said. "What do you thee?"

"A room, kind of messy. I seem to be on the ceiling. There's a lot of junk around. Messy room, messy mind, as my mother used to say."

"Did she, dear?" Lobelia asked. "How prosaic."

"She was my mom," I said defensively.

"I'm sure she was right about a great many things," Lobelia said, without a sincere syllable in the sentence.

"Thimeon," Pansy said. "Can we get back to it? Ahmed ithn't going to give you the Eye forever."

Ahmed said something affirmative in a fictional language heavy on throat-clearing sounds.

"It's a little odd," I said. "Everything looks kind of flat."

"You're only looking through one eye." It was Patsy this time, sounding extremely patient. "No depth perception. That's why Ahmed flies into things all the time. Come on, come on. Give, share. You're the only one who can see it."

"Well, it's a small room. In a house, is my guess. It doesn't feel like an apartment. It feels like a crappy little square house with one bedroom, a kitchen, a living room and maybe a dining nook. Sort of like my house, but with linoleum. The world outside the windows is extra-bright, like the sun dropped in for a visit. The house has that awful, yellow-wax feeling that says it might be stucco on the outside."

"Check it out," Pansy said. Since there were no "s" sounds in the sentence, it took me a moment to decide which twin it was.

"How?"

"Jutht back up, right through the theiling, and keep going. Don't move your head, thtupid, the Eye ithn't in your head. Just think yourthelf back and up."

"Wow," I said. "An attic with a rat in it. Insulation. Good Lord, asbestos, this place is old. Wood that termites have—"

"Can you go a *little* fathter?" Pansy's tone was the verbal equivalent of a tapped foot.

"Wheee, this is fun. Okay, we're outside. Yup. Stucco. Square as a chessboard, and all by itself on a whole lot of sand enlivened here and there by the occasional rock. The sun is almost down and everything's got long shadows, sort of threatening, that look like someone grabbed them and stretched them until they're about to snap forward and bring the rock or whatever it is with them."

"*Listen* to him," Patsy said.

"It's that old hack, Alan Westmore," Lobelia said. "That was how he wrote. Simeon, sit on the purple prose, okay? Just because you're using the Eye doesn't mean you have to talk like someone in a penny dreadful."

"It looks hot," I said. "And boring. I'm going back in. I'm going down the chimney this time."

Ahmed gargled and Patsy translated: "*No.* Don't. It's full of soot, and if you get a bit of grit in the Eye, Ahmed will be quite rightfully put out."

"Rats. I've never gone down a chimney. Okay, I'm back inside and I've gone lower now so I can look at her tennis shoes and her face. And she *is*, she's the woman who found Ferdy. The one with the odd haircut. Her name is Madison, although I don't know how I know that—"

"Do the wordth all-theeing mean *anything* to you?" Pansy asked.

"Madison Jefferson. Good Lord, that's awful. A name like a dollar bill. She's not happy. There's someone named Jake, and he's why she moved to the desert but something went wrong and now the whole world seems bleak and empty—"

"Empty is good," Patsy said. "Empty is what you want. Move into that space. Take over."

"Is this—" I said, and stopped. "Is this ethical?"

"Ferdy," Lobelia said. "Don't you want to know who killed Ferdy?"

"Well, yeah, but—"

"What's the worst that can happen?" Lobelia said. "She has to entertain two thoughts at the same time? From the way you describe her, she could use a little practice."

"Anyway," Patsy said, "it's like hypnosis. You can't make her do anything she wouldn't normally do."

The remark had come just a bit too quickly. "Are you sure?"

"Of courth," Pansy said. "You think we're *evil* or thomething?"

The girl on the couch looked unhappy and loose-limbed, as though the current flowing through her nervous system had been cut. The lower lip was generous, the upper a sharp-cut little M with a laugh lost in it somewhere. Her cheekbones were parentheses, and nothing seemed seriously wrong with the face between them. The asymmetrical hair was a streaky blond with a million hidden colors that blazed into life wherever the late sunlight through the window released them. *Good Lord*, I realized, I was even *thinking* purple prose.

She sighed and opened the book on her lap.

With some misgivings, I said, "Here goes." I tried to close my eyes but I didn't have any. So I put all my effort into sending her a thought.

* * *

Ferdy, Madison thought for the fourth or fifth time. He'd been sweet, if a little bit oozy, just a sort of general impression that the skin under his shirt might be damp. And he'd smelled like old paper, but then, Madison supposed, she probably did, too. All they did all day was handle old paper.

Portuguese, he must have been, with that name. What she knew about Portugal would fit on the inside of a book of matches, if there even were books of matches anymore. Prince Henry the Navigator, typical nobleman, claimed the title and sent hundreds of sailors into danger to explore the coast of Africa while he stayed safe at home and hogged the credit, signing all the maps. Probably got seasick. Portugal, Portugal. *Lisbon.* Something about earthquakes. There, *that* was something she knew about. Nobody lives in San Francisco without learning about earthquakes.

It probably wasn't *Ferdy's* fault he was kind of thick in the waist and broad in the—okay, he'd been fat. But it was probably glandular. At the word *glandular,* Madison's internal hyp-check flashed a deep, warning-light red. All right, he ate like a pig. They'd only gone to lunch together one time, one of the few days Henry—not the navigator, but the owner of their landlocked bookstore—was actually working in the shop and could cover for them. Ferdy kept asking for more mayonnaise and ate two orders of french fries. He'd swallowed them in little log-jams of ten or twelve, and every single time he'd gotten a bunch down he'd licked the oil and salt off his fingers. And said, "Mmmmmm."

But so what? So he had terrible manners. Maybe it was because he always ate alone, the poor guy, maybe he didn't even know he made those *mmmmmm* sounds all the time. For all I know, Madison thought, *I* make those sounds now. And even if

he did know and made them anyway, even if he was kind of...
dank, he'd been a *reader*. He'd been open to the worlds between
the covers. He wasn't one of the fish in human form who can
walk past a bookshelf without even slowing down. No, he was a
member of the crick-in-the-neck community, the people who
spend too much time with their heads cocked to one side, reading
the titles printed sideways on vertical spines.

Like her.

That was the only thing, Madison thought—well, *almost* the
only thing—she really liked about herself. That books could
make her vibrate like a crystal chime. That she'd been issued at
birth the passport to the imagination. And Ferdy'd had that, too.

Unexpectedly, her eyes were wet.

Who was she kidding? Miss Higher Sensibilities. She was
alone in the middle of the desert, a fool who'd followed a liar,
even if he was a really cute liar with a great butt, and her life was
as barren as Joshua Tree. She had this crappo rental house, her
books, her job, and—for a while, there—she'd had Ferdy. He'd
been so hopelessly, so transparently sweet on her. Following her
around the shop with those brown eyes, moving everything that
weighed more than five pounds to spare her back. Coming in on
days when he wasn't even scheduled. Shoving books at her all the
time, books that had nothing in common, novels about South
Africa by Alan Paton, nonfiction about Patagonia by Bruce
Chatwin, stories about the future by William Gibson, about the
past by Anthony Trollope, about everything else by Margaret
Drabble, Raymond Chandler, Haruki Murakami, Anthony Pow-
ell.

Ferdy had even tried to introduce her to Balzac. It was one of
the few times she'd been self-consciously kind to him, accepting
gratefully that terrible translation of *Père Goriot* without telling
him she'd read the entire *Human Comedy* twice, in French.
Without saying that Balzac was her internal world, that the big,

thickset coffee addict, wired out of his skull and writing his arm off by candlelight in his Paris garret, had given her the life she'd always wanted, the life she'd been looking for when she followed Jake to this wretched salt lick in the precise, magnetic center of Bumfuck, Nowhere.

Balzac Among the Cacti. What in the world had she been thinking?

And now she didn't even have Ferdy. Just her and those bookstore shelves, sagging under old, fading, dusty books. Books that resembled her. "Fading" was too obviously metaphorical to take seriously, but she found herself taking it seriously. Madison on the fade, slowly growing transparent in the middle of a crowd of no ones. This empty house, that bookshop, now, too, empty.

She hadn't even noticed: Ferdy had been her friend.

All right, she thought. Let's accept for the moment that Madison is fading, vanishing, that the nicest thing that could be said about her is that she's like a diamond hidden in a glass of water. A little sparkle of value that probably no one will ever discover. So put that in the closet and close the door on it. What would a Balzac heroine do?

She'd make sure that her friend was avenged, that's what. Even if she had to do it all behind the scenes because of the social restrictions on what was acceptable for a woman; even Balzac permitted no women in the avengers he called The Thirteen. She'd be on the case, but *indirectly*, moving people around from behind her fan like chess pieces, to make sure justice was done.

Of course, there was that detective. He was the one who was supposed to solve it. Not very confidence-inspiring, that detective. With his trumpeter's lip and his baggy skin and the melancholy that came off him in waves so thick that things behind him seemed to waver and shift. Those little eyes, too close together and too sad to be forceful.

What did he remind her of? She closed the book but left her index finger marking the first page of the story.

A Basset Hound, she thought. He looked like a Basset Hound.

Was he capable of finding out who killed Ferdy? Could he identify the one person, out of a whole world of people, who had slipped in and broken the neck of her only friend in the desert while she was choking down that unwanted piece of pie at the Merry Go Round?

She sat up straight. Maybe *this* was what had been coming down the time tunnel. Maybe it had cleared the curve and streaked into sight at last. The thing that would transform her life: Finding Ferdy's killer.

Madison had goosebumps again, and it wasn't the air conditioner.

So. Learn to think like a detective.

She opened the book on her lap, which was, after all, about a detective, and began to read.

All dressed up for the Fourth of July, McGinty's of Malibu was even more of a slag-heap than usual.

14

It Always Begins with a Question

"SIMEON," LOBELIA CALLED. "COME IN here and look at this."

The spell was broken. I found the Eye once again focused on my knees.

"Give it here," Patsy said. "Ahmed wants it back."

The Eye revealed that Ahmed was, in fact, standing, towering over the two seated twins and gazing down at me with his very odd blue eyes. The gun in his hand would have looked a lot more menacing if I hadn't known he didn't have anywhere to put it. "But how will I see her?"

"Your problem," Pansy said. "Let'th go."

"She's a Sensitive," Patsy said. "You've established a contact. You'll be able to feel some things—extremes of joy or fear, for example."

"You mean, she's on her own?"

"Oh, spare me," Patsy said. "She's an adult. You're just revealing your conviction that women aren't competent to take care of themselves without paternal guidance."

"Stratemeyer never wrote anything like—"

"I've had a century," Patsy said. "I've been reading."

"Come in here and look," Lobelia called again. "She's in your window. Pretty little thing."

"Coming." I turned my head, and then cold little fingers touched my neck, the chain was lifted off, the world went black and rolled over a couple of times, and I felt a sharp line of pain, like someone had taken an ice-cold scalpel to my face just below my eyebrows, and then I could see again. I rubbed my eyes, and they were there and they weren't bleeding. It was more of a relief than I allowed the twins to see.

I went down into the living room and looked at the window.

Lobelia was right. Madison *was* pretty, in a highly individual way, a way that made the sum of all her features, animated by big, intelligent eyes, even more attractive after looking at them for a moment. She was on her back, her head on a pillow, with a crumpled bedspread beneath her. She was holding the book in the air as she read, so we were looking down on her. She wore a pair of well-worn jeans and a black T-shirt that said CAUTION: SOFT SHOULDER on it. Half a dozen cheap plastic bracelets circled her left arm, most of them well up her forearm since her hand was in the air. No watch, which automatically moved her a couple more notches up on my personal esteem scale. She'd put on an enormous pair of glasses that had the effect of dwarfing her already-tiny nose, and she was chewing the ends of her hair. The words she was reading came into my mind.

I said them out loud:

Red, white, and blue beach balls had been tossed into the ropy fishnet that hung from the ceiling. They nestled among seashells, starfish, old floats, weights, and other nautical bric-a-brac to create a landscape that looked like the place where drowned children go to play.

"Your first-person narrative?" Lobelia said. "Not bad in a slightly overwritten way."

"Sort of mine. I mean, he wrote it, but it was me, really. I suppose. I probably wouldn't have used that finicky series comma in between *white* and *blue*."

The flow of words stopped and Madison's eyes began moving in that distressing pattern that meant she was skimming. A bunch of words tumbled by in my mind like bits of paper tossed in front of a fan. She looked up, past the book, and sighed.

"You're not holding her attention," Lobelia said.

"Since we're going and taking the Eye with us," Patsy said from the doorway, "we'll fix it so you can hear her. Ahmed?"

Ahmed, behind her, said something in Sci-Ficlish, the language of bad speculative writing, and suddenly I was hearing the trailing end of Madison's sigh. She said, "I don't even know how to begin."

"It begins with a question," I said without thinking. "It always begins with a question."

"The question," Madison said aloud, "is who killed Ferdy."

"Boy," Pansy said. She almost looked impressed. "You've really got a link."

"The problem is always where to start," I said, waving Pansy off. She grunted assent and came down into the living room.

"Start in the center," Madison said. She got off the bed and dropped the book, face-down. The window went dark.

"Put Ferdy in the center," I said, raising my voice as the hawk materialized in the night sky. Behind the bird, most of the stars were gone, probably on their way wherever the twins were going next.

"You've got a link," Patsy said, echoing her sister. "You don't need to yell."

I heard Madison's voice, stuttering and broken like a bad cell phone connection: "Some... over here... paper."

"I don't hear her very well," I said, as Ahmed poured all seven feet of himself into the room. "That makes me nervous."

Patsy shrugged. "You've got the best connection I've ever seen," she said, heading for the door.

Pansy said, "Much better than—" and not only stopped talking but stopped moving, one hand over her mouth.

"Better than who?" I said. "Who have I got a better connection than?"

"*Look* at the time," Patsy trilled, pulling a gold pocketwatch on a chain out of some linen pocket or other. "Haven't we just had a perfect *whirlwind* of an evening. But now we must—"

I got two disconnected syllables from Madison, afloat on a sea of silence, bright little life-jackets of sound. "Better than who?"

"It doesn't matter," Patsy said airily. "Life, after all, is not a competition."

"You're dodging me," I said. "I want an answer."

"I'm *most* sorry." Patsy was moving into *grande dame* territory. "I'm not at liberty to—"

"Come *on*, Ahmed," Pansy said. She practically bolted for the door.

"Sassafras," Lobelia said.

Pansy stopped dead. Patsy looked at Lobelia in much the same way King Lear looked at Cordelia in Act One. "You—" she said, just barely not sputtering. "You, you can't—"

"You weren't written as liars, of course," Lobelia said, her voice serene with certainty. "No little hero or heroine of that time could tell a lie. Legacy of that drippy little George Washington in Parson Weems' totally bogus story about the cherry tree. *I cannot tell a lie.*" She looked up at the window, still dark and largely starless. "But you *could* evade a straight answer. Am I recalling this correctly?"

Patsy was giving total attention to her watch but Pansy's glare could have punched holes in tin. Her back was stiff, her fists clenched, her shoulders raised to her earlobes.

"Therefore, *sassafras*," Lobelia continued, as unhurried as someone addressing herself in an otherwise empty room. "The word that people, usually your parents, could use to make you tell the complete truth."

"A corny little plot devithe," Pansy said, her voice trembling with fury. "When the old thtinker couldn't think of a way to wrap up the thtory, he uthed *Thathafrath*." The Eye on the chain around Ahmed's neck kept looking from the floor to Pansy and then back to the floor, like a dog that knows it's probably in for it later. "It won't work," she said, getting a bit shrill. "It won't, it won't, it won't, it—"

"Sassafras, sassafras, sassafras," Lobelia said over her, and the room went completely silent. Patsy had bright patches of red on her cheekbones, little badges of fury. "The question, Simeon?" Lobelia prompted.

"My connection is better than whose?"

"The. Other. Two," Patsy said, the words coming slowly, separated by periods, not commas.

"Which other two?"

"Two. Other. Characters. We. Helped." I felt like I was prying coins out of a piggy bank.

"What happened to them?"

Patsy waited until Pansy had turned to face her, and they exchanged a long twinny glance, full of meaning only they could decipher. When the exchange was over, Patsy said, "Many things."

"This won't do," Lobelia said, but I raised a hand.

Feeling like an idiot, I said, "Will your sassafras cover me, or do I have to say it myself?"

Lobelia said, "Girls?"

"He didn't address the question to us," Patsy said, looking at a high corner of the room.

"Okay," I said. "Here goes. First, *Sassafras.*" Pansy made a little spitting sound, like a drop of water on a hot frying pan. "What *exactly* happened to the other two, and if something went wrong, what was it?"

"They lost their Sensitives," Patsy said.

"What does that mean? They lost *contact* with their Sensitives, or they lost them completely?"

"No way for us to tell, is there?" Patsy said with unconcealed satisfaction. "Since they couldn't establish contact, we had no way to know whether the Sensitives were still there. And since—" If she'd stopped talking any more quickly, there would have been a syllable trainwreck.

Lobelia and I said, simultaneously, "Since?"

Pansy said, with a certain amount of malice, "Thince the *characters* dithappeared, too."

"Oh," I said. "The characters lost touch with their Sensitives and then the characters disappeared. Any other downsides? I mean, the death of language or anything?"

"No." Patsy brushed something off her linen sleeve.

"Why did the characters disappear?"

"We don't know." She examined the sleeve and looked up, satisfied. "And you can ask us all night long, and that'll be the answer."

"And these Sensitives…" I paused to make sure the question was phrased correctly. "Were these Sensitives engaged in investigating a crime down there?"

Patsy turned the gold watch at an angle and breathed on it, then wiped it on the sleeve she'd just cleaned. The pause stretched so long I could hear the watch ticking.

Finally, Pansy said, "Thertainly."

There was a sudden pressure behind my eyes, a little baby-step in the direction of a headache. "And you're packing up and taking Ahmed and the Eye and going back to Parker World with its beautiful, starry skies, your consciences as clear as daylight after we've launched that girl into a murder investigation."

"See?" Patsy said to Lobelia. "What did we tell you when you insisted we come? We don't do well with long-term relationships."

"The answer to my question is *no*," I said. "You are not abandoning that girl."

"Young woman," Patsy said.

"You got her into this," I said. "I mean, I did, but on the assumption that you weren't going to set this into motion and then pull the rug—"

"*Assume,*" Patsy said in a tone that might have gotten her slapped if she'd been closer to anyone, "makes an *ass* of *you* and *me.*"

"Not happening." To Ahmed, I said, "Give me that Eye."

Ahmed lowered the Mauser and pointed it at my chest. His hand was as steady as the average tree, and the Eye was riveted on me.

"It's a profound mistake to get Ahmed angry," Patsy said. "Even *with* those shoes."

"I'm telling you, this is not the way the story goes," I said. "You'll come here tomorrow and let me look at her again, and whenever I need you, you'll—"

"We'll what?" Pansy asked. She crossed her arms and the safety pins swung back and forth with a little clicking sound. "You can't even find uth."

"Don't worry," Patsy said soothingly. "That's *real* life down there, what she's going through. It's not fiction. Nothing ever happens in real life except that people get older and lonelier and sadder."

"Tell that to Ferdy," I said. "I'm not kidding. You're going to help me stay in touch with Madison or I'm going to do something very unpleasant."

"Blah blah blah," Pansy said. "Let'th go."

"Like Sassafras," Lobelia said over her. "Like the two of us telling everyone up here, and I mean absolutely *everyone*, about Sassafras. And don't forget, *I* know where to find you. Just imagine it: everyone up here dropping in on you day and night, and you have to tell them all the truth. No entertaining made-up stories. Just your bleak, boring, identical little selves. Forever and ever and ever."

Patsy said, "You wouldn't."

"Did you see how many people I got into this room on two hours' notice? And I wasn't even trying. I can give you a very rocky eternity, I promise you."

For a moment, I thought Patsy was going to attack Lobelia physically. Her face was the color of paper. Finally, she nodded. "All right for now," she said. There was none of the little Edwardian girl in the reply; she'd been replaced with a century's worth of malice. "We'll come back tomorrow afternoon."

"And then?" Lobelia had her harmless muffin-lady smile on.

"And then we'll see," Patsy said, and she swept out, dragging the other two in her wake like satellites. A moment later, I heard Pansy say, "Hit anything and I'll tie your shoeth in *knoth*."

Lobelia stood there, her arms folded, looking quite pleased with herself.

I said, "My my. Where did *that* come from?"

"Oh, honey," Lobelia said, "I always wanted to be hard-boiled."

15

Shaped Like Texas

THE DOT IN THE CENTER of the circle (a pretty good freehand circle if she said so herself) said *Ferdy*. To Madison, the dot had two implications: Ferdy as a person, a concept, an active verb in the world, and Ferdy as a cooling body on the floor of the Pack Rat bookstore's back room.

The circle with the dot marked *Ferdy* at its center was labeled **Geography** in tentative, easily-erased light pencil. Madison started to rub out the word and then pulled back from the page—one of many blank sheets in her long-unused sketchpad—to get a better perspective. She'd had to flip through only eleven pages of penciled Joshua trees, rock monoliths, sun-blackened hills, dirt roads snaking over empty desert rises, and attempts at capturing the curve of Jake's butt before she hit white space. Talk about perspective: the sketches were doodles of the enthusiasm she'd once felt for the desert, attempts to lasso what she saw then as its beauty. Before it turned into the world's biggest, dullest sandbox, without a single kid in it worth playing with.

Jake's butt, unfortunately, was still interesting.

Okay, the circle. She reversed the pencil in her hand, taking the eraser out of play. Probably best to think of the circle—the *first* circle—as purely geographic. It would be confusing to go all cosmic on something as simple as location. Within the circumference of the Geography circle, Madison wrote the names of the businesses within sight of the Pack Rat. There were four of them, or three if the proprietor of the one farthest away didn't have good vision. Then she put another dot on the edge of the circle and labeled it *Ferdy's Apartment* and drew a circle around *that*. She'd taken him home twice when he locked his keys in the car, something he did frequently until she suggested to him that he have a spare set made and hang it under the Pack Rat's counter. She looked at the circle representing the apartment, trying to figure out what it reminded her of.

The solar system, she thought. The big ellipse of the earth's orbit with the earth a dot on it, and around that dot, a smaller circle representing the orbit of the moon. Or, in this case, Ferdy's apartment. In the circle around Ferdy's apartment she wrote *supermarket, laundromat, coffee house, bank*—the bank was a guess, since people don't always use the bank closest to their house— *restaurant(s), library, gym.* Madison realized she was chewing on the eraser, dried it on her T-shirt, and erased *gym.* It looked messy, the way wet erasures always did. However Ferdy spent his time away from the store, it probably didn't involve frequent visits to a gym.

She thought, *How little I know about him. He probably knew ten times more about me than I do about him.* On the heels of the thought, like the vibration of a gong, came a pang of guilt. She'd been thinking about herself, about her unhappiness, about—okay —about Jake. Mr. Lost Cause. Mr. Nice-Smile, Cute-Butt, World-Class-Liar, Lost Cause. She'd been thinking about herself, and it was time to stop doing that.

The unaccustomed sensation of virtue at the concept of not thinking about herself—*look, I'm rising above being so self-centered* —was immediately drop-kicked by the realization that, even if she was thinking about *not* thinking about herself, that was still thinking about herself. Whatever was coming down time's tunnel to change her life, it had to be bigger than she was.

Ferdy had been bigger than she was. Ferdy's murder was

much bigger than she was. Actually, now that she considered it, any time a person stopped thinking about herself, it was more or less automatic: things got bigger. Everything sort of boiled down to you, on one side of the mirror, and on the other side, the world. The world was bigger.

Some kind of lesson there somewhere.

She rolled onto her back and balanced the pencil between the end of her nose and her upper lip and then she curled her upper lip to create a pencil mustache. In her mind, she drew the larger circles that would surround the circles she'd already drawn. They would be labeled *Personal*, meaning relationships, and (she supposed) *Spiritual*, assuming that there had been a component in Ferdy's life that he'd thought of as spiritual.

She didn't know *anything*. At least not anything that mattered. He'd been fat, he'd eaten french fries by the handful, and he liked detective stories. She'd been working beside him every day for almost eighteen months.

And he might have been in love with her.

The thought prompted a nervous yawn, and the pencil fell to the floor. The windows were black rectangles. The temperature of the room was safely in the seventies, a comfort zone the air conditioners achieved only when the temperatures outside had plummeted. She rolled onto one side and looked at her cell phone on the rickety table beside her bed. Her eyebrows lifted, almost on their own.

It was nearly eleven.

She had gotten through the entire evening without looking at her phone once. Without even eating dinner. And she wasn't hungry.

That had to mean *something*.

She picked up the pencil and began to draw the outer circles. The next morning's activities were taking shape in her mind.

* * *

"Who you s'posed to be, sweetheart, Nancy Drew?"

Burt, the proprietor of Burt's Boot Barn, had the kind of creases in his face you saw only in long-time desert dwellers and below photos with captions like *World's Oldest Eskimo*. His generous nose ended in a bulb that looked like it would honk if it were squeezed. A few restless whiskers had migrated to its tip, making Madison ask herself whether the man shaved his nose and then answer her own question: *not recently*.

"Of course not, Mr.—um, Mr. Burt." She should have been prepared for this.

"The cops already asked me all this stuff. It's *their* job, right? Not yours."

"Of—" She stopped, unwilling to say "Of course" again. "Of… of all the people in Joshua Tree," she finally managed, "I'm probably the one who's most frightened. I mean, I have to work in that store all by myself now. All day. Every time I hear a car pull up, I'm going to wonder—well, you know." She widened her eyes in her best pass at female helplessness.

"Awww," Burt said. He reached up and manfully pushed his stetson, patched with dirt and sweat, farther back on his head to reveal a nasty little scattering of skin irregularities that Madison immediately diagnosed as precancerous. "You're scared, huh?"

"Well, yes," Madison said, all candid. "I have to admit it. I am."

"Aw, gee, honey. Should have figgered that out myself. You understand, I'm a workin' man in here. I can't keep my eyes on old Henry's store all the time."

"Oh, no. But, you know—the gravel. When a car stops for us, it might be stopping for you. Or vice versa. Since we're, like, next door? You hear the gravel, same as we do. I always look. It's just automatic."

"Puttin' it *that* way," Burt said. "I look most of the time, I guess. I told the cop yesterday, I 'membered four cars. A little white Japanese something, with two doors—"

"That's mine," Madison said. "Stopped in front of the store for a few minutes and then pulled away?"

"Yup. You, huh? Whyn't you just park there?"

"Henry says it's for customers. But I'd picked up a box of books from a seller so I stopped in front and carried them in, and then went and parked on the back street."

"Ol' Henry, he's not a very givin' person, cute little thing like you, havin' to walk all that way." Burt batted the side of his nose with a thumb, as though its presence had startled him. He sniffed a couple of times, apparently to make sure it was still working. "So now you'll be all alone over—"

"Yes, and it does worry me, I have to admit it. What if he comes back?"

"Who? Henry?"

"*No*, not Henry." Madison had to put a little work into her tone. "The guy who killed—"

"Oh, him. Well, I doubt he'll come—"

"What were the other three cars?"

"Oh. Yeah. A pickup truck with bad primer all over it, but that's Melvin Price's. He just got out and looked at his rear tire, driver's side, for a minute, like he'd heard something? And then drove off. Probably on his way to the Hitching Post. Melvin likes to launch early."

"Does he." The Hitching Post was your basic small-town bar, with rodeo trimmings. Jake had taken her there twice.

Burt tilted his wrist and tossed an air-shot of, presumably, whiskey. "Higher than the Empire State by noon, old Melvin. And then there was that Caddy with the big rust spot on the trunk, and a little red sporty, a, uh, whatchamicallit, an Aurora or something."

"Acura?"

Burt cocked his head like an interested dog. "Could be. Why them Japs can't name their cars right—"

"So, counting me, that's three cars after, um, Melvin, right?"

"Far as I can remember."

"What time did the Caddy arrive?"

Burt squinted at a bunch of boots in a far corner of the shop. To Madison, they looked like every other bunch of boots in the shop. He popped some air in their direction, just a little P with a breath behind it. "Twelve-thirty, twelve-forty," he said. "I was getting a mite peckish. I get hungry pretty much the same time every day. Creature of hab—"

"I was at lunch then," Madison said, trying to keep her tone conversational, hardly aware she'd interrupted him. "What color was it?"

"Horsefly blue. You know, that blue that's got some silver under it. Probably some cholo paint job, no way the folks at Caddy would ever paint—"

"With a rust spot on the trunk."

"Shaped like Texas."

"Could you see the driver?"

"Windows was tinted. Real dark." Burt's eyes flicked over Madison's head. "Honey, I got boots I gotta dust."

"Almost finished. What about when the driver got out?"

"Didn't see him. Car stopped at your place. Stopped watching. Weren't no way he was comin' in here."

"And the little red one?"

"Looked like a thimble," Burt said. "Kind of car is that for a man to drive?"

"*Was* it a man?"

"Don't know. Stopped in front of your place, just cruised on by Ol' Burt's like we wasn't here." He bent down below the counter and came up with a rag in his hand, stiff with old wax.

"What time?"

"'Bout the same time." Burt used the rag to polish the chunk of turquoise in his bolo tie. "Little later. Caddy was gone. Know that 'cause I heard its tires as it left and I looked up. And then, maybe five minutes later, the red thimble rolled in."

"And stayed how long?"

A shrug. "Three, four minutes. I was busy, so coulda been a little longer."

"And the Acura arrived when?"

"'Bout ten minutes later. And before you ask, nope. Didn't see who was drivin' that one neither."

"Close together like that?"

"Yup. Then nobody until the cops come squealin' up. Well, that got me to wonderin'."

"I'll bet it did. You've been very helpful. I appreciate—"

"All them people comin' by in a row like that. Happened two, three days a month."

Madison had been backing toward the door, but she stopped. "Sorry?"

Burt grinned, exposing teeth of an unusual, perhaps even unique, shade of yellow. "Yup. This'll be news to you. One time, two times a month, maybe every couple of weeks, when you went out for lunch, there'd be a bunch of cars. Nobody there all morning, then you'd head out to get a bite and they'd be two, three, four cars like they was lined up for burgers to go, and then you'd come back and poor old Fatso would go out, and then there wouldn't be but one, two more cars all day long." He buffed the nails on his left hand with the waxy rag and studied the shine. "Enough to make a man wonder."

"Wonder what, specifically?"

"Like was he havin' a lunchtime sale, all alone in there," Burt said, widening blue eyes that looked like they'd been bleached more often than his jeans. "And maybe not books."

16

Horsefly Blue

AN HOUR LATER, MADISON HAD met all the shop's neighbors and realized that she hadn't been missing much by not knowing them.

Mrs. Terwilliger, at Wumsy's Craft Shop, looked like one of her own dried flowers and had a weighty antique-perfume smell that suggested a sachet from an Egyptian tomb. Mrs. Terwilliger hadn't seen any of the cars the day before but she saw Madison's clothes clearly enough, her eyes skipping over the tight jeans and the sleeveless T-shirt as though she were trying to spot the place where the scarlet A had been sewn before Madison picked out the stitching. She'd been downright unpleasant, affronted apparently by Madison's very presence, her well-preserved Southern accent making the words sound even ruder, and by the time Madison banged the door closed behind her, she'd been provoked into saying something she shouldn't.

Ronnie, behind the counter of The Little Brown Jug, woke up from a nice, peaceful-looking snooze behind the cash register and allowed as how it seemed to him, now that he thought about it, there *was* a kind of business spike over at the Pack Rat in the middle of the day once in a while, although his job demanded most of his attention. "I'm studyin' IDs day and night over here," he said. "Got a bunch of thirsty 17-year-olds. Got bums coming in to buy for kids in the parking lot: guy who hasn't taken a shower since the last time it rained waving a bunch of twenties and saying, *That'll be five six-packs and a bottle of Thunderbird.*

Hard enough to hang onto my license without making notes on who's in and out of Henry's store. Noticed *you*, though."

"My, my," Madison had said, backing out. "How sweet of you."

"I still got the old eye," Ronnie had said, pointing at his right.

"Really. Is the other one new?" Madison asked, in retreat.

The fourth of the business names she'd written in the *Geography* circle, the one with the worst view, was King Arthur's Inn, a moated, peeling motel sitting in the middle of a rocky lot a long block away and on the same side of the street as the Pack Rat. When Madison asked whether he'd noticed anything the day before, the Indian guy behind the desk had done a subcontinental head-waggle that could have been either a yes or a no. He'd had a long, leisurely, elbows-on-the-counter conversation in mind, but she'd finally pried a "no" out of him and escaped only by promising to come back for a chat. He'd heard nothing about Ferdy, and the cops hadn't talked to him.

A little alarm pinged in her head, telling her it was about 10:30 and she was on the verge of being late for work. For years in San Francisco, she'd won bets by telling people what time it was within two minutes. Another useless talent, but at least, when she was a kid, she hadn't had to choose a watch. She had enough trouble choosing a pair of cheap earrings without something as potentially disastrous as a watch. For most of her life the plastic bracelets have worked just fine: they look cheap so people see them (she hopes) as whimsical, as opposed to clueless. And, since her armful includes at least one bracelet of practically every color God tilted into the spectrum, they go—sort of—with everything.

I think "sort of" too much, Madison thought. *Got to stop hedging bets. Just take a stand once in a while. So what if I'm wrong? What're people going to do, throw rocks at me?* She pulled the car around to the back street and braked in a cloud of alkaline dust, waited a moment for it to clear, and then hiked across half an acre of sand, scrub, and thorns. She had her head down, observing the perpetual cholla cactus avoidance alert, so it wasn't until she had her keys in her hand that she saw the yellow tape across the back door that said, CRIME SCENE DO NOT ENTER in a no-nonsense, blunt-force, unpunctuated font that brooked no argument.

Why hadn't Henry called her? If the shop was going to be closed surely he owed her the courtesy of—

She fished her cell phone out of her bag and looked at it. On mute. Two missed calls. Both from Henry.

"Well, hell, Madison," she said. The day yawned in front of her, empty and enormous. It hadn't occurred to her that the shop would be closed, although now that it was, she felt like kicking herself for sheer thickness.

And then, unexpectedly, she felt relief. No spending the day alone in the shop where Ferdy had died—no, where he'd been *killed*. The relief wasn't because she feared ghosts or believed that violent events left some trace behind, tainting the places where they happened. Although, she thought, more than half the population of San Francisco would argue with her about that. In San Francisco, there'd already be half a dozen people in there, burning sage in the corners, chanting the names of discount deities, and setting crystals all over the place, to neutralize the evil. Or repel it. Or reflect it back at itself. Or borrow five bucks from it. Or *something*. Madison had never been quite clear about crystals.

She dropped the keys back into her purse, along with the phone, and took out the stiff sheet of sketch paper with her circles on it. She smoothed it against the door, located a ballpoint, and drew lines through the names of the four businesses in the circle.

And as she crossed out the fourth feature in the *Geography* circle, she realized there might be a fifth one she'd forgotten.

The back of her neck prickled. Was someone watching her? That's what it always meant in the movies, someone watching

you. Exaggerating her actions, she refolded the paper and dropped it into her purse, then tried the doorknob again, shook her
head, feeling like a bad actress, and turned to go. And there it
was, gleaming in the sun, across the scrubby half-acre between her
and the back road. The fifth feature. Ferdy's car.

Was she being watched or not? She took the first steps toward
her car, scanning everything she could look at without actually
moving her head. Behind her was the shop, and on the other side
of that, the highway. In front of her was a gentle roll of desert
sand cut into rectangles by three empty streets, straight as rulers,
intersecting each other at right angles. She could see for more
than a mile in either direction, and in that expanse she saw only
two cars, both heading away from her and too far away for her to
worry about. But of course, there was always traffic on the highway on the other side of the shop.

Right on cue, a truck rumbled past behind her, and she
turned in that direction, checking out the whole visible world as
she pretended to watch the truck bump its way east. There were
no cars parked on the shoulder, nobody ambling along in the
hundred-degree heat. As far as she could tell, she could burst into
flame where she stood without attracting attention. She suddenly
saw herself from high above, a small figure in an empty landscape
of thorns, free to go in any direction she chose.

Her heart did a rimshot: if that were true, if she was truly
free, that meant it was all down to her, no longer theoretical. She
could move or not move. Take action or go on as she was. De-
pending on which way her next eight or ten steps took her, she
either would or would not actually be risking something in the
hope of learning more about Ferdy's death. Not *sort of* risking
something, *actually* risking something. Playing in traffic for a
change, instead of sitting wistfully on the curb with the braver
kids sneering at her.

Starting, perhaps, with Ferdy's car. She either could, or could not, search Ferdy's car. Up to her.

A thought drilled its way through her consciousness with the direct impact of a cosmic ray: *Be careful.*

It felt like all the times the name Ferdy had been pushed into the center of her mind recently—as though someone was talking to her or she'd picked up a fragment of talk radio on her fillings.

And it said exactly the wrong thing.

"I've *been* careful," Madison said to the air. "I've been careful my whole life and look where it's got me—standing in the middle of this crap desert, all by myself with a rock in my shoe, marginally employed, missing somebody I don't want to see, and waiting for something to come around the corner and drag me into the kind of life everybody else seems to have." It was a long and complex sentence for a person all by herself to have spoken aloud, and she made a quick check once again to make sure no one was squatting behind a cactus and watching the crazy lady. She was still alone.

"Careful, my *ass*," she said.

She strode toward the bookstore, pulling out her keys with a decisive jangle. Once at the door it took her only a second to make a defiant slash across the yellow tape with the edge of the door key, and then to insert the key into the lock, turn it, push the door open, and step through the shreds of tape and onto the wrong side of the law.

The smell of old paper bloomed out at her, and the dark, cool air of the shop invited her in. She pulled the door closed behind her, squinting in the gloom, breathing in books.

The building that housed the Pack Rat began life back in the 1940s as some desert refugee's house: a big living room right inside the front door, a short hallway leading to two bedrooms, one to the left and one behind it. A door in the right wall of the hallway opened into a kitchen in back, with a little laundry room directly behind it. When Henry bought the place, he'd hung shelves on every inch of living-room and bedroom wall that didn't have a window in it and a few that did. In the front bedroom he'd installed an old, overstuffed armchair and a plump maroon footstool, both from a local thrift shop. The two of them huddled together near an old brass floor lamp, absolutely surrounded by books. Both Ferdy and Madison sometimes sat there and read when things were slow, which was pretty much all the time. Ferdy had also liked to read in the bedroom where he'd died.

Been killed.

The store's stock had come in faster than it had gone out, so Henry had put shelves on one wall of the hallway too, making it awkwardly narrow. The room in which Ferdy had breathed his last housed the shop's sorting shelves and its nonfiction, a mix heavy on biographies of vaguely remembered film stars, old Time-Life books, and those irritating ye-olde-style classics from the 1940s and 50s, sold by the millions to people who would admire their spines. A short, stubby shelf labeled *First Editions* housed books nobody wanted in any edition. This was the dustiest of the rooms and the darkest, because the shelves covered the space's sole window. There was always grit, sifted mysteriously down from the ceiling, on the rough wooden floor.

The little utility room behind the kitchen had only one window, facing west. Henry had covered it with newspaper to keep the afternoon sun from turning it into an oven. The newspaper, maybe twenty years old now, had gone parchment-colored with age, and the light that filtered through it was a faded, old-photograph yellow that Madison liked: it was both nostalgic and cheerful, and it seemed to her that those two qualities rarely went together.

Well, she'd liked it *before*, anyway. Now it was just the sour, rancid yellow of butter that had been left out too long. For some reason, someone had made a hole in the newspaper at just about eye level. She tried the door handle to make certain it was open in case she needed to make a quick exit, put her head down, and gritted her way across the floor and down the hall toward the front of the shop, a route that would take her past the back bedroom. As she strode down the hall, Madison averted her eyes from the open door, where the thick-waisted yellow outline had been chalked on the floor, marking the spot where Ferdy's reading had been permanently interrupted. But a few steps past the door, she stopped, backed up, and forced herself to look.

Ferdy had landed with one arm thrown upward and one knee sharply crooked in a parody of a dance position, one that Madison had seen on Chabad telethons. Next to the rough circle that marked the position of Ferdy's head was a yellow rectangle.

A *book*. The book Ferdy had been reading. The police must have taken it with them. Suddenly, Madison wanted to know badly what Ferdy's last book had been. Something wonderful, she hoped. The *Rubaiyat*, maybe, or Rilke's *Duino Elegies*. Emily Dickinson. "The Tempest." Something that would have lifted his spirit high above the body drawn so roughly on the floor.

The sorting shelves, as always, were jammed: horizontal books lying on top of upright books that were wedged together so tightly there wasn't room for a stray idea. The only gap she saw was two books wide, a literary missing tooth, on the shoulder-high *First Editions* shelf just the other side of Ferdy's final silhouette. Hugging the wall behind her, Madison edged around the yellow chalk and then, as though walking a balance beam, navigated the narrow space between the shelf and the outline.

The Man with No Time, said the book to the left of the gap. By the same guy who wrote *Skinny Dip* or whatever the title was of the book Ferdy had pressed upon her. *Skin Deep*, that was it. And on the right side of the gap was another copy of *Skin Deep*, which suggested that might also be the title of the one the cops had taken, since the one Ferdy gave her was back at her house. On an obscure impulse of guilt, she slid it out. Ferdy *had* wanted her to read it. She stood there a second, book in hand, looking at the shelves. Even if she was wrong about the title, he'd been reading a private-eye novel. Ferdy had met the Great Mystery while engaged in a somewhat lesser mystery.

"You could have done better," Madison said to Ferdy's outline. "The last thing we see, it should be, I don't know, something sublime." She edged the rest of the way past him and left the room without a backward glance, although it took some effort, since in her imagination the chalk outline was silently peeling itself from the floor and getting to its two-dimensional feet. She might have hurried just a little down the narrow hallway to the front room of the store.

The building creaked and groaned as she walked, its planks expanding in the heat and the floor boards sagging slightly beneath her weight. The sag was just enough to bring the heads of the nails at the ends of each plank *up* a quarter of an inch every two or three weeks. The thought of the nails gave her a pang: that had been one of Ferdy's chores. Whenever anyone stumbled over a nail, he scrambled over all the shop's floor on hands and knees with his big butt in the air, pounding all the offending nails with a hammer until they were once again flush with the surface of the wood.

Madison snagged the toe of her shoe on a nail and felt her eyes fill up. What a dolt she had been, not to recognize Ferdy's offer of the thing she needed most: friendship. Well, okay, maybe not precisely friendship, but something with an element of friendship in it. Something she could have pretended was friendship, could have *managed* like friendship.

As she entered the front room, she went, out of sheer habit, to turn on the lights, but stopped with her finger on the switch. The wall facing the highway had a big picture window in it, and

Henry had glued a sheet of gray-colored gelatin film over the inside surface to protect the books displayed there from fading. The tint dimmed the room and made it difficult to see into the shop from outside until the fluorescents were snapped on. With them on, the room was, if not easily visible, at least more visible. Madison voted for less visible.

Things had changed in here since she left the store at the end of her dreadful shift yesterday. Some books had been pulled from shelves and stacked on the floor. Two stacks had toppled, spreading a clutter of books over the floor. Here and there were irregular splotches of black powder, which she knew (from television) was part of the cops' fingerprint paraphernalia. She put the copy of *Skin Deep* on the counter, avoiding a patch of the powder, and opened it at random.

Stillman laughed as though I'd said something funny. He was the sort of man who's always a little shorter than you remember him being, as though he'd shrunk while you weren't looking.

No, thanks, she thought, and looked around at the mess. Her instinct was to straighten the place up, but who knew? Maybe the cops wanted it like this. Maybe they were coming back. Anyway, she wasn't even supposed to be in—

Maybe the cops will come back?

Whoops. Get it in gear and get out of here.

She put her purse on top of the counter next to the book, and knelt below the cash register, reaching in to fish around in the dark for Ferdy's car keys. The first hook she touched, the one he usually used, was empty. So maybe they were on the one farther back, on the one—

Crunch of tires on gravel.

Madison ducked down into a tight crouch behind the counter and held her breath. The wheels stopped moving. Despite a stream of silent wishes, they didn't start up again. In fact, the motor cut out, and Madison heard nothing but the shop creaking around her.

Very slowly, she edged to her right to get one eye clear of the counter, and in the window she saw the front one-third or so of a big horsefly-blue car, the sunlight splashing brilliantly, despite the gray gel, on the curves in its hood. The passenger door was out of sight.

But *opening*. A click and the squeal of an un-oiled hinge announced the fact, and a metallic protest from the car's springs suggested that someone with a lot of mass had gotten out. One boot crunched in the gravel, and then another, and then the car door thunked closed. The man had to be at or near the shop's door.

Even as she pictured him standing there, studying the front of the building, a metallic noise that sounded close enough to be inside Madison's head drew her eye to the doorknob, which was being jiggled back and forth.

Her forehead and upper lip were wet. Cramps seized and wrung out the muscles in her thighs and calves, and the temperature in the room seemed to inch upward as the man outside inserted something into the lock and began to probe it.

And probe it. It seemed to take forever. Very slowly, she edged sideways, positioning herself for a quick dart to the hallway, a race for the back door, but then the noises stopped.

A *bang* as he kicked the bottom of the door. The door buckled inward and then snapped back into its frame, sending Madison a couple of inches into the air, and then she heard the sound of his boots again, saw his outline—he *was* big, both tall and broad through the shoulders and chest—as he stepped in front of the window. His face was shaded by a stetson. He cupped his hands to either side of his face and leaned up against the tinted glass to peer in, and she ducked back behind the counter and remembered, a thought like a bucket of cold water being poured over her, that she'd left her purse sitting up there, next to the cash register.

Big as a watermelon and twice as green.

Did it look like a purse? Could it be mistaken for a, a, a—oh, shit, what *could* it be mistaken for? A purse, it didn't look like anything in the world but a purse.

A new sound. The man was rapping his knuckles on the window. The kind of thing you'd only do if you were pretty sure someone was inside.

The boots on the gravel again, more scraping of something metallic inside the lock. Then a brief silence and another kick, this one sounding like a shot fired right beside her ear. Madison abandoned the concept of being furtive and reached up and grabbed her purse, ready to run for the back door.

But the man opened the door of the big car and slammed it closed, and the engine caught, and Madison peeked again around the edge of the counter as the car slid forward and stopped, the darkened driver's window all the way up, and she could feel his eyes through it. She froze. He was more likely to see movement than he was to recognize a face, so close to the floor, in the gloom.

To be on the safe side, she closed her eyes.

And heard him gun the motor and spin his wheels, spraying a hail of gravel on the side of the building.

It took her a moment to put her mind back together. Why was she—? Oh, right. Ferdy's keys. Her sleeveless T-shirt was soaked beneath the arms, the damp patches cooling her sides as she felt beneath the counter for the other hook. As she reached back just a little farther, her knuckles hit the keys and made them jingle. A moment later she had her hand wrapped around them and she was standing, breathing as though she'd just run a mile.

Get *out* of here, cross the acre of scrub, and open Ferdy's car. Go through it quickly, looking for God only knew what, and then get into her own car, go home, crank up the air conditioning, and, just maybe, get into bed for an hour or two. Yes. Bed sounded nice.

She picked up the purse and immediately dropped it as she heard the back door open.

17

People Communing with Rocks

"TELL ME WHY I SHOULDN'T just arrest you," the police detective said. He tried to holster his gun, caught it on the lining of his jacket, and started over. This time, he got it in.

"Arrest me?" Ferdy's keys were burning a hole in her hand. She wanted to drop them in her purse, which was back on the counter, but it felt yards away. "Why would you arrest me?"

"This is a crime scene." The detective's voice was so deep it sounded like a joke, like something generated at many fathoms by a cartoon fish with a mouth a yard wide. It was disorienting, coming from the mournful face. "There was lots of bright yellow tape all over that door telling you not to come in. You came in."

"I work here."

"In case you hadn't noticed," the detective said, glancing around at the shop as though double-checking, "the store is closed."

Madison said, "I'll bet you have to get your jackets fixed all the time."

The detective squinted at her so strenuously his eyeballs almost disappeared. "What? Why would I need to get my jackets—"

"Because you snag your gun on them. I'll bet you do that all the time. I'll bet your wife is always resewing the lining in your jackets."

"I *don't* snag my gun 'all the time,'" the detective said. "Most of the time, I don't have any problem at all with—"

"And I'll bet you snag it when you pull it out too," Madison

122

said. "Your poor wife. Not to mention that it could get you killed. Or you could shoot yourself in the foot."

"I don't have a wife, cops aren't gunfighters, I almost never snag my gun, my foot is fine, and what the hell are you doing here?"

"Detective—" Madison said, banging into a conversational concrete wall as she realized that she'd forgotten his name. "Detective, ummm—"

"Barnes," the detective said.

"Detective Barnes," Madison said. "Of course, Detective *Barnes*. I knew that. We talked just yesterday."

"I'm waiting," Detective Barnes said. He looked down at the inside of his sport coat, checking the lining.

"Well, Detective Barnes, I had *horrible* dreams last night, just one nightmare after another. Sleep for a little bit, *bang*, a nightmare, wake up all scared and sweaty, get back to sleep—"

"I get it," Barnes said. "Bad dreams. What's that got to do with why you're—"

"You have to face up to bad dreams," Madison improvised. "If you run away from them, they'll beat you every time. I needed to come in here—"

"Right through the crime scene tape—"

"—and go into that room where Ferdy was… was killed. And stay there until I knew that I'd *confronted* it. *Internalized* it. Wrapped myself around it and made it mine." Even to her, it sounded like a self-help article written for a teenage girl. "You know what I mean?"

"Not the faintest idea."

"Oh," Madison said. "Maybe it's a San Francisco thing."

"Wouldn't surprise me. Nothing about San Francisco would surprise me."

"You should talk," Madison said. "*Joshua Tree*. Hippies with bongs all over the place, Volkswagen buses everywhere like 1968, people communing with rocks. Gram Parsons, for heaven's sake, getting *cremated* up—"

"Ms. Jefferson." Barnes showed her a palm. "I realize you have an unusual amount of personal energy—"

"Why, thank you, that's very sweet of—"

"And I want you to stifle it. This is not actually a conversation."

Madison reached for her purse but felt Detective Barnes's eyes on her and put the hand that didn't have Ferdy's keys on the counter instead. "How come you're not married?"

"Ms. Jefferson," he said in his ridiculous voice, "and no, don't ask me to call you anything but Ms. Jefferson. Now move your hand and don't try to pick up the purse again."

"Don't pick up the purse," Madison said, not picking up the purse.

"That's right. Exactly the way you're not picking it up right now, just keep doing it. And don't reach for it again until I say you can."

"Oh. Oh, my God, you think I've got a gun or something."

"Just procedure."

"If I'd picked up the purse, you could have shot me. Except you probably would have snagged your gun on the lining of—"

"I *would not* have snagged the gun. Not on anything. But stay away from the purse. Look, maybe we'd better go down to the station."

"But—why?"

"I was gonna talk to you anyway. Better there."

"What's better?"

"Well, for one thing," Detective Barnes said, looking like no one had ever asked him the question, "we could sit down."

"We have chairs," Madison said. "In the other room."

"The—oh, yeah." He nodded toward the hallway. "In there, right?"

"Very comfortable. Much nicer than the hard, old metal chairs down at the—"

His chin lifted slightly. It made him look less hangdog. "You've been to the station?"

"*No*. I mean, you know. Television."

The edges of his mouth were tugged even farther down and his eyes were very steady. "Mmmm."

"Really. I've never been in any police station anywhere."

"If you say so."

"So." She took a small nip at the tip of her tongue while she tried to remember what they'd been talking about before he suddenly turned into a real cop. "You want to go in and, you know, sit down?"

"Sure," he said. "You first."

"Thank you," she said automatically. Then she said, "You mean because I'm like a suspect?"

"You're not *like* a suspect. You *are* a suspect, like everyone is, until you're eliminated."

"Wow. You're kidding." She looked longingly at the purse but then picked up the open book instead, dropped Ferdy's keys into the center, like a bookmark, and closed it the best she could.

Detective Barnes looked at the book with the keys hanging out of it, blew out some air, and said, "After you."

"I wouldn't have hurt Ferdy." She got to the hallway and paused. "I liked him. We were friends."

"Only friends?"

"Well, sure. I mean, come on. I live alone, I think Ferdy lived alone. Alone, you know? Like *not with* each other?" She sat down on the footstool and dropped the book on the floor. It fell open, the keys prominently on display. Absolutely not looking at them, Madison waved Detective Barnes toward the armchair. He eyed it with some mistrust and perched on the arm.

"Not romantically involved," he said.

"Me? Ferdy? No. Maybe if I wasn't such a ditz, we might have been, but I hardly noticed him, even though he was so nice to me all the time, always… always…" She wiped the back of her hand angrily over her cheeks. "Why don't women like the men who would be good for them? Why do we always like the lizards?"

"You're out of my area of expertise. But maybe it's because the right guys are a little dull. Maybe women want the ones who seem harder to corral. The ones who look like they'd kick the fences down."

"That's not bad," she said. "For a guy and all."

"The differences between men and women are usually exaggerated," he said. "I was actually talking from a man's perspective. We're the same way."

"You are? You mean you passed up someone who would have been—"

"Stop," Detective Barnes said. "We are not talking about any of this. We're talking about the case."

Madison sat back and began to pick at the cuticle of her left thumb. When it was clear it was her turn to talk, she said, "I told you everything I know yesterday. I went to lunch and Ferdy was okay, I came back and he was dead. Ferdy was just this guy I worked with, although he was dead—I mean, *sweet*. I called 911. That's all."

"At the Merry Go Round."

"Beg pardon?"

"The Merry Go Round. You ate at the Merry Go Round."

"I always eat at the Merry Go Round. The food's okay and they keep the air conditioner on high."

"How did you know he was dead?"

"You're kidding, right? His tongue was longer than his necktie."

"You made no stops between the Merry Go Round and here?"

"Where's to go?"

"Is that a no?"

"Yes. No. No stops. I mean, ask at the Merry Go Round."

"I have," Detective Barnes said. "You left at one-thirty, approximately."

Madison lifted her hands and let them drop into her lap. "Well, then."

"What I don't know is what time you got here."

"What is it, three minutes away? Maybe one-thirty-three, thirty-four."

"You didn't call 911 until almost five till two."

"And? I mean, hold on. You can't think that I came in here —"

"I'm just trying to get the time straight—"

"And strangled a guy who was twice as tall as I am and weighed more than Rhode Island. I mean, have you looked at me? I have trouble with *staplers* if there's more than like five sheets of paper. I am seriously not a strong person."

"Why the delay?"

"What delay? I didn't know he was dead. I came in, went to the counter, put my purse away, yelled hello, and picked up a book."

"What book?"

Madison looked down and mumbled something fast.

"Sorry?"

"*Splendeurs et misères des courtisanes.* Balzac."

"In French?"

A bit defiantly, Madison said, "So?"

"What's it mean in English?"

"They usually call it *The Splendors and Miseries of Courtesans*, or *A Harlot High and Low*. It's about a whore, but it's really about all of Paris."

"Paris."

"*You* know," Madison said, suddenly angry, "a city in France? They've got baguettes and stuff?"

"Yes, I know where Paris is. So you just sat there, reading in French—"

"Until I realized that Ferdy hadn't answered me. Did I say I yelled hello?"

"You did."

"So okay, it hit me that he hadn't answered. I figured maybe he was in the john, he was shy that way. I mean, if I'm in the john and someone comes into the shop and shouts hi or whatever, I'll just shout back, *Be right with you* or something, but not Ferdy. It was like he didn't want people to know he went to the bathroom."

"Mmmm." Detective Barnes scratched his nose. "So he was shy about being on the toilet?"

It was an uncomfortable question. Stated that way, it seemed to take for granted a certain level of intimacy between her and Ferdie.

"What I know about Ferdy's bathroom habits is based just on what I told you. If he was in the john and you called him, he probably wouldn't answer."

"The toilet here. In the store."

"It's the only toilet he ever used while I was around, Officer Basset."

"Barnes." He leaned back a little, an unsuccessful imitation of relaxing, and Madison's stomach muscles tightened. "He's dead, right? Balzac, I mean."

"Well, *yeah*. If he wasn't he'd, like, have a reality show. He was born in 1799."

"Why Balzac?"

"Who cares? Or did some profiler wizard describe the killer as someone who read books by dead French guys?"

"I'm curious." Barnes let himself slide down the arm of the chair to the seat. "I like to get to know the people in my cases."

"Well, why *not* Balzac? Who else had the gonads to call his work *The Human Comedy?* All these big fat novels and little stories, all interlinked, just the whole world of Paris. He went to bed at six in the evening, got up at midnight, and then chugged black coffee and wrote all night long and forced himself to create something wonderful. And a woman in Poland wrote him a letter anonymously, and they fell in love without ever laying eyes on each other. How could you not like a guy like that?"

Detective Barnes started to say something and, apparently, thought better of it, because he shook his head. Then he said, "Without *ever* seeing her?"

"Not for years. Turns out she was married to a man, a nobleman, about a hundred years older than she was, and twenty years later he died and Balzac went to Poland and they took one look at each other and, bang, got married. She wasn't beautiful anymore, not a babe, I mean, if she ever *was* a babe, but he stayed with her even when she made him miserable, and did she ever. What a guy."

"I've seen pictures of him. He wasn't exactly Mr. France himself by then."

"Women don't care so much about that."

"Oh, no," Barnes said with barely subdued bitterness. "Of *course* not." Her silence drew his gaze and he saw her upraised eyebrows. "So," he said, coloring slightly. "You were reading Balzac."

"I think we've established that."

"For what?"

"For *enjoyment*, okay?"

"No, I mean, for how long?"

"Eight, ten minutes. I wasn't running a down-timer or anything."

"And then."

"And then—you know. I went to look for, um, him."

"And called 911."

"Well, sure. I've never—" Her throat threatened to close up and she made a *harrumphing* noise. "I'd never seen anybody, you know—"

"Dead," he said.

"And this was someone I *knew*. Poor, sad, fat Ferdy."

"Was he sad?"

"Oh, geez. I don't know. He seemed sad. He never got phone calls and he never talked about other people or what he did when he wasn't working. Never."

"Got it." Detective Barnes levered himself out of the armchair. "So you came back here today just to confront your fear. *Make it yours*, I think you said."

A little bell, like the one that tells you that whatever's in the oven is about to burn, rang in Madison's head but she ignored it. "Like I said."

"Just here."

Madison looked at him.

"You weren't, for example, going around to everyone in the neighborhood, talking about cars."

"Oh," Madison said. "That old crow in the hobby shop. Wumsy or something."

"Mrs. Terwilliger. Edina. Two of them, actually. Her and Boot in the burt store, I mean Burt—skip it, you know what I mean. Why were you asking about the cars?"

"Because I'm going to be here all—"

"It wasn't so you could—let's see—play amateur sleuth?"

She could feel her face burning. "Really, Inspector Basset—"

"Barnes." It was sharper this time. He raised an admonitory finger. "Breaking into a crime scene. Questioning witnesses. No amateur sleuthing on my patch. Clear?"

"Fine."

"Do you know how many actual amateur sleuths there are in the world?"

"It's not of the slightest—"

"None. And you know why? Because, little lady, the only real amateur sleuth is a dead amateur sleuth."

Madison stood and picked up the book, closing it as best she could around Ferdy's keys. "Are we finished here? Are you done patronizing me? Have you had the all-important last word?"

He remained seated, looking up at her. "Almost. Have you ever been to Mr. Carvalho's apartment?"

The question had a weight to it that made it seem as though this was what he'd been working toward the whole time. "To it or in it?"

"Is that an answer?"

"To, yes," Madison said. "In, no."

"Why?"

"I drove him home. He didn't have his car. It was being repaired or something. So I drove him home. Just dropped him off in front."

"Never went in."

Madison just looked at him.

"Not even for a second. You know, 'Come in for a minute, have a cup of coffee.' Not even that."

"Not even."

"You couldn't describe the place. His couch, for example." Barnes leaned forward half an inch. "What's he's got hanging on his walls."

"Not unless someone turned the building inside out."

Detective Barnes said, "You *don't know what's on his walls.*" The tone was flat but intense, and the upraised eyebrows turned it into a peremptory question. Madison stood there, concentrating on not fidgeting. He gave her a leisurely assessment, then shook his head. "Fine," he said, "if you say so. No amateur sleuth-ing, got it?" Then he got up and walked past her and out the back door.

Madison was most of the way out herself, doing everything she could to keep herself from running, before she remembered her purse.

18

Intergalactic Black

"THAT'S AN INTERESTING YOUNG WOMAN," Lobelia said, standing at the window. She'd been there so long—ever since Madison first opened the book—that Billy had decided she'd taken root and curled himself around her feet.

I said, "I *hate* this." I was sitting on the couch with a crumpled map of Joshua Tree, circa 1993, in my lap. It was a rotten substitute for the All-Seeing Eye.

When Madison shut the book around the keys, the room she'd been in had disappeared from the window, leaving the sky outside pretty close to black: no stars, no variations of gray that might suggest clouds. No hawk visible yet. A little unsettling. A change up here, as I seemed to be learning, usually announced something unsettling.

"She's going to be just fine," Lobelia said. She'd picked up on my agitation even before I did and moved instantly into comfort mode. "Weren't you listening? She tied that cop in knots."

"I'm not so sure. He's got to be smarter than he seems, or he'd be in a jar somewhere. What was all that stuff about Ferdy's walls? And how come we could both hear it, out loud like that? Before, all I got was the words from the book, and they were inside my head."

"You remember what Pansy said. You've got the best connection she's ever seen."

I said, "Mmmm."

"I know, I know. It doesn't sound like much of an explanation to me, either." She looked down at her hand as though surprised to find it empty and brought up the other one, as though to double-check. "I wish I had something to bake."

I was still feeling the smoky little curls of whatever it was that had begun to tighten in my chest when the conversation between Madison and the cop turned personal. In order to avoid analyzing it, I said, "I wish I could just forget about the whole thing, getting her involved like this. Roll back time and not have gone all detective on Ferdy's murder."

Lobelia gave me a bright, brief, birdlike glance. I had the impression she'd cocked her head at me, although I was certain she hadn't. "Dear," she said, "if you'd been written a little later, you'd realize that women actually can handle difficult situations." She turned on the old brass lamp on the sideboard in front of the window.

"Yeah, well."

I got hands on hips this time, and Billy got up and took a couple of prudent steps away. "*Really*. Would you be all a-twitter like this if she were a man? Or don't you think the harmless little thing can get along without you?"

"Oh, don't preach—"

"*You* managed to get through four, or five, murder cases—"

"It was *six*. Six, okay? There were six books. And I got beaten up, cracked over the head, had a fork shoved under my fingernails, got shot full of vodka by a Chinese gangster in a yellow suit—"

"But you survived, didn't you?"

"I had skills. I was willing to hurt people, kill them if I had to."

Lobelia either wrapped her right hand around something invisible or made a fist, and I brought my knees up to rock the chair back, away from her. "And were you *born* with those skills?" she demanded. "Or was there a time you had to find your way, like she's doing?"

"Of *course*, there was." I shut up for a moment. "But I don't remember them being in the books."

"So the big strong man can do it, but the pootsy-cutesy little girl can't?"

"She's *not* pootsy-cutesy."

Lobelia said, with infuriating sympathy, "You poor thing."

"Damn it, Lobelia, this is not some cornball vicar in a quaint English village who's eaten fudge poisoned with an exotic Amazonian toxin in a book that ends with a recipe for Healthy Choco Balls that disguise the taste of kids' vitamins."

Lobelia's eyes were so narrow I couldn't tell what color they were. "That vicar was as dead as anybody in any of your books. He'd thrown up lots and lots of a really foul-smelling mess, one of the telltales for that poison, all over the front of his—his hassock or haddock or whatever it—"

"Cassock, probably, but—"

"And I can tell you, he died *badly*. What is it about you hardboiled guys, you think you're so much more realistic than cozies? We're both just a bunch of words that—that…" Her eyes flicked down at the carpet, then at me, then over to the right, and then back to me. "You," she said. "You *have* read me."

"A little."

"My, oh my. Watch me not gloat here for a moment or two. How many?"

"I don't know. Two? Three? They all sort of blend together."

"They do, don't they? She was limited, poor thing. Not that your guy was much better."

"Right," I said. "And then there's that, isn't there?"

"What?"

"That we were *written*. That we were *supposed* to live through it, however bad it was. We didn't know it at the time, but we had to survive, or the series was over."

"Simeon," Lobelia said. "That's exactly why you don't need

to worry. She's not in a book. She's a nice, bright little girl playing detective, and the cops will catch whoever killed your fan long before she can get anywhere near him. It's *real life*. She's not the heroine of a thriller, okay?"

"*That* cop? I don't know," I said. "I worry about her."

Billy made a sound surprisingly like a human snicker, and Lobelia's mouth fell open. "Oh, Lord," she said. "It's true. You've fallen for her."

"Spare me," I said. "I've seen her twice, okay? Once reading a book and drawing circles, and then today, hiding and putting that cop in his place. All right, three times, when she found Ferdy and then the cop came, and we could see her in the background with that, that haircut—"

"*Let me not to the marriage of true minds admit impediments*," Lobelia said. "Shakespeare, Sonnet Sixteen. Not to hit you over the head with a rolled-up copy of *Romeo and Juliet*, but she's human and you're fictional."

I said, "I don't feel fictional."

There was a moment of silence. Lobelia looked at me with something that was probably pity, and Billy came over and put his head on my knee. I petted the silky ears.

"He smells like a dog," I said. Billy pushed a cold, wet nose into the center of my palm so I petted him some more. Something solidified in the region of my heart and sank a little. Billy sighed, which was what I felt like doing.

"You know what you need?" Lobelia said. "Hot chocolate."

"She's a complicated girl. Full of self-doubt, doesn't know how smart she is, how different she is. She wants her life to change, so she's challenging herself, putting herself in change's way. Somebody puts up a fence, she's going to kick it over. I mean, she had a chance to get out of it. All she had to do, if she didn't want to play amateur sleuth, was give Barnes those damn keys."

"As an amateur sleuth myself," Lobelia said, "I didn't like that part, either." She pushed her lips out thoughtfully. "But, you know, there must be an evolutionary reason why guys in real life don't know what women are thinking. It's kind of an unfair advantage."

"For whom? Men or women?"

She headed for the kitchen, probably to find something from which she could improvise hot chocolate. "I'm working on that."

Looking up from Billy's soft brown eyes, I saw the window. I said, "Um."

Lobelia stopped and looked at me, then turned and followed my eyes. "Oh," she said. "Um, indeed."

The gray afternoon sky was back even though it was night-time, even though it had been nighttime for hours. Cut into it, exactly the right size and in exactly the right place, was a patch of absolute-dead, intergalactic-black space, in the shape of a hawk.

Billy whimpered.

I said, "I'm being messed with."

19

Two Pale Europeans,
Freezing to Death In the Sun

EVEN WITH THE SUN FLAMING directly overhead, she could still feel the anger burning in her face as she closed the back door and left Detective Barnes to nose around the shop like a Basset Hound. *Stop it*, Madison thought, or you'll call him that again. Across the acre of scrub, her car glittered at her, and a few hundred feet to the right, Ferdy's car answered the glitter, a little more dustily.

Well, she thought, sliding the keys out of the book and dropping them into her purse, *this is* not *the time to go prowl Ferdy's car. Detective... Barnes, Detective* Barnes, *will haul me down to the station for sure.*

She tucked the book under her arm, cast an attentive eye over the terrain for cholla, and listened to her shoes scrape the scree. Why is it always *down* to the station, she wondered. Aren't stations ever up? She stopped a few prickly yards short of her car. Like she was going to let him frighten her. Like she was the helpless little ingenue in some crap TV show or some cheap, shoddy mystery novel.

The book squirted out from under her arm and hit the dirt.

Sorry, sorry, she thought, stooping to pick it up and not even asking herself whom she was apologizing to.

* * *

Well, if the sun was at its high point, it was time to eat. The usual desert rats were at their usual tables at the Merry Go Round, and *Madison's* usual table, the hottest one in the restaurant because it was right up against the west-facing window, was empty, also as usual. She nodded to Corinne, the waitress, wondering idly how long Corrine had worn her hair in that beehive above all that Cleopatra eye makeup. As she pulled out her chair, she considered the Universal Waitress Time Warp. Even their names: Corinne, Dottie, Edna. She put the book on the place mat and sat, looking out the window at the parking lot, just a stretch of flat, bulldozed sand, until a slight drop in volume told her that Corrine was behind her, between her and the other patrons.

"The usual, please, Corrine," Madison said without turning. "And can I get some ice water?"

"How do you make ice water?" a falsetto voice asked, and she swiveled her chair and looked into the cool blue eyes of Jake. He was tan and lean and slightly dusty and looked like the man for whom blue jeans had been invented. Corrine was all the way across the room, looking at them wide-eyed as she stuck her pencil into her beehive.

"You get a swimming pool, fill it up, and throw you into it," Madison said, keeping her voice steadier than she would have thought possible a day ago. "Listen, as long as you're standing there, Corrine isn't going to come get my order, and I'm hungry."

"No problemo." Jake sat down opposite her and then lifted an imperious hand. Corrine, who was watching the two of them as though she expected gunfire to break out at any moment, said something to the cook on the other side of the pass-through window, and came over to them. She glanced down at Jake, then widened her eyed dramatically and aimed them at Madison.

"She'd like the usual," Jake said. "Oh, and a glass of ice water."

"*Thank* you, Jake," Corinne said in a tone so flat it had only two dimensions. "What would you like, Maddy?"

Madison took a breath. In an inch, in all the way. "A can of bug spray."

"We've got one of those," Corrine said. "And what would you like after the bug is gone?"

"Hey," Jake said, "I'm a paying customer, too."

Corrine said, "I hadn't noticed."

"When I ate here with Ferdy," Madison said, "he had some kind of grease sandwich on rye."

Corrine didn't even have to think about it. "A Reuben. He ate it all the time. Sometimes for dinner, too. With every fry in the place. You want one?"

"And the fries, too."

Jake said, "Kind of heavy, don't you think?"

Corrine said, "Did somebody say something?"

"No one who matters," Madison said. She was feeling better by the second. "And a glass of ice water. No, two glasses of ice water."

"Reuben, extra grease, multiple fries, couple of coldies," Corrine recited. "Got it. And one bug spray, coming up." She turned her back on Jake and left. Like most waitresses, Corrine had back-turning down flat.

"I don't get it," Jake said, his blue eyes watching her go. "I've lived here most of my life, and you've been here, what? Fourteen months? And ol' Corrine is on your side."

"Twenty-five months." She gave him a smile. It felt a little stiff, but it was a smile. "Two years and a month. That's how long since I came here to be with you. But as you say, you've lived here most of your life. She's had time to get to know you." She opened the book and started to read.

"So somebody killed Fat Boy, huh?"

"It never ceases to amaze me," Madison said to the air, "the way people who don't read—people who, in fact, may *never* have read—just strike up a conversation with someone who's got a book in her hand."

"What do the cops say? Nobody's hearing much."

"What were you expecting? A murder telethon? Live hourly updates? A stream of tweets? And that chair looks better empty."

Jake lowered his head to get a look at the book. "Hey, at least it's not in French."

"It might as well be," Madison said, "as far as you're concerned."

"Listen, listen, Maddy—"

"*Madison,*" she said, suddenly furious. "Corrine can call me Maddy. You have permission to call me Madison, and I'm thinking about rescinding that."

Jake shook his head slowly, a mannerism that hadn't worn well. "You're in your head too much, you know that? *Rescind.* That book. *All* those books. Your problem is you can't just *freestyle,* can you? Can't look life in the face."

"Wo *ho,*" Madison said. "A metaphor. Almost."

"It probably looked cool in San Francisco," he said. "With all those other leftover beatniks. Here, it just looks like somebody who's afraid of life."

Madison said, "Define *life.*"

He lifted the handle of a fork up with one fingertip and let it drop again. "You're not the only one who got hurt, you know."

"I may not be. I may just be the only one who didn't tell lies. But you know what? That's enough for me. So just freestyle yourself away from this table and leave me alone with my book."

"Alone with your book," Jake said, giving her the puppy eyes she'd once sighed over. "Boy, those are some sad words."

Madison surveyed her internal landscape, something she'd recently gotten good at. Saw anger where she half-expected the regret to be. "So go find someone who can't read."

And then Corrine was standing beside her, putting a big glass of ice water next to her placemat.

"Where do you want me to put this one, honey?"

"On his head," Madison said.

Lifting the glass, Corrine said, "Fine by me."

* * *

Madison was still vibrating from the look on Jake's face when the water hit his hair as she pulled onto the street behind the bookstore. Barnes' unmarked car, which had been back there when she left, was nowhere in sight. Which meant that it was time, once again, either to step up or to go back into hiding. How many times was she going to have to make this decision?

She pulled to the curb and cut the motor. The moment the air conditioning died, she broke out in a sweat. She grabbed a scalding breath, squeezed both eyes shut, and shook her head, making a noise like *bugabugabugabuga*. With her eyes open again, she blotted her upper lip with the side of her index finger, then angled the rearview mirror down so she could mess with her hair. *Stalling*, in other words. Thought about going home and maybe having a cold beer.

The eyes in the mirror regarded her.

Madison said, "*What?*"

The expression in the mirror didn't change, but after a pause long enough for one tumbleweed to chase another past the car, the girl in the mirror shook her head. There was reproach in the gesture. It seemed to Madison that a lot of people had been shaking their heads at her lately.

"Easy for you," she said to the mirror. "You're staying here."

And so are you, the reflection didn't exactly say.

"You just watch me. You and old denim-butt Jake." And she opened the door and climbed out.

The heat slammed her with the force of a plank swung directly at her chest. Ferdy's car, only about twenty feet away, shimmered at her, its sides and top wavering as though it were at the bottom of a fishbowl. Madison stood straight, pushed her shoulders back, flipped through Ferdy's ring of keys, and marched herself to the car.

The passenger side, she thought. She had no idea what she might be looking for, but it seemed likelier to be on the passenger side, since all that driving stuff was on the other side. She put the key into the door, looked left, looked right, said an abbreviated prayer, and gave it a twist.

The air in the car was so awful it should have had a color. All the fresh grease in Madison's stomach immediately detected a family resemblance and began to come on up, as though it wanted to see if it recognized anybody. Madison slammed the door, straightened, took three long breaths, rested her hand for a moment on top of the car, yanked it back as her skin began to cook, and decided to do her first survey through the windows.

Fast-food autumn, a scattering of wrappers, mostly yellow and white, all waxy and transparent with fat. French fries congregated in yellowish bunches, especially in the creases between seat and seat-back. Squeezed plastic packets oozed yellow and red. Part of what had probably begun existence as a burrito was midway through the process of turning itself into a viscous mystery fluid on the back seat, passenger's side.

On the front passenger seat she confronted a miscellaneous ziggurat of stuff topped by a couple of paperbacks, one a faded and creased old fatso by someone named James Gould Cozzens, and the other a very fifties-looking thing with crinkled covers that seemed to be called *Marjorie Morningstar*. She grabbed a breath, pulled the door open, leaned in, and pushed the books aside. Beneath them were two more books, and the day stopped cold for a second as she recognized one of them as a beaten-up copy of Stefan Zweig's life of Balzac, Zweig's intended masterwork, left unfinished when he and his wife committed suicide together in the Brazilian resort city of Petropolis, two pale Europeans freezing to death in the sun. Madison had read the book several times and mentioned it to Ferdy on half a dozen occasions.

She looked under the biography, and things immediately got worse: the book beneath it was a paperback, an English/French dictionary. She found herself blinking quickly, taken so off-guard that she grabbed a breath without remembering to pull her head out of the car.

She fought her lunch back down into her stomach and swallowed twice, and the edge of something metallic glittered from beneath the dictionary. She lifted a corner of the dictionary and saw a small black digital camera, about the size of a pack of cigarettes. It said LUMIX.

She bent over it, breathing pure grease, her back roasting in the sun, and confronted an ethical dilemma. Look through the pictures in Ferdy's camera or not? On the one hand, who knew what he'd been pointing it at? On the other—

"For heaven's sake," she said aloud. "Stop nattering." She pulled the camera, hot to the touch, from under the book and put it on the edge of the seat, where she'd be sure to take it. Then, feeling slightly tarnished, she popped open the glove compartment. What she saw made her pull back so fast she cracked her head on the roof of the car.

"Oh, Ferdy," she said, one hand to her mouth.

At least twenty little plastic bags nestled there, each wrapped tightly around a golf ball of densely packed white powder. The day seemed to get much darker, and the sudden heartbeat in Madison's ears kept her from hearing the big car pull up behind her.

She had reached forward to remove one of the bags—to smell it or taste it on the tip of her finger or whatever it was they did on television—when she heard the idling of an engine. Guiltily slapping the glove compartment closed, she turned to face the horse-fly-blue Cadillac, only two or three yards away. Up this close, it reminded her of nothing so much as a hearse, glittering its way toward eternity on a sunny day.

The Caddy coasted to a stop beside Ferdy's car. The window that was nearest to her was the one on the Caddy's passenger side. It was rolled up. Madison swallowed hard and sighted it across the roof of Ferdy's car, trying to see through the tinted glass. The desert on the other side of the car was bright with sunlight, and against the brightness she saw a silhouette: a big man, heavily shaped, with a prominent, hooked nose, wearing a ten-gallon hat.

The engine idled with an occasional metallic rattle. The sun condensed itself into blindingly bright points of light on top of the fenders and just above the windshield. The *windshield*. It wouldn't be tinted. Madison summoned her courage and took a step to her right, thinking she'd get a look at him through it, but the big car rolled slowly forward.

He's afraid of me, she thought.

And then, in an instant, the game changed. She heard the car's engine go silent and then the door locks popped open. *She* was the one who was frightened.

Without an instant's thought, Madison dodged back, reaching through the open passenger door of Ferdy's car, hearing the Caddy's door open as she backhanded the books and papers and grabbed the camera. She whirled and bent her knees so the man inside the Cadillac could see her face, and put the camera to one eye, her index finger feeling frantically for the shutter release.

She found it and squinted past the camera, which had no viewfinder and no LCD screen on the back—oh, my God, yes it did have a screen, but she hadn't turned the camera on. She stood frozen there as a long line of hot water found its way down her forehead, through her left eyebrow, and into her eye, bringing with it the fierce sting of sunscreen. She was still blinking, trying to clear it, when the door closed and the engine started, and the car, to her surprise, reversed, its unexpected backward lurch actually making her feel seasick for a moment, and backed away down the street.

No license plate on the front of the car.

A hundred feet from her, it backed into a three-point turn and then the driver gunned it, throwing up a low, thick funnel of dust that would have obscured the rear plate from even the camera's zoom lens.

As an alternative to falling down, she sagged back against Ferdy's car and immediately jumped away, a long brand burned into the skin on her back where she'd put her weight against the edge of the roof.

Reaching behind her and rubbing the burn on her back with one hand as she kept trying to blink the stinging sweat from her eyes, Madison watched the car turn left, toward the highway. It disappeared from sight behind the little line of stores that included the Pack Rat and reappeared a moment later, roared past, going to Madison's left. West, down the long hill to the lower desert. West, away from town.

20

A Mere Girl

FOUR HOURS LATER, HER car was angled into a space in the vast parking lot behind a McDonald's almost two blocks away from her apartment, half-hidden behind a dumpster in the darkest corner she could find. She'd been driving mindless circles and zigzags, one eye on the mirrors, afraid to go home and afraid not to. Ultimately, she'd decided to risk her house for at least a little while, if she could get there before the moon rose. One good thing about the desert—good for the furtive, at least—was that a moonless night there was dark in a way San Francisco never was. So, with the car tucked away, she'd taken a spooked start-and-stop, cholla-wary hike across open sand to get home, and then sneaked in through the back door.

All the shades were drawn, all the doors locked, all the lights out but one, a small table lamp Madison had put on the floor and covered with a red scarf for an unintentionally hellish effect. She settled herself on the floor beside it. On the coffee table in between her and the couch lay the wrinkled white wrappers she'd peeled from the bandage now covering the holes some fucking cholla had punched in her leg. Which itched madly. Should she be worrying about infection?

Probably not. At the rate she was going, considering that the big horsefly-blue monster had sneaked up on her without her even hearing it, she might not live long enough to get infected.

The only real amateur sleuth, Detective Basset said in her ear, *is a dead—*

"Give it a rest," Madison said to the empty room. Then she bit the inside of her cheek as her memory aid: *Barnes*, not Basset.

Two of the plastic bags from Ferdy's car gleamed on the floor, stretched wrinkle-free around the balls of snowy whiteness they enclosed. Madison reached out a finger and poked one of them, and it rolled around a little bit. The powder was packed quite tightly.

She picked up the one she had poked. Should she open it? Smell it? Taste it? And if so, why? It's not like she knew what anything illegal tasted like. If the basic ingredient were French fries, she thought, I could spot it instantly. Amaze everyone. "French fries, my dear Watson, and from a genuine Idaho potato." Murmurs of appreciative awe went up from the assembled policemen in their thick blue uniforms and heavy shoes. One of them whispered to another, "And she's a mere girl." He had a British accent.

"Right," Madison said. She looped a fingernail under the rubber band holding the baggie closed and worked it off. Then she put it on the table beside the cholla spines, slowly opened the bag, and lowered her face to it.

Sniffed.

Yipes. It smelled bitter. Puckeringly bitter. She'd never known how *bitter* would translate into a smell, but here it was.

What it smelled like, she thought, was poison.

Not a reassuring thought, since the next step was to taste it.

Just a smidgen. Just enough to *nearly* kill her, maybe put her in bed for a day or two, or, if it's a powerful psychedelic, to turn her temporarily into a piece of salt-water taffy. How bad could that be? She moistened the tip of her finger with her tongue, wiped off some of the moisture, and just *barely* touched the powder. Then, with some hesitation and a good deal of anticipatory grimacing, she brushed her finger very quickly across the tip of her tongue.

Sour, no, not sour—she made a tight-mouthed little face—rather, as the smell should have warned her, *bitter*. Bitter as a Minneapolis winter, bitter as useless regret. She gave herself a moment or two to die or for the walls to start writhing around. A long time later, maybe three or four minutes, she was still there with her heart keeping Sousa march time, and the world still looked solid, and she was wiping her tongue on the bottom of her T-shirt to get rid of the, the—taste wasn't the word, flavor wasn't the word, the word was *yutz*. Yutz *plus*, yutz with unripe cherries on top, concentrated yutz, ancient, mystical, medieval-saint-relic-tomb-intensity yutz. Yutz for the ages.

"Let's summarize," Madison said, partly to hear a voice and partly to make sure that her tongue still worked. "It smells bitter and it tastes bitter. We can safely conclude that it's neither artificial sweetener nor pastry flour. *Well* done. A mere girl, indeed."

Wind had come up outside, hard enough to fling handfuls of sand against the windows. With no nearby houses or trees to slow it, the wind hissed beneath the windows and through the gaps under the doors, making the scarf over the table lamp wave and flutter. It also made a cliché moaning sound as it passed over the opening at the top of the chimney. Cliché or not, Madison wished it would stop.

The house felt loose and ramshackle. A Big Bad Wolf with a three-pack-a-day habit could have blown it down. All the privacy that had seemed so desirable when she took the place, anticipating nightly visits from Jake, now seemed foolhardy, even arrogant. The house sat there, an orphan on its street, surrounded by nothing, as distinct and conspicuous as the center circle on a target. A very good place to leave. And soon.

Her eyes flicking to the darker corners, she made the phone call that would get her out of there, and then went into the bedroom. By the wavering light of a couple of candles, she threw into a shoulder bag everything she would need for a few days, pausing for a moment over the current Balzac, which weighed more than a pound, before passing on it.

T-shirts, underwear, extra jeans, the serape Jake had bought her in Tijuana (along with a silver bracelet that had turned her arm as black as gangrene), a few hair scrunchies. Shampoo, three small cakes of hotel soap, two pairs of running shoes. Moisturizer, not that anything short of bathing in a tub of sweet light crude could moisturize anyone in Joshua Tree's zero-percent humidity. Her one and only lipstick, just because she figured she should probably have some lipstick. She'd been carrying this same tube for a couple of years and no longer had any idea what color it was. As long as she was packing her toothbrush, she took a moment to brush her tongue, which dulled the edge of the bitter aftertaste, at least a little. For the first time since she was eleven or twelve, she ate some toothpaste.

On her way out, she took another look at the Balzac, chewing on her lower lip, but left it where it was. She blew out one of the candles and carried the other into the kitchen, only a few steps down the narrow hall. She put the candle and her bag on the painted wing-drop wooden table from the 1930s that was the only thing she liked in the house, and opened the refrigerator. Moving by its light and the glow from the candle, she put away the dishes that had been drying in the rack and ran a damp cloth over the counter. With the rag hanging forgotten in her hand, she stared into the refrigerator, falling immediately into the familiar Refrigerator Trance, in which she looked with an equal lack of interest at everything on the shelves until she realized she'd forgotten why she opened the door in the first place.

For light, she remembered. She stuck the wet rag beneath her arm and grabbed the quart of milk from the top shelf, pried open the top, and drank it all. *No sense in letting it sour*, she heard her mother say. Rinsed the carton (*good girl*), dropped it into the trash, and went back into the living room, where she realized she still had the rag under her arm.

She tossed the rag on the couch with a little more force than was required and picked up the two bags of powder. A quick twist of the rubber band closed the one she'd opened, and she took them into the kitchen and zipped them into a side compartment on the shoulder bag. Then she took a last look around the kitchen. It was as good as it was going to be.

A gust of wind slammed the side of the house as she returned to the living room, the bag dangling in her hand. She tossed the bag on the couch, noticed the damp cloth next to it, and stood perfectly still, her eyes closed, for about thirty seconds. Then she went to the couch, picked up the rag, and tore it in half and then in quarters. With the pieces clutched in her left hand she went to the front door, opened it, stepped back as the wind hit her, shouldered the screen door open, and threw the scraps of cloth out. The wind snatched them and took them into the darkness, where they would undoubtedly snag on some bush and bleach to the white of old bones.

As long as the door was open, Madison took a look up the street. Nothing. She closed the door against the wind and went back to sit on the floor again.

The battery icon on top of Ferdy's camera showed only about half a bar, and she was pretty sure that four bars meant *full*. She had located the power switch and pushed it, but the LCD screen on the back was just barely glowing, a very deep gray the same color as the dark spots in the silver backing on old mirrors. Somewhere on that surface, if she could energize those sleeping pixels, she might see the face of whoever, ummmmm, killed Ferdy.

Right on cue, the cholla punctures started to itch again. She slapped them impatiently, and the itching stopped.

She pushed a few buttons on the camera, and heard a little

whirring noise as the lens slid out. The LCD screen brightened. Holding it up, she peered at the little screen and saw her messy couch. When she pushed the big button on the camera's top right corner, the camera beeped. The little status screen on top said STORAGE FULL.

Tilting the camera so the scarf-covered light illuminated the back, she found a control in the form of a little wheel, with milled edges like a quarter's. In the center of the wheel was a button, and Madison pushed it.

And looked at herself.

She was sitting behind the counter in the bookstore, an open book lying flat in front of her, her left hand tucking her hair behind her ear.

She felt a surge of irritation, first at Ferdy—*how dare he?*—and then at herself. How could she not have noticed that he was taking this? What was she, vegetation? Her anger abated a little as she saw that it was a very good picture of her, actually an *extremely* good picture, and that she was obviously completely lost in the book. Her neck, which she had never particularly liked, looked long and elegant, and the curl of her fingers was—

Was the *curl of her fingers*, for heaven's sake. She made an impatient clicking noise with her tongue, something she'd learned from Angelique Kidjo records in San Francisco, and turned the wheel. Looked at herself again. Turned the wheel. Looked at herself again.

Ferdy had shot her and shot her. In the front room, reading in the armchair in the side bedroom, sitting on a stool in the used-to-be kitchen, shelving books, walking across the desert to get to the back door, her car and his glinting behind her. He was either a very good photographer or he'd erased all the pictures that didn't make her look like a movie star. She'd never been photographed this well in her life.

And she'd been impervious to him. She hadn't seen him,

hadn't heard him, hadn't felt the energy of his attention. The in-difference, though, was obviously one-way.

Ferdy had been smitten. And she'd *known* it.

A tug of guilt made her look up just as a pair of headlights swept across the shade over the front window. Madison put down the camera, turned off the little lamp, and went to the window. Hooked a finger around the edge of the shade and looked out to see a white car with CONCIERGE RENT-A-CAR printed on it, pulling into the drive. Went to the couch and began to grab her stuff.

* * *

An hour and a half later, she was almost fifteen miles away in a cheap motel in Twentynine Palms, her rental car ticking away in the space down below her second-story door. With a sigh that seemed rooted in her toes, she plopped down onto the hard bed with its nubby, scratchy bedspread and piled up the two pillows, meager and hard as bran sacks, and powered on Ferdy's camera again. She flicked the wheel back, finding four more candid shots of her, and then, in an aluminum folding lawn chair with white and yellow nylon webbing, a woman who could have been anywhere from forty to eighty and who weighed perhaps sixty pounds. Her eyes, their cushions of fat long devoured, were so deepset as to be almost invisible, and they were peering into the light like the eyes of someone who's been in a cave for years. Her hands gripped her knees with an intensity that looked like pain. Her hair was as dead as a snarl of thread.

But she was laughing.

21

High-School Heartbreak
in One-Third of a Haiku

FERDY'S APARTMENT BUILDING WAS a featureless, charm-free, two-story, vaguely Spanish stucco oblong that had been economically painted the dirty white that everything in the desert eventually faded to anyway. It occupied half of a short, dusty block off of Smoke Tree Avenue. The air conditioner in Madison's rented car wasn't working so she sat there at the curb, stuck to the fake-leather seat, and looked at the building. Waiting for it to tell her something.

It didn't. And the car smelled like that awful old pink bubble gum, what was it called?

Eleven-ten AM. She'd been up since seven, regretting the motel coffee, weak enough to have filtered for years through a mile of sandstone. It had taken four cups just trying to pry her eyes open. For the past three hours, as the heat of the desert day staked its claim, she'd been spiraling around the places she'd written on the circumference of one of the circles in her sketchpad, the one with Ferdy's apartment at its center. And now she had a post-coffee case of the drowsies and a full bladder, which were the exact opposite of the effects she'd been hoping for.

She needed a bathroom. The nearest bathroom was in Ferdy's apartment. There was no locked gate between her and Ferdy's front door, just an open, welcoming Spanish archway. Thanks to the keys Ferdy had hung beneath the counter, there was probably no lock on Ferdy's front door she couldn't open.

There was, in short, nothing to keep her out of Ferdy's apartment. Away from Ferdy's bathroom.

Except a strong personal revulsion at the idea of prowling a place into which she hadn't been invited and an ingrained reluctance to use a guy's bathroom, with all the spatter on the seat. And —no denying it—there was also a healthy dose of fear about, well, the same old thing, really. Stepping across a line she couldn't recross.

But this wasn't really amateur sleuthing, was it? She just needed—wait, stop, back up, edit that—she really, *seriously*, bordering-on-urgently, needed to pee. Even Detective Barnes wouldn't arrest her for peeing.

Okay, a deal, she thought, feeling like the nine-year-old Madison who had negotiated her world via a series of deals she made with herself: if Mom isn't home, I'll eat three cookies; if the next car isn't red, I'll call Patty and ask why she's mad at me. If there was no yellow tape on the door to Ferdy's apartment, if no one answered when she knocked (and who would?), she'd let herself in, avail herself of the facilities, and then vanish into the light of day, leaving not a rack behind.

"*The Tempest*," she said out loud, getting out of the car. "Leave not a rack" was *The Tempest*, but what the hell was a *rack?* The car's interior had been so hot that the day felt almost cool. As she crossed the street she pulled the sopping blouse away from her back. The moment she let go it plastered itself to her again.

She didn't know which apartment he had lived in, and despite the pressure on her bladder, she experienced a pallid flicker of hope at this glimpse of a reason to turn around. But there was a directory in the archway, big as a bullfight poster, one of those black officey things with the little white push-in letters, the ones that always looked like mints to her.

Carvalho, the directory said mintily, *14*.

So she had the apartment number, the only thing she'd lacked, and one more reason to pull out vanished into air, into thin air. "Thin air"—*The Tempest* again. As she entered the pool area of the apartment house, Madison cast a quick look around for Caliban, for a monster of some kind.

Number 14 had yellow tape crisscrossing its door, and at the sight, she almost tripped over her own feet. *No*, she thought, it's too much. She couldn't cut through another—

But the tape had *already* been cut, very neatly, obviously by something sharp. Not only had the tape been cut, but the door stood open by eight or ten inches. The brilliant sun, beating on the white door, made the space beyond it seem darker than it undoubtedly was. Madison took a look around the bright, empty courtyard, all the big windows with people presumably behind them, ears just cocked for a cry for help. Nothing scary out here. She went to the yellow-taped door, swallowed twice, straight-armed it hard enough to bang it against the wall, and, standing safely in the sunlight, called out, "Detective, um, Barnes?"

No answer. Nor did anyone appear in the door with long black claws and blood dripping from his teeth. And then her eyes adjusted to the darkness inside, and she saw herself, five feet high, on the opposite wall of what had to be the living room.

She was laughing.

You don't know what's on his walls? that doggy detective had asked.

The picture. When could Ferdy have taken —?-

She was inside before she knew it, staring at herself, her heart banging against the skin on the side of her throat. Her image filled twenty square feet of black-and-white, her head thrown back in mid-laugh, and there she was again on the wall to the left, a different photo, wearing different clothes, and—on the wall beside the door—an enormous picture of the agelessly gaunt woman with the sunken, luminous eyes, the one she'd seen in Ferdy's camera. She was sitting in a high-backed armchair, open newspapers at her feet and a cigarette in her hand.

Farsighted, Madison thought automatically. Her own mother read the paper that way. The woman's feet were sunk into big furry slippers, puffs of fluff exploding like dandelions at the end of stick-thin legs. Gleaming beside the armchair was the aluminum skeleton of a walker.

Listening to her blood boom through her veins, Madison realized how silent the place was. She steadied her breathing and slowly turned to survey the room.

It had been searched furiously, with no attempt at concealment. The couch cushions were cockeyed, a couple of them torn open, the couch pulled away from the wall. Books had been yanked from the row of shelves beside the door, obviously installed by Ferdy; no cheap California apartment house has built-in bookcases. Some of the books had been ripped down the spine, an act of violence against all civilization, and one that would have probably moved Ferdy to tears. These were *his books*, most likely his only constant and reliable companions.

She fought the impulse to soothe the books, to return them to their shelves, and instead took another look around. Above the pass-through counter separating the living room from the kitchen, she saw the refrigerator standing open, its little light still burning yellow. Broken dishes on the counter, empty cabinets.

Madison thought: *This is not a police search.*

Still not a sound.

She felt eyes on her back and turned to face the photo of the skeletal woman. She wasn't laughing in this picture, as she had been in the one on Ferdy's memory card. The shutter had clicked as she raised a hand in half-irritated protest. The hand was a claw but the eyes were soft, not angry. Affectionate, even.

If anyone else was in the apartment, he or she was absolutely silent.

Go fast, Madison decided. By the time the intention was fully formed, she was halfway down the hall, darting into the bedroom, trashed as though by a furious genie, but empty. Then the bathroom: no one behind the door, no one behind the shower curtain. Didn't smell too terrible. One more quick pass, taken at an urgent trot: bedroom closet, unoccupied; no one under the bed; kitchen, empty. Living room, same as she'd left it, with herself laughing down from the wall at whatever had happened here. Beneath the pain-glazed gaze of the spectral woman in the armchair.

She went back into the bathroom, closed the door, popped the lock button in the center of the knob, and stood immobile for another long moment, waiting for any sign that she wasn't alone in the place. Heard nothing.

Two minutes later, wiping her hands on her jeans and feeling much better, she went to the front door, closed it and locked it. Then she went into the bedroom and began to go through Ferdy's things.

* * *

He looked out from the page of the yearbook with an expression simultaneously hopeless and half-expectant, steeled against the disappointment he knew would come. His eyes announced that he was intimately familiar with disappointment. Already fat at seventeen, with a stiff bird's-nest of hair that looked like he'd put it on crookedly, ill-conceived sideburns of different lengths, and a really unfair case of acne. *Surely*, Madison thought, surely the acne demon could have skipped Ferdy, who had lacked *only* pimples to fill out a royal flush of teenage misery.

Beneath his picture were the five words the yearbook staff had chosen as commemoration: "Ferdy. Big Bird. Tries hard."

High school heartbreak in one-third of a haiku.

His whole life had been spent beneath this merciless, cheerless sun, rolling around, friendless, in the high desert as the world bleached itself to bone around him. The kid no one remembered two years after graduation. The one they'd pass without a flicker of recognition in the Stater Brothers supermarket. Never one of the stars, one of the ones who gathered the light.

Wait a minute. *How* old had he been? She looked at the cover of the yearbook: 2000. Just about right. Feeling faithless—how many other people had turned away from Ferdy to look for someone else?—she flipped through the pages until she found him, grinning knowingly up from the page, a beacon of confidence: Jake.

Hmm. Real name, James; she hadn't known that. *Among other things,* she thought. And a knot of type beneath his photo as long a paragraph in *Finnegans Wake:* "Ooohhh, *Jake.* Whistle bait. 'Don't ask me—I was born this way.' Bats 320, and that's in the *daytime.* 'Yo, hey, *sure* I remember your name.' Class president, junior year. 'Lemme see the pictures from that party, Jakey.'" And on and on.

The kid Ferdy would have avoided in the halls like a funhouse mirror: *This is who you could be like if God liked you.*

She licked the pad of her thumb and rubbed at Jake's picture until she'd managed to smudge it quite effectively. Shame no one had done that to him in real life. Then she paged back to Ferdy.

The photo had told her everything it could, but the pages around it added a little sizzle of pain. Two hundred and some photos, and not a single signature. No *See you soon, I hope,* no *Have fun in college,* not even *It's been great sitting next to you in Spanish.* The rest of the yearbook was similarly unblemished by affection, except for a blank double-page spread in the front. Someone named Fawn—*never trust a girl named Fawn,* Madison thought—had scrawled in purple ink, *Your a real sweat guy.* No

LOL or anything to say whether the illiteracy was intended to be ironic, although Madison thought not. And facing that, on the snowbank of an empty page, someone called Mr. Monroe had written in a tight little corner as though reserving space for more important signatures, *Keep your eyes on the stars but look out for the drainage ditches. If you can do both of those things, you can do anything. And you can, Ferdy!!*

The second exclamation point seemed immensely sad, almost as sad as the fact that the only even faintly affectionate thing in the whole yearbook had been written by a faculty member.

Mr. Monroe, she wrote on the piece of sketchbook paper with all the Ferdy circles on it, and then she closed the yearbook, which was a paperback, printed on coarse-feeling paper, cheap as well as melancholy. At the bottom of the cover, as though to assure the graduates that time would, indeed, roll on, were the words 100% BIODEGRADABLE: WE STUDENTS CARE.

Care about whom, you wretched, self-obsessed little jerks? To the book, Madison said, "So hurry up and biodegrade, fucker," and tossed it halfway across the room. She was sitting on the carpet of a bedroom that had probably been neat before the cops went through it and then someone followed them in and tore it apart. The drawers in the dresser had been pulled out, flipped upside down, and dropped onto the floor. The closet looked like it had exploded: clothes lay any old way on the floor, still on their hangers, and boxes and other odds and ends had been swept from the long shelf above the length of cheap wooden doweling over which the hangers had been looped. One of the sliding doors had been ripped off its track and leaned against the wall. The bed looked like giant cats had fought on it, blankets torn and crumpled, the sheets peeled from the slashed mattress.

Someone had been angry, angry enough to make noise in this fully-inhabited apartment house.

She'd found a couple of photo albums, but they were full of

pictures of the desert, pictures of the ocean, pictures of Disney parks, pictures of the Grand Canyon, pictures of Hollywood Boulevard. No one stood smiling in front of the camera, standing in front of the view. No one had been with Ferdy when he saw these places, no one to put her shoes into the footprints at Grauman's Chinese Theater, no one to take a picture of Ferdy with Mickey and Minnie in Anaheim. No one to take a picture of Ferdy anywhere. One person, alone, seeing things with no one to say *lookit* to, taking pictures because that's what people did.

Take pictures.

Without consciously deciding to do it, Madison got up, gave the yearbook a parting kick as she passed it, and went back into the living room. In the laughing photo, she was wearing a T-shirt that said UNRELIABLE NARRATOR, something she'd bought online when she went to work at the bookstore. She'd worn it to a Mexican restaurant with Jake and he'd asked what it meant. She'd let it pass, just said it was a joke, and he hadn't been curious enough to ask for it to be explained to him. Bad sign, lack of curiosity. How many bad signs had she sped past without slowing down? In her hurry to get someplace that didn't exist, in the company of someone who wasn't who he said he was and didn't want to go there anyway.

That's where she was in the photo: on the patio of that Mexican restaurant. A man sat behind her, out of focus, at another table, his glass raised. She was undoubtedly laughing at something Jake had said. A lot of what he'd said had been funny, the first time he'd said it.

When *was* that? About a year and a half ago, she guessed. She'd been working at the bookstore for a while then, so she would have recognized Ferdy if she'd spotted him, but she hadn't. Either she'd been completely wrapped up in Jake, or Ferdy had used a long lens.

She got the creepy feeling again, and instantly batted it away.

She *knew* him. He'd been sweet to her, sweet *on* her, this guy no one remembered, this overgrown casualty of high school. The only girl to write in his yearbook had called him *a sweat guy*. What was he supposed to do, walk up to her, ignore Jake, and ask permission to take her picture?

Sure, what with Jake being a pal from school and all. He'd probably invite Old Ferdy to sit down, join them for a drink.

Ferdy would have understood what was written on her T-shirt. Or, if he didn't, he'd have looked it up. Ferdy had been try-ing to read Balzac when he—

Madison said, *"Shit,"* unlocked the door, and went back into the heat of the day.

22

Life Rubs Away At You

IN HIS OFFICE, MR. MONROE said, "I write that in a lot of year-books." The light through the window behind him made the frizz of gray hair gleam like short-circuiting ideas. "The kids think it's funny."

"Ah," Madison said, feeling the hope seep away.

"I barely remember him, actually." Mr. Monroe obviously dimly recalled the Sixties and had kept one foot firmly planted there. He'd raked his rebellious hair back into a gray ponytail, gathered through a thin, braided leather strap with a bit of turquoise woven into it. He had a drinker's veined nose, a doper's muzzy eyes magnified behind thick glasses, and a woman's mouth, incongruously plump and shapely in what was, all things considered, a face that had probably seen its share of bad use.

Madison put her hands on the arms of her chair, ready to get up. "Well. I suppose this was silly of me."

"What—" He raised a hand to erase the opening and started over. His tongue slid over his lower lip, right to left and back again, a drinker's tic. "Excuse me for asking, but what was Ferdinand to you?"

"Ferdy," she said with a ripple of irritation. "He called himself Ferdy."

"I remember that much." Mr. Monroe patted the pocket of his Hawaiian shirt, an automatic check for cigarettes, felt the pack, and remembered where he was. Did the tongue-thing again.

With a sigh, he tilted back in the wheeled chair behind his dis-
ordered desk, apparently in no hurry to move the conversation
along. Through the ice cubes of his glasses, his eyes roamed the
office as though he wished he could see through the walls. Out in
the hall, a bell rang for what seemed like a long time.

"Fourth period," Mr. Monroe said, leaving unspoken the obvious remainder of the thought, *and two more to go.* "How did
you know him?"

"We worked together," Madison said. "At the Pack Rat? The
used bookstore over near—"

"I know the Pack Rat. Don't get in there as much as I should.
Don't read the way I used to, nope, nowhere near as much as I
used to." He seemed quite interested in the change in his reading
habits.

"People get busy," Madison said automatically. "They settle
into their lives, they get busy."

"You've noticed that," Mr. Monroe said with a slow, magnified blink. "At your age."

"Life rubs away at you."

"It does, it does." Mr. Monroe lifted his watch close to his
eyes. It was strapped to his wrist with a strip of dark suede an
inch wide, studded with more turquoise. The tongue made its
little tour again. "Look, I've got a few free minutes. Let's take a
walk. Get out of the building." His hand strayed again to the
pocket with the cigarettes in it.

"Sure," Madison said, as though she had a choice. She got up
and followed him into the hallway, thick with students.

"Slow down, slow down," Mr. Monroe said to the kids, not
seeming to expect any results. "Classroom's not going anyplace."

A kid with a Buddhist monk's shaved head grinned as he
shoved past. "Ciggie break, Mr. M.?"

"I cannot tell a lie," Mr. Monroe said. "Actually," he continued to Madison, "I can, but it sets a bad example. You worked together, you and Ferdinand."

"He was sweet on me."

"Very perceptive of him. I don't think he got much practice here."

"You mean, while he was in school. No, probably not."

"Everyone says it, but that doesn't mean it's not true." He shouldered open a glass door, and the heat wrapped itself around Madison and squeezed.

"What's not true?" she asked when they were both outside. "Or true, whichever."

"Hmm? Oh. True. That kids are cruel. Worse than adults."

"They *feel* it more than adults, too."

"Double whammy," Mr. Monroe said. He heaved a major sigh, cast a furtive look back at the building, and pulled a flip-top box of Marlboros from the hibiscus-printed pocket of his shirt. He popped the pack open, pried one out, stuck it between his lips, started to close the box, and remembered Madison. "Mmmm?" he asked, extending the box, his lips pressed closed to prevent the cigarette's escape.

"No, thanks."

From the center of a nimbus of smoke, Mr. Monroe said, "Good girl. You could pave a mile of Twentynine Palms Highway with the tar in my lungs." He inhaled deeply again, coughed all the way to the soles of his shoes, and said, "So, what is it you want to ask?"

"I don't know, actually."

"Well, that makes it difficult." He dragged on the cigarette.

"All right. I had the feeling he was alone in the world."

Mr. Monroe looked at the building again and let his eyes drift above Madison's head. Then he sighed smoke, met her eyes, and said, "He was alone *here*, that's for sure. A lot of them are. He was one of the kids who stand out in the wrong way. Fat, needy. Kids just sharpen their teeth on neediness. It's like a shark sensing blood." He looked down at the cigarette with some fondness: it would never betray him, at least until it killed him. "Every year we have two or three kids who just exude discomfort. It surrounds them, like an aura. It draws the, um, the wrong kind of interest. They're afraid, they're alone, they hate themselves, and they expect everyone else to hate them, too. And everyone does. Once in a while, one of them kills himself, herself. If you want the awful truth, I was relieved when Ferdinand graduated." He broke Madison's gaze and looked down at his feet, which were encased in beaded moccasins. "He'd be somebody else's problem."

"I thought you didn't remember him," Madison said. She wanted a cigarette for the first time in three years.

"I didn't want to remember him. I'm a counselor, but we all know that's a meaningless term." Mr. Monroe used the heel of his hand to muscle sweat off his forehead and scrubbed the hand on his shirt. "What's a counselor? Someone with skills, a psychologist or a specialist of some kind. I'm a burned-out English teacher with a sinecure. All I could do was talk to him, and I couldn't even do that very well." The magnified eyes searched for her and found her. "It's sobering, when you've defined yourself by being on one side of a generation gap, to find yourself on the other side. I barely spoke his language."

He looked so lost that Madison put a hand on his arm. "I'll bet you helped."

"*Nothing.*" He sucked down half of what remained of the cigarette. "I did nothing. And then his father got killed—automobile accident, drunk as a skunk, and his mother got sick, and there he was. No friends, father gone, and he's suddenly his mother's caretaker. I have to tell you, Ms. Madison, I worried for him."

"It's Ms. Jefferson," Madison said. "Madison's my first name."

His big, empty eyes, a diluted blue, settled on her. "Madison Jefferson. That must have been tough in school."

She shrugged. "Not the hardest thing I ever lived through."

"See, but you have a sense of self."

"*Me?*" Madison found herself pointing, like an idiot, at her own chest. "I'm whoever anyone wants me to be. My self-assurance is as thin as the glass in a light bulb."

"Oh, I think not." He dropped the cigarette to the sidewalk and twisted a moccasin on it, beaded fringe dancing. "Or, if it was, you've changed."

"That would be nice," Madison said. "Sick with what? His mom, I mean."

The glance she got was stricken, its impact magnified by the glasses. "I don't actually know. Isn't that unforgivable? I don't know. The *counselor* doesn't know."

"Well, don't beat yourself up over it." Once again, she felt the impulse to comfort him. "You've got hundreds of kids—"

"Five or six," he interrupted. "In any given year, only *five or six* who are on thin ice. Ferdy was on ice so thin you could see the water through it. She, his mother, she had something... wasting, you know? One of the real buggers that just eats away at you until you die. Takes everything, hurts you and humiliates you, and puts the people who love you through hell. Then it kills you."

"*Is* she dead?"

He shook his head. "I don't know, but I'd be surprised if she weren't. As I remember it, the prognosis was short and horrible. He got special waivers for absence because of it." He pulled out the pack again but Madison surprised herself by reaching out and pushing it back into his pocket. After a couple of surprised blinks, Mr. Monroe nodded. "Right," he said. "Right you are. You're a nice young woman. Ferdy was lucky to have you in his life."

"Oh," Madison said, and suddenly she was blinking fast. She cleared her throat. "Oh, well."

"Look at the two of us." Mr. Monroe slipped the tip of an index finger under his glasses and wiped something away. He looked fierce. "Isn't it unbearable to be too late?"

23

Lame Horse Lane

THE BAGS OF POWDER WERE troubling her.

They were evidence, although she had no idea of what, and she was concealing them from the police. She couldn't face the idea of taking them to Detective Barnes. Just the idea of coming up with a plausible story made her head ache. He'd go all deep-voiced-insufferable on her, probably call her "little lady."

Maybe threaten her with jail again.

She had, in fact, broken into someone's car and played amateur sleuth. She thought she'd rather be put in jail than be called "little lady."

It was almost three. She'd left Mr. Monroe—or, as she found herself thinking of him, poor Mr. Monroe—and gone to the library, where she'd dug up a phone book from ten years earlier, back when people still used phone books. Carvalho wasn't a common name unless you lived in Portugal, and she easily found the address she needed. It was about twenty minutes, slightly uphill, from the library. Grab something to eat at the Merry Go Round, and she could probably be there by four or four-thirty.

But the bags of powder were a *problem*. She'd only taken two; Ferdy's glove compartment had been stuffed with them.

She made a deal with herself, her second of the day: if Ferdy's car was gone, if the police had finally figured out where it was and taken it, they'd have the powder and she could stop worrying about it. If the car was still behind the Pack Rat, she'd make an anonymous call to the cops, tell them where it was.

Anonymous call=voice prints=phone-trace technology=that cop= deep bark, I mean voice=*jail cell=little lady.* It felt like she was watching clothes going around in the dryer. She was already sweating because the car's cooling system was on the fritz—*do they have air conditioning in jail?*—but by four o'clock, as she left the Merry Go Round with her meal a tangle of jellyfish in her stomach, an hour of the restaurant's air conditioning hadn't cooled her. She blew through her lips, making a *b-b-b-b-b-b* sound as she turned right off of Twentynine Palms Highway, past Burt's Boot Barn and the Pack Rat.

The desert rose in shimmering waves on all sides, the hills in front of her climbing toward the mountain wall that cradled the Joshua Tree Monument, and then, to the right, the long road she and Ferdy always parked on, and she slowed without hitting the brakes—no telltale brake lights, although she knew no one was watching—and sighted down the road to see exactly no automobiles parked anywhere. A little weight lifted off her heart. The cops had it. She could relax.

About *that*, anyway.

* * *

The shadows stretched eastward as she made the turn onto Lame Horse Lane. The neighborhood, if it was sufficiently organized to be called a neighborhood, probably had a population of 20, most of which had four or more legs. She drove past only five houses in three-quarters of a mile, three of them boarded up and well into the process of being gnawed by the sun that would eventually bring them down in stages: first a tilt, almost a curtsy, to one side or the other, then a swaybacked sag in the roof line, and, finally, after all the nails dissolved into rust, a pile of disjointed firewood in the sand.

The first occupied house was actually a couple of trailers flanking a big, rickety-looking corral with three horses in it and a pack of badly matched dogs, five or six of them, that came bounding out to gang up on her car. The other inhabited house was an adobe of great apparent age, a thick-walled, pumpkin-colored cube with small, protective windows, squinting into the afternoon glare.

Not a soul in sight.

The fifth house, around a mystifying bend in the road—there was nothing Madison could see to bend it *around*—was a clapboard cottage that had been painted a festive blue twenty or thirty years earlier, but had faded since to the color of the sky seen through thin cirrus clouds, a blue so faint it seemed to recede. Someone had boarded up the two front windows, but the plywood rectangles had been pried off and dropped to the ground, where they'd gradually been leached of their color in the desert's eternal bleach cycle. The hills to the West were clipping the bottom of the falling sun, and when Madison got out of the car, she cast a shadow fifteen feet long.

The front door had been yanked off its hinges, probably by the same vandals who'd pulled the plywood from the windows. The door was tilted up on one corner, the opposite corner propped against the wall. As Madison approached it, she saw the tattletale fan of darker sand that announced where a coyote had dug beneath it in pursuit of some burrowing thing. Madison gave the door a little extra room as she walked past it, just in case either the predator or the prey was still under there, and went to the yawning frame where the door had once hung.

The house's floor was one concrete step up, the usual futile precaution against scorpions, tarantulas, and baby rattlers slipping under the door. It was brighter inside than she'd expected because the wood that had covered the windows on the left and right had been pulled away, too. Broken glass caught dying fire in the window to the west, grabbing hold of the sun's last rays, and raggedy curtains made of some cheap diaphanous fabric hung absolutely still, dyed orange by the light trapped in the glass. There was no wind at all.

The fabric curtains were the only thing in the room that looked human.

And holes had been knocked in the walls.

In eight or ten places, at apparently random intervals—down near the floor, just below the ceiling—someone had taken a sledgehammer to the drywall. Big, roughly triangular chunks of inch-thick plaster littered the floor, and here and there through the openings Madison could see the dull silver spiral of electrical conduit, draped in brownish cobwebs.

A short hallway bisected the rear of the house. To the left was a kitchen, nothing remaining but a pitted white porcelain sink blooming rust, doorless cabinets, a lemon-yellow formica counter, and the lingering smell of long-ago damp. An unfaded patch of wall, the paint protected by a thick layer of grease, announced where the stove had been, and beyond the kitchen she found a small utility room—another rusting sink, a small, rectangular re-frigerator with its door missing, a bare, broken light bulb in the center of the ceiling, and cigarette butts on the floor.

The butts, two of them, looked new. They'd been squashed flat, probably beneath the sole of a shoe. The paper was still white; it had never been damp, and the oils in the tobacco hadn't had time to leach through it. Someone had stood there, smoking and probably thinking, not long ago.

The back door hung open, the window in the top half punched out. Madison found herself on tiptoe and breathing shallowly as she approached the doorway, and she hung back and surveyed as much of the yard as she could see before stepping through it.

About thirty feet behind the house was a wooden shed, one

wall yawning wide and unbuilt, probably designed as a garage. Madison took her last step through the door and followed a faint path across the sand so she could look inside. An empty shelf, about five feet off the ground, went all the way across the back wall. The shed was dim and windowless and, in her frame of mind, deeply forbidding, so she stood there, looking for anyplace that might conceal anything, something she'd have to go inside to look into, and was relieved not to see one. With a mental dusting of her hands—*been there*—she turned to go back to the house.

But stopped after her first step, her eye drawn to the thing nailed above the rear door, trailing rust like a red veil down the weathered wood. A horseshoe hung in the approved keep-the-luck position, its rusted ends pointed up.

For all the good it did, she thought. She sighed without knowing it and followed the fairy-path back to the door, climbed the step, and stopped again.

On the wall of the kitchen, just beside the door to the hallway, was a series of fading marks, a vertical chart of short horizontal lines with writing next to them. As she neared it, the writing resolved itself into dates: October 13 of eight successive years, the most recent of them eleven years ago. Then a measurement in feet and inches: Ferdy's height.

She had a quick vision of the boy on his birthday, back against the wall, trying to make himself taller without going on tiptoe while someone—his mother, his father—made the mark and then measured it. Another year, another inch or two. Growing toward God only knew what.

The little ceremonies of optimism, she thought, feeling like she was about to cry. Sometimes it's a mercy we can't see the future.

Ferdy, growing bigger and more inward with every year, just as she had. The body taller, the shell thicker, the disappointments more deeply entrenched, little emotional dents in the interior landscape, deepened and broadened and transformed into permanent housing once it became apparent the disappointments weren't going anywhere. That they had to be *accommodated*, like the color of one's eyes or a speech impediment or the sense that everyone else is real, that he—or she—is the only one who's *pretending*.

There would have been the smell of food here then, the soft contours and colors of furniture. Books in the rooms; Ferdy's parents must have loved books. Birthday cakes with candles on them. First, two parents, then one. For a while in his life, Ferdinand Carvalho had come home to love. It made a kind of deeply pessimistic sense that the place had been destroyed.

Time to go, before she burst into tears. She forced herself to look into the two bedrooms and the little bathroom on the other side of the hallway, the interior growing darker now, making it harder to see the holes that had been punched in the drywall everywhere, to see the place where the floorboards had been pried up. Just to confirm what she didn't want to know, she picked up a fragment of drywall and found its edges clean.

Newly broken. Such a short time ago that she imagined she could smell the dry, itchy scent of the plaster, billowing through the air as the hammer struck.

The shadows were in their last and longest stages as she came back out through the front door. Long enough to throw everything into chiseled relief, including the oversize, heavy boot-prints leading to and from the door. Size 12, 14 maybe. An enormous guy.

It had been so windy the previous night she'd thought her house would blow down. She remembered the wind tearing the damp rag from her hand and fluttering it, like a discarded flag, into the darkness. So. The boot-prints were hard-edged. They'd been made after the wind, which meant today. The walls had been punched out *today*. Those clean white cigarette butts had been smoked—

Half a mile away or so, she saw a glint of blue, the setting sun fingering something shiny and blue.

Behind it, a funnel of dust.

On the move, toward her.

Lame Horse Lane was a dead end, a scratch in the dirt that ended in a turnaround. The whole thing was probably bulldozed twice a year to scoop off the sand-drift. She was three-quarters of a mile from the paved road, Utah Trail, that led up into the Monument in one direction and down to Twentynine Palms Highway in the other. The blue car was between her and Utah Trail, on the only road she had.

There would be people and cops in Twentynine Palms. There would be a ranger on duty at the entrance to the Monument.

The engine in the rented car caught with no argument the first time she pumped the accelerator. Without questioning the impulse for a moment, she backed up a few yards to get a better angle and then swung to the right and took the old driveway back behind the house, angling right again and bumping over the sand to miss the shed, completely dark inside now, and pointed the car at the bloom of orange just above the hard rim of the mountains: the sun, going now. She goosed the gas a little, needing to cover as much ground as she could while she could still see without headlights, fighting off visions of stranding herself in a dry stream-bed, her wheels turning uselessly in deep sand, making fans of dark dirt just as the coyote had, going nowhere, nowhere, while the horsefly-blue Cadillac circled her, surveying its prey, a wolf looking for the weakest point of approach.

She'd driven the sand before, with Jake, but he had a four-wheel drive, a Jeep, and even so they'd gotten stuck a few times.

The terrain was bumpier at 25 miles per hour than she would have imagined. She bounced behind the wheel, sometimes hitting it painfully with the tops of her thighs. Twice, her head went past the flimsy roof liner to bang on the car's roof. The steering wheel argued with her, trying to follow the terrain, wanting to go left or right on its own, and after a minute or two of fighting it, she relaxed her hands, ready to grab hold if the turn went too sharp or started to take her back toward the road.

She knew there was a road running parallel to Lame Horse Lane, south of her, up toward the Monument. That road would also take her to Utah Trail, but she had no idea how far it was—half a mile? more?—and at any rate, the ground fell off slightly to the left, the direction she'd have to go in to get to the other road. In the desert, a falloff in terrain often signaled a dry streambed, which in turn meant deep, loose sand and an upward slope on the other side that she might not be able to climb.

Chollas and sage bloomed out of the dusk in front of her and went down flat beneath the wheels. It was getting dark faster now. The desert night was swift, as though the millions of bats towed it into place as they poured out of their caves at dusk, with the sky darkening above them and the first star punching a hole in the sky, nothing soft and poetic about it. And, in fact, there it was in front of her, burning away in the paling that signaled the vanished sun: Venus, or maybe Mercury, true west of her, toward Utah Trail and asphalt and park rangers and cops and safety.

But to her right, on Lame Horse Lane, she saw the blue car slowing, saw it skew around and away from her, saw the red lights coming on as the driver backed into his three-point turn to reverse direction and follow. She pulled herself higher behind the wheel, trying to see farther ahead, saw a relatively flat stretch and floored it, the desert whipping past, the little adobe house flashing by, a light in the windows now, then some big bumps that rocked her hard, almost making her bang her mouth on the wheel, and then—oh, *shit*—the dogs from the trailers, exploding out of the darkness in front of her, almost beneath her wheels, and Madison did her best to push the brake pedal right through the floor of the car.

The car slid left, the steering wheel spinning frantically in front of her. One of the radial supports inside the wheel banged her right hand, hard enough to make her snatch it back, and by the time she'd gotten both hands on the wheel again, the car was at a 90-degree angle from the direction she'd been going in, and the engine had died.

The dogs charged the car, barking furiously, giving her whole canine octaves, from bass to flute. Madison tried to start the car, but it turned over a couple of times, coughed, and flooded. She sat there, smelling the gasoline, keeping her foot off the accelerator as she ground on the starter, and then, down on Lame Horse Lane, she saw the Cadillac's headlights come on. It was moving slowly, deliberately, and though her own lights were off, she had a sickening remembrance of having hit the brakes, creating a long streak of bright red light, an ephemeral trail that led straight to her.

"Shut *up*," she shouted at the dogs, barely recognizing her own voice. They were milling around the car now, six of them, their pendulum tails giving the game away: they were a cheerful bunch of bozos, but they'd done for Madison very effectively. She watched the Caddy's headlights as they bounced once, announcing that the car had gone up, over the shallow bank of sand at the road's edge, not far from the trailers and the corral. Assuming, correctly, that she was stuck. Heading toward her.

Her right hand was a bit stiff where the wheel had hit it, probably swelling a little already. She flexed it repeatedly, one fist per second, as she watched the headlights approach, picking their way around sand hummocks and creosote bushes, while she counted to thirty. At the count of twenty, she closed her eyes, crossed the fingers on her left hand, and twisted the key.

The engine caught. Madison sat there, breathing hard at the windshield, terrified of putting her foot on the gas. After a second's thought, she slipped the car into reverse, rocked it back a little, and then pulled the gearshift down and into drive, and the car shuddered, threw up a veil of sand, and began to move. For a sickening moment the car slowed as the wheels spun again, but then they got a grip on a surface more solid, and the car lurched forward again.

And now people were coming out of the trailers, four or five of them, their backs to Madison, all focused on the oncoming Cadillac, and she saw that one of them, a shirtless, massively fat man, carried something that might be a shotgun, and she flexed the sore hand one more time, grabbed the wheel with all the strength she could summon, and pushed the accelerator down.

She was bouncing badly now, the car's left wheel lower than the right because of fall-off in the terrain, probably down toward the dry creek bed, and she instinctively steered right to avoid going downhill, even though the move took her closer to Lame Horse Lane and the Cadillac. But it was getting too dark to risk running without the lights. She rode her luck a few hundred blind yards more until she lost confidence. As she flicked on the lights, creosote jumped out at her, raising its spindly arms on either side, and a Joshua tree materialized prayerfully a hundred or two hundred feet off. She heard a deep *boom* that she identified automatically as a shotgun. With a twist of the wheel to avoid hitting the Joshua tree, she looked back and saw even more people, six or so now, running toward the Cadillac, which had taken out one section of the sagging corral fence and come to a stop.

And then it began to back up, and there was another boom.

She slowed just enough to take control of the car and survey the ground. A small hill rose in front of her, quartz crystals sparkling on it as her headlights swept over them. To the left, there was no question about it: the ground fell away downhill, virtually guaranteed to lead to a trap, a sandbox, at the lowest point.

The only way to go was right, right back to Lame Horse Lane.

She couldn't see the Caddy now; either something had happened to the car or the driver had killed his lights for some reason. Hoping that the shotgun had blown a hole in the radiator or taken out the front tires, she sped up slightly, looking for a relatively flat path back to the Lane.

Something dark loomed up on the right, taking a sharp-cornered piece out of the sky: the second of the abandoned houses, once an ambitious two stories high, now being hollowed out by sun and wind. Behind it she saw a level area about the size of a basketball court, perhaps once a parking area, and leading away from it toward Lame Horse Lane, as straight as a gunshot, the remaining ghost-track of a driveway.

She cranked the wheel toward it, and the car hit something hard, the front driver's-side wheel bouncing up and over it, and then a hollow *whump* as whatever it was struck the bottom of the car.

Within seconds, she smelled gasoline.

The blood drained from her face, succeeded by a cold film of sweat. How full was the tank? She'd filled it when she got the car. Then she'd driven to the motel in Joshua Tree and back, make that thirty miles, then maybe another twenty-five miles, free-wheeling from place to place in Twentynine Palms that day, so call it sixty miles. The tank held thirteen gallons, she knew that because she'd read the manual—Madison *always* read manuals—figure thirty miles to the gallon with sixty miles gone, and she had about eleven gallons left.

Leaving her face to face with the only missing piece of data: how fast it was leaking.

Well, whether it was a drip or a pour, the sooner she got someplace where she could run out of gas without being killed, the better. The front wheels bumped up slightly onto the edge of the parking area. It was smooth and even, and she accelerated as she headed for the driveway, hoping to get back down to Lame

Horse Lane before the driver of the Cadillac could extricate himself from the situation back at the trailers. A lot of meth got cooked up here, and she found herself hoping he'd driven straight into a bunch of cranked-up, heavily armed, highly paranoid, ill-tempered tweakers who had him under perilous control.

No such luck.

Within twenty seconds of her left onto the Lane she saw the Caddy's headlights burning up the darkness in her rearview mirror.

The only possible response was speed. She jammed the accelerator again, remembering that the Lane was, at least, straight. She'd seen five houses in all when she drove in, and she'd passed four of them now, and here came the fifth, also abandoned, on her right, and the cross-street was only about a fifth of a mile farther: just twenty, twenty-five seconds, and she'd be on Utah Trail, with help in both directions, assuming she didn't run out of gas, and her luck was better than that, *surely* her luck was better than—

Utah Trail, coming up. And pulled across Lame Horse Lane, a car.

Madison braked, seeing the headlights in her rearview mirror leap closer in the amount of time it took to stop. The car blocking her way was red. An Acura, at a guess.

Its lights were on, so it was certainly running. Whoever was in it was sitting there, waiting for her, and waiting for the Caddy. Waiting to take her.

For what felt like a very long moment, Madison just sat there and thought about screaming.

24

Custard-Yellow Suit

THE FOG HAD MADE A reappearance, heavier, whiter, ropier, and wetter than before. I stalked up the hill feeling like I was trying to bat my way through clotheslines sagging with damp sheets, wishing I could burn a tunnel through the white with the heat of anger.

God knew I was mad enough. Years and years of paralyzing boredom vaporized in a flare of fury and fear.

One thing the designers of this place hadn't stinted on was fragrance. The moisture floating in the air released the sharp, treble scent of sage. I passed a big star anise bush and grabbed a blossom, crushing it between my fingers and inhaling the black smell of licorice, strong enough to be intoxicating.

A fragrant flower in one hand, a heavy Glock in the other, I scuffed my way up the hill, making as much noise as possible.

And at the center of my chest, I felt the heart-catch of Madison's fear.

Lobelia had dropped in, looking worried about me, with a bag of brownies and some kind of hyper-fragrant tea. She'd found me staring out the window at the hawk-shaped hole in the sky, still dark and sharp-edged. Then, as Madison's panic reached across the distance to squeeze me, the first twists of fog made their appearance, long, trailing tendrils untangling themselves over the chaparral.

And somewhere *down there*, I knew that things were going wrong.

Lobelia had barely put the brownies down and uncapped the dreadful tea when I turned her around and pushed her out the door again, sent her to go get the only people who might be able to help.

Just a minute or two after she left, I heard voices from the hilltop.

I hadn't had the gun in my hand for a long, long time. It felt good, it felt as natural and as direct as a clenched fist. It almost made me feel *real* again. I pressed the hand gripping the gun tightly against my leg, as though I thought something might emerge at my side from the fog to snatch it away.

I wouldn't say I was hoping to kill someone, but the fact that I wouldn't say it didn't mean it wasn't true.

I hadn't killed many people in the books, and when I had, it hadn't been an experience I'd been eager to repeat. But right then, with things going wrong for me up here, and something terrifying Madison down there, killing someone seemed like it might be… therapeutic.

The wind took a swipe at me at the top of the hill, sending the fog skidding from right to left. The area up there is about the same size as the construction pad that holds my house, which means I had about thirty feet to the rear of the lot, with a sheer drop-off beyond that, and roughly seventy feet in front of me, to the cliff that falls twenty feet to the parking area in front of my shack. The unbuilt pad stretched about sixty-five feet from left to right, and I was on the right edge, at least the way I was facing. Once again I was struck by the new density of the environment, its details, its lack of the usual first-draft sketchiness. *Someone* was funneling a lot of imagination my way. A whole book club, all taking a nostalgic swipe at the 90s with one of my books? So why hadn't I seen any of them in the window?

Up here—for now, at least—nobody was talking.

Could have been a scrap of conversation echoing up from the canyon below, I thought, not believing it for a second. But canyons are funhouse mazes for sound, unpredictable echoes ricocheting from all sides. Oh, don't be silly, it had come from up here. But *where* up here?

The noise I'd made on the way up stopped seeming like a good idea. Barry, the needle-nosed sadist I'd punched out last time I'd been up here, had been more solid than any of the bad guys and girls I'd met up with since being transported to wherever this actually was. And, since I'd heard conversation, I was either dealing with more than one heavy or with a single who was unhinged enough to chatter to himself in multiple voices. Neither possibility was very attractive. Edging just far enough left, toward the center, to make it harder for anyone to push me off the right edge, I felt my way back through the fog until I was within six or eight feet of the rear edge of the pad. This was a fall I *really* didn't want to take, maybe forty feet straight down to a large bed of prickly pear cactus, a stand that might have been expanding its territory for a hundred years.

Mapping it out mentally, I figured the best thing was to zigzag as quietly as possible, right edge to left edge, then forward, then back again. The world was visible for a distance of only six to eight feet, so when I came upon them, it would be a fast hello. And then I abandoned the plan.

Something went *clink*, as clearly as if the word had been written on the air.

Clink is metallic, clink is hard-edged, clink is not a noise we often encounter in nature. But clink *is* the kind of sound that might be made inadvertently by some asshole hiding in the fog.

The assumption was immediately confirmed by a sharp, irritated whisper.

It was directly in front of me.

It took me five minutes to take thirty steps. On the thirty-first, I saw two dark shapes, dim and soft-edged as a cave behind a waterfall. One of them looked a lot narrower than the other.

If I could see them, they could see me. But they didn't move.

I ran through several scenarios, including a pair of scarecrow decoys, as fast as my mind could process them, and wrote them all off at equal speed. The most obvious solution also seemed the most likely: they had their backs to me.

A couple of additional steps confirmed it, but I didn't need to see their faces.

One of them, wearing the same clothes as before, was my pal, Barry. The other, in a custard-yellow suit I knew to have been made from silk by pregnant girls in a Bangkok orphanage, was a mid-level Chinese triad executive named Charlie Wah.

I'd killed Charlie Wah once, and my only regret had been that I hadn't had time to enjoy it.

So I raised the gun, pointed it at the center of Charlie's back, and said, "Hey."

The two of them turned, taking their time. Barry saw the gun and began to back up. Charlie's eyes were on the gun, but he heard Barry move and backed up beside him. I paced them, moving forward, maintaining the distance.

"Do something for you guys?" I asked.

Charlie said, "Long time, no see."

"Nice idiom, Charlie."

"I try," Charlie said. "English is trickful."

"Look at the two of you. I mean, how ill-matched can you be? You look like you met on a cruise." I took a step forward, and they both edged back.

Charlie said, "Appearances can be—"

"What do you want, Charlie? Actually, who cares what you want? Who sent you?"

Charlie smiled and said, "Sent me?"

"You know, dug you out of the compost and set you loose on me. Why so solid?"

"I am solid citizen," Charlie said proudly.

I said, "That's what worries me," and stepped forward again,

Needle-nose—Barry—said, moving back, "You *should* be worried." But then his eyes widened and he teetered for a second and froze in place.

"Oh, keep going," I said. "Let's see how high shit splashes."

Charlie halted suddenly, windmilling his arms for a panicked moment, and then put a hand over his heart as though fighting panic.

"Take the hand away," I said.

"Of course," Charlie said pleasantly, and when the hand came away from his chest it had a little mouse-gun in it, and I shot him twice, putting one on either side of the hand.

Charlie's eyes opened so wide there was white all the way around his pupils. He looked down at himself. There were two good-size holes in his awful yellow suit, and as he stumbled back, little wisps of fog blew through the holes. And then he dropped out of sight.

"Your turn," I said to Barry. "Who sent you?"

Barry just smiled, shook his head, and said, "Nobody had to, asshole," and then he stepped back and straight down.

I didn't hear any impact.

But I did hear something crash into the woodpile, followed by a relatively obscene string of complaints in a childish voice.

25

As a Practical Matter, I'd Shoot Ahmed First

"MY, MY," PATSY PARKINSON SAID. "That really *is* a good connection." She was standing in the middle of the living room, still wearing her white linens and her picture hat, but her sister, who was picking splinters out of her hair and smoking a cigarette in the door to the roof, had added a mordant fashion touch in the form of a wide black leather headband worn low on her forehead. Behind her on the roof, silhouetted mountainously against the fog, an embarrassed-looking Ahmed kept the All-Seeing Eye firmly on me. Now that the landing was over, he apparently saw me as the only threat to the twins. He'd scratched his nose on the firewood, and he kept pressing the cut with the back of a hand the size of a leg of lamb. In the kitchen, Lobelia, whom I had invited to this meeting, fussed with a plate of something or other.

"I'm not looking for an Olympic score," I said to Patsy. "I need to know what I can do."

"About what," Pansy said flatly around her cigarette, returning my tone with compound interest. If she'd been a cartoon, her words would have been printed on a balloon of smoke.

"About Madison. She's been terrified off and on for the past day. She hasn't had the book open, so I can't see what it is—"

"That's what I mean," Patsy said. "What a connection."

"I got her into this," I said. "With your—"

186

"*Girlth*," Pansy said derisively. She shrugged. "Probably thaw a thpider."

"I know her better than that."

Both twins looked at me. Ahmed was already looking at me, so that made three. I glanced over at Lobelia, who had frozen with a baked good in her hand, and she made it unanimous.

"What?" I said.

Patsy smiled to herself, and even though her back was to Pansy, the exact same smile appeared on Pansy's face.

"And you're the ones who hooked her up to me and got her into this," I said. "So stow the smiles of childish tolerance and tell me what the hell to do."

"Tell her to stop doing whatever it is," Patsy said, with an obvious attempt not to roll her eyes. "With a connection this strong—"

"I've been telling her to stop all day."

"And what are you getting back?" Patsy leaned forward a fraction of an inch. She seemed academically interested, like someone discussing an anomalous cancellation on a rare stamp. She ran her fingertips down her right cheek as though she enjoyed it. "What's it feel like?"

The question stopped me. What *had* it felt like? "Sometimes it's like I'm... talking to someone who's not listening. Busy or preoccupied, or—or wearing earphones. She's got her mind on something and she's not paying much attention to anything else. And then some of the time, she's just scared, and I feel like background noise, like I'm yelling at her over the sound of a jet taking off."

"Aaaaahh," Pansy said. "She'll be okay."

Patsy said, "You're sweet on her."

Pansy said, "Tee hee" without bothering to sound amused. "Fathe it, you *like* the idea that the helpleth little twit ith thinking about you. Even when her *life* ith in danger. Oooooh, my big man, *pleath* come down and *thave* me."

"I know the good-twin bad-twin thing is mostly role-play," I said, "but—"

"A typical, pitiful twin way of saying, 'I am, *too*, an individual,'" Lobelia said.

Pansy said, "Why don't you go eat thome lard?"

"—but I really do like *you* a lot less," I said to Pansy, "than I do your sister."

Pansy got up and came down the stairs into the living room. "Fine. Tholve your own problemth." To Patsy she said, "I'm taking Ahmed."

"Well, send him back when you're through with him." Ahmed appeared in the doorway, the Eye jerking back and forth between the twins. Patsy said to him, "*Her*. You're going with *her*. Why do we have to say everything twice?"

"You're written that way," Lobelia said. "It's not his fault, the poor lug."

Pansy said, "*Ahmed*," and stomped out, and Ahmed followed, the Eye looking down at the carpet.

"Poor guy," Lobelia said.

"You have no idea," Patsy said. "We've brought him out of himself, made him feel useful—"

"He was supposed to be a hero," Lobelia said, "not a limousine service."

"It gives him something to *do*," Patsy said, just barely keeping it short of a snap. "He can't oil his chest *all* the time."

"With all due respect," I said, "I'm not worried about Ahmed. I'm worried about that young woman down there, who's only in this mess because I wasn't smart enough to argue with you. And now you're going to help me help her."

"Or."

"Lobelia?" I said.

"Yes?" She looked up from the things she was arranging on the platter she'd brought with her.

"What happens if I shoot them?" Patsy's eyes came up to mine. She had one end of her lower lip between her teeth.

Lobelia thought about it for a second and said, "I have no idea, dear. As far as I know, no one has ever shot anyone up here. Do you know, Patsy?"

Patsy's expression was tougher than anything I'd ever seen on Pansy's face. "Yes."

"And what happened?"

Patsy held my gaze and then shrugged. It was a good, solid, insolent shrug with lots of suppressed information behind it.

"It's an interesting question, dear," Lobelia said to me, "but as a purely practical matter, if I were you and they were all together, I'd shoot Ahmed first."

"I shot someone a few minutes ago," I said, watching Patsy's eyes, "and he seems to have disappeared."

"How corporeal was he?" Patsy asked. She was disconcertingly calm.

"Enough that the bullets punched holes in him."

Patsy said, "Hmmm."

"I said, *hmmm*, too," I said. "And I thought about you. Since the first time you came here and brought that sky and those wolves, this place has been a lot more solid, with more detail. I even feel *heavier*. And the bad guys from my books are more solid, too, solid enough to come after me."

"Well, *obviously*," she said.

"Why obviously?"

"That damsel in distress down there. She's totally focused on you, probably with more energy than a roomful of readers. That's going to... enrich your existence up here."

"I'm not sure I think of it as enrichment."

"It has its uses. Are you going to threaten me again? Where

there's a stick, as our papa used to say, about halfway through every single boring story, there is usually also a carrot."

"I've got some *lovely* brownies," Lobelia said brightly.

I said, "What do you want?"

She looked at me for so long that I more or less snapped. I said, "Don't forget the stick," and pulled the Glock out from under my shirt.

"You'd shoot a little girl?" Patsy said. She dimpled for maximum effect.

"Oh, come on. You're a hundred and eleven years old."

The dimples disappeared.

"*Would* you shoot her?" Lobelia asked. She sounded only mildly interested.

I had no idea. She *looked* like a little girl. "If I have to."

"Once it's over, you tell me everything," Patsy said. She turned to her right as though she expected to meet her sister's eyes, and she held the pose, so perhaps she *did* meet Pansy's eyes somehow, because she nodded. Turning back to me, she said, "Absolutely *everything*. Is that agreeable?"

I looked down at the gun and said, "Sure."

She gave me a smile that was more an idea than the thing itself. "Assuming you get back, of course."

"Back from where?"

The smile emerged a bit further, but it would have been difficult to describe it as *pleasant*.

"From down there, of course," she said. She cocked her head to one side, regarding me with impressive neutrality. For all the emotion it suggested, I could have been a dust ball. "Where did you *think* I meant?"

26

Austerity Hours

IT WAS OVER. DEFINITELY, UNMISTAKABLY, unarguably over.

The small red car was *not* going to get out of her way. The big blue car was coming up fast.

To the right, between her and the Lane, the ground rose in a gentle, treacherously soft-looking hill. To the left, the ground was flat, with rocks.

On an animal level she knew that neither was good, but flat was better.

She twisted the wheel left and punched the gas pedal, and the car exceeded her expectations by lunging forward, banging off some rocks that were big enough to shrug off the encounter, hitting the bank at the side of the road so hard she smacked her head into the roof again, and then—fishtailing across the sand—she tore across the stony desert scree toward Utah Trail.

Immediately, the red car pulled forward, and for a moment Madison thought he was going to try to head her off, but instead he turned sharply ninety degrees and stopped, now blocking Utah Trail, which was very narrow, in both directions. Cutting off her access downward, toward Twentynine Palms Highway.

So that left up. Toward the Monument. As she felt the wheels grab the paved surface of Utah Trail with a squeal, she also heard a high screech of protest from the Caddy's brakes as it skidded sideways over the sandy surface of Lame Horse Lane, trying not to slam into the red Acura.

The air in the rental car was thick with gasoline fumes. Madison blinked away tears as she pushed the speedometer toward 100 miles per hour. Utah Trail ran as straight as jet vapor, at about a five-degree grade upward. With the world falling away behind her in her rearview mirror, she saw both cars motionless. Her heart leapt for a second, but then the Caddy's backup lights came on, so they were coming after her, after all.

A conference, she thought. One of them had gotten out of the car and gone to talk to the other. Making a plan of some kind.

Which apparently involved hauling ass after her. Both sets of headlights were now following, a couple of car-lengths apart. They hadn't gotten up to her speed yet, and for the moment at least, her lead continued to increase.

Madison's foot was so heavy on the gas that her calf began to cramp. One hundred and eight miles per hour, and that seemed to be all there was, at least going uphill, and uphill was all she had available.

Or was it?

She leaned left, toward the open window, to grab a breath of clean air and then risked slowing slightly so she could pay attention to the rear-view mirror. She imagined herself letting them get closer, and then making a sudden breakneck, three-point u-turn, flying past them at more than a hundred miles an hour, not giving them time to stop and block her, clear all the way down to Twentynine Palms Highway.

But the second car—which, from the size, she guessed was the Acura—was falling back: fifty yards, a hundred yards. Even if she could get past the Caddy, and that was a long way from certain, the driver of the Acura would have the road blocked long before she reached him, and by the time she did, the Caddy would be on her tail again, and she'd be right where she'd been before. In between them.

They'd anticipated her.

The desert unscrolled on either side at heart-attack speed and then, too fast for her to do anything about it, another little lane hurtled by on her right, the windows of a house gleaming all safe and yellow partway down it. And then the lane was gone, lane, house, and all, swallowed up in the night, and to her left, winking just above the hills, she saw a hairline moon making its first appearance of the month, adrift in a powdering of stars.

And then she was seeing it waver and ripple through a hot film of tears, not from the gasoline. The world was so uselessly, so extravagantly beautiful, and it didn't give a shit. She glanced back at the mirror and saw that the front car had gained on her. She punched the gas again, surprised to find herself twisting her foot on the pedal as though it were a cigarette butt.

The cigarette butts. The big one in the blue Caddy had been at the house.

He'd been at Ferdy's car.

He'd been at Ferdy's apartment. Who else would have ripped it apart like that?

It had to be the bags of powder. If he'd gotten to Ferdy's car before she did, if he'd broken in and searched it and taken the bags, would she be safe now?

She had a sudden chilling thought: *They think I took all of them.*

The car stuttered, hiccuped, died, and then caught and jerked forward again, and Madison heard herself saying, "Jesus oh Jesus oh Jesus oh Jesus," and she didn't even believe in Jesus.

The gas gauge was leaning lazily left, close to empty.

She pounded the heel of her hand against the top of the steering wheel, urging the car forward, willing the engine to run smoothly, peering at the darkness, trying to see through it. The entrance to the Monument, with its ranger hut, had to be coming up soon.

She said, "Uuuuhhhhhh," all the way from her gut, because

there it was, in the center of the road, right where the rangers could talk to people going in or out. And as she lifted her foot from the gas to the brake, she realized the structure was dark. There was no light behind the window.

But she braked anyway, not believing it, and as she saw the headlights blossoming in her mirror, she also saw the big sign taped in the hut's window: AUSTERITY HOURS.

She didn't slow further to see what the new hours were since the hour she was in was the only one that mattered. Instead, she crossed her fingers on the wheel and flattened the gas pedal again, feeling the car cough and lag twice and then recover, and she accelerated into a thousand square miles of desert, empty as the face of the moon.

* * *

The road inside the Monument was smooth and dark, newly paved, and it took her up and up some more, the desert transforming itself around her as it rose: the sand replaced by a litter of broken stone, the congregations of Joshua Trees thickening, here and there the looming silhouettes of big rock structures, giant stone monoliths the size of apartment houses and office buildings, starless shapes raising themselves against the spangled black of the sky to the east and the paling at the horizon to the west, the huge stones perhaps a quarter of a mile from the road.

Population zero.

The only way out, since she couldn't turn around, was to follow a big looping U through the Monument, first up and then down again, ultimately coming out in the town of Joshua Tree. Estimated distance: thirty miles.

It might as well have been Morocco. The gas was running out fast, the fumes so thick she could practically see them, making the horizon undulate in front of her as it would on a hot day. She looked down for a second, searching for the button to lower the passenger-side window, and when she found it and raised her head again, she was headed off the road, straight toward a pile of rocks as big as refrigerators, glaring at her in the headlights.

For an extremely long instant, she thought she was dead, but the tires caught as she steered into the direction of her spin and then she turned and accelerated again, straight and true down the center of the road.

The car choked, stuttered, and caught again.

Curves, she thought. She'd forgotten; inside the Monument, the road curved often, unlike Utah Trail. The old Caddy had more horsepower than she did; it would catch her eventually on the straightaway, but it probably cornered like a pig. She accelerated through half a dozen more bends, glimpsing the headlights falling back, the safety zone between them and her lengthening. Advantage, Madison.

For the moment. What she needed was a strategy. What she needed was a *plan*, solid, ingenious, dependable, the leap of intuition that would turn the fleeing rabbit into the patient chameleon, invisible, motionless, cunning, able to out-think, out-anticipate the men behind her.

Yup. That was what she needed.

What she *got* was a fit of coughing from the engine, and then the sudden stiffness of the wheel as the power steering cut out, and the dead weight of the car beneath her, slowing toward a stop. And refusing to catch again, even when she turned the key so hard it bent in her hand. The last thing she did was steer the car across the road, turning it sideways, hoping the Cadillac would slam into it. And she yanked the key and sat there, feeling the desert: dark, silent, haunted, still, stretching uninvitingly away from the disabled car.

Two seconds later, she was running.

27

23:59:59

I said, "You're sure about this."

I was standing uselessly in the middle of the living room as Lobelia and Patsy pulled the old sideboard away from the window.

Patsy said, "Certain enough."

"Enough for *you*," I said. "But you're not going."

"Nobody's making you go," Patsy said. She stopped dragging the sideboard, and Lobelia leaned forward and rested her elbows on it as though exploring the idea of leaving it in the middle of the room. "You're the one who waved the gun around."

"She's right, dear," Lobelia said, sounding like someone who was being fair. It's one of my least favorite traits.

I said, "And what about you?"

"Me?" Lobelia put her splayed fingertips on her plentiful bosom, the society dowager in a 1930s movie. "I have no idea."

"Well, what do you *think* I should do?"

She looked faintly surprised. "Well, you want to help her, and no one can think of any other way for you to do that. And, from my own perspective, not meaning to sound selfish, I have to say that I'd like to see what happens."

"Let's explore this from a new angle," I said. "Would *you* go?"

"Certainly not." She looked around at the room as though she'd designed it and was pleased with her work. "But I'm not like you. I'm perfectly happy here. It suits me. I have a nice kitchen and a never-ending supply of baking goods. And, although I wouldn't normally tell you this, it's been years since anybody read me. I'm sort of clinging to my time up here, trying to enjoy it before I fade."

"I'm sorry," I said.

"That's sweet of you, dear. Even when I did have readers, though, I didn't get as... *involved* with them as you do."

Patsy snickered.

I turned to her, and her face went blank. "Neither you nor your awful sister has gone down there."

"No," she said. "But we've known people who did."

"Did you know the two who disappeared?"

Her ears practically went up, so at least I knew that Bradley Zipper hadn't been making it up. Then, unexpectedly, Patsy laughed, the merry, innocent laugh of a young girl who's never so much as sneaked a chocolate in her life.

"Of *course*," she said. She laughed again and delicately wiped away a tear of mirth. "Clowns," she said. "Idiots. They knew what to do, and they didn't do it. They thought somehow they were *special*, as though being a failed and largely forgotten fictitious character and being sentenced to a cut-rate limbo like this one weren't enough evidence that there was nothing special about them. Honestly," she said. "Some people."

"What rule did they break?"

"The time rule. The most important of them all. We'll get to that in a moment."

My eyes went past them to the window, which looked the same as it had always looked, if you didn't count the hawk-shaped hole in the sky. It looked like a window.

"It looks like a window," I said.

"We've covered this," Patsy said, using the precise diction of exasperation. "And we don't have time to go over things four and five times." She rapped her nails on the sideboard's dusty surface, demanding attention. "You've had Seeings through it." She waited for me to say something, and then made an exasperated *tsk* sound. "Haven't you?"

"Sure—"

"I mean, if this were just a window, you wouldn't be half in love with this silly girl, would you?"

"I'm not—"

"That's not the point. Is it? *Here's* the point. She's in trouble. You want to help. You have a very strong connection. You have a portal, right here, the same portal that let you see her in the first place. The thing you insist on calling a window. It's like—to use a quaint metaphor from the time when we were published—it's like a coal chute. It connects two places, and energy can flow through it. Under... certain... circumstances, you can use that connection the same way pilots use a landing beam. You can follow it to her. The portal, the coal chute, this thing you keep calling a *window*, will take you there."

"But—"

"Should we put the furniture back, dear?" Lobelia said.

"I have a quirk," I said. "I like to *understand* things. That's why I became a detective in the first place. I don't know what the —the medium is. I mean, you say there's a connection, a beam. And I know there is, I know that's right, because I can feel it right now. But she's a real person, down there. And I'm—I'm whatever I am, up here. When you jump, you fall through air. When you swim, you go through water. What's the fucking *medium*? What's carrying the connection? What am I going to be traveling through?"

"When someone reads you," Patsy said, sounding as resigned as someone who has spent a lifetime explaining things to the extremely slow, "where are they seeing you?"

"In," I said, and stopped. "In their imagination."

"And when you see them, looking up at them through the

page—*in this window*—what part of them do you think reached up to you and put the image there?"

"So what you're saying," I said, "is that the medium is imagination."

Pasty widened her eyes in mock appreciation. "It's the conductor *and* the medium. We discussed this endlessly the first time we were here. Imagination is where you've always been. Even Pansy and I, we started in Mr. Stratemeyer's imagination, fighting for air with all those *boys*, but when people read us, they re-created us in their—"

"Okay, okay. So, through the portal, follow the coal chute and some tenuous connection to Madison. Get there, do what I can, and come back."

"Actually, it's a little easier than that. You've also got words."

"Words."

"The last time she read you. The words she read are still strung out between you and her. They'll be backwards, beginning with her end and ending with you."

"I'll see the *words*, is that what you're saying?" It seemed absurd.

"What do you want?" Patsy said. "A video? The people who came back said they followed a trail of words sometimes, and sometimes they just homed in on the orange warm spot."

I thought about it. "If it's that easy, why aren't there fictional characters all over the place down there?"

"How do you know there aren't? How many times have you looked at someone and thought, *He can't be for real?*"

"She's teasing you, dear," Lobelia said. "Remember, you can only be down there a certain amount of time."

"Twenty-four hours," Patsy said, sounding weary. "As I said, you've only got twenty-four hours."

"Or I disappear."

"And not just for a while. Always and forever. You can't exist longer than twenty-four hours outside the imagination. And I mean, you'll really disappear. *Completely.* You'll evaporate. As far as I can tell, your books won't even exist down there any more. The people who read them will forget them. Even your writer won't remember you."

"There are amphibians," Lobelia said helpfully, "that can only exist a certain number of hours without getting their skin wet."

"Thank you," I said. "That's what I need. The Nature Channel."

She looked hurt. "It's a metaphor."

I turned back to Patsy. "And I'll know how long I've been gone because—"

"Look at the window," Patsy said, making no effort at all to be pleasant.

I looked. In the upper right-hand corner, almost too small to see, was a red digital read-out that blinked **12:00 12:00 12:00,** the way the clock on my parents' video player had for years.

I said, "Not that. Please, not that. It's in every bad movie ever—"

"We're in a *genre* limbo," Lobelia said. "What did you expect? Originality? Production values? You may not have noticed, but there's a cliché under every carpet."

"In Lit-Fic," I said, "it's probably a medieval water clock or an 18-carat Vacheron Constantin tuxedo watch."

"For someone who's burning to rescue someone," Patsy said, "you're being pretty picky."

"Yeah," I said. "I probably am."

"Think what she might be *going* through," Patsy said, all but wringing her hands. "In *extremis*, even. Just *begging* for a savior." To Lobelia, she said, "I don't suppose you smoke."

Lobelia's eyebrows went up. "I thought it was Pansy who—"

"In public. I'm the good one, remember?"

"Not to bore you," I said, "but I can get back here through a portal, too, right? And the portal will be—"

"Wherever. That. Is," Patsy said, wiggling her index finger in the direction of the digital read-out. She sounded miffed, but to be fair, it was third time she'd said it. "It won't always be there, though. I mean, you have to face the fact that you can get killed down there, and if you do, you'll disappear from up here, too. So you shouldn't think you're Superman or Captain Atlas or—"

"Who?"

"Went out of print in 1943," Lobelia said. "They needed paper for the war effort."

"—or anyone," Patsy said, as though no one else had spoken. "So, one, don't get killed, two, don't lose track of time, and three, keep your eyes peeled for a portal." She paused, one finger ticking off another, then spread her hands, palms up. "Simple, really."

A bolt of panic hit me, burned straight through, and kept right on going. I took a step back, with Patsy's eyes following me. She pursed her lips, and Lobelia, to my surprise, mirrored it perfectly. I stood there and felt the sizzle of it, deep inside me, and knew I didn't have a choice.

"Open the window," I said. I looked down at the Glock, popped the magazine, and took two shells from my pocket.

"We don't *have* to open it," Patsy said. "I keep telling you, it's not really a—"

"Fine," I said. "Been painted shut for years, anyway." I pushed the last bullet into the magazine, rammed it home, and stuck the gun in my pants.

"I don't know whether that's going to work down there," Lobelia said.

"It's a perfectly good gun," I said, hurrying back into the bedroom. I grabbed a nice, heavy blackjack and a penlight. I was pocketing them when I came back into the living room.

"It's a *fictional weapon*," Lobelia said. "Down there, I'm not sure it'll—"

"It's the gun I've got," I said. I backed up to give myself room for a running start. "You're sure we shouldn't try to open it."

"No need," Patsy said. "Just do it or don't. I haven't got all day."

"Well," I said. I fought the urge to cross myself. "See you."

And I grabbed a deep breath, ran across the room, and jumped toward the window, my hands instinctively extended in front of me in diving position. The next-to-last thing I heard was glass breaking. The last thing I heard was a little girl laughing her ass off.

28

Yalp Ot

THE GLASS BROKE BUT I didn't feel any sharp edges. Instead, I had the sensation that it *yielded* somehow and then draped itself over me, like a layer of gauze or a membrane, and then everything was absolutely dark and I felt myself penetrate another membrane, and the stuff swathing me felt thicker and heavier, as though I were plummeting through layers of fine silk, and the silk draped itself over me without slowing me at all, and then I hit *another* membrane and the blackness eased just a tiny bit.

Except for the fact that I kept passing without resistance through the membranes—one after another—there was no sense of motion, and there was no sound, just one soft, yielding barrier after another, each coating me in something, and each time I passed through one I saw a little more light in front of me, and then, for some reason, I felt myself begin to drift sideways and downward into darkness, and immediately had the shriveling sensation of being suspended over a great height, and at the same time adrift on the skin of a vast and black and trackless sea.

I panicked.

There was supposed to be a beacon, wasn't there? A lighthouse, a point of some kind, or something at the other end of a string of layers of blackness?

Madison.

I thought her name again, harder. If it had been audible, it would have been a peremptory snap. I waited for the response.

Nothing.

A wave of dizziness seized me, spinning me around like the needle on a game board, and when it was over, I had no idea what direction I was facing, nor which way was up or down. Just me, a point suspended in darkness.

The other two, I heard, so clearly I might have been right next to Bradley Zipper, Eagle Scout. The two who didn't get back.

Get *back*? I couldn't recall asking if they'd even gotten all the way *down*.

For all I knew I'd just leapt through my window and straight into the Abyss, the Maw of Forgetting, Region Zero, the Event Horizon of Absolute Nothing. An infinite and trackless waste in which the laws of genre fiction, which might have protected me in a novel, were a punch line.

Oh, shut up.

It's not about me. It's about Madison. And though I didn't know what to do, I knew I had to do *something*.

Since I had no reference point I could use to estimate my position or my velocity, I just focused my attention on my own center, seeing it as the center of everything around me, which, for all I knew, it might be. I still had no idea whether I was traveling forward, backward, right, or left, but I put out a sort of *intention*, to use a New-Age term my ex-girlfriend Eleanor Chan had crowbarred into my vocabulary, and my intention was to slow, to stop, to hang wherever I was until I could—well, until I *could*. What the hell, I was just hung up on a sentence.

So I envisioned a period.

And had the sensation of gliding to a stop. Where I was, I hypothesized, was in the gap between imaginations, Madison's and mine, and that probably meant that she was fully occupied with something that had nothing to do with me, nothing to do with reading, nothing to do with anything except—and the next two words arrived as noisily as the last two cars on a train—*staying alive.* The thought galvanized me, filled me with useless urgency that had the effect of making me spin slowly, tumbling in the middle of all that darkness, and far, *far* in the distance, something tiny and pale slid by at the edge of sight, and I grabbed a breath and held it until that thing slid by again, and I stopped rotating just by willing it, as I had moved through Madison's house using the All-Seeing Eye, and stared at it.

Now that I had a reference point outside myself, I suddenly felt that I was very, *very* high up, looking down at a formless paleness, not a point, not a dot, but a suffused aura, as breath-edged as a breeze, and as I slipped through another membrane, and another, I suddenly had a definite feeling of movement,

of

of

of

well, of *falling.*

And I saw **23:59:39** blinking in red, and fell past it, thinking *thanks for nothing*, and the thing below me expanded and resolved itself into a round dot—a *real* period—and just beyond that, a lower-case *y*. And beyond that, quite a distance away, an *a* and then an *l* and then a *p*. ***Yalp?*** I thought as the *p* drifted past, and out on the horizon, if a featureless vista can have a horizon, I saw an *o* and then a *t*.

yalp ot?

What was this, Science Fiction?

But I was gliding now, not falling or tumbling, over the stretch of pale spots, and as the next blur resolved itself into another *t* and then an *n*, followed by an *e* and a *w* (tnew?), I remembered someone saying something like "The sentence begins with *her* and *ends* with you," so I turned and looked back and saw, trailing off and getting smaller in the direction I'd come from, the words *went to play.*

Looking ahead again, more alphabet soup spilled out in front of me, like stepping stones in the dark, getting smaller as the characters receded, but I knew that was a trick of perspective, and I spelled out **nerdlihc denword erehw ecalp eht ekil dekool,** which I translated into "looked like the place where drowned children went to play." The end of the paragraph of *Skin Deep* Madison had looked at in her house.

Hot damn. Piece. Of. Cake. A hopscotch Scrabble grid to the real world. I even (sort of) knew the words that were coming at me.

Okay, I'll admit that I'm downplaying the fact that I was terrified, but really, how many times can I say it and have it continue to mean anything? It shouldn't be too difficult to intuit the emotional state of someone who was falling/gliding/flying through emptiness, following a backwards sentence that had been written for him by an undependable author in the direction of God only knew what.

What I had going for me was that a sentence had been predicted, and *there it was*, streaming by below me, a sort of sign that there *were* rules someplace, and then, at the precise moment I relaxed, the letters in front of me seemed to crumple a bit, squeezing around something that looked like—no, that definitely *was*— a comma, between the words **etihw** and **dna**, or "white, and" which I recognized as a fragment of "red, white, and blue"—one of Hallinan's damned redundant series commas, and the letters on either side squeezed the comma harder and harder until it began to bulge at the top the way a water balloon does when you tighten your hand around it, and then it popped out, rocketing toward me like a meteorite, getting bigger and bigger, until it was the size of a Porsche Carrera, and it clobbered me on the shoulder and sent me into free fall, past the long, comforting pathway of letters and into the darkness beneath.

It had been edited out, I guessed. As it should have been.

But that was small comfort because I could see nothing. No letters above me, nothing at all below. I knew I'd been traveling right to left, since I'd been following the letters backward across the page, and now, if the directions held true, I'd fallen farther down the page, except that the sentence seemed more like an un-spooled ribbon than a series of parallel fragments, by which I mean more like a single unbroken stream of words rather than lines on a page, which might have explained why there didn't seem to be another line of text farther down, where I was, and then I got a glimmer of *something*, way, way down there, and I aimed myself toward it and saw that it was a…

2

A number that small would have been written out in the text, meaning that this was a *page number*.

Above me, nothing. And all at once, I knew why. The begin-ning of the sentence was on page one, and I had no idea in the world how to get to page one.

In the center of a cyclone of panic, I screamed mentally, *Madison, think about me*, and nothing happened. I was doing it for the sixth or seventh time when, far below me, I saw an undif-ferentiated oval of dim rust-red, and it drew me to it as, for the second time, I felt gravity seize hold of me and yank me down through the darkness, faster and faster, the orange blur getting bigger and bigger and…

…there was moonlight, the rush of air past my ears, and I heard myself—well, might as well say it, *scream*—and then, as sudden as a light going off, I wasn't falling at all, I was standing someplace dark with big rocks all around me and a trillion stars overhead and a young woman staring at me with one hand over her mouth as though I'd just materialized out of thin air, which I supposed I had, and then my full weight hit me, maybe eight or ten times what I'd weighed up there, and my legs gave way and I went down like wheat when the sickle goes through it, and the young woman jumped backward as I fell, and as I hit the ground, she said

29

Who the Hell

"WHO THE HELL ARE YOU?"

part three

the twain
shall meet

30

The Only Alien I've Got

I SAID, "I KNEW YOU'D ask me that." I raised myself on one elbow and was surprised that it held me up.

I *had* known, of course. Even as I tumbled through the dark zone between there and here, distracting as it was, I'd known she would ask me that. If I'd been challenged to predict the first words spoken between us, I'd have predicted them accurately.

But I'd been too busy to come up with an answer. So I lay there, still leaning on an elbow, trying to focus my eyes and feeling my blood bubbling in my body as though I'd been shaken hard enough to carbonate it.

She backed up a couple of paces, which I thought was an entirely sensible thing for her to do. A pale curl of hair had fallen over her left eye, and she blew it away but it promptly came back.

"I just need a moment," I said through a throat that felt like it had been sewed shut, "to get used to my weight."

"You need a moment," she said, taking another step back and sounding like someone doing simultaneous translation, "to get used to your weight."

This was not going well. "You never have a day when you just feel heavy?"

"All the time," she said. She had backed up against a boulder, just about knee-high, and she stepped up onto it like she was afraid I was going to turn liquid and stain her shoes. "But I thought it was a girl thing."

I sat up, feeling so dense and heavy that it surprised me, even though I'd realized when I was up there that I'd been a pretty skimpy version of me. Down here, at my real, solid, physical weight and with all this surplus gravity, it felt like I'd been dipped in lead. And I'd twisted my knee when I fell to the ground. It gave a pathetic little twinge, just a bid for attention. I said, "Ow," and rubbed it.

"Where did you *come* from?" she said. I had the feeling she was about to call the bad guys for help.

"Back there," I said, gesturing at the big rocks—two or three times my height—behind me.

"*I* was just back there," she said. "You weren't."

"Wow. I didn't see you, either."

"What are you doing up here?"

"Um," I said. "Lost?"

Her eyes were narrow enough to slip quarters into. She was definitely in the *not going for it* camp. "And what brought you *here*?"

"Oh. *Here.*" I pointed at the ground in front of me. "You mean the thing that, that brought me, you know, *here...* "

A guy down below yelled something like *Come out of there*, and Madison jumped.

I grabbed it like a life raft. "Did you hear a guy yell?" I said.

"That's the first time—"

"No, I heard him before. He yelled, uh—"

"Yeah? Yelled what?"

"Madison," I said. "He yelled *Madison*." I pumped some innocence into my face. "Who's Madison?"

"He did not," Madison said. "This stinks."

"Not your friends?"

"No," she said. "Not."

"Maybe I can help."

"Right. Of course. The man from nowhere, maybe he can help."

I sat all the way up, inadvertently making a *whufff* noise that made her jump again. "Sure," I said. "Two are better than—"

"I have no idea who you are or whether I can—"

"Come on. They chased you up here, right?" I grabbed a couple of breaths. "I mean, you're up here, they're down there, and they're yelling for you." I put both hands down on the sand. "Hold on."

"What are you doing?"

A man yelled again, maybe a different one. He sounded closer.

"Going to try to get up. Give... me..." I got my legs under me. "...a second." I launched myself to my feet, wobbled, grabbed the nearest upright anything, which was covered in thorns, yanked my hand back, said something unpleasant, and stuck my finger in my mouth as I stood there, wobbling harmlessly in her direction, sucking my index finger. Your basic friendly, reassuring, finger-sucking wobble.

She nodded. "Yeah. You're going to be a lot of help."

One of the men below changed the emotional atmosphere by firing a shot. The sound of it bounced off rocks all the way around us. It was followed by a garbled, echoing shout that seemed to say, "We don't want to hurt you."

"Maybe not the guy with the gun?" I said. "Are there two?" and immediately I heard a second voice. It said, "Can you hear us?"

Madison said, "*Eeeeeeee*," but not very loudly.

"It'll be fine," I said. "You just have to trust me."

"Ho, ho," Madison said. Then she hugged herself as if she were cold and said, "*Eeeeeeee*" again. "I've got nowhere to go, and I can't stay *here*. You'd think I'd feel familiar with this by now. It's the story of my life."

"Look, they chased you, right? So what are you thinking? They stashed me up here days ago or something? So they could chase you up here at some vague time, to this exact spot, and I'd be right here and I could pretend to help and then, I don't know, turn you over to them?" I stopped talking and panted and sucked my finger again. But I was still standing.

She chewed her lower lip for a moment. "I guess not. But that doesn't explain…" She let it trail off.

We were in a sort of bowl, rocks all around us, various species of ugly scrub sticking up out of the sand wherever they felt like it. Those damn Joshua trees doing their vegetable worship thing, arms upraised to heaven, here and there. The moon was a crescent micro-slice in the sky, more for decoration than light. The rocks behind us were higher than the others, and I had a general sense that the ground fell away on the other side of the rocks in front of us.

"How many of them?"

"Two." She winced as though something had stung her. "I think."

"You think?"

"Well, I know there was only one in the blue car," she said, "because I saw him, but the red car, the red car could have had two in it." She looked over her shoulder as if trying to see them through the rocks. "Or three?"

"Two cars," I said.

She nodded and swallowed. "That I'm sure about."

"And where's your car?"

"Down there." She pointed straight through the rocks in front of us. "But it's out of gas."

"Okay," I said. Talking seemed to be calming both of us down. "Tell me if I've got it straight. Two cars, with at least two guys in them, chased you up here, wherever *here* is, and you ran out of gas, presumably when you were far enough ahead of them to let you get up here on foot before they arrived, and they've parked their cars down there and now *they're* on foot, looking for you."

The gun boomed again. The sound banged into a dozen rocks with a new *spang* every time. The echo ricocheted around us like a flock of imps, and Madison put her hands over her ears and squeezed her eyes shut, then opened them and glanced over at me. I'd managed to be looking elsewhere by then, and she lowered her hands and made a show of brushing something off the left sleeve of her T-shirt.

Down below, someone shouted, "Knock that off, stupid."

"And one of them has a gun," I added.

"At *least* one of them," Madison said. "Seems to be a little disagreement about the gun, doesn't there? Unless, I mean, it's a trick. You know, get us to think they don't *all* want to kill us when actually—"

She seemed to be sliding into panic so I said, "I'm going to move around a little. Don't get all weird, okay?"

"Just stay over there. Walk in little circles or something." She held her hands a couple of feet apart. "Circles about this big. What do you mean, wherever *here* is?"

"Did I have it right? You here, cars there, them in between?"

"Yes." She held up a fist and then pointed a finger at a spot between her fist and her chest. "Us," she said. She pointed at the fist. "Them." She pointed to a spot beyond her fist and opened her mouth.

"Cars," I said.

She squinted at me as though I was going out of focus. "Wherever *here* is?"

"What we need," I said over her, "is a vantage point."

"If we can see them, they can see us."

"If we *can't* see them, there's not much I can do."

"I don't know what you could do if you *could* see them. You can barely walk."

"It's coming back to me."

"Walking? *Walking* is coming back to you? Do you have any idea how much of an alien you sound like? Oh, and do you have a gun?"

"It's just a first impression," I said. "I grow on people. Yes, I have a gun."

"That is *so* not reassuring," she said. She backed away on the rock. Another couple of steps would have brought her to its far edge.

"Look," I said, "if you don't want me near you, why don't you get off that rock and let me up on it? I can probably climb up the bigger one." I took a step forward and then another one—not entirely planned—to the side. Big friendly-looking spots bloomed in front of my eyes.

"No," she said. "You stay there and practice walking, and I'll go up and look."

"That's not going to do us much good."

"You're condescending to me," she said. "You're disempowering me."

"What the hell does that mean?"

"I don't know," she said, taking a lithe giant step from the rock she was on to the taller one in front of it. "I've always wanted to say it, though."

"Shame there's almost no moon," I said. "I'm not sure what you'll be able to see." I was taking a certain amount of pleasure in watching her climb.

She was going up the rock on hands and knees now, the toes of her sneakers upturned against the stone for extra purchase. I'd seen her through the Eye and once or twice through the page of an open book, but always from the front; this was my first look at her goodbye side, and as objectifying as it sounds, it was worth the wait. The men of this world owe an ineradicable debt to whoever invented women's jeans. The way they fit Madison justified the entire complex history of cotton agriculture, the discovery of indigo, the creation of the spinning wheel and the loom, the invention of rivets, steam power and the Industrial Revolution, the development of global trade and the rise of capitalism, just to deliver that precise pair of jeans to that precise rear end. Who says history doesn't have a direction?

She said, "What are you looking at?"

"Your climbing. You're a great climber."

"So maybe you're not an alien," she said, pulling herself higher. "You were looking at my butt." A little more scrabbling, and her head was higher than the crown of the rock. She went flat on her stomach and lay still.

I looked at the moon, at the stars, at anything except her butt. I was cold, colder than I'd been in a long time. It hadn't occurred to me that where I'd been had been climate-controlled, but here I was, in the middle of the desert, half-freezing.

"I see the big one," she said in a sharp whisper.

"How far off?"

"Couple hundred yards. He's poking around a rockpile, like he thinks I'm on the other side and moving just enough to stay out of sight. *Oh.* There's the other one." She ducked down. "Yipes, he's looking right up here."

"Are they straight in front of you, or to one side?"

"They're both a little to the right." She raised her head again. "The little one is farther right than the big one."

"I should really look for myself."

She turned back to me. "Don't you even think about coming up here with me."

"Okay, you come down and I'll go up."

"Actually," she said, "I kind of like it up here. You really did appear out of thin air, you know."

"All I did was step forward," I said. "It was dark, you didn't see me. Fine, I'll find my own damn rock."

She looked back at the men and then at me. "You mean you're going to leave me?"

"The word for this is *conflicted*," I said.

"You may or may not be an alien," Madison said, "but you're the only alien I've got."

"Good. Then come on down."

A minute later, I'd fidgeted my way to the top of the rock, where I promptly got dizzy. When the desert stopped spinning I could see that it rolled generally downhill in the direction of the moon, still low in the sky. About a quarter of a mile away, I saw the road, a straight dark line drawn in soft pencil across the desert's surface. On the road were three cars, one of them white and two darker. The white one was on the far side of the road, facing north, and the other two were facing south, parked on the near side of the road,

"The white car yours?" I whispered.

"Yeah. It's a rental." She kicked her left calf with her right foot and said, "Good, Madison, tell the nice alien everything, let's not confine ourselves to what's important."

I oriented myself for a moment, a task made much easier by the rising moon, which might as well have had *East* written on it. "Why is the car facing north?"

"North?" She tapped her chin with an index finger. "Oh, the direction I came from. I left it blocking the road. They must have pushed it out of the way. Probably didn't want to attract attention."

"Lord, he's big," I said, looking at the nearer man, who was standing on a rock about four feet high and slowly turning in a circle. "Looks like the road slopes downhill to the north. Is that right?"

"Umm. Yeah. When I ran out of gas I slowed pretty fast."

"Okay. Good."

"Come out of there," the big guy shouted. I saw his hands cupped to his mouth. He was facing in our direction, but then he ruined the effect by turning about forty degrees to his left and shouting again.

"He doesn't know where we are," I said. "He's broadcasting in a semicircle."

"So—what? What does that mean? We should stay here? Just sit here and freeze to death? That's how you're going to help? And what did you mean, wherever *here* is?"

"You're cold too? Good. I thought it was just me."

"Why? Why would it be just you? Do you usually live closer to the sun?"

"Is your car open?"

"Do you ever answer a question?"

"I'll answer them when we're out of here. Is your car open?"

She gave me a long, unfriendly look. "You mean unlocked?"

"Yes," I said, perhaps a bit impatiently. "*Yes*, I mean unlocked."

"You don't need to bite my—"

"And the road slopes downhill to the north, right?"

She didn't bother to respond.

"Right," I said. "Asked and answered. How far back was the last curve?"

"Why?"

"Because it's important."

"Oh, sure, because it's important. Maybe a minute's worth, maybe a little less. I was doing about 100 until I wasn't."

"Good."

"Well," she said, nodding. "It's good that it's good." She said, "I'll just be *over here*," and walked sideways in the direction I'd first appeared in.

"Here's what you do," I said. "*Wait*, stay there. I need to whisper."

She stopped, but she didn't look particularly receptive.

"I'm going to find a way down there." I gestured to my left. "They're still off to the right, so I should be able to get around them by heading left, all the way to the cars. I want you to follow me to see where I climb down, so you can do it."

"So I can do it," she said. "That's so *thoughtful*."

"And then come back here and go as far in the other direction as you can without having to climb anything too hairy. I know, I know, you can climb better than I can, but you're going to have to get back here in a hurry, and I don't want you breaking anything."

"No," she said, "out here in the middle of the desert with two guys looking for me with guns, I wouldn't want to break anything."

"What time is it?"

She looked up at the sky. "Eight-twenty."

I looked up at the sky, too.

"I always know what time it is," she said.

"Good." I glanced at my watch, which said **23:39:27 23:39:26** in blinking red numerals. I slapped it, and it read **8:21**. "First, you follow me to see where I climb down, and we both check our watches, I mean, you check your mental watch, and we both start timing. Work your way back, as far past this point as you can, and seven minutes after I start down, you scream your head off. As loud as you can, two or three times. Yell for help."

She was looking at me as though she was hoping for a commercial break. "Scream," she said. "For help." It wasn't a commitment. It was just to prove she was listening.

"Scream yourself silly. Then haul ass all the way back to where I climbed down, and you climb down the same way I did. They'll be running in the other direction, toward your scream."

"Or one of them will," she said.

"Both of them will. They're going to think you're hurt. And alone. They have no idea I'm up here."

"Jeez," she said, "*I'm* not sure you're up here."

"You remember that pile of rocks the big guy was searching around? Go there, and wait on the left side. Just keep your eyes open and stay on the far side of the rocks, where you can't be seen from up here. Stay there until you see my signal. Then run like hell to get to me."

She actually seemed to be listening. "What signal?"

I said, "When the second car leaves."

31

Groobits

THE CLIMB DOWN WAS EASY, especially since I lost my footing on the slope and did most of it on the seat of my pants. When I stood up, several pounds of sand and small rocks fell out of my jeans. My watch said **23:36:52** so I slapped it again and then held my breath for a few seconds. Between the little landslide and the watch-slap, I'd been making quite a bit of noise. When I looked again, the watch said 8:24. It had been 8:24 when I started my descent, too, so I had a little less than seven minutes before Madison would let loose.

The route down had put me beside a big pointy boulder in the general shape of a bishop's hat. I went to the left edge of the rock and looked around to the right, in the direction where I'd seen the two guys.

Empty desert. Just to establish that its emptiness wasn't entirely wishful thinking, I counted to thirty as I stood there, eyes unfocused on the middle distance, waiting for anything to move. And, sure enough, something did. Maybe 200, 300 yards to the right, I saw the little guy approaching the castle-size rock structure on top of which Madison was hiding. He had his right elbow crooked, and the thing in his hand was probably the gun we'd been hearing.

He was obviously looking for a way up, and even from my perspective there seemed to be quite a few of them. Maybe seven minutes was too long; maybe he'd be up there by that time.

The big guy wasn't in sight. My watch had gone to 8:25, so I didn't really have the luxury of buttoning down every little thing. Time was accelerating: the little guy was starting to climb, there were only six minutes or so before Madison screamed, and I had to go a quarter of a mile before I could do anything that mattered.

Bent double, I took off at a scurry, heading at a leftish angle, away from the men but toward the road. I immediately realized that a quarter of a mile at this weight was just this side of a pentathlon. Thirty seconds in, my lungs were on fire, my heart was pounding, my legs were shaky, the bad knee was practically squeaking, and I was filmed with sweat.

On the other hand, I wasn't cold anymore.

Over the course of the first hundred yards or so, the scurry degenerated into a sort of urgent limp, which I pushed into a crab's scuttle. Back in the days when I was still being written, Hallinan had me running all the time. Whenever I was hung over, which was quite a lot, or when I needed to think things through, I went to UCLA and ran. He didn't know how much I hated it; he didn't know that the only way I could keep myself from despairing at how far I still had to go was by keeping my eyes on the ground in front of me for long periods of time. That way, when I looked up, I was occasionally pleasantly surprised by how much distance I'd covered.

Not an available tactic here. The place was full of things that could kill you if you ran into them: rocks, cactuses, Joshua trees, holes, more rocks; for all I knew, man-size gila monsters with hypodermic fangs, and vampire bats the size of Siamese fighting kites. Laboring for breath, pressing my right hand against a stitch in my side, I lumbered toward the road.

No one shouted at me. No one shot at me. My sore knee was doing its best to bring me down, and the rest of the body was pitching in to help it out, but I remained alive and, as far as I could tell, undetected. And the cars were now a realistic distance off.

And time was passing. I stopped and put my hands on my knees, bent double, seeking new ways to wheeze.

The nearer of the two cars was the smaller, which, up close, was a dark red. It was Japanese, and it was locked, which was just as well because I couldn't have messed with the ignition system. I needed an old simple, Detroit system, and there one was, right in front of me.

It was a big fat conspicuous-consumption Caddy from the seventies that probably got eight miles to the gallon, a fossil from the days when Detroit believed not so much that Bigger was Better, but rather that Bigger Was Everything and thereby set the stage for the appearance of smaller, nimbler, more agile cars from across the sea that ate the big cars' eggs right out of their nests and drove them to extinction.

It was a great relief to find that the driver's window was wide open. I leaned in through the window, into a fug of old cigarettes, to find the overhead light, which was right where it should have been, just behind the driver's seat and midway between the doors.

Eight-twenty-eight. Three minutes before scream time. No way to know about the climbing guy.

In the seventh book, the one the publishing houses turned down, I got set up with a car thief who taught me how to hot-wire a car. Hallinan was always casual with research, so I had no idea whether what I'd learned would actually work, but this probably wasn't the best time to worry about it. I pulled the blackjack out of my pocket, reached in, and tapped the plastic cover over the interior light, which obliged me by breaking into a couple of thousand old, brittle pieces. The little bulb popped out without an argument, and I dropped it back into my pocket with the blackjack, and opened the door.

I shielded the tip of the little penlight with my hand and turned it on, keeping it low in the car. The steering wheel was housed in a big plastic shell, but it was just two modular pieces, and it only took me a few seconds of using a key as a lever to pop them apart. I jimmied the ignition unit out of its hole in the column and let it dangle down, and there they were, the famous wires—not the furious squirrel's-nest tangle of computer-rich modern cars but the relatively spare and orderly assembly of older ones. And in a General Motors car from the 70s, only three wires really mattered. It took me a few seconds to strip off the insulation from the last four inches of each of them.

Eight-thirty. A minute before the show was supposed to begin. I had twisted the two starter wires together, using my wadded shirt as insulation, and was maneuvering awkwardly to replace the steering housing and push the ignition assembly back into its hole when Madison let go.

It was a bravura scream, a Jamie Lee Curtis scream, a *Grand Guignol* scream that scaled an octave and a half, broke into pieces at the top of the arc, and shivered back down again like a stunned flock of birds. I got goosebumps just listening to it.

Then she topped it.

I raised my head and surveyed the territory. The scream had come from a point quite a bit farther left than where I had first seen her, and now I spotted a big dark figure at full run, heading for a sloping ascent that looked like it was plentifully supplied with loose stones that would have him sliding down two feet for every four they went up. And sure enough, there was the little one, fighting his way up.

There was almost *no* time left, so I hurried. Hurrying is never a good idea. Without worrying enough about the power wire, I replaced the ignition assembly back into its hole and started to tighten it. I wanted the driver, who had to be the big guy, to be able to turn the key without it being obvious that things had been monkeyed with.

And into all that urgency, all that hurry, a thought pushed its way forward, claimed center stage in my frontal lobe, and announced, *I'm* real *again*. After what seemed like an eternity of feeling not much more tangible than smoke, not much more involved than the reader of a dull novel in a disliked genre, here I was, *back* again: heavy, clumsy, terrified, and loving it. The revelation distracted me from what I was doing just enough to get a shock strong enough to melt my fillings.

* * *

He really *did* appear out of thin air, she thought as she picked her way from rock to rock. It was as though the dark had rippled, like the surface of black water, and he kind of floated up through it. Or out of a bubble. *Pop*, and there he was. So he can duck the question all he wants, but I saw it. I was looking right at the rock, thinking about going around it, and all of a sudden he was there, in between me and it.

And then, standing on a stretch of ground as level as a bowling alley, he fell down like his legs couldn't hold him.

So let's not dismiss the fact that *something very odd is happening*. Something that would scare me senseless if I weren't already scared senseless of something else.

And even beyond the fact that he, ummm, spontaneously generated, there's something—odd about him. Like he's only completely filled in on the side I'm looking at. Like if I got behind him without him knowing it, his back would be blank. Just a silhouette, an outline. Sort of—what? *Two-dimensional*. Like a character in a not-very-good book. Not, in other words, someone with *substance*, someone you could *lean* on. And here I am (she thought), leaning on him.

She took a look around and confirmed that she'd backtracked all the way to the place she'd been when she first saw him. There was the rock they'd both climbed. A dozen steps straight forward would take her around the round, Olmec-head-shaped stone he'd materialized in front of.

She did not take the first of those dozen steps.

That head. Or, rather, rock. It's just a rock, right? she asked herself. It isn't like a materialization zone or an alien bulls-eye or something. It isn't like there are probably a bunch more of them, with big teeth and yellow eyes, back there. Waiting to eat her.

Certainly not. That was just plain silly.

But he *had* appeared out of nowhere. *Ordinary rules do not apply.*

She looked at the sky, mostly to stop looking at the rock. It had been roughly three minutes since he said, "Now, you be careful," and then more or less fell down that hill. And he was, oh, hell, unexpectedly sweet for a zombie. Kind of clueless. Sneaking a peek at my butt and then trying not to look at it again, like a kid who's got his hand stuck in a jar but wants to deny any interest in cookies. A doofus. You know, your basic mysteriously-appear-from-nowhere-in-the-dark sweet, clueless, sneak-a-peek doofus. If there were more of them back behind the rock, they'd probably just want to tell her bad jokes and show her their palm buzzers and whoopee cushions.

She went around the rock.

More rocks. No new astral doofii. Keeping the sliver of moon on her left so she wouldn't get turned around, she picked her way around the bigger stones, between a pair of gargantuan Siamese-twin rocks joined at the base, asking herself whether *Siamese twins* wasn't politically incorrect these days. Thai twins? Double-value babies?

Five minutes.

She realized she was scuffing her feet and put them down more carefully.

What in the *world* was he doing down there below her? Why had he needed her keys if the car was out of gas? Was he going to siphon gas out of their cars? What would he use as a siphon? What, exactly, *was* a siphon? There ought to be a word, she thought, a group noun describing things you accepted as real even though you had no idea what they were.

"Groobits," she said experimentally, out loud. No, too made-up.

One of the men below shouted, "Come down. We don't want to hurt you." He sounded pretty close.

She walked a little faster. *They* said they didn't want to hurt her. *He* said, or at least implied, he was a real person. She didn't believe any of them. People who don't want to hurt you don't shoot at you. Real people, which is to say *human beings*, don't assemble themselves out of dark air.

But, on the other hand, she asked herself, not entirely rhetorically, what was so great about real people? She'd been disappointed by a lot of them. Come to think of it, every single individual who'd disappointed her in her entire life had been a real person. So. Real people or an alien?

Balzac's heroines didn't face this problem.

She stopped, her way blocked by a rock so big its top disappeared in the darkness. This was as far as she could go. X marks the scream. The way she saw it, she had three choices. She could try to sneak out of there without getting caught by the bad guys or running into the alien, spend the night alone in the desert, surviving long enough to get lost and die in it tomorrow. She could surrender to the guys with guns and forget all about the alien, and maybe they'd kill her. Or she could scream and hope the alien could get her out of here. Preferably without taking her to Shadowland or wherever he'd appeared from. The choices surrounded her in a malign game of Ring Around the Rosy, coming closer with every passing second.

When the time to scream came, she had no trouble making it sound real.

32

The Second-Largest Rockpile

THE MOMENT I RE-ENTERED MY body from wherever the shock had put me, I smelled burned hair and knew that it was mine.

I was lying on my side on the seat, my knees tucked protectively against my chest. I straightened as much as I could and listened. Shouting rolled over the desert floor, the voices of two men echoing off rock faces in all directions. One of them seemed to be calling out to someone and the other was just swearing, loudly and monotonously. I took all the noise to mean that they hadn't found Madison yet and that they were both too busy to be watching the road.

I managed to reassemble the Caddy's steering column cover without killing myself and pushed the ignition assembly with my index finger. It held. It probably wouldn't fall out when he stuck the key in. I got out of the car and left the door standing open. Still feeling kind of sizzly from the shock, I crossed the road, which seemed to be shaking beneath me, and opened the door of Madison's car. The interior light came on, and that was fine with me.

Even though I was still jittery, it was amazingly easy to turn the car to the left and point it down the long hill. In fact, I had to jump in and hit the brake to keep it from rolling away. I sat in the car for a moment to steady my breathing as the two men continued to shout. Then I took my foot off the brake and, a moment later, the car started to roll. When I lifted my hands from the wheel, the car pulled just a little tiny bit to the right. Not enough, I hoped, to spoil the effect. But just in case, I knew how to correct it.

I put the car in park and got out. The tip of Madison's key fit nicely into the valve on the front left tire. All I could do was guess. I pushed the stem in the center of the valve and let the air hiss out into the night for about twenty seconds. The slightly lower tire might compensate for the car's innate tendency to pull right. For a while, anyway.

Madison would be down from the rocks by now, if they hadn't caught her. She'd be waiting behind that rockpile. I straightened up from the tire and surveyed the terrain, trying to pick out the rockpile I'd told her to hide behind. I failed. There were three rock structures that looked pretty much alike. I tried to intuit which one she was behind, and immediately experienced a little surge of *warmth* in the center of my chest when I looked at the second-largest rockpile. That's where she was. I knew it. Behind the second—

So what was *that* about? Warmth? I can feel where she is?

She's a *Sensitive*, I thought. It's just business as usual, she's a reader and I'm a character and there's a natural connection. Perfectly natural, doesn't mean anything.

And once again I heard Patsy laughing when the window broke.

Without even looking at my watch, I could tell it was blinking red so I smacked it with the palm of my right hand. Nine minutes, going on ten. More than enough time for her to be down from the rocks and watching the road.

I reached in and turned on the headlights of Madison's car. Nice and bright. Then I went to the Caddy and slammed the door as hard as I could. It was a heavy, loud door. Just for good measure, I opened it and slammed it again.

The shouting stopped.

I ran back to Madison's car and sounded the horn for a count of three. Then I bent my knees and duck-walked to the passenger side. If I stayed low enough, I'd be invisible from the side of the road the men were on.

One long, enraged bellow from the rocks. Still bent over—and, one seriously hoped, invisible—I began to push the car.

It moved slowly at first, straight and true down the middle of the road, which was about three car-widths across. I figured even if it drifted—and it would—it would be a few hundred yards before it ran off into the sand and the brush. The car sailed away from me in a stately fashion, headlights blazing, and I crawled on my hands and knees to the Cadillac and rolled under it.

It felt like a very long minute before I was sure they were coming.

They were still yelling at each other, and I could hear them get nearer and separate, jabbering away, and then I saw a pair of big-ass cowboy boots at the Caddy's door. The door opened and someone landed in the passenger seat, someone heavy enough to push the car so far down it touched the back of my head before bouncing up.

The other car started.

Above me, the door closed. I waited and heard nothing.

The other car's lights came on and angled across the road as the driver started a three-point turn.

"Come on, fatso," I said between my teeth. "Move it." If the other car got away, we were screwed.

Then I heard "SHHHHIIIIIIIT!!!!" from directly above me, and the Caddy's door opened again. The car rocked upward as the driver's weight was lifted, and I heard him running across the road.

He shouted, "Ridley! *Wait*!"

The other car stopped moving. I heard a moment of what would probably have been slapstick if I could have seen it—some swearing and then banging on the roof of the car and the words, "Open the fucking *door*," repeated several times at top volume. "My *car* won't start." Then a second's silence, then a door closing, and then the taillights flaring red as the driver backed up. Your basic soundtrack squeal of tires.

I gave them a couple of seconds, rolled out into the road again and hauled myself up, almost vibrating with anxiety, and searched out the second-biggest pile of rocks. Something brightened and bloomed inside me as I saw a small figure come around it and start to run toward me.

"Hurry, Madison," I called, mainly because I wanted to say her name. It felt so good I said it again.

By the time she got to the driver's door of the Caddy I'd tossed the steering-wheel housing into the back seat. She got in, saying, "But how will—" and at that moment I laid the power wire across the starter wires with a satisfying spark and the engine rolled over and caught, and I folded the power wire back again and wished to hell I had something to insulate it with, and she said, "Oh," and we were rolling.

The car was weighty and cumbersome, heavy-metal testosterone on wheels and subtle as a bull. I was driving as fast as I could without turning the lights on or hitting the brakes; I didn't want anything flashing in the other guys' rearview mirror. That meant I had to be fully alert to curves because the car didn't handle them well. Or at all, actually.

I could feel her looking over at me.

"Where can we pull off the road?" I asked. "Someplace the car won't be seen."

"If you go straight," Madison said, "it'll take you to Joshua Tree."

"Is that, like, a town?"

"Yes," she said with some resignation, "since you apparently arrived here without passing through anything at all. Joshua Tree is a town."

"Then no," I said. "That's what they'll expect. They'll figure we're just going to try to outrun them."

"But we're not?"

"This car's center of gravity is so high it could roll over on a straightaway," I said. "They're going to find your car next to the road, figure out that no one was in it, and turn around. Then, when this tub isn't where it's supposed to be, they're going to break the sound barrier trying to catch up to us."

"So we're going to pull over, let them pass, and then go back out the way we came in," she said.

"You got it, partner."

She kept looking at me. I kept looking at the road. "Partner, huh?"

"Well," I said, as my face went all hot. "Sure."

After a moment, she said, "Jumbo Rocks. Maybe three, four miles, on the left. It's a campground."

"Can we hide the car?" Her gaze brushed my face like a flow of air.

"Just off the road. We can pull behind a boulder."

"Fine," I said.

Half a mile later, after she'd had time to commit my profile to memory, if that's what she was doing, she turned to face the road and said, "Fine."

33

A Pumpkin At Midnight

I WAS STANDING AT THE counter, waiting to take our coffee to the table. The waitress had volunteered to bring it but I wanted to delay the beginning of The Talk for a few minutes. On the way out of the Monument, I'd been able to postpone her questions on the pretext that the Caddy was a wretch to drive and we had to haul ass, but obviously we couldn't drive forever.

But I wouldn't have minded it if we could. I hadn't smelled any real people in a long time, and there was something fine about the way Madison smelled, like a loaf of fresh bread that had just shampooed. Well, maybe not, but two good smells, anyway. It made me want to buy a house and put nice, soft stuff all over the place, maybe even kind of frilly and pastel, and help her make a nest in a room with a lot of windows that would be just hers and maybe some power tools if she wanted them, and a man-cave for me, maybe even with a pipe rack, although I'd always thought most guys who smoked pipes also secretly practiced raising one eyebrow. And the two of us would nod at each other in a friendly fashion in the hallways and develop shared hobbies and eat together once in a while without criticizing each other's manners and trade books back and forth, and never fight over who got the remote. And who knew what else?

* * *

The waitress put the two coffees on the counter, mine black and hers almost entirely cream. As I picked up the paper cups and turned, I saw Madison get up and come toward me. Passing, she said, "Bathroom," without a lot of obvious hidden meaning and kept right on going. I wondered whether she was *also* postponing The Talk.

Great, I thought, our first avoidance.

The Wonder Garden was a perfectly nice little coffee house in Twentynine Palms. It was softly lighted, a hell of a lot warmer than the desert night, and right on the highway, no more than a couple of miles from the point where we'd emerged from the Monument. We'd passed her rental car, lights burning away, just to the right of the road at the first curve, the front right fender crumpled from hitting a boulder. She'd turned to look at it as we passed and said, "That'll cost."

I'd said, "Don't you have insurance?"

She'd said, "We're not anywhere *near* discussing anything as prosaic as insurance."

I'd said, "Oh," and we'd come the rest of the way in silence.

Now the Caddy was parked behind a supermarket across the street, which was the best I could do to get it out of view, and according to my watch, it was 9:31. According my watch, it was also **22:33:25**, so I was well into my second hour.

I looked at the watch again. The red digits. Surely *that* wasn't the portal. I wasn't supposed to jump into a wristwatch, was I? Wasn't it sort of *little?* Just as a quick check, I tested it by poking my index finger, hard, at the face of the watch. I bent my index finger in kind of an interesting way that was a lot more painful than it probably looked.

So maybe I'd clarified something: while all portals may have the red digits in them, not everything with red digits in it was a portal.

"Got a train to catch?" Madison asked, pulling out her chair.

"Do you turn into a pumpkin at midnight?" She sat, blew on her creamy coffee, put an elbow on the table, and rested her chin on her hand. "So?"

I said, "If you had them leave out the coffee and just give you cream, you wouldn't have to blow on it."

"You might not know this up on Altair or Aldebaran, but dairy goods cost a fortune," she said. "The only way to get cheap cream is to let them put some coffee in it. I'm waiting."

I said, "It's complicated."

"Spontaneous generation is complicated. Assembling yourself out of air is complicated." She dipped the tip of her index finger into the beige fluid and tasted it. "I'm actually *expecting* something complicated."

"I didn't generate spontaneously." I sipped my coffee automatically and lowered the cup. "Are you *sure* you won't accept that I was right there but out of sight until I took a step forward?"

"Absolutely not. I saw you arrive. I was staring at that rock and then I was staring at you. The end."

"Okay." I took my hand off the coffee cup and looked out at Twentynine Palms Highway, which was too narrow and too empty to qualify as a highway. "I was somewhere else," I said, turning back to her. "And then I came here."

"Somewhere else." Her eyes flicked to the door as a couple of big, conspicuously fit guys with military haircuts and bruiser shoulders came in. Almost the only thing I knew about Twentynine Palms was that it was home to some sort of military base. She gave the guys a big smile, and one of them returned it. They took a table only two away from us, even though the place was empty. "Goodie," she said. "Reinforcements."

I said, "It's silly for me even to try to explain. You're not going to believe me."

"I already don't believe you. I don't believe that you've *never once asked me* why those guys were after me. I don't believe what I saw when you—appeared. So if it makes it easier for you, all we're doing is moving to the *next* point that I won't believe, okay? Maybe three's the charm."

"Fine. Let me start this way." I looked again at the watch, which was back to blinking red numerals. I polished it on my shirt to get rid of the big fingerprint in the middle of it. "What do you think about me?"

"What do I—"

My palms, upraised in surrender, stopped her. "Humor me. What do you think about me?"

She filled her cheeks with air and blew out. "Sure. What I think about you. You came out of nowhere. You had trouble with how *heavy* you felt, and you could barely walk for a while. You didn't know where you were. That's all alien stuff. If you were a *person*, what would I say? You have no curiosity at all but you're smart. That thing you did to get us out of there, well, that was pretty impressive. Especially for someone who was only about ten minutes old."

"Thanks," I said.

"Though a lot of things could have gone wrong," she said.

"I know. I wasn't sure how long your car would stay on the road. I really needed it to keep rolling long enough for them to pile into the red car and take off."

"So you're also lucky," she said. She took another sip of coffee. Raised her eyebrows to say *your turn.*

"Maybe it was *your* luck."

A decisive shake of the head. "Oh, no. Not a chance. And you're changing the—"

"Tell me more about me. Come on, you're doing great."

"Women learn early to talk about the man. If we didn't, we'd all live alone in the middle of a cabbage patch." She sipped the cream mixture. "So you're kind of… resourceful. And brave, I guess. Oh, and you know how to steal a car. And you *absolutely* helped me out, although I'm not going to figure out how I feel about that until I know why. And you're carrying something tucked into your pants under your shirt, and I think it's a gun."

"I told you I had a gun. Or *had*. It's in the car now."

She looked automatically at the guys two tables over, both of whom suddenly stopped staring at her. "Why?"

Here we went. "It's my job. I'm a detective."

She nodded slowly, the absolute picture of someone who's trying to look like she believes something that she wouldn't believe if it were sung in barbershop harmony by a quartet of angels hovering in the air in front of her. "A detective."

"Right."

"Like—like a cop? I mean, are you, you know, Space Patrol or something?"

"No, not a cop."

"Not," she said, and stopped. Her eyes got kind of hooded. "Not an amateur sleuth."

That stung. "I am *not* an amateur sleuth. Amateur sleuths are a self-extincting species. Like lemmings."

She said, "Lemmings aren't extinct."

"Not much in the way of prospects, though."

Her chin came up. It was a pretty strong chin. "Let's humor you. What kind of detective?"

"A private eye."

"Just start over," she said. "Good-looking private detectives are only in books, and not very good books, either. *Real* private eyes are grease spots who subsist on misery. And I suppose you live all alone in some picturesque dump and nurse a broken heart and drink too much and have a cop friend."

I said, "I'm good-looking?"

"Don't be pathetic. It was a slip of the tongue."

"Well, you're right on all counts: live alone, picturesque dump, broken heart, cop friend. I even drink too much. Okay, as *you* said just now, private eyes like that—private eyes *exactly like that*—exist only in books. Hold onto that one, and tell me more about me."

She put down her cup. "I don't want to play any more. So you're a private eye. So to get your license, you had to learn to— to teleport or whatever they called it on *Star Trek*?"

I leaned back in my chair, which squeaked, and instantly the two military-looking guys were staring at me. I gave them a little wave, and one of them looked down. The other let his face harden to show me that he wasn't a guy who turned and ran when someone waved at him. I felt better about the nation's security.

"Since you don't want to do it my way," I said, "let me ask a couple of questions. What's your definition of reality?"

"Oh, well," she said. She picked up the cup and folded part of its rim into a point, tilted the improvised spout above her mouth and half-drained it. "Let's start small and work our way up, shall we? Reality is what I can see and feel. This room is real, that road out there is real. Those rocks we hid in were real, and so were the men who were shooting at us. Those guys over there who probably want to hit you are real. You're real, too. The problem is that you *weren't* real an hour and a half ago."

"So reality changes?"

"Anybody whose notion of reality doesn't change is a fire hydrant."

"Everything that's real has a physical presence?"

"Oh, we're not going to talk about God, are we? Because I'm a wuss on God."

"No, not God. Other things that you can't touch or see. None of them are real?"

"Well, *sure*." She might have been on the verge of rolling her eyes, but she settled for releasing a martyred sigh. "Ideas are real. Hopes and fears, they're real, at least in the sense that they exist.

They're not necessarily going to come true or anything, so they're not real in that—"

"Words?"

She closed both eyes and put the back of her hand against her forehead, looking like a fever victim in a silent film. "This is *so* first-year college. Words are—you know—symbols. They're real in the sense that the word 'rock' is something that everyone who reads and speaks English can see when it's printed on something and say out it loud, and it's real in the sense that there's such a thing as a real rock. It *denotes* a real rock, okay?"

"But what about—"

She held up a hand to stop me. "But then, as you were about to say, there are the words that denote things you can't see or touch. *Real*, for example. We all know the word and we all think we know what it means, but what's real to you might not be real to me, even though we use the same word. And there's nothing in the physical world we can take a picture of and put a caption under it: *This is the essence of real.*" She shrugged. "I mean, obviously. Otherwise, we wouldn't be having this little chat."

"So something *that abstract*—a written symbol for a spoken sound that describes something we can't see or feel, or even agree on—that's real."

She shook her head, quickly and impatiently. "This is the kind of thing that usually interests me, but right now it just feels like a delaying tactic."

"Please," I said. "Just a minute more. What about stories? You love to read—"

The force of her gaze stopped me. She was looking at me hard enough to make the back of my head itch. "How do you know that?"

"Good," I said. "A great point of entry. You love Balzac. Are the stories in Balzac real? Are the characters—"

"How the hell do you know I love Balzac?" She slapped the table. "Have you been—have you been *snooping* around me?"

Her voice had risen, and the guy who wasn't afraid of being waved at stood up.

Madison turned to him and said, "Sit. If I need you, I'll scream."

"You sure?" The guy's voice was deep enough to plow the trench for the transatlantic cable.

"Do I look indecisive?" she asked.

He said, "Ummmm..."

"And it's not that I don't appreciate it," she said. She laced her fingers together and brought them level with her heart, one hundred percent *Rebecca of Sunnybrook Farm*. "And when I do need help, I'll be *sooo* grateful."

The soldier blushed and sat down, but he shot me a quick, mean glance before he turned away.

I said, "You should be ashamed."

"Piss on that. How do you know I read Balzac? Have you been in my house?"

"Do you think Balzac's characters are real?"

"I asked you—"

"Lucien? Père Goriot? The little harlot, the, the—"

"The Torpedo," she said. "Sure, they're real. Not the same as a rock or a tree, but they were real in Balzac's imagination and they're real in mine."

"Because? Because, when you read them—"

"They enter *into* me. I see them, I hear them. I build the rooms around them. I create the Paris they live in. I *worry* about them. What in the world are you getting at?"

"Do you think it works both ways?"

"Do I think *what* works both ways?" She shoved her coffee so hard it began to topple and she had to catch it. "What does *it* modify?"

"You see them, they enter your awareness. Do you think they're aware of you?"

Her mouth was partly open, and it stayed that way. With her eyes on mine, she lowered her head half an inch, a gesture that was the silent equivalent of "Huh?" Then she closed her mouth and sat back decisively. "Of course not." If she'd written the words on a page, the pen's tip would have ripped the paper.

"Okay," I said. "I'm going to say a couple of things you're not ready for." I paused, trying to find the first words.

"What am I supposed to say? 'I'm ready'?"

"You haven't just been reading Balzac." I said. "You've been reading a private eye novel."

A vertical crease appeared between her eyebrows. "How the hell do you—"

"Ferdy gave it to you. He wanted you—"

"Stop." She pushed her chair back a few inches, and Captain America swiveled toward us. "You can't know that."

"It's called *Skin*—"

"—and I have *never* mentioned Ferdy to—"

"—*Deep*. You opened it for the first time at home—"

"I'm leaving." She started to get up.

"—and you had it with you when you were talking to that cop, Detective—Detective Basset."

"*Stay where you are*," she hissed at the soldier, who was halfway up. She moved her chair back another couple of inches and sat there, looking at me as though she expected something with a lot of teeth to jump out of my mouth and attack her. She was gripping the edges of her chair with both hands. The straightened arms made her look like she was ready to bolt. She licked her lips and said,

"Detective…"

"Basset," I said. I sat back myself, just to give her more space. Her eyes shifted past me and then came back. "He—he told you," she said. "The cop. I called him that, just once, by accident, and he—"

"But you almost always *think* of him as Detective Basset."

She shook her head and started to say something, then waved it off like smoke, and put both hands around her cup as though protecting it from an anticipated attack. She was staring down at it.

"I've never met him," I said. "You were right. Until a couple of hours ago, when you saw me appear, out of thin air, I've never been here in my life. Wherever we are."

"Twentynine Palms," she said, but it was just a place marker, a little dog-ear in the conversation so she could pull back from it and still find her place when she was ready to come back. "Any other… revelations?"

"Ferdy was sweet on you. You didn't know it but Ferdy—"

"I'm not ready to talk about Ferdy." Her eyes came to me and then went kind of unfocused. "Wait. I mean, you might know that Ferdy liked me, but how would you know that I wasn't aware—"

"The same way I know about Detective Basset." I leaned toward her, lowered my voice, and took a deep breath. "The same way I know that you think time is like a tunnel and you hope it's curved."

She blinked twice, but nothing else moved. Even the soldiers were quiet. She touched the tip of her tongue to the center of her upper lip. "And how—" she began, and then stopped, swallowed, and cleared her throat. "How would you know that?"

Here we were. It was either going to fall apart completely in the next thirty seconds, or we'd be able to move on together. I borrowed a mannerism from her and cleared my own throat. "The Simeon Grist book you were reading. You stopped when you got to a sentence that said, *It looked like the place where drowned children went to play.*"

She said, "There's *no way* you can—"

"The book is about a private detective," I said. "Simeon Grist."

"I—um." Her eyes went to the window for a heartbeat and then came back to me. "I remember his name."

I said, "I'm Simeon Grist."

* * *

The soldiers trailed us, fifteen or twenty feet back, after the waitress announced that it was closing time. They followed us across Twentynine Palms Highway and around the supermarket until we cut across the parking lot, where they stopped, watching from the sidewalk.

I opened the passenger door for her, and Madison turned back to them and called, "I'm okay, guys. Really."

The big one, the one with the deep voice, looked at the Caddy and said, "Sweet ride."

"It was a steal," I said. "Thanks for looking out for her."

"You don't deserve her," the big one said.

"Nobody does," I said, "but she's a fool for cars." I went around to the driver's side and got in. Madison was leaning back, looking up at the car's cloth ceiling as though she was afraid it was going to drop over her like a net.

After I closed the door, I said, "What is this *smell?*"

"Don't change the subject. I still don't want you to think I believe it."

"I have trouble with it myself. But it does smell in—"

She interrupted me with a punch to my arm and leaned back again. "You're so... solid."

"Not a word I hear often."

"But on the other hand," she said, "I have to believe *something*. I did see you appear out of nowhere. So it might as well be this. Something with—with books in it."

"If you didn't love books, I wouldn't be here. I couldn't have found you. It's like a beacon. A light powered by imagination."

"That doesn't mean it's not creepy. You were *inside my mind*, and I didn't even have a chance to straighten things up first. You know, not that there are piles of awful, ugly stuff in there, but it's pretty cluttered. I hoard maybes. I have piles of hypotheticals."

"It's a nice mind," I said.

"Neither too cluttered nor too empty?"

"Right down the middle, I'd say. Well appointed. A fine blend of aesthetics and utility. Tasteful but not stuffy." I reached the end of everything I remembered from *Architectural Digest* and stopped.

She nodded. "Well, at least it's a new line. A little… patronizing, but different. Not anything I'm likely to get in a bar." She settled herself in and sniffed the air. "Do you really drink too much?"

"Oh, you know," I said. "The usual semi-morose, too-sensitive-for-this-world cliché. It's not like he ever had me get bat-faced and beat up the defenseless."

"He?"

"The guy who wrote me."

"That must be on the far, dark side of weird," she said. "To know somebody *wrote* you. Not that I totally believe it yet."

"Oh, well. Lots of people think God created them, and they seem to have a lot more questions than I do. At least I know why things happened in my world."

"Yeah?" She rolled her head around to look at me. "Why?"

"For the story."

"But how does it feel? To be written?"

"I never knew I *was* until it was over and I was up there. We don't. That's part of the joke, I guess. It always felt real to me."

"Like you had free will."

"Sort of. Although there were times I asked myself, *This is stupid, why in the world am I doing it?* I didn't know it was just bad plotting."

"We all do that," she said. "Do something stupid, and then do it over and over. I call it a dimpulse."

"Yeah, well, he gave me a lot of them. Although, to give him credit, not more than once or twice a book."

"Wo," Madison said, sitting up very straight.

"Wo?"

"How do I know I'm not—"

"You don't," I said. "And you can't, so it's better not to think about it. What are you going to do, buy a giant eraser to eliminate your mistakes?"

"I wish we hadn't had this conversation."

"I think we just do the best we can, Madison. Whether we're real or fictional. Assuming there's such a thing as real."

"Gee," Madison said. "Thanks."

34

But He's Dead to Me

WE WERE DRIVING. NOT ANYWHERE in particular, just looping around on back streets where we were less likely to run into the dwarf and the giant, and talking to get used to each other. "When I was in the books," I said, "I had no idea that the game was fixed, that it was preordained that I'd survive. I had no way of knowing that Hallinan *couldn't* kill me because he had a six-book contract. It felt to me—it still feels to me—like I was in charge, like I was really risking everything and doing everything I could to stay alive. Solving all those problems on my own."

"You're not being written now," Madison said. "I mean, as far as we know."

"No. This time out, I think it's real."

"And you did great up there in the Monument. When you *were*. Risking everything, I mean."

I thought of a couple of words but nothing to follow them with.

She smiled and looked away. "Turn right here."

I did, and thirty seconds later we came to a dead end. "Why here?" I asked.

"I just wanted to see if you'd do what I told you to do. Jake would have—" She stopped and swallowed and said, "I don't remember you being all shy in the book. What I read of it."

"Yeah," I said, doing a three-point turn. The car felt bigger than a Rose Parade float "Well, right now I'm not in a book. Who's Jake?"

"This guy."

"I figured."

She had turned to look at me. "You don't know who Jake is?"

"How would I know who—"

"Because you were in *there*, in my mind."

While I was trying to frame an explanation, a coyote, all ribs and tongue, ambled through the headlights without giving us a glance. Like most Topanga coyotes, he walked at an angle, his body at a slight diagonal, rather than pointing straight ahead. I've never known why they do that. "It wasn't like that," I finally said. "There was a connection, like a phone line or a sort of hidden camera, while you were reading, but if you visualize your mind as a house, I was pretty much limited to one room. I was right up front, right where you were reading and, you know, looking around the room and stuff. Just inside the front porch. I was where the current thoughts and sensations were, but if you didn't think about, say, Jake, I wouldn't have, um, come across him."

She said, "Well, that's a relief. A girl wants to thinks she's got *some* mysteries."

"So his name is Jake?"

"Was, and no, he's not dead."

"Suppose you *were* being written and your writer had you—this isn't very good, but what the hell—suppose he had you put your hand on your heart and say, *But he's dead to me.*" A few seconds passed. I said, "Could you?"

"You move pretty fast for someone who's only been real for a couple of hours."

"Okay. Sorry. Forget it."

"I could," she said, "but I'm not a hundred percent certain I'd mean it."

* * *

Unending was the only word. I was on the Twentynine Palms Highway, heading west at what felt like a brisk pace, and no matter how much desert we drove through, there was more of it in front of us. I said something to that effect, and Madison said, "It's like lime Life Savers. The more you hate them, the more there are in the package."

"So," I said, "who killed Ferdy?"

A shake of the head. "I have no idea."

"If you were a writer and Ferdy was your character, and someone asked you to describe him, what would you say?"

She crossed her legs and slipped her hands between her thighs as though she was cold. "Ferdy? Ferdy was the, um, the bus everybody missed. Big and conspicuous, with the same series of stops every day, and nobody ever stayed with him long enough to find out where he was going or where he came from. He was big and sweet and… undiscovered. Even by me. And I'm supposed to be so sensitive and understanding."

"Are you?"

"If I were putting up a billboard for myself, it would say, *Sensitive and Understanding*. And maybe *Self-doubting*. With the left three-quarters of my face showing."

"Why the left?"

"Because that's the side of this haircut that works." She turned to face me.

I took my eyes off the road, although I didn't actually need to look. "Both sides look good to me."

"Sure, but you're an alien. Did you *see* the women in your books or just the words the writer used to describe them?"

"I saw them."

"Were they pretty?"

"Women in books are always pretty. If they weren't they wouldn't be in books."

"But they're made out of words, right? Pictures from words. I see the women in Balzac, and *they're* all words, I guess." Her face lit up, like she'd just thought of a secret she could tell me. "You know, there was an American painter named John Sloan, and when he saw something he wanted to paint, he didn't sketch it or take a picture of it, like everybody else. He wrote a description while he was looking at it, and then he went home and painted the description."

I said, "Really."

She leaned toward me. "Don't you think that's at least a *little* bit interesting? You've got a man with tremendous visual talent but he didn't paint a scene directly. It wasn't real to him until he put it into words. I mean, you know, speaking of *real* and everything."

"Was he any good?"

She was rubbing her forearms with her palms. "John *Sloan?* Was *John Sloan* any good?"

"Give me a break," I said. "There weren't any museums in my books. They weren't the kind of books that—" The penny dropped about the way she was sitting. "Are you cold?"

"I thought you'd never ask."

"Why didn't you say anything?"

"Oh, you know. Girls. You guys will use any excuse to eliminate us from the good parts of the story. *Oh, no, honey, it's* way *too cold for a little cupcake like you.*"

I found the heat and turned it on. It tripled the strength of the car's smell, which I finally identified as the scent of raisins that had fermented for centuries in the center of a mouse nest inside the Great Pyramid. "So," I said, "why *would* someone kill Ferdy?"

Madison put a hand on the heating vent and aimed it at herself. "The dope. They want the—"

"Ferdy wasn't selling dope," I said. "You know he wasn't."

"I do know it," she said. "But it looks like it."

"He couldn't. Dope kills people. Ferdy wouldn't have slapped a mosquito."

"You really sound like you knew him."

"I know just about as much about him as I do about you."

She shook her head. "Right. I keep forgetting. Jeez, it's really embarrassing."

"What is?"

"Well, I get—you know—kind of, uh, *interested* in some characters in books. Personally interested. Maybe a little over-happy."

"As long as they stay in print, there's no chance you'll run into them." I pointed at the glove compartment. "Can you hand me whatever's in there?"

"What are we going to do about Ferdy?" She popped the door. "And if it's not dope, what is it?"

"No idea. They sure seemed to want it, didn't they?"

"Enough to shoot at us."

I pulled to the side of the road, such as it was, and took a wad of papers from her. "I don't think they were shooting at us."

"Well, not at *you*, obviously—"

I handed her a map book off the top of the pile and a wad of unused paper napkins, a long white feather and then a pair of sunglasses, and looked down at the card in my hand as she returned the other junk to the compartment. "Not at either of us. They were just trying to scare you into giving up."

"And you know this how?"

"They're a quarter of a mile away from us, on the other side of a wall of rocks, and for all they knew, you were actually on the other side of the road altogether, and they're firing a gun at nothing. It was for effect, to scare you."

"What a brilliant strategy. I'm *so* much more likely to reveal myself to someone who's firing a gun."

"Nobody said they were smart," I said. "But I think only one of them was that stupid."

"Which one?"

"The little one. I saw the gun. Which is a good thing."

"Why is it a good thing? Can you look at that and drive at the same time?"

"It's a good thing because this car belongs to the big one. And his name is Ruben Heller, and he lives in Yucca Valley." I handed her the registration slip. "Is that far?"

"Twenty miles in the direction we're already going."

"Good." I looked back and pulled into the right-hand lane. "Let's go bother him."

35

Add *Duplicitous and Faithless and Hopeless Asshole*

YUCCA VALLEY LOOKED A LOT like Twentynine Palms and Joshua Tree, both of which we had driven through to get there. As a drive, the journey totally lacked dramatic structure. A scrubby little town, then miles and miles of rolling desert—low-budget landscape without an idea anywhere—then lights ahead to announce the next scrubby little town, a crowd of stores and motels and maybe a stoplight if the town had pretensions, and then desert again. The third cluster of lights we drove into was Yucca Valley.

"How does anyone decide which one of these towns to live in?" I asked, slowing for the new speed limit. "I mean, it would be like choosing between cornflakes."

"The bigger question is why anyone lives in any of them."

"Why do you?"

She looked over at me just as I looked over at her, and there was a little electrical *zetz* as our glances met. "A dimpulse," she said, turning back to the road. "A guy with a lot of plausibility and a real talent for wearing jeans."

"Jake."

"Not just another almost-pretty face," she said, "and I'm talking about you."

"And he's past tense?"

"He would be if I had more faith in my ability to stick to a

255

plan. Slow down, I can't read the sign." She was squinting. She looked good squinting. "Does that say Sundown Trail?"

"Yes. Who named this place, the Lone Ranger?"

"Turn right. Then it'll probably be about a quarter of a mile."

I made the turn. "*Trail* doesn't begin to describe this."

She said, "Who do you think this guy is?"

"You mean Ruben?"

"Of course, I mean Ruben."

"I think he's a big, tall, fat guy who has bad taste in friends and drives a crap car. I saw his boots, you know. When he killed Ferdy. They were big boots."

"I've seen the prints from his boots. They're big prints." She leaned forward, craning into the darkness. "You have to explain to me how you saw Ferdy get killed."

"Same way I saw you. He was reading me when it happened."

"Jeez," she said, peering through the window. "No street lights at all. Even Twentynine Palms has street lights. It's like Midnight at the Oasis, minus the oasis. Why does he want the powder?"

"I don't know. I haven't seen the powder yet."

"Turn coming up. Do you think you'll be able to tell what kind of powder it is when you see it?"

"Probably not."

"So you were showboating just then." She lowered her voice. *"I don't know. I haven't seen the powder yet."*

"You know," I said, "the name *Jake* is kind of retro, like formica or log furniture or Pac-Man, a little on the simple side, probably got spaces between his teeth—"

"And you came down here, from wherever it was, because of Ferdy?"

"Shouldn't we be there by now?"

"Here's the turn, on the right," she said. "Fix the teeth and add *duplicitous* and *faithless* and *hopeless asshole*, and you'll be closing right in."

"But cute." I cut my lights as I made the turn onto Heller's street.

"You came down only because of Ferdy?"

"Well," I said, pulling over, "lookit here."

Here was a long, dark line of vintage mega-cars, Cadillacs, most of them, with a couple of old-style Lincoln Continentals to keep things interesting. Two of them had big-ass steer horns on the end of the hood, Texas-fifties style. Big Detroit iron all along the line. They were parked in an untidy line at the side of the road, their right wheels all the way up on the sand.

"What does this tell us," Madison asked, "about the size of his equipment?"

"Six of them," I said. "Maybe we should keep this one. He'll never miss it."

"No lights in the house," Madison said.

I looked at my watch. It said **19:49:44.** I said, "Holy shit," and slapped it.

"Holy shit what?"

"It's late." More than *four hours* gone? "Almost one."

"Why do you keep beating up your watch?"

"Never mind. At this hour, no wonder there's no light on."

"So does that change anything?"

"Probably makes it easier for us to creepy-crawl. Or me, anyway."

"I'm in this, too."

"Then stay behind me, okay?" I kept going to the cross-street, turned right, and parked the car behind the house on the corner. I turned off the lights and opened the door.

"You're leaving it on?" She got out, too.

I lowered my voice. "That's why you stay behind me. Any-

thing happens to me, you turn and get back to this thing and get
out of here."

She looked at me as though she was trying to translate what
I'd said into a language she understood, then shook her head.
"Jeez. How long have you been out of circulation?"

"You mean, up there? Since 1997, '98."

"Things have changed. See, these days, women generally
don't—"

"I know all about it. We've got female private eyes up there
now."

"Oh, well, then you're an expert." She rubbed her palms on
her jeans as though wiping the question off, and started toward
the house ahead of me, quite briskly.

I had to trot to catch up. "Seriously," I whispered, "I want to
go first. This is a big guy."

"Fine, fine, fine." She slowed and fell behind. "I'll just shrink
back here and hope he takes long enough to kill you that I can get
away. Even though we girls run so funny."

"Listen," I said. "The time to discuss this is probably *not*
while we're sneaking around the house of someone who could kill
both of us with a cough."

"Wait," she said. "Can you even *get* killed?"

"In more ways than you, and don't ask me about that now,
please. Make a list or something. Just stay back a little."

"Suppose I see something you don't?"

"Tap me on the shoulder."

"So you want me far enough back to be able to run, but close
enough to tap you—"

"Oh, for Christ's sake," I said. "Please. *Make* conversation.
Hum your favorite song." I started walking.

She made a noise that might have been a snicker and fell in
behind me.

The fine-line crescent of the moon was high overhead now,

but it didn't make enough light to cast shadows beneath the trees Madison had identified during the drive as cottonwoods. That meant it was dark everywhere: it was pretty dark between the trees and *really* dark beneath them. I settled for really dark and stayed under the cottonwoods whenever I could.

Five of the trees lined the narrow street on the side that the fleet of big Detroit gulpers had claimed, the side that Ruben Heller's house was on. The street was as straight as a stripe, with only four houses on it, widely spaced. Heller's house, from what I could tell in the dark, was an efficient one-story zigzag, probably stucco, that looked like it had started out as the basic desert cube and then had rooms tacked on here and there, creating something that reminded me of an awkward Tetris composition—a cube of probably four rooms, with three others straggling off in a two-steps-forward, one-step-sideways pattern.

The roof was flat, and as we neared it, something high up went wuh*WUH*wuh*WUH* and inhaled all the air in the neighborhood, stopping me in my tracks. Madison, who had apparently been watching her footing, walked into my back. She said, "Whoops."

I whispered, "What the hell is that?"

"Swamp cooler. Everybody's got them. That's why the roofs are flat." She pointed at the roof in case I was having trouble following her.

"Oh, well, then, talk about anything. Sing Wagner. Nobody can hear anything over that."

"You're wrong. You get so used to them here the noise disappears."

"If you say so." I started forward but she grabbed my arm.

"Look," she said, pointing.

"At what?"

"The ramp. Leading up to the door."

She had sharp eyes. The porch was a three-step affair, and to the right of the steps was a gently-sloped concrete ramp.

Madison said, "Ferdy's mom."

"Sorry?"

"I *think* it was Ferdy's mom. There were pictures of a woman on the wall of his apartment and in his camera. She had a walker, maybe even a wheelchair."

"You are certainly not suggesting that Ferdy's mom lives with this guy."

She grabbed a handful of her hair and gave it a yank. "No, she should be dead by now. Mr. Monroe, the man at the high school? The way he talked, she should be long gone. She got sick ten, eleven years ago."

I looked back at the ramp. "I hate this. I hate when the bad guys get human. I like it when they're just bad."

We were whispering, but Madison put a hand over my mouth. "Listen."

I listened. I heard the swamp cooler.

"A car," Madison said. "There's a car coming."

I said, "Let's go," and moved at a trot toward the back of Heller's house. When I looked back, Madison was about eight inches behind me, looking back over her own shoulder, toward the road. I couldn't see anything coming but I thought I might just barely hear an engine over the giant iron-lung gasps of the swamp cooler.

As I passed the zigzag wing that had been tacked onto the original house, I saw another doorway with another concrete wheelchair ramp leading up to it. It was hard to tell in the dark, but the ramp seemed to have been painted pink. Behind the house I saw the dark, angular bulk of a garage, weathered wood, older than the house. The entire structure leaned slightly to the right, and the door, wood on a rusty hinge, was closed.

The sight slowed me. What good was a garage when you had

a fleet of antique gas-guzzlers parked in front? What did he keep in it, anyway?

I was torn. If I only had a few seconds left—house or garage? The garage meant opening a door, which could make noise. Looking through a window was quiet. I chose the house.

As we angled toward the right, I saw a square concrete pad at the back of the house with a sliding glass door opening onto it. A round table with an umbrella poking up out of its center had staked out part of the paved area, and a frayed-looking aluminum-and-plastic chaise claimed most of the rest of it. A ramp had been built across the entire width of the half of the door that slid open. The room on the other side was dark.

I held up a hand for Madison, and she stopped beside me. I was short of breath but she wasn't, so apparently I wasn't completely used to my weight yet. I pointed to the sliding glass door and she nodded.

We crossed the concrete on tiptoe.

I cupped my hands at the sides of my eyes to shut out light and leaned against the glass. Madison did the same. The glass felt cool and smooth. The room on the other side was as dark as an underground river.

And then a dark face—all round, pale eyes—swam toward me and stopped not eight inches below the end of my nose. The unnaturally wide eyes widened even further, and white teeth appeared below them, and then the owner of the eyes and the teeth screamed.

Madison screamed.

I screamed.

Headlights swept the desert on the far side of the house, revealing a pile of old car parts, probably diseased organs ripped from the fleet parked in front.

I didn't need another cue. I grabbed Madison's hand and ran like hell for the idling car.

PAGES FROM A COMPLETELY DIFFERENT NOVEL

(1)

The crag's surface was gray rock, barren, wind-shaped and wind-scraped to an almost glassy smoothness, now nearly black with moisture. The wind, cold and malicious, whipped Aaron's cape around his slender form, curled the fog around him like a larger cloak, and howled in his ears, a sound like the rage of the Earth itself.

"I have come an unimaginable *distance to stand here," Aaron shouted into the teeth of the gale. "To kill you would be a step so short I could take it without noticing."*

The Old Man laughed shortly and mercilessly. The laugh was high, brittle, thin, metallic, like a hinge that hadn't opened in centuries. "You kill me, *little beastling? I've destroyed and devoured characters more dangerous than you'll ever be. Throw down your sword, and I'll see whether I feel merciful."*

"Depend upon you for mercy? Knowing what you've done, the men, women, and children you've destroyed? The worlds you've turned to dust and ash? I'll plummet to hell first." Aaron brandished the cold and comforting weight of his sword, feeling his feet slip slightly on the slick rock, and a tongue of lightning flicked fire in the sky, reflected blindingly bright and snakebite-quick down the blade's silvery length.

The Old Man raised an empty hand, fingers spread wide, and a gust of wind struck Aaron, sending him a step backward, toward the yawning abyss. Satisfaction sparked like a struck flint in the drooping but still-powerful eyes. The Old Man waved the wind away effortlessly, lifted his chin, and said

And said

and said...

...and *said*

What the hell did he say?

Kind of a lot of adverbs, weren't there?

the rage of the earth itself. What was the earth pissed off about?

He leaned back, tilted the chair away from the desk, and stretched his arms wide, making fists. He mimed a yawn, hoping to provoke a real one. It must have been one-thirty, two in the morning. Maybe the Voice was finally running out of steam.

The Voice.

He reached past the beat-up laptop, the hard drive of which had lately been making an alarming gnawing noise, moved the wine bottle aside, and picked up his Catty Award. It was worthless but satisfyingly heavy. He did twenty curls with his left hand, sitting at the trestle table in front of the dark window and trying to avoid looking at the laptop's screen.

He realized he was ready—he'd been ready for hours—for the Voice to call it a night.

Swiveling the office chair ninety degrees, he transferred the Catty to his right hand and started a new set of curls. On the base of the award, it said: *For outstanding achievements in catalog prose, 2002, Timothy Hallinan.* Two thousand two, the year he'd come up with *The Twill is Gone* as a headline for a new, smoother gabardine shirt in the *Off the Map* catalog.

It had been a while since he'd written anything that good. On the other hand, the old muse hadn't exactly leaped at the bait of a new braided belt or another stupid photographer's vest.

He'd once spent two days trying to name the inside pockets on a vest. The ones they'd liked had been *smuggler's snugs* and *contraband compartments.* It had seemed to him at the time that designers who put pockets inside a vest would have had *some* idea of what people would use them for. But no. In the world of the faux-photo vest, function follows form. They went with *smuggler's snugs.*

So: the Catty. Not exactly an Oscar or even an Edgar. Its two upturned hands—applauding, he supposed—mimed the curve at the lower part of a roast chicken's stomach, and he privately thought of the award as The Pupik. The only Pupik he'd ever won.

Nineteen curls, twenty. Swivel the chair, put the Pupik back on the table, pour another glass of wine—number three, or maybe four—and wait for the Voice. He ventured a look at the screen.

... drooping but still-powerful eyes. Can you call eyes *powerful?* Maybe *hypnotic? Mesmerizing?* Did he even know what *color* they were? Maybe he should Google Franz Anton Mesmer, maybe there was some 19th-century description of Mesmer's eyes he could bag, something with a nice, archaic feel, since they're on top of that fucking crag, wearing capes. Hit the wine, a long swallow, to see whether the old mind would clear. Okay, the capes he knew about, the capes had been in the story for a couple hundred pages, but where did the crag come from? They'd been fighting uphill for four or five thousand words, but this was the first he'd heard of a crag. Of course, he supposed that name of the place where they were fighting, in the center of The Jagged Realms, suggested at least steep, high hills, and it was logical that they'd be separated by crags. Otherwise, it would be the Plateau Realm, and there were zero dramatic possibilities in a plateau. He rubbed wearily at the bridge of his nose and caught himself going back in the thought to edit out "wearily." He'd been writing too long.

Obviously he needed to back up and fill in the setting. Maybe tomorrow. He put the cursor after the word *crag* and wrote RHUBARB. Tomorrow, he'd tell Word to find RHUBARB and he'd describe the landscape.

And stayed there, leaning forward with his eyes on the page. *The old man waved the wind away effortlessly.* Maybe should be *effortlessly waved the wind away. Effortlessly* was a weak ending. What was the strongest word? "Wind." *Effortlessly waved away the wind.* Awful. Sounded like he had a lace hankie in his hand. A *French* lace hankie.

The empty house let out one of the creaks that had alarmed him so much when they began, a couple of weeks back. When the book had begun to pour itself through him. Maybe just one more sentence...

Ahhhh. Enough. The Voice was going to leave him alone until maybe eight in the morning, if past nights were anything to go by.

But whenever it got him up, he was going to go to the keyboard and write what it said.

Not since his publisher rejected *The Wrong End of the Rainbow* had a story come to him so effortlessly. *Effortlessly waved the wind away?* Mmmmm. He was at 94,000 words now, with maybe another 8,000-10,000 to go. He hadn't gotten this far in a book since he'd been forced to retire Simeon.

And—his pulse gave a couple of extra thumps—his agent liked it. *His agent.* The same agent who'd neglected to call him to say he'd changed his email address. After he finally read the treatment, the agent had said, "There's a hair-tearing market for paranormal romantic suspense right now, even *with* capes, because that's the big genre in ebooks, and the big publishers think they've missed the boat."

Not precisely a rave, not a lot of praise for his specific book, but who cared? Publishers, he'd learned, operated most of the time from one of three positions: (1) Arrogance about their uncanny sense of the Market; (2) Resentful imitation of whatever had stolen the Market while they weren't looking; and (3) Blind panic that something was happening to the Market that they didn't understand.

They thought about the Market a lot more than they thought about Books.

But his agent thought that *The Stardark Chronicles* fit very neatly into Slot Number Three, the blind panic category.

Bye-bye catalogs. He could begin again to spell the word correctly again—to himself, anyway—as *catalogue*. It had been so long since anybody spelled it right that Word flagged it as a typo.

So, now he was writing—what was it? Paranormal romantic suspense in the fantasy sub-genre. He said it out loud, but it didn't help much. It still sounded like a literary goulash. But it was where his imagination had taken him. And his agent liked it.

He saved the manuscript, backed it up to a thumb drive, and pulled the thumb drive out so he could hide it someplace where it wouldn't be found by the burglar who was due any day to sneak in and steal the laptop with his whole life on it. As he yanked the drive from the USB port, he backhanded the wineglass and it went over—naturally—on the edge of the partially printed manuscript.

He caught the glass as it rolled off the edge of the desk, said an ancient Anglo-Saxon word somewhat corrupted by 21st-century overuse, and pushed the chair back as red wine dripped onto his knees. With his free hand, he grabbed the top half-inch of the manuscript before the wine soaked its way farther down. He stood there, glass in one hand, wine-edged pages in the other, listening to the wine hit the floor drop by drop. The smell of cheap Bordeaux tinted the air around him.

There were a lot of things he could have done: mop up the spill, separate the wet pages so they'd dry faster, take the glass into the kitchen. What he did was say, "Fuck it," drop the pages a safe distance from the spill, and put the glass back down. He paused on the way out of the room, with one hand already raised *to effortlessly wave*—no, no, skip that; no split infinitives—to turn off the light. His fingers touched the smoothness of the switch—

—and in the moment between breathing in and breathing out, his mind was ringing like a bell.

Aaron. *Aaron?* Was Aaron the right name? It didn't feel right anymore.

Maybe something sort of like it, with the same *not-now* feeling, but less ordinary. A sort of nudge somewhere in his mind produced *Elan*. Elan? Had anybody at any time in history ever been named Elan?

What about *Elen?*

No, too female. People would silently pronounce it as…

The skin all over his body puckered and popped goose bumps.

"Well?" he said aloud as he shivered. "What about it?"

He stood there, motionless. Wine dripped behind him.

36

What Outweighs What

MADISON THOUGHT: ALL RIGHT, SO there are some guys, you know right away, *instantly*, they're possibles. Even though they've got something wrong with them, since of course they've *all* got something wrong with them.

The art of life, as she was beginning to see it, was assigning a weight to what was wrong and another weight to what was right, and then putting those estimated weights up on a balancing scale, like the ones old Justice holds, to see what outweighs what.

The *problem* with the art of life was keeping your thumb off the scale, not letting things like blue eyes, a quick smile, just the right tone of voice, or a hint—beneath the masculine bravado—of being lost, add ounces to the positives and subtract pounds from the negatives.

He handles himself really well, he's cute in a kind of 1990s way, and he seems to like me. And he blushes like a lighthouse, which is, oh, well, dorky but endearing. He's tall, he's fit, he's smart, he's brave without going all cave man about it. He seems to have morals, unlike Jake, who would jump the entire line of Rockettes if they'd hold still for a minute. So, all those good traits, and he's also *not Jake*. All to the good.

On the downside? He's fictional.

So? What's wrong with that? Might even be a positive. The problem with most guys is that they're one knot of complications inside another knot of complications. Maybe he's not so complicated. He doesn't talk about his—his writer—as though he was Joyce or anyone. Maybe the surface is all there is.

Wouldn't that be restful?

I like the surface.

And it is, after all, genre writing. How deep can it go?

Oh, no, I'm not messing with the weights here *at all*. He's a *fictional private eye?* Ideal. Bring it on. What could possibly go wrong?

Assuming that any of what he says is true.

But he's *something* out of the ordinary, that's for sure, what with the popping into existence and the rummaging around in my mind. I don't believe in aliens or vampires or witches or warlocks. On the other hand, I know thousands of fictional characters. And he really did seem surprised when he tried to pay for the coffee and the waitress told him it was play money. Why would a real guy carry play money?

That's a nice profile. Regular but not pretty. Guysy. The hair is 90s but I could do something with it.

And he drives really, really fast.

She sat back to look at him again, and she could sense the spark when he felt her gaze.

* * *

"What?" I said. The side of my face actually felt warm. "What are you—"

"You can slow down a little," she said. "They're not back there."

"Let's keep it that way. Where are we going?"

"I have a motel room," Madison said. "Oh, that sounds classy."

"Where is it?" I was tilting the mirror to check it myself.

"Men actually don't believe a woman can tell whether there are headlights behind them," she said. "It's in Joshua Tree."

"On the highway?"

"Everything's on the highway."

"I'm not parking this boat on the highway. It'd be like putting up a sign. *Kill us here.*"

And I like the way he talks, Madison thought. I like the way he handled those two soldiers even though they could have split him in half and spread him on toast. And here's what maybe I like best of all: he—

"Hey," she said. "Can you still see inside my mind?"

I kept my eyes on the road, trying not to look like I was taking a pass at reading her while I took a pass at reading her. I got nothing. "I haven't tried. Maybe not, though. The way it was explained to me, the medium was imagination, and we're both down here now. Not to knock your neighborhood, but it's no monument to imagination. And also, being with me isn't the same thing as reading me." I shrugged. "Apparently."

"Should I believe you?"

I was checking the mirror again. It was hard to believe we'd gotten away clean. "Up to you."

"One thing I like about you," she said, "is that you have the sense to know when to run."

"That's one reason I don't think I'm being written now. Hallinan would have had me stay there until there were at least two guns pointed at me. He would have chosen the thrill of the moment over narrative plausibility." I shrugged. "Although it *would* have been more exciting."

"And then?"

"I'd have gotten out of it somehow. He had to keep me in one piece for the next book."

"Did you ever wonder if he could kill you? Say he got sick of you, and—"

"Oh, *thank* you," I said. "That may be the only thing I've never worried about, so now I have the complete collection."

"So rise to it," Madison said. "So far, you're doing great."

I glanced over at her, met her eyes, and looked back to the road.

"Yes," she said, "that was a compliment."

We rode in potential-rich silence for a minute or two, and then town lights blossomed ahead of us. I slowed the car. "After the way that waitress looked at the money," I said, "I don't think I want to show a cop my driver's license." I got the speed down to fifty, then forty, then thirty-five. "Did you like the book?"

"You saw how far I got."

"Oh," I said. "Right."

"Oh, poor baby. I got distracted, remember? But you know who loved it? Ferdy."

"Well," I said. "That's something."

"It really matters to you, doesn't it?"

I said, "Excuse me?"

"You didn't write them."

"No, but I—it—it's *who I am*. I don't have any existence except in those books."

"Sure you do. You're hanging around up there or *over* there, or wherever you usually are, watching us read and you're, you know, making friends and, and, thinking about things." She ran out of inspiration. "Maybe gardening, collecting the paper bands off cigars?"

"Not. Not much of anything, really. You probably can't imagine how little I do. Look out the window, wish I had a vacuum, stuff like that."

"And down here, you're being—well, really interesting." She literally kicked herself, the left calf with the right foot. "Isn't that the first thing you want in a character? That he's interesting?"

"I guess." I was trying to see myself outside the books and outside that pallid limbo I'd come here from, and not doing very well at it.

"And you're not just interesting. I've never met anyone like you. I mean, even aside from the things you've done since I met you, it certainly must be, I don't know, different to, um, to have those books behind you, with people reading them, and you can watch them when they do, but it's the same few stories over and over."

"I don't know," I said. "I'm no expert, but it seems to me that real people live the same stories over and over, too."

Madison said, "Ouch." Then she said, "You can speed up now."

"That was Joshua Tree?"

"It was. And there goes my motel. So," she said, changing the subject so abruptly he could almost hear it being shoved aside. "Who was that very small person we saw through the window?"

"That's who the ramp was built for," I said.

"Wheelchair," she said.

"Exactly." I checked the mirror again. "We need a new car."

"Well," Madison said, "I know where we can get one."

37

Golden Arches

"Pictures of me," she was saying as I made the turn off the highway. "Big blowups, all over his wall. And then the woman, just emaciated, sitting in a chair like a throne. And a walker over to one side."

"Walker," I said. "Ramps. Wonder if we knew who the other guy was, whether we'd find ramps at his place, too."

"The woman in that house... did you see what color the ramps were?"

"Hard to see. I thought maybe pink."

"What I thought, too. If they were for the woman," Madison said, "that's kind of sweet."

"He's a bad guy," I said. "Probably. Where am I going?"

"The Golden Arches. Right up there."

"Why did Ferdy want you to read *Skin Deep*?"

"He liked it."

I pulled into the parking lot. The McDonald's outlet was dark and empty but the air was almost gelatinous with saturated fat. "You're up to your ears in Balzac, reading it in French, no less, and he's shoving obscure, out-of-print mysteries at you?"

"Oh, boy," she said. "Why don't you keep pushing at that sore tooth?"

"It's not a sore tooth," I lied. "It's detective curiosity. Guess that's your car, by the dumpster?"

"That's it."

I angled the car across the lot.

"I didn't mean to snap at you," she said. "But the way it happened was sort of silly, and I didn't want to talk about it. I've got... issues... with abandoning plans, which means I sort of float around saying I want to do things but not doing them. I mean, that's how I got here and that's how I stay here, one day at a time. So he knew, Ferdy did, that I wanted to write. Or that I *talk* about wanting to write, and he was trying to be practical. He thought I should read one or two of your books and then, after I had something to talk about, he'd introduce me to the guy who —I mean, you know, your writer."

I braked so hard that she had to put out a hand to keep from hitting the dash.

"*Ferdy knew him?* Knew Hallinan?"

"That's what he said. He said maybe he, I mean, Hallinan, would talk to me, maybe even read some of my writing. If I had any writing, which I don't, but Ferdy didn't know that."

I drummed my fingers on the steering wheel for a moment, just trying to absorb it. "Wait, wait, wait. That means that Hallinan is here? Somewhere near here?"

"He lives in Joshua Tree, I think."

"Oh, boy." I closed my eyes. "This is so completely *wrong*. I need to think."

"Wow," Madison said, lighting up. "Maybe you could meet him. What do you think would happen? Maybe you'd both explode. Like anti-matter, or—"

"Wait, wait, wait. This isn't—this can't be a coincidence." I opened my eyes again and peered through the windshield at the nothingness of the night. As usual, no answers were written there.

"Why? He has to live somewhere."

"Yeah, but not *here*. Of all the places in the world, not here. Oh, man I knew it. This is all tied up somehow with what's been happening up there."

"You mean, up where you—do whatever you do." She broke off and then grabbed a breath. "So what's been happening?"

"Holes in the sky, wolves, more detail, higher resolution, guys getting solid. I'll explain it to you when I think I understand it, okay?" I pulled the car forward until the tires bumped the stanchion at the end of the space, and opened my door.

"You're going to leave it running again?"

"I don't actually know how to turn it off," I said, getting out. "I learned how to hot-wire in the book but I never had to turn the car off."

"*I'll leave it running for you,*" Madison said in a deep, authoritative voice. "*Anything happens to me, you get your helpless little girl butt back to the car—*"

"Okay, okay."

"*I haven't seen the powder yet.*" She opened her own door. "No, you hardly showboat at all."

"I'm just trying to raise your confidence level."

"You know what *else* we haven't covered?" Madison said. "What else we haven't covered is why you're here."

I cleared my throat. "Why I'm—"

"Here." We regarded each other over the top of the Cadillac, which displayed a nice sense of timing by shutting itself off with a cough that practically cried out for a tune-up. "Why you actually came here."

I said, "Oh."

"It's not a trick question. What really brought you here?"

In the silence, someone who was neither of us said, "We was wondering about that, too."

38

Rat-A-Tat-Tat

THE BIG MAN LUMBERED TOWARD us from the edge of the dark McDonald's. Now that I wasn't fixated on getting out from under Madison's question, I heard the other car idling around the corner.

"Who are *you*?" the big man said. "We didn't know she had nobody with her."

Madison said, "I'm right here. You don't have to discuss me in the third—"

"Quiet," the big man said. His voice was deep and ragged, as though he'd been shouting himself hoarse for years. And he really was big; I guessed him at six-seven, six-eight, maybe 300 pounds, and not fat, other than a hemispherical belly suspended over a cowboy's slender hips. He wore a big lopsided stetson and had something in his hand. "So?" he said. "Who are you?"

"What's in your hand?" I asked.

The big man brought his hand up. It held a black automatic. "You have fucked with me enough," he said to Madison. "Stealing Ferdy's stuff, taking my car. Coming to my house tonight, that was the last mistake. Now who is he?"

"He's my friend?" Madison said, but her voice was a little watery and over-loud.

"Too bad for him," the big man said. He pointed the gun at me, and my legs went a little watery, too. "Open the car, friend."

I swallowed, and when I was finished, I said, "Fuck you."

"Ummm," Madison said.

The big man seemed to grow an inch. "You think I'm jacking you around? I'd shoot you for fun at this point, scaring my wife like that."

"Simeon, this is not an ookbay," Madison said.

"So shoot me," I said, suddenly furious. "Come on, fatso, *do* something. Don't just hulk there. Big man. Chasing a girl all over the goddamn desert. Scaring her half to death. Do something."

Madison said, "*Simeon.*"

"He's not going to shoot anybody," I said. Ignoring the big man, I walked around the front of Madison's car. "He's a bag of wind with a big hat. On the other hand, *drop, Madison—*" I said, and then I was leaning my elbows on the roof of the car, pointing my automatic at the center of the big man's body. "I'll shoot you *right this second* if you don't put that gun down. No? Okay, you're dead." I raised the gun in a two-hand grip, but the big man lifted his hands and took a step back.

He said, "Keerful now, keerful," and slowly bent to lay the gun down.

"Step away. Hands on top of your head. I have almost no time left here, and I *will* shoot you."

The big man put his hands on his head, fingers laced. "I believe you. You cain't shoot me. I've got to take care of—"

"Madison, get the gun. Where's your runty little friend?"

Madison's eyes came up over the top of the Cadillac's hood. She said, "Get the gun? Are you kidding me?"

"Just get it. He won't do anything."

"I won't." The big man took another step back.

"Your friend. Where is he?"

Madison ran around the car and up to the gun. She threw an anxious glance at the big man and said, "Excuse me," as she picked up the automatic.

The big man said, "No problem, missy."

I said, "I asked you a question."

The big man watched Madison back up, holding the gun between thumb and forefinger, as though she could scarcely force herself to touch it. "Prolly back home," he said. He seemed dispirited. "How'd you know I wouldn't shoot you?"

"I didn't. I just didn't think I was going to get shot by anyone who paints a wheelchair ramp pink. And the runt isn't with you but you left your car over there with the engine running?"

The big man said, "I'm a trusting soul."

"Come on, come on, come closer." I gestured with the gun. "Three steps, four, and stop."

Madison whirled away from me, said something that sounded like "Heeep," and dropped the gun to the pavement with a clatter. She darted back behind the Cadillac.

Keeping my gun on the big man, I ducked a little lower behind Madison's car and called out to the man around the far corner of the restaurant, "Throw your gun out now, or I'll shoot your friend."

"What the fuck do I care? Shoot him over and over. Use up your bullets."

"I'm not playing with you. Count of three, are you listening?"

"Nothing else to listen to," the hidden man said. "We're in the fuckin' desert."

"One," I said. Madison scooted from the Cadillac to my side of her car. Her eyes filled half her face.

"Two," I said. "I don't see you yet."

"You'll see me just before I shoot your left eye out."

"First shot is in his gut," I called. "He'll survive it, but it won't be pretty. Second, if I need it, is through the heart. You coming out?" The big man lowered his head and waited.

No answer.

"And *three*," I shouted. I raised the gun just high enough to fire over the big man's head, inadvertently squeezed my eyes shut, and pulled the trigger.

And the gun said, "Bang." In a not-very-deep voice.

It said, "Bang, bang."

* * *

"What I liked was when it said, 'Rat-a-tat-tat,'" the big man said at the wheel of the car. "Dang near pooped myself." He laughed, a laugh so deep it sounded like something the car was dragging.

"Funny as hell," I said. "Always a big hit at a party." My hands were tightly cuffed behind me, and I was in the front seat of the car the men had arrived in. Madison, also cuffed, was in her own car, which was being driven by the smaller man, its taillights visible through the windshield. The Caddy had turned out to be out of gas and been left at McDonald's.

"What I don't understand," the big man said, when he was all chuckled out, "is why you pulled the trigger when you knowed it was a toy."

"It's not a toy," I said, nettled. "It's a fictional gun."

"You mean a fake."

"If you like." They were most of the way back to the town of Joshua Tree. "How did you find us?"

"Her car. We knew where she lived and we figured I spooked her and she might hide her car so it'd look like she wasn't home. Micky D's was the closest parking place. Simple."

"How did you know where she lived?"

"My friend has connections with the PD. Someone looked her up for us."

"I figured he was a cop or an ex-cop. These cuffs are too tight."

"Ex. That's what Ridley said you'd say." Heller took his eyes off the road to glance at me. "How'd you figure he was an ex—"

"Most civilians don't carry a couple pairs of handcuffs."

He gave out a sort of subterranean chuckle. "That's old Ridley."

I looked out the window. Desert unscrolled itself past us in an uninteresting fashion. "This is the dullest place I've ever been. If it was in a book, I wouldn't waste a bookmark on it, even a free bookmark."

"Some of us like it."

"Not that it matters when it's all alike, but where are we going?"

"Got me. Wherever she tells him to go."

"You mean *Madison* is in charge?"

"Of this part," the big man said. "Pretty little thing."

"She'd love to hear you say that."

"Aahh, sure, right. They're all militants now."

"Who?"

"The girlies. I remember when they was sweet and polite."

I looked over at him. "How old *are* you?"

"Sixty-six. But I'm right proud to say that I lag behind the times. What about you?"

"*What* what about me?"

"How old are you?"

"Well, now," I said. "That's an interesting issue. I was thirty-seven for six years, until I went out of print in 1997, but I've been living at a different rate of time than you ever since then, so—"

"Never mind," the big man said. "Just making conversation. Thought it was an easy question."

"I'm Simeon Grist," I said, operating on the assumption that someone who knew my name was marginally less likely to kill me. I think that was in one of my books.

A brusque nod. "Ruben Heller."

"And your little friend?"

Heller laughed, this time sounding like colliding bowling balls. "Oh, that would make him real cranky, he heard that."

"Ridley his first name or last?"

Heller shrugged, and his shirt creaked. "Got me. Just Ridley."

"He's your partner but you don't know his full name?"

Heller's eyes were too close together, making him look puzzled by default, but the look he aimed at me was *deeply* puzzled. "Partner? We're not partners."

"Well, then, what's your interest in Madison?"

"No interest at all. You know, pretty and all that, but I'm a married man. As you saw at my house tonight." And Heller balled up his oversize right fist and swung it sideways into the center of my chest.

It felt like my heart had exploded. I folded forward, banging my forehead on the dash, and straightened back up with a ball of pain expanding into my lungs and the tops of my arms, my attention divided between that and the sting of torn skin on my forehead, plus a line of warm blood dripping off the lashes of my right eye. I squeezed the eye shut and wheezed against the pain.

"Jist shut up," Heller said. "That's for frightening my wife. Be quiet and don't piss me off again, and we'll git along fine."

The left-hand turn signal on Madison's car began to blink.

"Looks like we're here," Heller said.

Through my open eye, I saw the lighted sign that said M TEL.

The car glided to a stop with a high, nervous whine of bad brakes. Heller turned off the ignition and said, "I'm going around to your side to git you out, and then I think we're going upstairs. You give me any trouble and you'll come down them stairs on your face, got it?"

"Got it."

"Good. I plumb hate being unfriendly."

The door to the other car opened, and the little man got out. A moment later, Madison climbed out of the passenger side, unaided. Her hands were not cuffed.

"Guess they're gittin' along," Heller said as he got out. I watched Madison lead the smaller man—Ridley—up the stairs to the second floor.

The motel was a dilapidated two-story dump that looked like it had been kicked out of a budget chain for failing to meet standards. It was, as far as I could see, the universal high-desert no-color that lurks beneath all paint jobs, no matter how ambitious.

Heller opened the door. "Don't hit your head."

"I don't have to," I grumbled. "You did it for me."

"Awww, I told you why I done that. Quit bitchin' and follow them." He let me take a three-step lead and then fell in behind. "Don't have to remind you not to get stupid, do I?"

"I've used up my stupid supply for the day." The steps were steep and far apart, each requiring an instant for me to center my weight before climbing it. "This would be easier with my hands free."

"Ridley's got the key." At the top of the steps. Madison turned right, with Ridley at a companionable closeness beside her. They seemed to be getting along great.

"Of course he does," I said. "Why did I ask?"

"Go right at the top," Heller said.

"I'm handcuffed, Ruben, not blindfolded. And to think I was going to shoot over your head."

"Turn right," Heller said again, with a prod this time, and he followed me to the open door of room 204.

39

Sold for Spare Change

RIDLEY, A SHORT, SKINNY GUY with a down-turned mouth and an Adam's apple like an elbow, his hands jammed into the pockets of his jeans, was standing in front of a grimy-looking, floor-mounted air conditioner, and Madison was sitting on a grimy-looking bed, her knees together and her hands folded in her lap like a chastised child. If the décor had a theme, it was *grimy*.

"Hey, it's Deadeye," Ridley said cheerfully. "Get into a fight?"

"Simeon," Madison said, starting to get up. Ridley made a little cautionary noise, and she settled back, eyes on my forehead. "Did that big ape—"

"He hit his head on the dash," Heller said, pushing me farther in so he could close the door.

"Whatever he says." I looked around at all of them, blinking away the blood and trying to act like I got hit all the time and had learned to like it. "Well, here we are."

Ridley laughed, kind of a happy rasp. "I love it when the bottom puppy tries to take charge. Ruben, uncuff him."

Ruben said, "Sure," pulled out a key, and went behind me.

"Liar, liar, pants on fire," I said.

"*He's* the liar?" Ridley said. He was redheaded and buzz-cut, balding on top and long-chinned on the bottom, producing a face shaped in the long oval of a coffee bean. His upper lip was as long as his forehead. "What about *The first shot is through the arm* or whatever you said? With a cap gun."

"Fictional," I said, stung. *"Fictional."*

"He always talk like this?" Ridley asked Madison.

Madison said, "Yes," still eying my forehead. "I'm going to get some wet toilet paper for his head."

She started to get up again, but Ridley waved her back.

"If anybody's going into the bathroom, it's Ruben, especially since he helped old Deadeye hit his head in the first place. Argument, Ruben?"

"I just want to git to bed," Heller said. He finished fiddling with the cuffs, and I stood, opening and closing my hands as they were flooded with needles. Heller trudged toward the bathroom.

Ridley said, "C'mere." With a glance at Madison, I went to him. "Behave, now," Ridley said, going up on tiptoe. I felt Ridley's fingers, callused like leather, on either side of the torn skin. He pulled the split wider for a moment and I gasped, but then the man put his hand back down and backed away.

"You're not even gonna scar," he said. "I've had a dozen worse than these and lookit me."

"No, thanks," I said.

"Go sit with your girlfriend. How you coming in there, Ruben?"

"Really cheap toilet paper," Heller complained from the bathroom. "Falls apart when you git it wet."

"He won't care," Ridley said. "Just wad some up and soak it and bring it to little nurse Madison out here."

Madison made an irritated little *pssssss* noise.

"I want *him* to nurse me," I said. To Madison, I said, "Opdray itay."

Speaking over me, Madison said, "Please hurry, he's swelling."

"Yeah, yeah, yeah," Heller said. He came out of the bathroom with a wad of wet paper in his right hand, water dripping onto the carpet. Standing in front of me, he held out the sop of paper.

Madison took it, said, "Whoops," and dropped it, and Heller

automatically went down to pick it up for her. As he did, I leaned forward and lifted the automatic protruding from Heller's pocket, encircled the big man's neck with my free arm, and touched the gun to his temple. Heller went completely still.

"Keep your hands where I can see them, Ridley," I said. "This one shoots bullets."

"Simeon," Madison began.

"I didn't rack the gun," Heller said, but not with much authority.

"You one hundred percent sure of that?" I said. Heller answered with a loud swallow. "You're a cop," I said to Ridley. "Why'd your big lummox friend kill Ferdy Carvalho?"

Ridley squinted at me as though I'd spontaneously split in two. "*Ruben*? Ruben kill Ferdy?"

"Simeon," Madison said. "They didn't kill Ferdy."

From his kneeling position, Heller startled me by saying, "Last thing we'd do in the world would be to hurt Ferdy."

"Has this thing got a light trigger?" I asked.

Heller said, "Yup."

"Then don't surprise me."

Heller said, "Right."

"You got it totally backward," Ridley said. "We loved Ferdy."

"We did," Heller said. Then he cut his eyes to me and said, "Sorry."

I felt my adrenaline level drop, to be replaced by about three hundred pounds of exhaustion. "Madison, is there any reason I shouldn't take the gun away from this man's head?"

"I don't think so," Madison said. "And anyway, I can't clean up your cut while you've got him like that. Suppose it stings and you kill him?"

"Might mess up this nice room," Ridley said, and laughed. After a beat, Heller laughed with him.

"Well," I said, pulling the gun back. "Since we're all friends."

"We never wanted to hurt you or this little sweetheart here," Heller said, still on his knees.

"Ruben," Ridley said, "you planning to propose?"

"Naw." Ruben said, "Kin I have my gun back?"

"Not just yet," I said. I got up just to move. "So you wanted the dope? And you chased her all over hell and gone and fired guns at her? To get the dope? And that somehow makes you the good guys?"

"Old Madison here says you're a private detective," Ridley said. "One of the first things I learned when I made detective is that as long as you're talking, you're not learning."

"So talk."

"We never meant her harm," Ridley said. "We thought she had all the stuff from Ferdy's car, and we needed it bad."

"And Ferdy," Ruben said, still on his knees, "Ferdy was the Angel of Light."

* * *

"That's it, huh?" I asked. I was sitting on the bed beside Madison, with a wet, cold, but clean forehead.

The two plastic-wrapped golf balls of white powder were at the foot of the bed, and Heller and Ridley were looking at them with expressions of mingled longing and disappointment.

"The cops got the rest," Madison said, "when they took Ferdy's car."

"Mmmm-mmm," Ridley said, shaking his head. "How many?"

"S'posed to be twenty," Heller said, looking woebegone. "Enough for evvybody, and some left over."

"When I smelled it," Madison said, "it was kind of bitter."

"You should be the detective," Ridley said. "Not old Deadeye here."

"I never smelled it," I said and caught a glance from Madison that made me wish I could unsay it.

"Apricots," Ridley said. "What she smelled is apricot kernels. Bitter as hell."

"Wait a minute," I said. "Apricots? Are we talking about *lae-trile?*" I rubbed my forehead and immediately regretted it. "The wheelchair ramps," I said. "The woman in the picture."

"What pitcher?" Ridley asked.

"On his wall, right, Madison? The apartment wall."

"Oh, right," Ridley said. He looked ashamed of himself. "Ferdy's place."

She said accusingly, "So you guys were the ones who ripped—"

"Sorry, sorry," Ridley said. "We just needed to get the stuff. For everyone, not just us."

"I don't get it," I said. "This is all about a bogus cancer cure?"

Madison said, "Cancer? That's what Ferdy's mother had?"

"It was, sweetheart," Ridley said. "And as for you, Mr. Smartass, we'll see how bogus you think it is when the doctors tell you there's nothing more they can do for somebody you love."

"'Cept dope them up for the pain," Heller said. "And then they're not hardly there any more."

"So, Ferdy—what, sold you this stuff?"

"It's like a co-op," Ridley said. "We all put in money every couple weeks, and Ferdy goes down to—*went* down to—Mexico, and got the stuff and snuck it back into the country."

"Done it for free, too," Heller said. "Never took a cut."

"How many of you?"

"Fifteen, counting us. All over the high desert."

I transferred Heller's gun from my left hand to my right, thought *the hell with it*, and laid it on the bed.

"But it doesn't work."

"When you been told *nothin's* gonna work," Heller said, "and then someone offers you something new and says it *might* work, guess what? It works. Maybe only for a little while, maybe only a little bit—"

"Maybe only in the mind," Ridley interrupted.

"But it works," Heller said. "And even if it only works ten percent, that's ten percent I'd give my life for." He hooked a thumb at Ridley. "*He'd* give his life for it."

"I would," Ridley said.

"So, what, then?" Madison said. "He started with his mom?"

"That's it," Ridley said. "And for a while, she felt better. Wasn't in pain all the time, wasn't trying to claw her way through the walls of that little house. And people like us—like Ferdy and Ruben and me—we all go to the same hospitals and sit around in the same waiting rooms. Nothing to do but talk, and we only got one thing to talk about: Does anything work? And here's old Ferdy, whose mom was dying, but he thought the laetrile had helped through a couple of years she wasn't supposed to have had in the first place." He looked over at Heller, whose close-set eyes were focused on the opposite wall. "Well, that was some powerful information."

"So he said he could git us some," Heller said to the wall.

I said, "It's that hard to get?"

"Well, sure." Heller swiveled to face them, and the close-set eyes were practically sparking. "The fucking government can't do nothing about crack," he said, the deep voice almost breaking under the weight of his anger. "They can't do nothing about heroin, nothing about opioids, can't do nothing about the Meskins killing each other for pot all over the place, but they got laetrile *under control*. Locked down tighter 'n a tick's ass. Gotta make you wonder about all them millions of dollars from the pharmaceutical lobby, don't it? Man, I been conservative all my life, but this country's been sold for spare change. By the people we *vote* for, the sonsabitches."

"It's true," Ridley said. "This'll turn a man radical. Oh, they sell the stuff in Mexico, call it Vitamin B-17, and you can order it on the Internet. Trouble is, if you do that you don't know what you're really getting, and then there's those crackerjack assholes from the government. They got nothing else to do, what with terrorism and opioids and crime being all under control, so they set up sting operations every now and then and bust somebody who's trying to help somebody they love. I'm telling you, I wish I could spit on every politician in Washington."

"So," I said, and then I sighed. "This is all about faith."

Ridley said, "Huh?" And then he said, "Yeah. I s'pose it is. Faith is all we got."

To Madison, I said, "We're at zero."

"You may be at zero," Ridley said. "We're a lot worse off than that."

Heller said, "Now we don't even got the faith."

Madison said, "You don't know where he got the—laetrile?"

"Naw." Ridley sat on the plastic shell of the air conditioner which creaked a complaint. "We never asked. You know, after his mom died, he could make the trips and we had to—had to stay, had to take care of people here." He looked over at Heller. "Looks like we kind of took old Ferdy for granted."

"You and everybody else," Madison said. She sniffled.

Everyone looked at the floor for a minute.

"So who killed him?" I said.

"You talkin' to the wrong guys," Heller said. "If we'd known anyone was gunning for Ferdy, we'd have been with him night and day."

"Anyone in the—the co-op—lose a loved one recently?"

Ridley shifted his weight, accompanied by a new protest from the air conditioner, and squinted at the suggestion. "You mean, maybe someone got mad at Ferdy because the stuff didn't work?" He looked over at Heller, who shrugged. "Naw, naw, not that I know about. And they wouldn't be mad at Ferdy anyway. He never promised it worked, just said he thought it helped his mom. We all knew he wasn't making no money off it."

"It was a *service*," Heller said. "Everybody was grateful."

I said, "Well, shit."

"Honest to God," Madison said, "if Ferdy hadn't been strangled, I'd think someone killed him by accident. Nobody in this world wanted Ferdy dead."

Ridley nodded and said, "Word."

I said, "Maybe you're right."

40

Santa Claus Is a Committee

16:19:32. I YAWNED AND SLAPPED my watch. 4:11 AM.

Nearly eight hours gone.

"You said you didn't have any time left," Madison said. She was under the covers, fully dressed, with the sheet pulled up to her neck. "You said that at McDonald's. And you spend half your life looking at that watch. Where do you have to go?"

"Back." Using the ancient and honorable male tactic, I changed the subject and surveyed the room, my mouth pulled to one side. "Jesus, what a dump."

"I suppose we could go to my house." Madison turned on her side, punched her pillow a couple of times, and then settled back onto it. "They're obviously not much of a threat."

She was right beside me, her head on the pillow. I was sitting up but I felt her throw me a sidelong glance. "So when you said that thing about time, you meant before you go back to wherever it was?"

"That's what I mean."

"Permant—I mean, permanently?"

"Oh, I don't know." I took a deep sigh to try to shift the weight off my chest. "I have no idea."

"I see." She pulled the covers up to her nose.

"I don't mean I wouldn't *want* to come back. What I mean is, I don't know whether I can. I had help this time, and I don't know whether they'll ever be willing to help me again."

"They?"

"Two girls," I said. "Twins."

Madison closed her eyes and said, "Mmm. Twins. Lot of men have a thing about—"

"They're eleven years old," I said. "But they've been up there longer than anyone. They were remaindered around 1904. They know more about the place than anyone."

"Nineteen-oh-*four*? Who are they?"

"Patsy and Pansy Parkinson."

She shook her head. "Never heard of them."

"Written by the Stratemeyer Syndicate. A whole bunch of hacks writing under various names. They wrote Tom Swift and the Bobbseys and, I don't know, Nancy Drew—"

"Ohmigod, Nancy Drew. *The Secret of the Old Clock*. I bought a magnifying glass after I read that and made my parents let me fingerprint them with charcoal and Scotch tape. I was ten, but I disguised myself as an old man, with a white cotton beard and one of my father's sport coats and a big hat and a pair of sunglasses, and hobbled down the street."

"Fool people much?"

"First person I saw was Mrs. Sato, next door. She said, 'Hello, Madison. I didn't recognize you.' It took me half a block to identify the contradiction."

"Childhood is so cruel." I leaned heavily back against the headboard, looking up at the ceiling. "Growing up is just one disillusionment after another."

She kicked me through the covers. "How would you know?"

"Just trying to be sympathetic."

"What's with the Strate—Strate—"

"Stratemeyer."

"I thought it was Carolyn Keene."

"I hate to pile disappointment on disappointment, but Carolyn Keene and about a hundred other writers were actually a bunch of freelancers, and the Carolyn Keene who wrote most of the books was named Mildrid Wirt. I guess Carolyn Keene sounded better than Mildred Wirt."

"Well, that's bitter," Madison said. "It's like learning that Santa Claus is a committee." She scissored her legs beneath the covers. "You really *have* to go back?"

"If I want to continue to exist, I do."

Madison said, "Foo." Then she said, "When?"

"In sixteen hours and twelve minutes. And some seconds."

"Oh. How, um, how *many* seconds?"

"Seventeen. Sixteen. Fifteen."

"*Stop* that." She swallowed. "Well, you've been pretty colorful. I don't remember anyone risking their life for me before. And three times, too."

"Three?"

"Sure. In the desert, in the parking lot with that fake gun, and when you disarmed old Ruben, right here."

"He wasn't very dangerous. And my gun isn't—"

"But you didn't know that." She shifted to her left and scrabbled her fingers against my ribs through the blankets. "Aren't you ticklish?"

I'd never thought about it. "I guess not."

"Too bad. If you were ticklish and you weren't fictional, you'd be perfect. Of course, I haven't seen you drunk yet."

"It's a terrifying experience."

Madison said, "Mmmm," rolled over onto her side again, facing away from me, and sighed. I continued to examine the ceiling. One of my remaining minutes went wherever minutes go when they're finished with us.

"What do you mean, you'd cease to exist?"

"As I understand it, I literally won't be anywhere. Not there, not here. Even my books would disappear."

She didn't turn to face me. "That's kind of stiff."

"I don't even know whether it's true. But some of what they said has been."

"Non-existence. Not something to gamble with."

"No. Although it's not much fun there. It's mind-numbing, to tell you the truth."

"So that's why you came here," she said.

I found a faint stain on the ceiling and explored it with my eyes.

"Wasn't it?"

I cleared my throat. "Not entirely."

Madison waited a moment, then said, "This pillow is really lumpy."

"It, um…"

——"Yes?"

"It certainly… looks lumpy."

"Yes, well, it is, it's lumpy. It's like someone went out and found every lump on the block and put them all in here, and what *was* the other reason you came?"

I said, "You."

She started to talk, cleared her throat, and said, "Because—"

"Because I helped to get you into this mess. Because I was worried about you."

Madison said, "Ahhh."

"Because I, I saw you, and I thought, you know."

Madison said, "Ahhh" again.

"*You* know." The stain on the ceiling had exhausted its diversion value. "I saw you, and I thought, well, I'd like to get to know you. A *little*, you know, I mean, nothing—"

Madison said, "Are you *always* this awkward?"

"Yes." I reached up and touched the swelling on my forehead, very gently. "Always."

The bed bounced a little as she turned toward me, and I looked over at her and was stricken yet again by how blue her eyes were, the blue of sudden deep water. She said, "Can you see what I'm thinking?"

"No."

"That's good," she said. "Because if you could, you'd probably take advantage of me." She went after my ribs with her fingers again. "Would you *like* to take advantage of me?"

I said, "Would I ever."

"Well, as you said, you haven't got much time." She sat up and yanked her T-shirt over her head, and I stared at the pool of lamplight gleaming on the curve of her left shoulder. She folded the T-shirt neatly and said, "Are you safe?"

"I don't know why I wouldn't be. I've never been with a real person. Even if I had something, and I don't think I do, it would be, you know, fictional. You could probably cure it with a sugar pill."

"Like your gun." She brought up her knees and shoved the blankets down with her feet, then started to work on the button on her jeans. "Are you hesitating, or is this a dramatic pause?"

"I just don't know if—I don't know what the rules—well, has this ever happened before?"

She turned her head away a little bit but kept her eyes on mine. "So? What's the worst-case scenario? I give birth to semifiction? Or a novella?"

"Right," I said, getting up and pulling off my shirt.

"Come on, story boy," Madison said. "Time's wasting."

41

The Only Glimpse of Paradise
He'll Ever Get

"He was a whole new kind of heartbreak," she said. I was lying on my back, and she was curled on her side against me, her head resting on my shoulder. When she made the *h* and the *b* in the word "heartbreak," I could feel her breath on my skin, little puffs of Eden.

"It was like he was a bank that I put everything into, everything I cared about, and then one day I went to make a withdrawal and the building was gone. Just a vacant lot. And I mean everything. I'd folded up my whole life and followed him."

"From San Francisco," I said.

"How do you—right, I keep forgetting. Well, then, you already know the story."

"No. I have an impression of San Francisco, that's all."

"It's a good thing I've got a glow on, or I'd rethink this whole thing. You have a terrible advantage."

"We're not at war."

"No," she said. "That's right, isn't it?"

"You were saying you folded up your life."

She touched the side of my forehead, safely away from the swelling. "Your eyebrows are kind of bushy."

"It's an excess of male energy."

"You could shave them."

I said, "Shave them for me."

She sat up. "Would you actually let me?"

"No."

"Good." She settled back against me. "That kind of power isn't healthy."

"You folded up—"

"Okay, okay. San Fran was a counterfeit life, but it was the one I had. I wore black although though I like colors, I pretended I'd read a lot of things I hadn't read, I sneered at happy endings even though I hate sad ones, except for Balzac. I wore sunglasses at night. I drank quarts of coffee although I hated coffee back then." She pinched the skin at the side of my neck. "Do you hate coffee?"

"Go on."

"I was your basic pseudo-Berkeley girl. Hip, cool, disdainful. You know, dissatisfied with the general state of the world. It didn't live up to my superior standards. Gung ho for the rain forest and fair trade but hard on people. One hundred percent bullshit. But I think everybody else was, too."

"Cities are like giant ocean liners," I said. "People come from wherever and turn into whoever they want to be."

"Or whoever they want other people to *think* they are."

"What did you want people to think you were?"

"Just like them," she said. "Isn't that pathetic?"

* * *

I said, "Her name was—is—Eleanor." She had kicked off the blankets and turned sideways so she was lying across the bed, perpendicular to me, with the back of her head on my stomach. Seen from above, I supposed, we would have formed a human T.

"And?"

"Eleanor Chan. She's Chinese. She's smart. She's more honest than I am. Except that she's into New Age stuff."

"You're kidding."

"Well, she was in 1995. She probably would have grown out of it if we were still being written."

"Are *you*?"

"What? New Age?"

"Sure."

"No. I have enough trouble with the dimension I'm in without worrying about other ones."

"That's funny," she said. "Considering."

"Yeah, well, I formed that opinion before I changed dimensions."

"And Eleanor?"

"Eleanor's comfortable with multiple dimensions."

"That's not exactly what I was after, although I suppose it's interesting. How much longer do we have?"

I looked at the watch. "Fourteen hours and change."

"Then let's move along. Do you love her?"

"That's hard to answer. I did in the books. If I were still in a book, I probably would. I know that I can see her face with no effort at all."

"And?"

"And it kind of makes my heart ache."

For a long moment, I thought she was going to get up. Instead, she said, "We should form a club. Little black membership card with a red broken heart on it. Open a restaurant for the lovelorn. *Coffee, Tea, and Sympathy*."

"I think we're doing okay here," I said.

She nodded vigorously, digging her head into my stomach. "Two's a good number for a club."

I said, "I'm president."

"You can't be. You're fictional." She drew a deep breath and blew it out. "This isn't fair," she said.

"No," I said. "Not even close."

She reached for me.

* * *

She was lying on top of me, up on her elbows. I'd discovered a little mole, about the size of a grain of pepper, next to her right eyebrow and I was adding it to my mental map of her face.

"So I finally stopped sitting at home and waiting for the phone to ring," she said. The world on the other side of the window was beginning to pale. "And I got all dressed up and went out."

"Where?"

She shook her head, and her hair tickled my shoulder. "Who knows? Everything around here is a dump. Some dump or other. And it was maybe the third place I go, and I had maybe three Margaritas in me, and there he was in a booth with an insipid-looking blond girl with really ludicrously big tits, and she's got her arms in a knot around his neck. And he looks up and sees me and grins and shrugs his shoulders. Like, *What can I do? Just look at me.*"

"And you did what?"

"Well, I'd like to tell you that I poured a bottle of Tabasco into his Bloody Mary or aimed a swift one at his gonads, but what I really did was go home and cry all night. Like a total wuss."

"You had a right."

"And I went to work the next day with my eyes all red and puffy, and Ferdy was so sweet. We both pretended it was an allergy, but he just did everything all day. Wouldn't even let me pick up a book. When we closed up the shop, he kissed me on top of my head. Just the way my father used to."

She kissed the tip of my nose. "Actually, not like that," she said. She pulled herself up and kissed the top of my head. "More like that."

I said, "Do the first one again."

She did, and I tilted my head up at the last moment and our lips met.

"No fair," she said. Then she said, "Okay. Fair."

"So," I said. "Jake."

"Yeah. I erased him from my life, and a month or two later—" She shook her head. "Well, it was forty-nine days later. Forty-nine days later he figured I'd slipped off the hook and he called me up and gave me a huge bucket of swill about how he missed me and he couldn't sleep without me and how the bottle blond with the surgically enhanced jugs—she was just his defense because he was falling in love with me, see, and part of him was like *terrified* at the commitment."

"So he cheated because he was falling in love with you. Not very imaginative, is he?"

"It's easy to be clear and dispassionate when you're not involved. I know, it should have been like getting a BEWARE card in the mail—why aren't there BEWARE cards? They've got cards for everything else. At least a BEWARE card would be *useful*. But no one sent me one, and I fell for it all over again, which is really embarrassing to have to admit, and he got me all wound up and thinking about, I don't know, monogrammed pillowcases and new china, and then he did it again."

"Dumped you."

"Right on my butt, in the middle of the desert. And I went in and poured my heart out to Ferdy, and it never even occurred to me that he—you know—*felt* something for me. And now Jake is making his third move. And Ferdy's gone." She pulled a pillow over and rolled off me. She said, "Nothing is right."

"Forget about Jake. You're the only glimpse of paradise he'll ever get."

She lifted herself up and looked down at me. "Did you write that?"

"Far as I know."

"Well," she said. "It's very nice." She fluttered her lashes against the side of my neck. "But there's still Ferdy."

I said, "I'm pretty sure I know what happened to Ferdy."

PAGES FROM A COMPLETELY DIFFERENT NOVEL

(2)

The last quarter of an inch was the longest distance Elen had ever traveled.

It took an endless two minutes, the Old Man struggling and striking backwards with his elbows, kicking back with the silver spurs on his boots, until Elen's fingertips met at the front of the Old Man's throat.

Elen felt the air around him condense and thicken, and energy flowed from it into his arms and shoulders, and with a from-the-toes grunt of effort, he lifted the Old Man straight up by the throat. Two inches, four inches—

"I'll—I'll give you the world,*" the old man cried, his voice a strangled rasp.*

"And I'll make it worth having," Elen said, lifting the Old Man another inch, "by removing you from it."

And then he heard himself screaming as he raised the Old Man higher, and the Old Man kicked back, his rowelled spur gouging a line of fire across Elen's leg and...

Rowelled? *Rowelled?* One "l" or two? What the hell does "rowelled" mean? What's a "rowel?"

Okay, Google, do your—ah. *A sharp-toothed wheel inserted into the shank of a spur.* Where did I learn that? I've never worn a spur in my—

... and, the Voice said.

"Sorry," Hallinan said out loud. The moment his fingertips touched the keys...

...and Elen's scream scaled up into a shriek, and once again the air thickened and filled him with strength, and he lifted the

strangling man to the highest point Elen could reach, his arms fully upraised, and then let them drop: one foot, two feet, and STOP. *The Old Man's spurs jingled another six or eight inches of descent, but Elen heard the snap and the Old Man's head stopped exactly where Elen's arms had. His neck was suddenly eight inches long.*

A last choked sigh, an obscene parody of a cough, and Elen separated his hands.

The Old Man fell, dead weight, to the edge of the flat table rock, and the wind caught his black cape and swirled it up into an ebony spiral and then dropped it over the crumpled form. For a moment, as Elen looked down at it, it seemed as though the Old Man moved beneath the black cloth, and that he was moving more than four limbs, but then the wind died and the crumpled form beneath the cape was still.

The power left Elen as suddenly as it had come, and he let his head drop forward and his shoulders slump. For a minute or two he stood there, spent and gasping, until he could no longer prevent himself from turning and looking at the thing behind him.

It, too, was hidden by a cape, but this was a white cape, brilliant and unblemished, too pristine, too innocent, to hide the tragedy beneath it. One hand protruded, fingers open and loosely curled, as though raised in benediction.

A blessing.

As Elen studied it, his eyes grew wet. He blinked away the tears, feeling the space open beneath his heart, the core of dark emptiness he knew he would carry for the rest of his life. He could not force himself to go to the fallen form, to lift the cape, to look at the face he knew as well as he knew his own.

From this point on, he thought, he would be only half of himself.

A hot tongue of fury licked his spine, hot and forked and pointed, and he whirled to the fallen man beneath the black cape, raised a leg, and kicked with all his strength. The body rolled a foot, and he followed and kicked it again, and this time as it rolled he saw the pale

*blue eyes, open and unmoving but—he would have sworn—looking
directly at him. His kick this time was as much panic as hatred, and
at last the Old Man rolled to the edge of the table rock and over it,
and Elen went to the edge and saw the black cape flare out and then,
from above him, he felt the darkness solidify into giant black hawks
that plummeted past, met by others flying up from beneath; and before the dead man was halfway to the stones a quarter of a mile below, he was already the falling center of a tangled knot of feasting
hawks.*

Well, he thought. Where did the birds come from? And if I
was going to strangle him, why was I screwing around with all
those swords? His eyes on the screen, he reached for his wineglass,
but his fingers closed on air.

And he thought, *Right. I spilled it.*

There it was, right where he had left it, at the edge of the
desk. The bottle, mostly empty, stood next to the Catty, and as
he reached over to pick it up, he suddenly remembered what
happened when he spilled the wine, the soaking manuscript, the
spreading stain, and without even realizing it, he leaped to his
feet. Hadn't he quit? Hadn't he gone upstairs?

The Ambien. It had to be the Ambien. He licked his lips,
which were suddenly dry.

But the spill had been cleaned up, the wine-soaked pages
blotted and fanned neatly out, their red-stained margins exposed
to the air to dry. If not for the smell of the room, the stickiness of
the floor, and the burgundy bloom along the edges of those
pages, no one would know he—

He was loaded, that was it. He'd gone to bed drunk and
popped the Ambien in the hope it would drown out the Voice,
and he must have gotten up, floating in the center of a cloud of
Ambien and alcohol, and come back in here and mopped up—

Had he ever left *anything* as neat and precise as that fan of
pages?

But he was the only one here. Of course, he was. And it wasn't as though he hadn't experienced Ambien episodes before. He'd apparently phoned his former editor a few months back and told her exactly what he thought about her butchery, years before, of *The Bone Polisher*, the last published Simeon, and her refusal even to read *The Wrong End of the Rainbow*.

He had no memory of the call, but she'd recorded part of it on her answering machine and turned it over to the cops, and they'd contacted the San Bernardino Sheriff's office, and he'd had a very uncomfortable couple of hours at the station.

So. He had taken—taken the Ambien, gone to sleep, gotten up too loaded to remember it now, and cleaned up, and gone back to bed. Then he'd gotten up again, still loaded, and come back here and written all of this, which was pretty much the end of the book, minus a little trumpet flourish, some kind of affirmation as the hero exits to pursue the rest of his adventures in the sequel.

That's right, there's going to be a sequel.

The room still smelled of red wine. He sniffed his hands. They didn't.

That just meant he'd washed his hands.

Of course, it did. He just didn't recall it. But look at that language. *The falling center of a tangled knot of feasting hawks.* Had he written those words, with those two clunky *ofs*?

Of course, he had. Just now, right? He remembered keying them in.

He bypassed the empty glass, picked up the bottle, and drank from it.

What he didn't remember was *thinking them up.*

But the Voice, he thought. The Voice said…

And something cold began to spread in his stomach.

Was it *all* shit? Was it all as bad as "the falling center of a tangled knot of feasting hawks?"

And then some time must have passed, because the next thing he knew, he was back in his chair, his nose six inches from the screen, saying the words on the page aloud, hearing the thud of the bad ones, the ring of the good ones, and the manuscript had begun to assert its magic again, to weave the spell that had kept him there, bent over the keyboard for all those weeks. The *Stardark* world opened itself to him again, wet and cold and turbulent, sunlight glinting on wet stone, the sky darker than the one here, darker than the desert sky ever was, and beneath it were black hawks and enormous white wolves and an Old Man who could make and destroy worlds.

And a hero, a vulnerable hero who ends the story almost mortally wounded by the loss of his dearest friend, the person who has shared his journey for as long as he can remember. Leaving him there, still as the ageless stone itself, beneath that gleaming cape.

Outside the window, the sun began to rise *over the edge of the world,* he wrote, *and struck the white cape, turning it so bright it burned in Elen's eyes, and he had to step back and raise a hand to shield his vision until the steel returned to his spine and he lowered the hand and looked at the starburst of color that swirled up from the cape, a whirlwind of pale hues that seemed to flutter and lift the cape, and there it was.*

His face.

His eyes were open, as new and shadowless as a baby's, looking straight up at the center of the sky, like someone who has just discovered a rainbow through a window. Elen scrubbed his cheeks with his forearm and slowly knelt, and as he did so, something rolled out from beneath the spotless white cape, round and winking as bright as the sun itself.

The Mirror of Tomorrow. A final gift.

Elen rose and went to his fallen friend. He tugged the cape gently over the beautiful face and picked up the mirror. He slipped the mirror into the pocket of his jerkin...

Jerkin? What the hell is a—

... and turned to the abyss that had devoured the Old Man. He raised his arms as though in salute to the high stones, and called out, "Come. Come and take him. A warrior awaits you."

The words banged off the stones, and his shadow faded as the hawks gathered overhead, thousands of them, loosing shrill cries as cold as frozen wind, and as they circled, creating a black death's head against the dead gray sky, he began his descent to the broad valley and its glistening river, far, far below.

One *far* or two? Two. More final. Could he get away with three?

No. He tilted the bottle and emptied it into his mouth as he considered it again, rejected it again.

That personal pronoun. Why not just change it and look at it? What harm could it—

He put the cursor in front of "he" and...

... and heard a noise from overhead. Something or someone upstairs.

But there *was* no one upstairs. He touched the keyboard again and heard whispering on the stairs, and then he was up, his back to the screen, his arms prickling with gooseflesh, looking through the darkened door to the hallway, the only light available the one burning on the desk behind him and the watery sunrise framed in the window.

He hadn't breathed, he realized, in a minute or more. He released the air in his lungs as quietly as he could, and then he heard it again. A quiet whisper, quickly shushed.

What would Simeon do? A weapon, find a weapon.

He took the bottle by its neck, swinging it experimentally twice to make sure he could keep hold of it, ignoring the red arc of wine spilling through the air, and then edged toward the door.

The door led into the hallway, still dark. The stairs were on his left, and to his right was the front door.

The plan wasn't much, but it came quickly. Edge his way to the door and then break through it at an angle to the right, looking up the stairs as he ran, and if anything was up there that couldn't—couldn't be *dealt with*—keep going to the front door and through it, into the street.

At least he'd remembered to put his robe on.

By the time he reached the door to the hall, breathing hard, he realized that he didn't *remember* remembering to put his robe on, and that there had been several times lately when he'd lost whole pieces of time, found himself somewhere—in his car, twice or maybe three times, with no idea how he'd gotten there.

What in the *world* was happening to him?

Whispers, sounding like rats' claws in dry paper.

And he tossed his plan and bolted for the front door. He was almost all the way to it before he saw that no one was on the stairs, and then someone began to pound on the door from outside, hard enough to wake the woman across the street.

The wood frame of the door splintered.

part four

the clock

42

Bottled Light

THE CURVE OF HER UPPER LIP was a map of heartbreak.

Look at it long enough, I thought, and give up all possibility of ever being content with a life that doesn't have her in it.

She slept on her back with her head slightly to one side, the rough chop of hair baring enough of her face for me to commit it to memory, which, it seemed, was the only way I'd be able to keep her with me. I lingered again over the tiny upward curl at the corners of her mouth, as though she'd just thought of a joke, the smooth warm tones of her skin, the fine flare of her nostrils. One hand was raised beside her face, its palm pale and impossibly vulnerable. Her hair was smashed flat on one side, and I thought, *I know how it got that way*, and the thought flowed through me on a current of something I hadn't felt in a long time: happiness.

Above the ragged fringe of her lashes, Madison's eyes moved slightly beneath her lids. Dream time.

The light through the window was dishwater gray, the color of the world outside. I hadn't slept; my weariness had abandoned me as we made love and talked. It had moved on to plague someone more susceptible, leaving me awake, alert, and deeply conflicted.

What *would* happen if I stayed? Would I really disappear? I remembered Patsy's assurances about the window, her laughter as the glass broke. Still, if the twins were telling the truth—about, in fact, *anything*—would disappearing forever be *worse* than going

back up there to that shack, confined to the geography of my
books, to the endless company of benched and embittered private
eyes, to dead villains materializing in the fog, to a hawk-shaped
hole in the sky?

God, I was sick of detectives. Sick of my life up there. Truth
be told, sick of myself.

But I had to go back. Didn't I?

I took a long, deep breath and a short personal survey. Here I
was in this crappy motel at 6:11 AM, with a little more than thirteen hours to go, trying to rekindle my detective skills in this cac-
tus-strewn moonscape, trying to figure out how to trap a murder-
er as the red digits flashed their *hurry-up*, and the most beautiful
girl in the world slept beside me. The girl I couldn't take with
me.

The *real* girl.

In the real world.

Slowly, carefully, trying not to jostle her, I sat up and focused
on the cold strip of light beneath the room's door. Assuming that
the twins were being honest, at least about the time limit, and
that the red digits were accurate, I had until an hour or two after
dark that night to figure it out, to avenge Ferdy and—and what?
And make everything all right for Madison?

Who the hell did I think I was? She didn't need me for that.
As it turned out, she didn't even need rescuing. While I'd felt
briefly that I'd helped her up in the Monument, in fact, it probably would have been simpler if they'd just caught her. Real des-
perados, those two.

Madison would be fine. *I* was the one who was in trouble he
didn't even understand.

Which brought me face to face with the big one: the writer.

Hallinan was *here*. *Quelle* coincidence.

Al Hammond, like every other fictional cop ever written, was
fond of saying, "There's no such thing as coincidence." And—

since, in a mystery novel, coincidence is a no-no on the same scale as identical twins—he was always right. So it wasn't a coincidence that I found myself a couple of miles from my writer. It was an *arrangement*.

And I knew who was behind it. But that wasn't the same thing as knowing why I had been set up.

Or, for that matter, knowing what to do next.

So there were two possible ways to spend this day. One was to take some money from Madison's purse, go down, pay for another night, send out for food, and just lose the last hours of my—well, *life*, I supposed—exploring the soft surface of being in love. See whether I could assemble a mental graph of her fragrances. As I recalled it, sitting there with my mouth open so I couldn't cheat and take a sniff, that graph would be a long, smooth curve with a couple of memorable spikes. The data cried out for refinement. I thought it might simplify things if I just slipped beneath the covers again and held her until her eyes opened, to see what they would look like at the moment she remembered she was with me.

Then, assuming she didn't scream or push me away, do it. Stay with her until the last minute or two, then kiss her goodbye, walk into the desert and...

Pop. Gone.

Or.

Or get up, get dressed, and go out into the thin, shitty light of the new day and figure out whether I was anywhere near right about what it meant that Hallinan was here.

I had, after all, lost a reader. When a detective's reader is killed, he's supposed to do something about it. It doesn't make any difference what you thought of him. He was your reader and you're supposed to do something about it.

"Jesus," I said out loud. "That's *The Maltese Falcon*. Enough fiction."

Madison said something fuzzy to whoever was lucky enough

to be in her dream, and I sat there, looking down at her, feeling my resolve wane. She was wheat, she was wine, she was bottled light, she was everything that wasn't on the other side of that door. She wasn't unanswered questions and murder and people lying and the eternal dust and grit of the desert. She wasn't hard light on shiny cars or the greased-air halos of fried food or the road-howl of jacked-up truckers pushing sixteen-wheelers east and west.

And she wasn't my life up there, either.

She was here, and I was here. And I'd never be here again.

Why go back?

But Ferdy. *When a detective's reader is killed—*

"Okay," I said out loud. "Try to solve it and then, I guess, we'll see whether I go or stay."

Madison said, "But first," and reached up and pulled me down. I was off-balance, and I put an arm down so I wouldn't fall on her.

Madison said, "Fall on me, silly."

43

Nobody's Perfect

THE MINUTE WE WALKED INTO the restaurant, a waitress with a preposterous beehive looked at me, widened her eyes, scurried between Madison and me, and led her away like a cowboy cutting a calf out of a herd. They were whispering, so I figured I wasn't supposed to hear it and headed for the empty table at the window. I turned to ask Madison whether this was the right one and caught the waitress as she shook her fingers as though she'd touched something hot, and Madison laughed, leaned over and kissed her cheek.

As they neared the table, the waitress was saying, "… tell me this is breakfast and you just got out of—"

"It is," Madison said. "And I'm *starving*."

"Any carpet burns?"

"No. We had furniture."

The waitress caught me listening and went as red as a stoplight. "Well, I hate you," she said to Madison. "But sit down, and I'll bring you a menu."

"We don't need a—"

"Just shut up. I'm going to come back for another look at—" The waitress cut herself off in mid-word as I pulled out a chair for Madison.

"Oh my God," the waitress said, grabbing Madison's sleeve. "Is that for you?"

"Every inch of it," Madison said.

Corrine said, "I meant the chair."

"The chair's for me, too." Madison threw me a smile and the waitress struck out for the kitchen with a last glance back at me, one eye much smaller than the other, a pirate's grimace with a warning behind it: *Treat her right.*

"Friend of yours?"

"Sympathizer," Madison said.

I watched the men in the Merry Go Round watch Madison. This was new and familiar at the same time. Men in the books had always watched Eleanor. Not that Eleanor wasn't worth...

Madison said, "Pay attention to me. And don't shine any more brightly than is absolutely necessary. Desert women are fierce and predatory."

"Oh, good," I said. "You can fight over me." I sat down and looked around the room. "This is nice."

"Calm on the surface," Madison said, "but a seething cauldron of repressed emotion roils beneath."

"Wow. Do they have sourdough?"

"I think if you smile at Corrine, she'll run to the back and bake some. But don't."

"Who's Corrine?"

"The waitress. The one with the beehive from The Museum of Hair."

"She's pretty."

Madison leaned back in her chair. "I'm too satisfied to rise to that. What do you want?"

"Two eggs, sunny side, double bacon, sourdough bread, and hash browns burned. Coffee coffee coffee."

"Good." She watched Corrine tucking menus under her arm for the return trip. "Now go to the bathroom."

"I don't need to go to the bathroom."

She sat forward and picked up her knife and fork, holding them vertically. "Go take a fictional tinkle."

"Got it." I got up and headed past her, aiming at the sign that said *Longhorns*, which I figured was more appropriate for me than the one that said *Heifers*. I took a last look back just as Madison and Corrine turned in unison to look at me. I waved and went in.

* * *

"Where did you *find* him?" Corrine said. "If he'd been here longer than twenty-four hours, I'd have him tied up at my house."

"I've been keeping him indoors."

"Gosh, I hope nobody spits in your food."

"I met him in the Monument last night."

"Only last night? You move fast." She looked back at the direction Simeon had taken, and said, "He's so fine he should leave a sort of smear on the air, like perfume, but better."

"And visible." Madison picked up the menus unopened and handed them back to her. "He'd like the heart-stopper breakfast with the hash-browns burned. And sourdough."

"A guy. A real guy. No quinoa?"

"And an extra side of bacon."

Corrine fanned herself with her order pad. "Be still, my heart."

"And he's in a hurry."

"Well, of course he is. Nothing good lasts." She flipped the pad shut and said, "And speaking of nothing good." She wheeled around and headed toward the kitchen.

"You've got a glow this morning," Jake said, pulling out the chair.

"Someone's sitting there."

"Sure. I am. No coffee?"

"Jake," she said, "I am not kidding. Someone is sitting there. Go away."

"I'll just keep it warm." His face went all earnest. "Madison, we need to talk." He dumped earnest and turned to look for Corrine.

"She's not going to pay any attention to you. And neither am I."

Jake shrugged and turned back to her. "So. What about the news, huh?"

"What news?"

He gave her a skeptical glance. "You don't know?"

"If I knew, would I have asked?"

"Wow." He tilted back in the chair. "Can't believe you haven't heard. Where you been?"

"Well, Jake," Madison said, carefully unfolding her napkin and giving it all her attention. "If you must know, I've been in a cheap motel, getting my little pink socks fucked off."

* * *

Since I hadn't actually needed to visit the bathroom, I was close enough to hear that last remark, and by the time she got to the punch line, I was only about three feet behind Jake.

The front legs of his chair hit the floor with a *crack*. He said, "You wish."

"Honestly, you seem to think your equipment is unique," Madison said. "Or even moderately different."

Jake's hand on the table curled into a fist. "You met somebody?"

"What's the news? You mean, about Ferdy?"

"Fuck that." Jake pushed the chair back and started to rise, but stopped.

"Don't leave on my account," I said, one hand on Jake's shoulder. "You must be Mr. Blue Jeans."

"*This* guy?" Jake said, craning up at me. "Je*sus*."

"News?" I said, leaning in to him. "You have news?"

"I wasn't talking to you, faggot." He started to get up. "Far as I'm concerned—"

When Jake's jeans-clad butt was about six inches from the

seat of his chair, I threw a short, fast punch with the heel of my right hand, barely visible from a few tables away. It hit Jake hard on the side of his neck, snapping his head to one side, and he went over, taking the chair with him. I bent down, righted the chair, put one of its legs in the center of Jake's abdomen, and knelt on it, extending a helping hand.

"Sorry, sorry," I said. "Floor's really slick. Let me help you up." I grabbed his wrist and pulled Jake upward, putting even more weight on the chair. "Here, just hold on." Jake let out an agonized squeal as the chair's leg sank into his solar plexus. "What was the news?"

"Arrested," Jake said. "Get off—"

"Who? Who was arrested?"

"Some—some *writer.*"

"Really." I took my knee off the chair and picked it up. "Are you going to leave, or am I going to split your head open?"

"I'm going." Jake got up, his face rigid. "But you and me—"

"You and I," I said. "Five-thirty this evening. Just tell me where."

"Vacant lot," Jake said, dusting himself off. "Behind the Smoke Tree."

"You got it. You good to drive?"

Jake said to Madison, "We're not finished," and stalked out of the restaurant with everybody in the room staring at him. They all watched him through the window. Just before he got into his car, he flipped me—and, I supposed, Madison—the bird.

Madison said to the restaurant at large, "Really. You're not seeing him at his best."

I made sure the car was actually pulling out of the lot rather than coming in through the window before I let myself think about what he'd said. "What time is it?"

"You're the one with the watch."

"Right." I sat and looked around the restaurant. People went back to their food. "What's he look like?"

"Who?"

"Hallinan."

"I've never seen him. You mean *you* don't know what he looks like?"

"No. I mean, he probably looks like me, but not as handsome."

"Please tell me you didn't actually say what I heard—"

"No, no," I said, waving the remark away. "That's what everybody says about writers who work in the first person. Their characters look like them, but better." I looked for the waitress. "Isn't there coffee?"

"Coming. What kind of better?"

"More fit, more attractive. Younger. Better hair. Taller. And that means—" I broke off, running through what I'd just said.

"That means—"

"That means he doesn't have big feet. If he's shorter than I am, there's no way he has feet like the ones I saw."

She put her chin on her hand, looked at him, and then out through the window. "I liked it better in the motel."

"Me, too. But here we are. And here it comes."

Corrine glided across the room, coffeepot in hand. Madison noted that she'd refreshed her eye makeup.

"Sorry to keep you waiting," Corrine cooed. "You look like you could use a nice strong cup of—"

I was already getting up. "Sorry, can we get it to go? And some tea for the lady. She'll pay."

Corrine said, "I'll *bet* she will."

"He's only got play money," Madison said.

"So?" Corrine said. "Nobody's perfect."

* * *

OUT TO LUNCH, the sign read. SIT, PUT YOUR FEET UP, AND IMAGINE THEM IN A NEW PAIR OF BOOTS. The sign was hanging from a nail on the door, and beside the door was a rough wooden bench with a railing in front of it, presumably to help would-be customers visualize their new footwear.

"This the only place?"

"Burt's is it in the boot world, within twenty or thirty miles."

I said, "Where are we, exactly?"

"We're in the center of nowhere. Or, to put it another way, pretty much next door to the Pack Rat. Where I work."

I looked down the highway, which was rippling in the heat. The sign above the rundown house eight or ten yards away said THE PACK RAT. "Let's go."

"It's closed."

"Good. You have a key, right? That's how you got in when that cop was there."

"Sure." She followed me down the two warped wooden steps from the porch of the Boot Barn. "But why?"

"Look at the scene of the crime," I said. The sun hit me like a hammer. "Jesus. Is it like this every day?"

"No, some days it's hot." She made her voice deeper. "*Look at the scene of the crime*," she said, and then she grabbed my arm and said, "*Hold* it." A truck, longer than the Macy's Thanksgiving Day parade, roared by at about seventy miles per hour. The backwash slapped us, a hot, malodorous wave. She said, "I won't turn my back on one of those things." We crunched through a couple of inches of gravel that had been spread over the roadside in front of the two stores. Before we got to The Pack Rat, she cut to the right, around the store. "It'll be better if we go in through the back door."

"Why?"

"Because I already tore the crime scene tape on that door."

"My kind of girl."

I was following her through a kind of undergrowth that looked like it evolved on a planet called Scurrilon. "Look out for chollas."

"What are—*ow*." I leaned down, but Madison grabbed my arm.

"Don't touch it, you'll make it worse. I know how to get them out. I think."

"Son of a *bitch*," I said, looking down at the spike sticking out of my jeans.

"That's a jumping cholla. They don't really jump, but that's about all they don't do. Now, do you think you can get to the back door alive?"

I yanked the spine. "*That* door?"

"That door." She looked at the spine in my hand and sighed.

"Piece of cake." I dropped the spine and headed for the door, and she followed. "Is there a big mean dog?" I asked. "If there's a big mean dog, maybe you should go first."

"No dog."

"Well, then," I said, putting a hand out for her to drop her keys into, "let the man lead the way. You just hang back where you'll be safe." I pulled the door open, but she had her hand on my shoulder.

"Wait a minute," she said, turning me to her. She took hold of both my ears, pulled my face down, and kissed me. "I'm already crazy about you," she said. "You don't have to work at it."

"That's a relief. I was flailing, with only one cup of coffee." I pulled the door all the way open, then leaned down and returned the kiss, and stepped aside. "Lead on."

The air in the shop was hot, dry, dusty, and yellow with the sun through the faded newspapers taped to the windows. She led me out of the back room and down a short corridor to another one, larger and dimmer.

"In there."

I could see the outline on the floor. The room was darker in person than it had been during the Seeing. "Where were you standing when you found him?"

"Pretty much where you are."

"Come in through the front or the back?"

"The back. We—Ferdy and I—park on the street behind the shop. So there's room for customers in front. I walked right past him when I came in."

"Was the back door locked?"

She was rubbing the skin on her forearms. "Yes."

"And the front door?"

"Locked. I had to open it when the police arrived."

"Okay." I went into the room and stood at the far end of the taped outline, approximately where Ferdy's feet would have been. Then I lifted my hands, open and flat, to frame what I was seeing.

"What are you doing?"

"This is about as much as I could see, looking up through the book. I'm trying to figure out which way I was looking."

"Why?"

"Because the guy who strangled Ferdy came from behind. I want to know where he was." With my hands still cupping my eyes, I turned slowly left to right.

Madison said, "I figured he came in through the door."

I lowered my hands. "No. This is the angle I saw. He came from behind these shelves." I turned to face her.

Madison said, "Then Ferdy followed him in?"

"No. I think the killer was already here."

She shook her head. "How do you know?"

"I was *watching*. Ferdy thought he was alone. He was reading, silently. He had no idea anyone else was in here."

Madison looked at the bookshelf and shuddered. "Then that means—"

"Right. It means Ferdy didn't let him in. And Ferdy sure as hell didn't lock the door after the killer left. Who has keys?"

"Ferdy, me. Henry, he's the owner. Probably Mrs. Henry."

"Were Ferdy's keys here when you found him?"

"Yes. The cop took them. And his spares were under the counter. They're still in my purse."

"And you're positive both doors were locked when you came in."

"Sure." She looked behind her as though she expected someone to be there. "So somebody else had a key?"

"Either that," I said, "or it was someone who didn't need a key."

"Didn't need—" Her cell phone rang. She dug through the purse and pulled it out.

"Wow, what a cute little phone," I said, staring at it.

"Boy," Madison said. "Have *you* missed a lot. Hello?" She glanced up at me, mouthed the word *police*, and hit speaker. "Yes, yes it is, how are you, Detective Basset?"

"Barnes," the cop said over the speaker as I started to laugh. "Listen, Miss Jefferson, I know you've been worried, so I'm calling to tell you we have a suspect in custody."

I made the gesture for pulling taffy, which means the same thing everywhere: *stretch it out.*

"I'm sorry," she said as I squeezed past her and headed for the front of the shop. "You were breaking up. Can you say that again?" She followed me in as I rummaged under the counter and came up with a pen and a pad.

"I said we got the guy we think killed your friend. I remembered you were a little jumpy."

"Well, that's *so* sweet of you. What a thoughtful thing to do." She made a little circular *hurry-up* signal with her index finger as I scribbled. "The first time I saw you, I thought, this is an unusually sensitive policeman. Big brown eyes, like a—like a, uh, very sensitive—"

I held up the pad, on which I'd written, *How do they know?*

"Well, what I *mean* to say," Madison said, interrupting herself, "is why do you think this person did it? How do you know that—"

"We've got an eyewitness," Barnes said, and I started writing again. Madison came up and stood beside him me as I scribbled. "The witness saw the perp—I mean, the suspect—going into the shop about five minutes after you left. And then, about five minutes later, hurry back out. Said he was really kicking up dust."

I tilted the pad toward her. *Witness? Name? Description?*

"Who's this witness?"

"Sorry, Miss Jefferson. That's not something I can discuss."

"Well... vegetable? Mineral? Female? Big or—"

"What difference does it make?"

I was writing again.

"Oh, just—" Madison squeezed her eyes shut. "You know, small town and all that. Just wondered whether it was anyone I—"

The pad said, *Does he know where witness is now?*

Madison grimaced and covered the phone. "How can I ask—"

"Ask," I said.

She swallowed loudly and dived in. "Golly, I can't tell you how much I appreciate this. But listen, I mean, if there's only one witness, well, umm, I don't want to seem like a worry wart or anything, but if anything happened to that witness. I mean, what I *mean*, is do you know where the witness is right now?"

She closed her eyes and shook her head as the silence stretched out.

"Let me get this straight," Barnes said. "Are you asking me where my witness is?"

"Where your—oh, *no*." She tried a light little laugh but it sounded as dry as someone flipping pages. "No, no, *no*. I don't want to know where he—she, it—is. I was just making sure that *you* know. Since I've been worried and all, just wondered, you know? Where he or she. Is. I mean."

Barnes said slowly, "That's a very interesting question."

"Is it?" She fanned herself with her free hand. "I'm sure you're just being nice."

"Not at all. In fact, I think maybe we should have another chat. Where are you?"

"You mean, now?"

I made a slitting gesture across my throat.

"I'm on the way somewhere," Madison said. "Tell you what. I'll—I'll call you when I get there."

She tapped the phone with an index finger, hard enough to bend a nail. "Well," she said, shaking her hand in the air, "*that* was good, I mean, I'm practically a suspect now."

"His witness has disappeared," I said. "Let's go. Time to buy some boots."

44

Bigfoot Wants a Pair of Boots

"HEY, LOOKIT," THE LEATHERY GUY behind the counter said, glancing up from the boot he was polishing. "It's Little Miss Sherlock."

The scent of shoe polish was so overpowering it made the whole room look brown. I left Madison to talk to Burt while I wandered the aisles, trying to make sense out of things. Their conversation sputtered a couple of times before catching, like an outboard engine.

Well, well. They seemed to make cowboy boots out of pretty much everything anyone could put a heel on. Lizard, snake, rawhide, ostrich, eel, unborn calf, patent leather, a few with feathers. Some had two-inch heels, some had four-inch heels, some had spike heels, and some looked like they were designed for a woman to wear while riding Helmut Newton around on a bed of nails. I saw spurs, I saw steel tips, I saw tips that had been gold-plated.

"Who buys the patent-leather ones?" I called over the tops of the shelves.

"Well, that was a surprise," Burt said. "Fella who come up with them, he figured they'd be good for the ladies, back when evvybody was line-dancing, you remember line-dancing?"

"He missed it," Madison said. "He's from France."

"Voolay voo, huh? So anyways, turned out line-dancing didn't last any longer than any other stupid dance, and the boots get sold mostly to guys who come up from West Hollywood.

They got themselves a posse, The Riders of the Lavender Sage. It marches in some big parade every year."

I tried to find a response and settled for "Huh."

"He's the tall, silent type," Madison said.

Burt said, "He ain't that tall."

"He makes up for it," Madison said, "by being extremely silent. Really, Simeon, don't you have anything to ask good old Burt here?"

"I'm thinking," I said. I heard the conversation sputter some more, while I looked at boots and thought, *Gloves.*

I was certain I knew the general shape of what was happening but I couldn't get it right-side up. It was like trying to put on a pair of gloves in the dark. First, they're inside-out and your fingers won't slide in. Then you get one right-side out but it's on the wrong hand. Finally coax it onto the right hand, grab another and put it on, and the light goes on and you see you're standing in front of a box of gloves, all different colors, and you're wearing a red one and a white one. Then the light goes out again. "Gloves," I said out loud.

"Nope," Burt said. "Boots." Madison was looking at me as though she couldn't quite remember why we were together.

"Right, boots. What's the biggest size you carry?"

"Twelve triple-E," Burt said. "But that's only in the *real* boots, you know, workin' boots. You're not going to find them in patent leather."

"Real *men's* boots," Madison said.

Burt made a little pistol with his hand and shot Madison with it. "You got yourself a smart one here," he said to me.

Madison gave him her sweetest smile. "And we're so *rare.*"

"So," I said, "if you get Bigfoot in here and Bigfoot wants a pair of boots, what do you do?"

"Special order," Burt said. "Cash in advance, 'cause you can't just turn around and sell a pair of seventeen extra-wides."

"I'll bet," I said. "Sold any lately?"

Burt rubbed the boot in his lap. "You playin' Sherlock, too?"

"I'll take that as a yes." I went down the aisle toward the counter. "Madison, give the nice man twenty dollars."

Burt said, "What for?"

"For answering the question."

Burt shook his head. "Keep your money. Had a special order about six weeks ago."

"When did he pick up the boots?"

"'Bout four days ago."

"What size?"

"Biggest I ever seen." Burt shook his head in bootsy wonder. "Eighteen five-E. Cost a fortune. Ain't no machine last for a boot that big."

"I'll bet not. Big guy, huh?"

"That's the funny part," Burt said.

A few moments went by, and Madison said, "I've been a while between laughs."

"Not so big," Burt said. "Guy said they were a present. Wasn't any bigger'n you are."

"What did he look like?" I'd finally reached the counter, and I saw Madison's downward glance and realized that my fists were tightly balled.

Burt looked me up and down. "Looked kinda like you."

* * *

"You *knew* that," Madison said. "I watched your face. You knew what he was going to say."

"Well, that doesn't mean I know what to do about it." We were sitting in Madison's car with the windows down, waiting for the temperature inside to drop.

"I like to kid myself that I'm mildly smart," she said, "but I have no idea what train of thought you're following."

"And you wouldn't if you'd worked on it for a month. You haven't got the frame of reference." I looked at the watch, and it said 1:50. I slapped it, but the red digits didn't come up. *That* was interesting, but I'd have to hold it for later. "Damn, we've lost a lot of time." I closed my eyes against the monotony of the view and tried to calculate. "A little more than six hours left."

Madison said, "Oh." She didn't say it very loudly. She looked down at her lap. Then she said, "What's wrong with my frame of reference?"

"You're not fictional. All of this, every bit of it, from Ferdy on, it's all about a book."

"A book."

"Yeah. Where does he live?"

"What book?"

I said, "You haven't read it. Nobody's read it."

"Where does *who* live?"

"My writer."

"Wait, wait. He just got arrested. And... *oh*, he bought those boots."

"He did. Do you know where he lives?"

"Joshua Tree."

I yanked the door closed. She was behind the wheel. "Let's go."

"Joshua Tree is a *town*. I don't know where he lives in the town, Ferdy just said Joshua—"

"Well, we'll be closer to finding out where it is when we're there than we are here, right?"

"Boy," she said as she started the car, "if that's a sample of your dialogue, I'm sticking to Balzac."

* * *

The printer made its whisk-broom sound and another page slid out, face-down.

The person in the office chair took the page and turned it text-side up, scanned it for a moment, and then put it on top of the neat stack on the near left corner of the desk. The stack was almost three inches tall now.

Lying open beside the chair was a dark green plastic trash bag. The fumes of red wine emerged from it, and just visible on the bottom was a thick pile of paper—maybe four or five drafts of a novel. The one on top was stained with burgundy blotches.

Both of the two-drawer file cabinets on the wall to the right of the table gaped open. Three of the drawers were packed with paper, so tightly the files stood upright. The fourth was half empty, the files at the front of the drawer lying flat, those toward the back still vertical.

Someone was walking in the room overhead.

Another page slid out, and it, too, was pulled out, flipped, scanned, and added to the stack. The person in the chair picked up the stack, held it tightly by the left margin, and fanned the stack from the right, first quickly and then more slowly. The third time, the fanning was stopped in several places and each time an empty page was pulled from the manuscript. The blanks were crumpled and dropped into the trash bag.

Another page slid out, and the person behind the desk said something rude about the printer's lack of speed.

A telephone began to ring in another room, the living room, from the sound of it. The person sitting at the desk paid no attention to it.

It rang for a long time.

The person upstairs kept walking.

45

Darker Than It Should Have Been

"NO ANSWER," MADISON SAID. I slapped my watch again. "What did that thing ever do to you?"

"It's what it's not doing. It's not counting down anymore." I looked up and then around. "Where are we?"

"In Joshua Tree," Madison said. "Looking for your writer."

"I know what we're doing," I said. "I just wasn't sure where we were doing it." I held up the wrist with the watch on it. "This worries me."

"Maybe it means you don't have to go back."

"I doubt it's that benign. So, what the owner of the Pack Rat —"

"Henry," Madison said.

I nodded. "Thank you. No detail is too irrelevant. What *Henry* had was a phone number, not an address."

"Yes."

"If I were in a book," I said, "I could just go into a phone booth and look it up in the phone book."

"A phone what?"

"Book."

"No, the other one."

"Booth, a phone booth. You don't seem to have any these days."

"Well, I might not be your fictional honey, but you're still lucky to have me." She pulled her cell phone out of her purse. "Remember this?"

"Yeah, sure. Pretty cute."

"I wish we had time," she said. "The things I could show you. iPads and flatscreen TVs and the cutest shoes. But for now, this is a smart phone. See it? See how *tidy* it is?"

"It's adorable, and while I hate to interrupt your preening session—"

"I don't get to preen all that often."

"—my time is getting pretty short. Consider me dazzled by the IQ of your phone. What can it do for me right now?"

Madison was sliding things across the phone's screen, like some nerd showing off on a Rubik's Cube. "It can do this." She pushed a button and said, "Address for Timothy Hallinan in Joshua Tree, California."

I said, "You're shitting me."

"You live in the age of steam," she said, and the phone said, in a kind of dishy female voice, "Thirteen-twenty-five Alta Loma Drive."

"I give up," I said. "Nobody needs detectives any more."

"More than ever," she said, starting the car. She leaned across and kissed my cheek. "More than ever."

* * *

"My, my," I said on the first pass. "Front door's been broken."

"How can you tell?" Madison slowed the car. "The whole place is broken."

The house was a low clapboard sprawl with a single room serving as a partial second story. The upper room looked as though it had been dropped onto the roof like a big builder's block. The paint was a kind of disquieting green that the Post Office might have used on the inside of mail boxes. One of the windows, the farthest to the right from our perspective, had two missing or broken panes which had been replaced by what looked like cardboard. The yard was home to a thriving crop of desiccated, skeletal weeds that had scattered themselves over the open ground and clustered against the walls to form a kind of witchy shrubbery.

The house's edges looked a little rippled, as though viewed through intense heat. The door, drooping on one hinge, opened into a hallway that seemed darker than it should have been.

"Once around the block," I said. I looked at the watch again. Slapped it. No blinking digits.

"Not a really friendly-looking place," she said, accelerating a bit.

"You can see it, too?"

"*See* it? It looks like Dracula's vacation cottage."

"That's interesting," I said, looking over at her.

"Men never mean that when they say it to women. When a man says, *That's interesting* to a woman, what he really means is *Give me a minute to think about something else.*"

We drove in silence, the battered house receding to our left. As we neared the end of the largely vacant block, I leaned over and touched the backs of my fingers to the side of her neck.

"I'm going to miss you."

"Don't," she said. "My chin will dimple, and once my chin dimples, it's over."

I withdrew my hand, and she reached over and put it back. "On the other hand," she said, "I'm not wearing eye makeup, so at least you'll be spared the drunken prom queen look." She sniffled and then sniffled again.

I said, "I wish I'd gone to your prom with you."

"That's *exactly* the wrong thing to say." She wiped her forearm across her eyes.

"What's the right thing?"

"There isn't one." She sniffled again and then straightened

her spine and breathed deeply. "All right. Heading east. Heading east and *in control*. This left we're making right now? It's taking us north, and then two more turns around this wretched, abandoned block and we'll be back at Point A."

"Something is going on inside that house."

"Gee, you think? It's practically got a black cloud over it."

The house stood alone, dead center on perhaps two acres of gently sloping scrag. Its only company was a derelict-looking stucco cube across the street and a hundred yards or so east. Both houses were in the lee of the mountains that rose to shelter the Monument, and even at this time of afternoon an edge of shadow was creeping toward the structures.

"Why would he live here?" I asked.

"You really *don't* know anything about him, do you?"

"I can figure some things by looking at the way he wrote me. I lived alone and drank too much—way too much in the first four books—and I'm guessing the same went for him. Broken-hearted, maybe, or maybe just a disappointed solitary. Maybe nobody thought he was as cool as he thought he was. I think a lot of writers make up characters to keep them company. Later, around book five, I lightened up on my drinking, so maybe he quit but he was stuck with me drinking from the earlier books. But looking at this place, I don't know. What it looks like to me is home to an antisocial writer with an alcohol problem."

"Who was seen outside the Pack Rat around the time Ferdy got killed."

"No, he wasn't. He wasn't anywhere near it. That's why the witness has disappeared." I tapped Madison's thigh. "Slow down a little."

We'd made another left and were now behind the house, maybe 150 feet from it. Vertical pieces of wood had been driven into the earth on this side of the house, and string, originally a bright, optimistic orange, ran from stake to stake, right to the curb beside us. Someone measuring off a building lot, perhaps. The stakes were weathered, the string in the first stages of fading, signaling yet another abandoned plan.

"That's the back door," I said. "Four windows on this side. If you had to guess the floor plan, what would you guess?"

Madison pulled the car to the curb and put it in park. She squinted at the house for a couple of minutes and then said, "Front door into a little entrance hall that's got the stairway to that upstairs room in it. To the left as you go in is a bedroom, probably the only one when the house was built, since the upstairs is obviously an addition. To the right of the front door is a living room. Go past the stairs to the back of the house, and you've got the kitchen, where those two windows are, and a utility area with a sink, right at the back door. Desert houses are big on utility areas."

"Go ahead."

"There's something on the other side of the kitchen. I don't know—maybe a bathroom. It's probably a bathroom, put there so it can share plumbing with the kitchen."

"And upstairs?"

"Bedroom. That little window up there has got to be a bath."

"So the downstairs bedroom …"

"Maybe he works there, maybe it's an office now. I mean, to take a completely unsubstantiated guess. He's got to write somewhere, right? God, it's gloomy."

"Bad stuff going on inside," I said. "Okay." I popped the car door open and looked at the watch. No red digits. "It's two fifty-two. At three-thirty, be right here, okay?"

"Not," Madison said. "Not even vaguely okay."

"We're not going to have this argument."

"Yeah?" She crossed her arms. "How are you going to avoid it?"

"By blowing the whole thing off. Ferdy was your friend, not mine. Either I go in there alone, or I don't go in there at all."

She gave me a glare that rated pretty high on my Lifetime Glare Scale. Then she said, "Fine. If we don't both go in there, I'll go in alone."

I said, "Oh."

"So your choice is both of us or me."

"Not just a girly."

"A what?"

"That's what Ruben called you when we were driving to the motel. A girly."

"Is that so? Well, I *am* a girly, and I'm proud of it."

"Wait. I'm thinking."

"Are you getting better at it?"

I lifted the watch to show it to her. "It's still not counting down."

She pursed her lips and chewed on them for a moment. "And you don't think that's good."

"No," I said. "I highly doubt that it's good." I was bouncing my foot up and down until she put a hand on my knee to stop me. I sat there, looking down at her hand, and then I said, "Okay."

She looked at me suspiciously. "Okay?"

"Yes, but let's be strategic about it. We don't just blunder in there holding hands so they can scoop both of us up."

"They?"

"If I'm right."

"Male or female?"

"Probably one of each."

"And you think they killed Ferdy."

"I'm certain of it."

She said, "Jeepers."

"So I go in now. I try the back door first. You sit here and keep an eye on me. If I can't get in through the back, I'll go around to the front. If something goes really bad, you call the cops. Otherwise, you give it about ten minutes—in fact, from the time I get out of this car, you give it *exactly* ten minutes—you want to borrow my watch?"

"No. The phone is a clock."

"Fine. In ten minutes, you park in front of the house, go up to the front door, big as life, and shout out 'Hello.' Got it?"

"Hello," she said, imitating my tone. "And the reason is?"

"There are two. First, I might very badly need a distraction in about ten minutes. Second, it suggests you don't have anything to do with me. You're just somebody dropping by."

She turned to regard the house and then faced me again. "You think they'll fall for that?"

"Not for a minute. But it just possibly might be one-tenth of one percent better than you getting snagged trying to sneak in with me."

"Oh, well," she said. "With odds like *those*."

46

Fourfivesix

THE BACK DOOR WAS LOCKED. I worked the knob back and forth as quietly as possible, went up on tiptoe to try to ease it out of the latch, but I couldn't persuade it to let me in.

With one futile gesture out of the way, I waved to Madison, just in case I was never going to see her again, took a deep breath, held it for no good reason, and edged my way around the house. My mouth tasted like it was full of nickels, but part of me was exhilarated. Danger felt good in a familiar way.

The plant life was not only hideous, it was also noisy. It went straight down underfoot like miniature trees, with a lot of crackling, and I wound up trying to thread my way through it. Problem with that was that every time I found the slightest trace of a path, it had a cholla bristling in the middle of it.

So I made noise.

As I reached the right side of the house I saw two open windows, nothing between me and the room they opened into except a dusty screen and a layer of beige curtain. I stood completely still, listening to a creaking that might have been a swivel chair that needed lubricating and a whisking sound that I eventually identified as a printer.

If I could hear them, they could hear me. I stopped moving and surveyed the 180 degrees of crappy desert in front of me. Found a tenuous, curving, start-and-stop, dotted line of a path, and took it.

I felt ridiculously conspicuous, bending forward to present a lower profile—*Look at the man over there sneaking, Mommy*—so I stood upright and skirted the side of the house, following the path as much as I could and aiming for the front yard. When I reached it I cut left, heading for the broken door.

As hot as it was, I felt chilled. This whole thing was a setup, had been a setup from the time those hands went around Ferdy's throat. And I was pretty sure I was doing exactly what they wanted me to do.

And then there was Madison. The punch line, fate's leaden sense of irony, kicking in at the least opportune time. Me in the wrong place, the whole wrong fucking *dimension*, not belonging here, not able to remain here, and quite possibly unable to return to the place where I did belong. That obviously wasn't enough to satisfy the malignant djinns of the moment. I had to meet Madison, too, so losing her could be part of my experience. Total destruction might not have been painful enough.

One of those sad, ragged pathways made out of ill-fitting flat stones led up to the front door, and I took it. Even before I stepped past the sagging door and into the darkened hall, I could feel the cold in the house. It felt cold enough to see my breath.

Madison's floor plan had been spot-on. The stairway was in front of me with a hallway leading past it to the back of the house, and the living room, with an unexpected, highly polished hardwood floor, was to my right. The floor looked like something that absorbed a lot of nervous energy in the form of buffing when Hallinan couldn't write. The only pieces of furniture interrupting its gleam were a coffee table and a couch with a floral pattern, obviously ransomed from a yard sale. Light bounced off the floor but seemed to be devoured by the air before it could illuminate the room. The effect was something new to me: directional darkness.

The printer and the person who was using it were to my left.

I went toward them but stopped in the doorway and took it all in. The work table, the office chair, the filing cabinets, the printer, the laptop with the person in front of it.

Without turning around, she said, "Hello, Simeon. You're early."

"My watch stopped working. Finishing up?"

"Just about." The chair squeaked as Pansy Parkinson swiveled to face me. The safety pin in her nose glittered.

"What happened to the lisp?"

It wasn't the question she'd expected. She tilted her head to one side, someone studying a domestic animal that had just done something surprising. "I don't use it when Patsy's not around."

"One of many things," I said, "that Patsy's not aware of."

Her eyebrows came together. "How could you know that?"

"A guess. You're alone down here. You seem lighter, less repressed, than you do up there. It must be tiring for an individualist like you to be an identical twin."

"For more than a century," she said. "It's fucking agony."

I nodded at the manuscript. "What's the title?"

"Oh," she said, and something almost as warm as a blush took possession of her face. "It's not very good."

"I'm not a critic."

She licked her lips, a little nervously. "It's the first of a trilogy."

I said, "Good planning."

"*The Parting of the Ways*," she said, watching me closely. "*Part One of The Stardark Chronicles.*"

"You're right," I said. "It's not very good."

"Good enough to get me *back here*," she said, her eyes so small they almost disappeared. "In print again. Alive again. *Solo.*"

"Publishing takes a while," I said. "You're going to have to go back first."

"So what? My sister has no idea and she never will have, until

I'm gone. She'll never even suspect. She *loves* me. You're the only one who could tell her. And you—" She shrugged. "You're not going to be anywhere."

"But you'll be alive again, so to speak."

"As close to alive as any of us ever is," she said. "For at least six books."

I felt my eyebrows go up. "Six."

"Two trilogies. This one starts back in the days of yore, fighting ancient evil across the ages. The second trilogy brings me up to date." She showed me the closest thing to a real smile I'd ever seen on her face. "In New York City."

"Your writer's in jail. That's not going to interfere—"

"Oh, please," she said. "It's a dream come true. It'll make him *interesting*. Without it, he's nobody. A nonentity."

"Not exactly," I said. I came a little farther into the room, but she held up a hand, palm out, and I stopped. "He wrote me, remember?"

"You never existed," she said. She shrugged. "A couple of hours from now, you'll be gone, and all your books will be gone with you. Hallinan won't be a second-rate writer any more, with a record of no sales and a dropped series. The kind of writer publishers don't even want to read. He'll be a newcomer, the writer unjustly accused of murder and then freed in a sensational case, with a brilliant manuscript in the hottest genre going."

"Ancient evil?" I said. "Days of *yore?*"

"Paranormal romance-adventure," she said as though from a great height. "With capes. Don't even ask. You've missed it completely."

"I've missed a lot. Does it really work? Erasing a writer like that?"

"Poof," she said. "Gone. The books are gone, the contracts in the files are gone, all the memories are changed to something that's close, but *not*. Don't look at me like that. You *must* know.

Life is all first-draft until you're dead. And even then, after you're gone, you're just an element in other people's first draft." She leaned back in the chair, looking relaxed. "Are you alone?"

"Sure."

"You're not, of course. But you might be, without even knowing it. Think about it for a second. Let's say you were created at the instant you came through the door into this room, complete with all the memories you've amassed. How could you detect that? How would things be different?"

"Other people. They wouldn't remember the same—"

"Where are other people's memories written down? It's not even a first draft. It's the *idea* of a first draft."

"Have you actually done it? Erased someone?"

She shook her head, a bit grudgingly, I thought. "Not intentionally. Remember the writers who went back that we lost?" She covered her smile with her hand. "They didn't get back. It's harder to go back than it is to come here. Actually, people come here more often than you'd think. It's just that some of them don't get back, and everyone forgets about them."

"Who were they, the ones you lost?"

"Jennifer Marle and Spike Kinworthy. Jennifer was a drip but I actually kind of miss Spike. Hard-boiled, without feeling the need for redeeming qualities."

"Never heard of them."

She folded her hands in her lap. "I rest my case."

"But you remember them. You and Patsy."

"We're different. We've seen the whole edifice get put up, a plank here, an idea there. There are a couple of others who know almost as much as we do." She looked at her wrist, and I saw a watch a lot like mine. "Getting close to time."

"Really," I said. I came the rest of the way into the room, and Pansy used her feet to scrabble the wheeled chair away from me.

"Relax," I said. "What good would it do me to hurt you?" I tapped the manuscript. "I just want to take a look at this."

"I'd rather you didn't," she said, her voice scaling up a couple of notes.

"Don't be shy." I looked down at the title page, and the first thing I saw jumped out and struck me right between the eyes. My heart rate doubled. I picked up the top half of the stack and scanned the page I'd uncovered. There it was, again and again. And *again*. For a moment, I almost laughed.

"Don't you dare grin at that," she said. "It's going to put you away for good. And there's nothing you can do to it, because I've already sent it off."

"Have you."

"To his agent and the editor the agent is working with. So there's nothing you can do about it." My tone must have bothered her, because she kept pushing the chair back until it hit one of the filing cabinets. Then she rocked back and forth, studying me. "There's nothing anyone can do about it."

"Not even you."

She looked puzzled. "Why would I want to do anything about it?"

I looked at the last few pages. Yes, it was there, too. To cover my reaction, I said, "*The falling center of a tangled knot of feasting hawks?* Couldn't you squeeze in another *of?*"

"That'll be *fixed*," Pansy snapped. "Lot of, um, lot of touch-up." She looked at her watch again and pushed down on the arms of the chair to stand.

"Let me guess," I said. "The last thing you did to this manuscript before you printed it was a global search and replace, right?"

She stopped trying to push herself up. "What—I mean, how do you know?"

"It's a boring activity, global search and replace. And since you were in a hurry to send it off, you wouldn't have done it all manually: just tell the program to find the next appearance of the wrong word and push the button to insert the right word—"

"I know how to do a global—"

"—and you probably got a little, I don't know, drifty as you input the command, didn't you?" I picked up a pencil and circled three words, all the same word, on the page, gathered a dozen or so pages, and turned to her. As I faced her, I put my right hand on my hip, very close to my back pocket. "Maybe you got a little careless, maybe you didn't review it while it was in progress, just let it work its magic. But I *really* think you should look at this. Especially since you already sent it off and, as you say, there's nothing anybody can do about it."

I crossed the floor to her as she attempted to lean even farther back in the chair, trying to keep out of arm's length. I brought my right hand back from my hip, put the manuscript between my fingers by the top edge, so the whole top page could be read, and held the pages out to her.

For a second, I didn't think it would work, didn't think she'd take them. But then her eyes dropped to the top page and drifted over the text until they came to the first circled word.

She screamed.

Both hands flew up to her face, she went bright red, and she screamed again. Her hands were on either side of her face, about an inch from her cheeks, her fingers extended to their full length and so wide I thought she might tear the webbing between them. Then she was leaning forward in the chair, drumming her feet on the floor and grabbing at the pages and the scream was resolving itself into *NoNoNoNoNoNo*, and she didn't stop screaming until the handcuff I had taken from my hip pocket and was holding beneath the pages clicked closed on her wrist. Her eyes came up to mine, enormous, flooded with one horrific possibility after another, but by the time she tried to snatch the cuffed wrist away,

I'd yanked it beneath the arm of the chair and fastened the other end to the handle of a filing cabinet.

"Oh. Oh," she said, breathing so quickly she might have run a mile. "No, you can't, you can't, you *can't*."

"Watch me," I said.

"Please? *Please?*" She started yanking at the cuff, but it was one of Ridley's pairs, good, solid police-issue, a pair of cuffs even Hammond wouldn't have scorned. "The time," she said. "My book," she said. "My *life*." She tried to climb out of the chair but she was held in place by the cuff threaded under the arm, and she collapsed into the chair again, her eyes going everywhere in the room. She yanked at the cuff, then yanked again. "You, you, you —need me," she said. "It takes both of us to bring you back—"

"But you're not going to help, remember? You want me to vanish." I looked at my watch. "I figure you left my house about forty minutes before I went through that window, but I have no way of knowing how long it took me to travel here. Still, I figure your time will be up just any old minute now."

"I didn't really mean that we wouldn't—what I *meant*—you can't think I'd really—" She kept jerking spasmodically at the handcuff. Her eyes rolled almost all the way back in her head, and for a moment it was impossible to see her as anything but a terrified child, but then she grabbed a deep, *deep* breath and screamed, "Ahmed!"

And almost simultaneously, someone else screamed. And with a sinking feeling, I recognized the scream.

So then they were both screaming and Pansy was yanking at the cuffs and trying to kick me, and over it all I heard the front door being wrenched off its remaining hinge, and a huge shadow fell across the part of the hallway I could see. Then the door to the room darkened, and Ahmed filled it, Madison hanging over his shoulder like a sack of rice, her feet kicking his greenish back with no apparent effect. In his free hand was the Mauser.

Ahmed bent his knees to clear the door and came into the room. Madison said, upside down, "What a cliché. Girl thrown over monster's shoulder."

"Ahmed," Pansy said, panting feverishly. The Eye swiveled to her. "If he doesn't undo this cuff by the time I count to ten, kill her."

"You really don't want to—" I said, as Pansy said, "One."

Madison said, "Ummmmmmm."

Pansy said, "Two."

I said, "Put her down."

His left hand came up with the Mauser in it, but the Eye stayed riveted on Pansy, who said, "Three."

Something beeped behind me, and Pansy said, "Nooooo, nooooooo. *Fourfivesix*—"

I reached under my shirt and pulled out the automatic. Madison's eyes doubled in size and she said, "But that's the wrong gun, that's the one that—"

I shot Ahmed in his bare left shoulder, the one that didn't have Madison over it, and he staggered back a step, the hand with the Mauser in it hanging limply at his side. A hole had appeared in the shoulder, like something poked by an invisible finger, and greenish fluid began to flow out of it.

"Kill him," Pansy screamed at Ahmed, and I shot Ahmed again as he brought his gun up, but I was trying too hard to avoid Madison and the bullet passed through the muscle of his upper left arm. He shrugged it off and stretched the arm toward me, the Eye sighting down the Mauser's barrel, and Pansy's scream went so high and thin it was like a glass sliver through my eardrum.

"Grab the Eye," I shouted to Madison. "Get it in both hands. Cup your hands over it."

She made a swipe at it, missed, then caught hold of it and wrapped both hands around it.

I moved a few steps left and said, "Over here, stupid," and

Ahmed, blinded, turned and fired a shot in my direction, but by then I was on the far side of the writing table, and I said, "No, over here," and he dropped Madison to the floor with a really unpleasant sound of hard body parts hitting hard wood. The Eye swung to me and the gun's barrel followed, and I focused my entire being into aiming my own gun. When I pulled the trigger this time, the Eye shattered into a million pieces of porcelain and clear fluid, and Ahmed, his mouth hanging open, raised a hand to find the chain and the hole in his chest where the Eye had been, and he went down, first to his knees and then, stiff as a redwood, on his side. He hit the wood hard.

I dropped to the floor beside Madison and rolled her over. She darted her eyes at Pansy and said, "He was behind me. I didn't get a chance to yell *Hello*."

"No problem."

"Why is that poor little girl screaming?"

I'd actually stopped hearing Pansy, but I looked over at her and saw she was bleeding where she'd taken the skin off trying to pull her hand through the cuff. She kept yanking at it anyway, not feeling the pain, her face twisted to form that ear-splitting scream, but then the watch on the bleeding wrist beeped again, five times, fast, and her voice got softer and farther away although her mouth was still wide and her eyes huge with despair, and then her hand slipped easily through the cuff and dangled loosely over the arm of the chair as though she didn't have the strength to lift it. Her feet were no longer touching the floor, all the clothes too big for her now, hanging on her as she dwindled and turned yellow, like the newsprint in the windows of the Pack Rat. The voice died out altogether although her mouth remained open wide. Crinkled lines formed on her face and hands, like the irregular folds in a crumpled piece of paper that's been smoothed out, and then the crinkles sharpened and hardened and split and turned into tiny fissures, parting and opening like the ground in an earthquake, and, one at a time, the torn bits of paper began to fall from her face and waft to the floor, like dry leaves. There was nothing beneath them but darkness.

Her shoes were the only solid thing left. They kicked out galvanically in perfect unison, halted in mid-air, and then collapsed. There was a sound like cards being shuffled, and the black leather pants sagged flat and empty. A handful of old paper fragments, thin as onionskin, sifted down from the cuffs of the pants and the sleeves of the jacket. What was left was the black chair with the black clothes on it, and in front of it a little pile of yellowed, ragged pieces of paper, too frail even to pulp, with a few safety pins on top. And then the fragments burst into thin, chilly blue flame and were gone.

A *ping* and a sharp little sound drew my eyes to the last safety pin and a small black wristwatch, both of which had just fallen off the chair and onto the floor.

Madison said, "The poor baby, the poor, poor—*oh*!"

I turned to see Ahmed pulling himself up onto one elbow. The blue eyes were most of the way through the skin, and as I watched, they came the rest of the way through and focused on me. But then the watch on his own arm started to beep, and his face went rigid with panic. As Madison scrambled back, he got to his feet, threw a last, longing glance at Pansy's clothes on the chair, and ran.

I saw him enter the hallway, saw something red blinking in reflection on the polished wood floor of the living room. Then Ahmed launched himself into the air headfirst, horizontal to the shining floor, and as he flew through the opening into the living room, he disappeared. The air he'd vanished into rippled once, like water that's had a stone dropped into it, and was still again.

Madison and I sat in silence, not moving a muscle, until it became clear that we were alone in the house and that it was over. The smoke from Pansy's little fire scratched at my throat.

Madison swallowed once, loudly enough for me to hear her, shivered, and said, "So, um, are you going to tell me that this isn't fiction?"

47

For Me, Too

"But I still remember her," I said.

"Because she's a twin maybe?" Madison ventured from behind the steering wheel. "They were both in the books, so if one of them is still around, the books probably are too. And people still remember them. The people who ever did, I mean."

"You've been listening to me more closely than I have."

"That part's not so complicated. It's preposterous and completely unbelievable, but it's not so complicated. But that poor little girl."

"She wasn't a little girl," I said around the cold ball of dread in the center of my chest. I had just seen my own future and it hadn't looked pleasant. "She was one hundred and eleven years old. And she and that big green thyroid case killed Ferdy."

"Just to get into print again."

"All of us want to get into print again. You have no idea how much more alive we feel in a book."

The desert whipped past us, looking familiar by now, and why wouldn't it? This was at least the third time I'd made the Joshua Tree-Twentynine Palms trip. The sky above us was shading a much deeper blue in the east, which was the direction we were taking. Just above the earth's dark edge, the horned tip of a silvered moon had appeared.

"Oh, my God," Madison said. "At this time last night, Ruben and whatshisname were just starting to chase me into the park."

"Ridley. And I was getting ready to jump through a window."

"For me," Madison said.

"For you. And for me, too."

She took her eyes off the road for so long that I pointed my chin at it, and she turned back to it and snapped on the headlights. "But you may not get back," she said.

"I might not." I shouldered the fear aside, or almost aside. It was still there, but a little farther off, waiting easily, with its hands on its hips. "And it was worth it," I said. "No matter what." I put my left hand loosely over her right, which was on the steering wheel.

"Your twenty-four hours—"

"I don't even know whether they still count. The watch, for one thing, it hasn't been doing the countdown. And Pansy might have been telling the truth when she said it would take both of them to pull me back. You can get lost between there and here. Before I homed in on you, I was more lost than I've ever been, like being blown off-course at sea. I thought the dark was infinite in all directions and I'd just pinwheel through it forever. But then I found you."

Madison sniffled. "Don't make me go all silly girl," she said.

"So, yes. What they did was about getting back into print. You have no idea how much we envy the ones who are still being written, who think they actually live down here. They picked Hallinan because he was still writing and he isn't a really terrible writer, and because I was right there in the neighborhood, where they could use me. They chose Ferdy because he was a Sensitive and they could see him easily. Probably came down here and got an in-person look at him, maybe even went into the store once or twice.

"And because he was *so* sensitive, they could plant an idea in him. So they made a note of that and held Ferdy in reserve while they poured that stupid story about capes and black rocks into

Hallinan's mind, and when it was about finished, they waited until you went to lunch and then put a whisper into Ferdy's ear that it might be nice to go into that room and thumb through one of my books. Which meant that my window lit up and I was watching him read while Ahmed appeared behind the shelf, wearing boots Hallinan probably doesn't even remember buying. And Ahmed strangled Ferdy."

"Maybe you can still get back," Madison said.

"Maybe I can." Neither of us said anything about the way things had ended for Pansy. Didn't seem constructive. The little blue flame had pretty much creeped me out.

"They thought I'd want to come back here because I wouldn't be able to resist Ferdy's murder. This sounds kind of awful, but we all sit around up there wishing for a fresh murder. What they didn't plan on was you. They didn't realize I'd feel guilty about putting you in danger. They didn't realize—I didn't realize—that I'd fall in love with you."

Madison said, "Let's just go to my house."

"And I didn't, realize it, either. So here we are. On the verge of who knows what."

"I said, let's just go—"

"I don't know whether I have the time. Let's take care of this one piece of business and then we'll see where we are." Whatever happened, I was *not* going to be alone in a room with her when I crumpled and disintegrated, if that was what I had in store. I was going to run, get as far into the desert as I—

"Almost there," she said, pulling her hand out from under mine to press it against her right eye.

"So from the beginning," I said, pleased with the steadiness of my voice, "they planned to get rid of me. Pansy was right. Hallinan could do better without a failed series behind him. The whole thing worked almost exactly the way they planned it."

"You keep saying *they*," she said. "But the big green guy, he didn't look very strategic to me."

"No," I said. "You're right, of course. Listen, no matter what happens, I wouldn't have missed this for anything."

She turned to me again. "Let's skip this. I can take care of Jake myself. You don't need to waste time on this."

"Oh, come on," I said. "It'll be fun."

"Fun," she said, sounding like the word was new to her.

"You should have seen your face when I pulled out that gun." I laughed and actually meant it. "Ahmed was fictional. Those bullets were *made* for him."

"Here we are," she said, signaling left and slowing for the turn.

The Smoke Tree was a single-story building with no external clue to identify its purpose. A big, opaque-looking smoked-glass window faced onto the street, and a sign bearing the words SMOKE TREE was raised high on the front wall. As we turned, a light came on, probably on a timer, turning the sign an unwholesome, somewhat rancid yellow.

"What is this place?"

"I don't know," Madison said. She turned right into a barren, sandy parking lot. "It's a building with a name. I've driven past it for two years without having the slightest impulse to go in and find out." She pulled the car past the building onto the asphalt parking lot and gestured up at the east-facing wall. "Nice mural, though."

That side of the building had a fifty-foot long lizard painted on it. I said, "I guess. If you like lizards. What time is it?"

"Quarter to six."

"Maybe we missed him."

"He's not coming," Madison said. "Jake's real assertive with women, but you showed him your teeth. The most he'll ever do is flip you off through a thick pane of glass."

"Well, shit," I said. "I was going to pump him full of pulp-fiction bullets."

She opened her door and put an experimental hand outside the car. "It's cooled off some," she said. "Let's get out and neck without this steering wheel in the way."

"Sounds good. I'm too old to do it in a car anyway."

I reached behind me and got the green tote bag with the manuscript in it and then climbed out. She came around the car and put her arms around me and I wrapped mine around her and lowered my face and smelled her hair as we took tiny dance steps to music no one could hear. A breeze kicked up, and for a change it wasn't full of dust.

A spangle of stars had risen to the east.

I said, "Just for the record, I love you."

She said, "Sweet mouth," and hugged me more tightly.

I unwound one arm and put a finger under her chin so I could tilt her face up.

Something beeped.

I kissed her, or perhaps she kissed me. The bag with the manuscript was dangling from my left wrist and resting against her back and she reached back and said, "What's this?" and something beeped again.

I said, "It's the—"

She pushed at me and said, "Your watch, your *watch*."

"Holy hell," I said. I backed up a step and brought my left hand up, the bag swinging from it, and saw the red digits blinking at me as the watch beeped again. It read **00:00:13**. I said to it, "Where?" but it didn't answer.

"Where, where, where?" she asked. She looked right and then left. "What are we looking for?"

I grabbed her hand. "Come on." With her in tow, I ran around the building until we came to the big dark window. I held up the watch and saw the red numbers reflected in it. When I pulled the watch away, the numbers remained.

The watch began a series of rapid beeps.

"Listen," I said.

"Go, *go*," she said.

"You're worth fifty of him."

"I said go." She stopped. "Of whom?"

"Whoever he is, whenever you meet him. You're worth fifty of him."

"I know that," she said, and she hauled off and booted me in the rear. "Now *go*."

And I put the green bag in front of my face just in case, backed up, and ran for the smoked-glass window.

48

My Guess is a Lot of Rewrite

IT WAS DIFFERENT, GOING BACK.

The window went soft, as before, with a little breaking sound, and draped itself over me, and there was a brief interval of directionless darkness, but when the red glow appeared, it was brighter and its brightness never varied. And then, instead of going through membrane after membrane, I felt them peel away from me, another and another, and instead of accumulating weight and mass, I grew less substantial. I was beginning to feel as light as a dust mote when, all of a sudden, I wasn't, and I hit the floor in my own living room. The carpet emitted a puff of dust.

Lobelia was there, looking down at me with concern in her face. Beside her, her eyes swollen with crying, her hair a tangle, probably from her yanking at it, was Patsy Parkinson.

Lobelia said, "That wasn't easy, trying to beam myself at you like that." She blew out some air and stretched out a hand, and I transferred the tote bag to my right and reached up to her. When she pulled me upright, I had lost most of the heft I'd felt down there.

"Thanks," I said. "You were a good, strong, bright orange. The beacon I needed."

"Patsy's the one to thank," Lobelia said. She gave the child a pitying look. "She ran into my house, crying to beat the band, and practically dragged me here."

I said, "Thank you, Patsy."

357

Patsy burst into tears. Even as she rubbed her eyes, I could feel her watching me.

"The poor little thing," Lobelia said, putting an arm around her shoulder. "They were inseparable." She looked at the bag. "What's that?"

From Lobelia's ample bosom, Patsy darted an eye at the bag.

"It's a book," I said. I heard something move on the roof and looked through the open door to see Ahmed. He had three flesh-colored bandages stuck to him, although they would have been less conspicuous if they'd been green. There was a new eye hanging from the chain, but it was the size of a concord grape. It regarded me sullenly.

"Glad to see Ahmed got back," I said. Patsy's one visible eye remained trained on the bag.

"Patsy," I said, "I think you ought to see this."

"I can't," she said, and then she was crying again. "I couldn't possibly look at it."

"Please, Simeon," Lobelia said. "Give the child some time."

"The child, the child," I said. "How useful to be a child. I wish I'd been aware of that when *I* was one."

I pulled the manuscript pages out of the bag and extended them toward Patsy, who turned her head in the other direction and hugged Lobelia tightly.

"Won't look," she said.

"It's pretty slick," I said. "Probably only a twin could have done it." I rustled the papers. "Go on, look."

Patsy started to cry again.

"Okay," I said to Lobelia. "*You* look."

"This child brought you back here," Lobelia said severely. "And you're tormenting—" She stopped, looking at the text. She read further, then motioned me for the next page. The sound of the top page being dropped to the floor brought Patsy's head back around, and the eye I saw this time was small and cold.

Lobelia said, "Oh, my," and pushed Patsy away. She said, "You little stinker." Patsy backed up, arms at her sides, her fingers curved like claws.

I reached into the bag and brought out the title page. "Read it out loud," I said.

"*The Parting of the Ways*," Lobelia read. "*Part One of The Stardark Chronicles.* " She looked down at Patsy and then back at the page. "*A Patsy Parkinson Novel.*"

"One letter," I said. "I thought it was all about a book, but I was wrong. It was all about one letter."

"It wasn't supposed to be." Patsy took another step back, away from Lobelia, her face hard and set. There were bright red spots on her cheekbones. "It was supposed to be both of us. It was my idea in the first place. Pansy never had an idea in her life. The *Penis Pumps*, that was her idea of being creative, cutting yourself on stage and screaming about how sensitive you were. The whole idea was mine, the trilogy, the *two* trilogies, New York City…" She faltered, stopped, and grabbed a breath. "I would have loved New York City." The page on the carpet grabbed her attention, and when she looked back up at us, her eyes were clear. "In fact, I *will* love New York City."

"By yourself," I said.

"She hated me," Patsy said, and her voice, when it broke this time, sounded genuine. "All the work I put into this so she and I could get out of here. Together. To be in New York, to live in New York. All cool and hip, like the Olsen Twins. And she—she cut me out of the story. She changed my name and turned me into a *boy*, and then—" She closed her eyes and recited, in a voice that was pure acid, "*It, too, was hidden by a cape, but this was a white cape, brilliant and unblemished, too pristine, too innocent, to hide the tragedy beneath it.*" She stuck her tongue out and made a gagging sound. "*She could not force herself to go to the fallen form, to lift the cape, to look at the face she knew as well as she knew her own.* Is that cute? Knew it as well as her own? *From this point on, she thought, she would be only half of herself.* The little *bitch*," she said. "There was no room for me. When she'd finished, there wasn't a handhold I could use to pull myself into the story."

"So she restructured the book," I said. "She double-checked everything, and then she did the easiest thing of all. A global search and replace. First, being careful, replace *he* with *she, him* with *her.* Second, the easy one. Find *Elen.* Replace with *Pansy.*"

For a moment I thought Patsy was going to laugh, but she dropped her eyes. "She wasn't on guard," she said. "It was easy to make her hit the wrong letter, even from up here. After all she only had to do it once, and after that it was automatic. The hard part was keeping her distracted as she went through the story. Like you said, it would probably only work with twins."

"But you brought me back," I said. "Why?"

"Well, I didn't know you'd have *that*," she said, her eyes on the manuscript. "And Pansy and I had argued forever about whether to erase you. Pansy was wrong. Your books had a cult following. Some reviewers really liked them. It was stupid to throw all that away. It's practically impossible to get reviewed today."

"Ahmed?" The weensy little eye on the chain turned to me, but I was talking to Patsy. "Did Ahmed tell you what Pansy was up to? Was that how you found out?"

Patsy said, "He's my only true friend," and aimed a brave, tearful smile at Ahmed.

"Poor Ahmed," Lobelia said. "Having to make that choice."

"Poor Ahmed is right," I said, and Patsy's eyes widened in alarm. "After all he's been through, and he's not even in Patsy's book. Not even a mention."

Patsy put up a hand. "*Wait,* wait a minute—"

"Not even once," I said. "Not even a green giant under a different name. Nothing. *Nada.*"

There was a moment of absolute stillness, total silence and then Ahmed hurtled through the door so fast I could barely see him move. By the time I'd registered that he was in the room, he'd picked up the screaming Patsy, tucked her under his arm, and taken off, right through the front wall of my house. Lobelia and I stood there, watching pieces of the wall continue to fall, watching the door to the roof, ripped off its hinges, topple with a kind of elegant slow-mo grace to the deck, watching the dust billow. Watching Ahmed and Patsy dwindle into a speck in the sky.

"Oh, my," Lobelia said. "Whatever now?"

"My guess is, massive rewrite," I said.

"No, I mean over here," she said. "Look. Your hawk is back."

* * *

And back it was, visible again through the window in the side of the house, hanging in its old place in the sky. I thought it glared at me for a moment, but I was probably wrong.

"Tea for me," Lobelia said. "Coffee for you. My, my. What an afternoon."

As I watched her bustle into the kitchen, a change of light caught my eye.

The sky was darkening, the hawk—looking momentarily panicked—was fading. And then the sky was gone, and I was looking at Madison. Madison was looking at me, but from the expression in her face, I could tell she didn't see me.

What she saw was an open book. I felt the words. It was *Skin Deep*.

She bit her lower lip and then slowly turned the book to show me a laptop. It was on, the screen bright and empty. She did something with the book that jostled the picture for a second, but then the book stayed where it was, wide open and looking directly at the laptop, and her hands came back into the picture, poised above the keys. They waited.

I heard Lobelia come back into the room. Then I closed my eyes and worked as hard as I knew how.

When I opened them, I saw Madison's fingers on the keyboard and the words as they appeared on the screen: *I feel you there, Simeon*. My breath caught.

She leaned down to the book to show me the widest smile I'd ever seen, and then her face was gone again, and her fingers were flying over the keyboard and I read, *There's so much we didn't say to each other*. Her fingers started moving again.

Behind me, Lobelia said, "I'll leave you two kids alone."

I heard the door close, but I couldn't take my eyes away from Madison's hands.

Thirty minutes later, Madison was gone, leaving me with a full heart and my end of the conversation, which I hadn't been able to share with her. And I could feel a shift in my future, a widening of its potential, and I knew that

Epilogue

In Third-Person

THE STREAM OF WORDS STOPPED, for the first time in—what?—
thirty, thirty-one hours? For a moment, he almost felt lonely.

God, what a couple of days. Some kind of intruders, then the
cops, jail on those *idiotic* charges, and then, without even time to
get a sandwich, this novel started knocking on a little door inside
his head, *pounding* actually, and he ran for the computer the moment the cops dropped him at home early the next evening, and
he'd been right here, with a couple of brief breaks to open two
bottles of wine, ever since.

His forearms ached. When he relaxed his arms, his fingers
curled of their own accord. But, good Lord, he might have a book
here.

He blinked fast a bunch of times to try to clear the grit from
his eyes. There was daylight coming through the window for the
second time: dark, light, dark, light. A new record for him: his
personal best at endurance writing.

And maybe it was worth it. Why had he been so *unimaginat-
ive* for all these years—what was it, seventeen? Why had he been
so stubborn, writing the same book over and over, the mouthy,
semi-depressed private eye adrift in L.A. in book after book, as
though writing a book was like making a dress, cutting it to fit a
pattern. No wonder they'd turned him down time and again.

All he'd needed was to loosen up, to take *chances*, to depart
from the form he thought he'd mastered, but which, instead,

363

seemed to have mastered *him*. What he'd needed all along was to shake off the restrictions, get playful, turn out something like…

like…

like this…

… like this *mishmash* was the word that came to mind, but he shrugged it off. It was new territory. It was going to get him *published* again.

His shoulders were stiff, so he rotated them, lifted them and let them drop again, as he leaned in to read the most recent words:

… which I hadn't been able to share with her. And I could feel a shift in my future, a widening of its potential, and I knew that

It took less than a second for it to come to him.

… I would manage to be with her no matter what it took, no matter if it was only 24 hours at a stretch. Twenty-four hours can be a lifetime.

He hit the *save* button, slumped in the chair, and stared at his ending.

This would bring Simeon back.

Acknowledgments

This book needed, and got, a lot of help. I need to thank Peggy Hageman for a deeply perceptive story edit; Everett Kaser for a couple of typically invaluable spot-the-stupidity reads; James Egan at Bookfly for the brilliant cover design; Barb Elliott at ebooksbybarb.biz for a terrific copy edit and formatting; and my guiding light in the whole bewildering business of self-publication, the incomparable Kimberly "Hitch" Hitchens, proprietor and prime motivator at booknook.biz. I get dozens of request each year for someone who does what Hitch does, and the answer is always: Hitch.

Afterword

Thomas Wolfe notwithstanding, maybe you can go home again.

I last wrote about Simeon in 1994. By the end of that year I'd put him in six books over a period of five years, all published by NAL/Dutton/William Morrow to rapturous reviews and zero sales. The reviews were important to me because they compensated for the absolute deluge of indifference from the reading public.

Then came the long cold winter, when I stopped writing in order to make enough money to be able to write full-time, and Simeon and his world gradually made the sad descent from bad sales to no sales to out of print. And then from *out of print* to the final indignity of being *pulped.* I always liked old Simeon, so I asked myself, "How must he *feel?*" This book is my attempt to answer that question.

I had a a huge amount of fun writing it, even if it did take several years. Over that unusually long creative period, I was sustained by some great music. I listened to hundreds of albums, representing many genres. Madison had her own playlist, which included Aimee Mann, Emmylou Harris, Lake Street Dive, Lindi Ortega, Rachael Yamagata, Shawn Colvin, Neko Case, Ingrid Michaelson, Imogen Heap (and Frou Frou), Beth Hart, Kacey Musgraves, late Joni Mitchell, and a bunch of others. The music for the rest of the book was heavy on irony, with contributions from Craig Finn, James McMurtry, Randy Newman, Ray Davies, Little Feat, John Pryne, John Hiatt, Jason Isbell, Franz Ferdinand, and Elvis

Costello, plus a lot of classical music, most notably Mozart's piano concerti and Beethoven's sonatas for cello.

If you'd like to suggest some music, go to my website, http://www.timothyhallinan.com/ and hit the CONTACT TIM button.

Hope you liked the book. If you did, please don't be shy about reviewing it. In fact, review it even if you didn't. In either case, thanks for making it this far.

Made in the USA
San Bernardino, CA
10 June 2017